Balance of the Three

THE IVY CHRONICLES - 2

C. R. CUMMINGS

Printed in the United States of America by Sonder Publishing

Editorial advice provided in part by Practical Proofing; practicalproofing.com.

Cover Design by Nichole Cummings

ISBN-13: 978-0-9966050-1-4
ISBN-10: 0996605010

For Linda – You will never be forgotten

ACKNOWLEDGMENTS

I would like to thank my husband, Glen, for being patient, supportive and putting up with me disappearing into my own little world for days on end.

Nichole and Vale...you are both awesome, thank you for taking the time to review, give suggestions and for all your snarky teenage comments. (Many of which somehow found their way into the story.)

Special thanks to Jena at Practical Proofing for her wonderful editing and insights, and Suzanne Messer my BFF for helping with the Beta reads.

Balance of the Three

THE IVY CHRONICLES - 2

Hail the Oak Triad and their Scepters three,
That gives fire to the Orb and sets us free,
Hail to the Balance that gives us life,
That pours out blessings from the realms trice.

The Oak Triad

CHAPTER 1 - Edme

The three hooded men hurried down the passageway. The stone walls were close together, which helped, along with the darkness of night, to hide their movements.

"I do not understand why we could not blink to the Meadhan," came a grumble from under one of the hoods.

The fey in the lead halted and spun around to glare at the one that had spoken.

"Edme, stop your bewailing or else."

"Or else what Odive? The Elders did not put you in charge. They gave the mission to their Troikas, that means all of us," Edme responded still in his whining voice, though a bit of fear had crept in.

"I grow tired of you. All you have done since we left Firinn is complain. You complained about the smell of Alainn, you grumbled about the architecture of the buildings, you griped about having to refrain from magic when we retrieved the Valkyrie stick. I am tired of it." The fey's voice was laced with loathing.

Edme was not fond of Odive nor did he trust him. He had a perplexing odor about him and something always felt just a bit off. Edme was a good Minister; he loved the Elders and the fey in general. At times he disagreed with his superiors, but he always did as he was instructed...by them. But he did not trust the fey before him and he did not know for sure if the Elders had agreed to whatever this part of the mission was. There was no point to it that he could see. The Elders were right to be concerned about the young fey who had newly taken her

1

rightful place as the owner of the Meadhan…the girl worried him too.

The Elders had instructed the three to find a way to get the girl into Firinn and away from her guardian. The Woodsman had been a thorn in their sides for too long, and they needed the girl so that they had some leverage against him.

The renewed rumors surrounding the ancient prophecy were causing concern also. When the fey Seers had first spoken the words, no one paid it much mind. The Elders had dismissed it as unimportant, even though all the Seers had the same revelation at the point in time when the war with the Eilibear had ensued. It was nonsensical…little more than an absurd child's riddle.

But ever since the Woodsman had claimed the Hemlock Meadhan and taken the small **Frìth** fey, the prophecy had started to be spoken again. Gradually at first, as there were not many that even remembered it, then more and more fey started to refer to it. It had become almost a diversion among the fey. An interesting curiosity that now seemed to be at the tip of everyone's tongue. The Elders were unsure whether it was just for amusement or if for some reason the prophecy was now relevant.

What Edme could not wrap his brain around was why so many were linking the riddle to the Hemlock Forest, the Woodsman or the girl, Ivy. He did not see a connection and rattled the words of the prophecy to himself again. *The balance key is the three, who are the three who know the key, to restore the balance three.* It had a catchy rhythm to it, but still made no sense. Regardless, it did not matter what he thought. The Elders were troubled by it, so he needed to be also.

However, the greatest concern was the drain on Firinn's magic and the white mist that was slowly taking over their realm. The Elders had concluded that it was connected to the Hemlock Forest. They wanted the Woodsman hindered so he could not continue to do, whatever it was he *was* doing, and they thought that the girl, Ivy, was the solution. The Elders had demanded that their Troika, comprised of himself, Odive and Freman, find a way to capture and control the girl.

It sounded easy enough, yet Edme had been one of the first to try to snatch the girl away when she was still a small babe and that had ended up with the Woodsman locking the Meadhan from the fey. Of course, back then no one was concerned with an inane prophecy so the Elders had backed down and left the Woodsman and his family alone for all those turns.

Edme wasn't sure what had changed in the last few mortal weeks, but the Elders had now made this matter the highest priority. They wanted Ivy.

Odive had come up with a proposal the Elders had agreed to, but this part was never spoken of. Odive had not told him or the Elders about his plan to use the Valkyrie stick.

"I am the leader of the Troika for the Elders. I am the Minister, Odive. Even though you lead the Druid Counsel now *I* am the one who is to speak on *their* behalf. Just what do you think you could do to me?" Odive moved towards to him and leaned in close enough for Edme to smell his breath. It wasn't pleasant.

"You heed me or else I'll do to you as I did to Freman," he hissed with enough venom to strike a mortal dead.

That shut Edme up. He looked over at Freman

standing silently beside them. Freman had repeatedly complained to the Elders about Odive, even with Odive present, as well as to other fey in the Citadel. These two had fought on every issue since the day Odive had joined the Troika. Then one fateful day the fey had woken to find his ability to speak gone and now had no choice but to remain silent. There were rumors that Odive had somehow done this to Freman, but there was no proof...other than the fact that Freman never again challenged Odive.

There was little doubt that Odive had somehow been involved. The Elders hadn't cared and Edme knew that they wouldn't care if he too was silenced. It did not impede Freman from doing the Elder's bidding, nor would it him.

"Can we proceed?" Odive asked smugly.

Edme refused to be completely intimidated by Odive. He was able to keep his voice level, but he was shaking like a leaf. "Yes. Though you still haven't answered my question. Why could we not just blink into the Meadhan?" Edme asked.

The look on Odive's face told Edme that the other fey was amazed he still had the gumption to demand an answer. Edme hoped it increased Odive's respect for him and when he actually received an answer, Edme felt vindicated.

"Because this Meadhan is not like any other, you should know this. I used an enchantment to lock the Meadhan inside a spherical field. That is how we captured and stopped the Valkyries....and why we now need the Valkyrie stick. It is the damn key for the thing. You cannot blink inside the field itself. I put enchantments on where it is stored also so you cannot use magic to even get near. It is restricted, a secret and it would not be all that restricted if anyone could *just* blink into it," Odive replied making a snorting sound. "Now would it? And for added protection, just in case some imprudent fey did try to blink in, there is a spell in place that would send whoever tried into Ifrinn."

Edme digested this information. He hadn't known that it was Odive who had converted the Meadhan into the spherical field, he had thought it was the work of the Elders. Odive's power intimidated and worried him. The Elders did utilize Odive's unique abilities to wield the Mysteries in ways no other fey was permitted. He had always assumed it was due to the fact that Odive had come to the Elders from the Citadel where the Mysteries were preserved. Odive was the first Troika who was a druid, a fey who had given up his birthright in Firinn to live in another realm. But then everything about Odive was atypical, his looks, his manners, as well as his enchantment abilities. It was the same reason that the Elders were so concerned with the Alltha girl. She too had powers that no one could explain.

"Are your questions answered to your satisfaction *now*?" Odive asked with an amused look.

Edme didn't look at him. Instead he glanced at Freman. The other fey's face was as still as his voice. Edme nodded yes and pulled his hood tight around his head and pinched his nose with part of it. Odive snickered and Edme decided to overlook it. No matter what anyone said, he could not understand why a fey would choose living in Alainn over Firinn. It might be brimming with magic, but it had a stench of the Eilibear that he couldn't stomach.

The Elders had picked the location well the last

time they had relocated the curious portable Meadhan. Its original location had been in the rolling hills of France, which Edme had actually thought was very nice. However, that location had somehow been compromised and it had ended up here on this horrible island. The wind blowing off the water was frigid and the seagulls had left their marks everywhere, even inside the structure.

He remained silent as Odive sneered at him before he turned with a rough laugh and continued to walk. Edme followed sullenly. They continued on for a few more minutes, weaving in and out of a variety of corridors and stairwells. They came to a couple of stone pillars, and Odive squeezed in between. Edme and Freman followed him into an even tighter passageway, barely wide enough for them to walk single file.

"Here," Odive announced as he came to the end of the passage and it opened up to a small landing, edged by a rusted handrail. A set of narrow stone steps angled down and disappeared into the darkness. Odive didn't wait to see if they followed as he went down and disappeared into the shadows. Edme hesitated for a moment to look back at Freman. The fey's face was set in stone.

Uneasiness filled his soul, but he continued following and knew Freman was right behind him. Up ahead, a faint greenish light glowed and Edme rubbed his fingers together while whispering "gile." A small glowing orb of green appeared from his fingertips and hovered for a moment before it moved away from him. He continued to follow Odive, the orb of light moving along with him.

He looked back once to confirm that Freman was

still with them. The fey was calmly following, not even bothering to create his own light source. Their eyes met and Edme couldn't tell what he was seeing in the depths of the silent fey's eyes; fear or hatred? Edme turned, not wanting to ponder what the fey was thinking and started walking faster in order to catch up with Odive.

The passageway ended at a large metal wall. It rose up out of sight, the light not reaching that high. Odive stood before it, waiting for the two to draw near, as if he wanted an audience. When they were beside him, he turned to the door and laid his hand on it.

"Relachez les fixations, revelent le passage, somber a la lumiere que j'appelle sur le cercle de trois a liberer la magie!"

Edme watched in anticipation. Enchantments such as this were not as common as they once had been. He didn't know if Odive had set this enchantment also, but he figured he must have since he had no issues speaking the old tongue.

He wondered again about the Mysteries the druids had access to. Maybe when this mission was completed, he should spend time studying at the Citadel. Really he had never wanted to linger in Alainn since the Eilibear had begun to attack...but the Citadel had always been safe from the demons. It might be wise for him to overcome his disregard for the druid fey and study the Mysteries, also. He couldn't let Odive continue to be the one the Elders depended on to cast enchantments on their behalf.

Edme watched as the metal wall responded to Odive's command and began to reshape itself. The outlines of two wide doors appeared, with a round ornate plate set between them. Odive pulled out a large flat key from inside his cloak. He fit it into a groove on the plate and then took a step back. Nothing happened for a moment, then the key started to glow slightly as it began a slow vibration. When it exploded, all three of them jumped and then leaned in to watch the plate dissolve completely.

Beneath it were two handholds. Odive took hold of one and pulled, cursing under his breath as he fought with the heavy door. A weak clink sounded, and the door began to move outward as Odive continued to pull. When it had finally swung wide enough for a body to fit through, Odive pushed his way in and the others followed quietly behind him.

They were in a large chamber, the ceiling held up with square columns. Sitting in the center of the room was a large round cylinder. It stood over twenty feet tall and looked solid. The air had a scent of flowers that overpowered the dankness of the room.

Edme found himself looking at the unique Meadhan, reduced and sealed up. It resembled an oversized snow globe with a scene of a grassy meadow filled with flowers. A tree line could be seen in the distance and the sound of a waterfall echoed faintly around them.

Odive walked up to the cylinder as he pulled the Valkyrie stick out of his cloak. He mumbled a single word under his breath and a long blade emerged from the end of the stick. Odive gently touched the tip of the blade to the spherical field and it instantly started to shimmer before turning transparent. Pushing the blade through the field, he cut an opening large enough for him to enter and then started to walk through it.

"Wait!" Edme called out. "You are going

inside?"

"*We* are going inside," Odive responded, turning to give him a look of disgust.

"But if we go near the Valkyries, we will surely cease to exist," he screeched as his chest tightened with fear.

"There is no danger as long as I hold the Valkyrie stick," Odive responded firmly, but Edme caught the slight twitch around the fey's right eye. Odive's jaw tightened as he turned back to the sphere and moved inside the barrier.

Edme was terrified and his limbs felt weak. As far as he knew, no one had entered this Meadhan since the Valkyries had been imprisoned. He felt a movement beside him and looked over to see Freman walking forward. The silent fey followed Odive though the doorway and Edme didn't seem to have a choice but to do the same. Moving unsteadily, he followed the other two inside and immediately felt the difference in the air.

He couldn't stop himself, he had to breathe it in deeply. This was the Alainn he remembered, fresh and clean. It brought back memories of when the fey, good and bad, had still roamed Alainn freely. When all three kingdoms, Firinn, Alainn and Ifrinn, were still powerful and bursting with magic. He would never admit it to another fey, but he missed the way the realms used to be.

The landscape, which had seemed like a picture on the outside of the sphere, had expanded to a panorama countryside of green. A soft mist started to rise from the ground, blanketing the grass lightly, giving it a surreal feeling. The edges of the meadow were surrounded by tall stately trees, bowed inward by the invisible barrier that held the Meadhan. One large irregular stone stood in the center of the meadow, covered by brambles. Odive led the way through the wet grasses, the mist swirling around them as they did so, until they were standing before the stone.

"Klareras!" Odive ordered, holding his hand out towards the stone. Instantly the brambles broke away and fell to the ground, leaving the stone bare save for the intriguing runes carved around its sides. Odive put his hand on the stone and shouted.

"Valkyries! We bid you come!"

"Will they?" Edme asked.

"Yes, they have no choice."

The ground beneath their feet began to vibrate, and the mist billowed out in a wave towards the tree line. It rose into a sheet of swirling white before it reached the trees and six forms began to take shape. When the Elders had made use of the Mysteries to cast the ancient enchantment, the result was not what anyone had imagined.

The chosen female druids were expected to become strong warriors who could battle the Eilibear, yet instead the ill-fated druids had turned into monsters. The very sight of them led to instant death. Within days of their creation, the Elders had to figure out a way to get rid of them.

Edme watched as the forms solidified as they emerged out from the mist and began to move quickly towards them.

Horses.

The largest white stallions Edme had ever seen. Their manes glistened and flowed in long misty waves as the creatures galloped, unnaturally swift, straight at them. As they drew closer, he could make out riders on each, tiny in comparison to their mounts.

As they neared, they slowed to a controlled cantor and then to a uniform trot. The animals marched purposefully forward as steam rose from their nostrils. Edme started to tremble and felt the urge to flee.

One stallion moved out in front of the others, lowering its head and emitting a loud nasal snort that echoed loudly in the quiet of the meadow. Its ears were flattened back and it advanced threateningly toward us. It halted only inches from the stone, its neck muscles tensed as it pawed the ground and reeled its head back to neigh.

The other five horses had stopped also, back about ten feet from the first. Edme couldn't bring himself to stop looking at the stallion's eyes. The creature seemed to be staring right at him.

Then to his shock, it spoke in a light musical voice.

"A ghlaonn chugainn leis an Cloch Valkyrie, dúinn an damanta an Fey?"

Edme couldn't help but be impressed as he watched Odive step forward until he was within touching distance of the demon horse. He looked up at the rider. Edme realized it was she who had spoken, not the horse.

"English. Speak not in your common tongue!" Odive yelled up at her.

The horse reared, forcing Odive to stumble backwards. A deep laugh that sounded more like a snarl erupted as the rider flung herself down and gently patted the horse's flank. The white stallion calmed itself and stood like a statue next to the Valkyrie. Edme pulled his eyes from her to see the other riders had done the same and were now moving forward to stand beside the first.

They were women of unspeakable beauty, all adorned with long flowing silver hair that rippled about them as if a gentle breeze were blowing. Their eyes were like milky blue glass, clear and shining.

They were dressed for battle, wearing straps of blackened leather that barely covered their breasts and short skirts of the same. All six wielded massive swords that three of them were already beginning to swing as if to regain the balance and feel of their weapons. The Valkyrie that had spoken first took in her companions' readiness, a smile playing at the corners of her lips for just a split second before she raised her gaze to the three fey. Her eyes were but slits, filled with suspicion and loathing.

"I said, who calls to us with the Valkyrie Stone, us the damned of the fey?

Her voice peeled out like a chime, the sweetness of its sound unspoiled by the words themselves. It was hard to believe that this woman was as dangerous as the stories he had heard.

"Incredible," breathed Edme, who couldn't help but ogle the female fey standing before him.

"Quiet, you idiot! You are looking at the demon spawn of the druids!" Odive hissed over his shoulder at Edme.

She spoke again, her voice sending chills of desire though all three males.

"I am Kianna, and my battle sisters are Gunilla, Vada, Inger, Bertelle and Akneeta."

"I know you all. Gunilla the Seer, Vada the Siren, Inger the Healer, Bertelle the Mighty, Akneeta the Shield…" He looked at them one by one as he named them. "And you, Kianna the Shifter. The Sextet of

Valkyries." He sneered at her as if their very names were offensive. "You are an abnormality of magic, six fused as one."

"Did you bring us forth to insult us, or have the fey sent you here to ask our forgiveness?" Her posture was one of indignation.

Odive stood up straight and confident before her. "We have nothing to ask forgiveness for. You brought your banishment upon yourself by forging the Valkyrie magic. You trifled with the druids and have been living with their vengeance. It is them you should hate."

The Valkyrie moved closer to the fey. A hard look of rebellion flitted across her face, then was gone...replaced with a sweet smile. She strolled seductively over to stand before him, every movement pleasing and enticing.

"Oh, we do, fey...the druids will one day feel our wrath. We take responsibility for submitting to the magic, but we are neither the ones that wielded the Valkyrie stick nor the ones who made the feeble attempt to unweave the magic." Again, the sound of her voice did not match the words she spoke. "Come fey, you have called us. Name yourself. It has been many eons since any have come seeking us, yet you are the first to come inside and call out for us. What is the price for our freedom?"

"I am Elder Niall. These others are Elder Artair and Ronaic."

"You are not Niall. I know Niall...and Artair and Ronaic." Kianna snickered scornfully, giving all three imposters a hard look. Edme looked away uncomfortably from her gaze; he did not know that Odive was going to try to pass them off as the Elders.

She focused back on Odive. Leaning in, she sniffed the air around him.

"You do not smell like Niall, in fact you have an odor of another I know well." Taking another deep whiff, she leaned back with a knowing smirk. In a low whisper, she announced, "You are the one."

Edme wondered if she knew Odive was the fey who had cast the enchantment on her and the others. He knew the earliest stories of the Valkyrie warriors; they were shrewd, very powerful and *very* intelligent…as well as monstrosities that had been eradicated. The original Mystery that had created the first Valkyries had been locked away with the druids. Edme couldn't remember now if it had been the Elders who'd decided to use the Mystery to bring the Valkyries back when the Eilibear descended on them or if Odive had been the one to suggest it. He looked over at the fey and narrowed his eyes at him.

Odive laughed menacingly and seemed unfazed by the woman.

"So be it. I am Odive, a member of the Troika. This is Edme and Freman…the other members," he spoke their names flatly. "We have called you forth by the command of the Elders. The Eilibear are growing bold and draining the magic from Firinn, Alainn and all the Meadhans between. Your services and those of the other female druids are needed if we are to defeat them."

"Why the games, Oh-dive?" she asked, pulling the name out as if it were a foul word.

"In the world of Alainn, we are the voices of the Elders. Other than that, you need not know more…only that the Elders have sent us and desire your services…in return for providing you with freedom."

Kianna turned to look at her sisters. All had focused their attention on Kianna and the fey that had liberated them. Silent communication seemed to pass between the females until Kianna nodded as if in agreement before she faced Odive once more.

"You call us to battle? That is all?" she asked sweetly as she swung her sword. The other Valkyries moved toward the fey, encircling them, all the while swinging their swords. The one named Vada had moved to Edme. She leaned in towards him so that he could feel her breath on his face. He licked his lips and tried to keep his eyes from roaming downward. She moved closer still, until he could feel the outline of her breasts through his cloak. Two others had surrounded Freman who stood as still as a statue, but the one that had moved behind Odive was rubbing her body erotically against his back and whispering the same thing over and over again. *Is í an eochair iarmhéid na trí, cé hiad na trí cinn a fhios ag an eochair, an t-iarmhéid na trí ais… Is í an eochair iarmhéid na trí, cé hiad na trí cinn a fhios ag an eochair, an t-iarmhéid na trí ais… Is í an eochair iarmhéid na trí, cé hiad na trí cinn a fhios ag an eochair, an t-iarmhéid na trí ais.*

Edme felt a longing that had fallen silent long ago begin to grow. A whimper escaped from his lips and he looked over to Odive for help. Odive was glaring at Kianna, shaking with anger and looked like he was about to explode.

"What is this one saying?" Odive called out.

Edme gasped with disbelief. Even he knew what the Valkyrie was chanting. There was no way that Odive did not recognize it also. It was the prophecy. Even here, locked inside this Meadhan, their Seer was repeating the riddle.

"Nothing...it is just a poem she likes to say," Kianna replied coolly and licked her lips seductively at him. The one whispering was rubbing herself against Odive, leaning in until her mouth was almost touching his ear.

"Call your sister off," Odive screamed at Kianna. "And make her stop saying that!"

"And why would I do that? Did you not wish us free?" she asked him in dreamlike calmness.

Odive's eyes swept over the Valkyrie before him as he raised his hand, still holding the Valkyrie stick with the blade. He swirled in one quick motion and the Valkyrie behind him screamed just before she fell to the ground and the mist enveloped her.

Edme followed the action as if in slow motion and felt a silent scream erupt from his lips as the female's head rolled to his feet. He looked up from the grisly sight just in time to see the horses fade from being as the other Valkyries screamed in terror.

"What have you done?" Kianna shrieked as she ran around Odive to her fallen sister.

"Call them off!" he demanded once more, though he did not need to ask. The Valkyries had moved to where Gunilla had fallen.

"You killed her!" Kianna cried from where she knelt by the fallen body. "You have come to kill us?"

Odive had moved away and was looking down at the female he had so easily killed.

"Not to kill, though I have the power to do so. You see, I found the means to break the Valkyrie enchantment that turned you into fiends of death," Odive declared haughtily. "You *will* now obey me and the

Elders. I've only need for one of the Valkyries, but the rest may live if they obey."

He had gotten their attention, though even Edme knew that if not for Odive's apparent power, their swords would make short work of him. The five remaining Valkyrie stood and faced Odive, looks of abhorrence etched on their faces.

"We will obey...but a life for a life." The leader declared and before Edme knew what she intended, she had swung her sword and easily lopped off Freman's head. It sailed through the air and then only the sound of a thud was heard as it hit the ground in the mist. His headless body stood still for a few seconds more before it sank slowly down to the mist-covered ground.

Edme knew he was screaming, though no sound was forthcoming. His eyes were wide with fear and he looked from where Freman had fallen to the Valkyrie holding the bloodied sword, to Odive who ignored him and back to the head of the Valkyrie at his feet. Her face was set in a permanent look of shock.

"So be it. We understand each other. You will come with us. The Sumair stone has been found," Odive declared.

Kianna stuck her sword into the ground and glared at the fey. "The Sumair stone? What, pray tell, is a Sumair stone?"

"Don't play dumb with me. That one..." he said motioning to the now-dead Valkyrie. "was a Seer. You may have been sealed away, but we know you have knowledge. As I said, the Sumair stone is found, and being held in a Meadhan. That Meadhan is owned by a Frith fey, and she is using its power to her own end."

"You wish us to kill her?" Kianna asked with an

evil little grin. "You will us to rip this fey apart so that the magic can be released?" She had retrieved her sword and was gleefully beginning to swing it, slicing the air as she questioned.

"No, the Elders will take care of that. She has protection of another sort." He paused for effect. "A young Warrior Druid." At the mention of a druid, all of the Valkyries started to hiss until the air was heavy with their hatred. "Yes, I see you will like this undertaking. We wish to have you become part of the battle with the Eilibear, join once more the fight against the demons the Warrior Druids have been handling alone since your...untimely departure. All past animosities forgiven and forgotten. The young druid we wish you to focus on is the son of Rōber Edsmond."

A screech ripped through the meadow and Akneeta raised her sword high and screamed out. "Is é mo athar beo fós? Ba mhaith liom a mharú go diabhal!"

"Yes, I see I was correct. I thought one of you was also the spawn of that particular druid and you have been watching the events as they played out." Odive laughed easily as he kept his eyes trained on her gleaming sword. "I'm rather glad it was not you I had slain."

"We will be able to do as Akneeta asks? She will be allowed to avenge her mother and kill her sire?" Kianna asked with bright eyes.

"Yes...but only after you do what we ask. It is the young druid we need to curtail. We do not wish his death...only the death of the affection between him and the Frith fey. The Elders wish the druid, Zaccheus Edsmond, otherwise occupied so that the Frith fey will be alone and he will not be able to complete the Gorffen.

Can you do that? Work with the Warrior Druids? Battle alongside them against the Eilibear? Will you enthrall the young druid? And most importantly, assist with the retrieval of the Sumair Stone?"

"Tell me Oh-dive, why is this stone so important to the Elders that you would release us back onto the world?" she asked narrowing her eyes at him.

"I'm sure that the one there knew the answer," he replied motioning to the fallen Valkyrie. "The prophecy speaks of the balance key is the three. It is the Elder's belief that the Sumair Stone is connected in some way. Whether it is or is not does not matter to me. The Elders wish control of it for the benefit of all fey and it is our duty to achieve that for them."

Kianna looked around at her sisters, each nodding agreement, before she turned once more to Odive. "We may not be six, but we are still Valkyries," she declared strongly. "We will have our revenge on Rōber Edsmond and possibly others of the druids. And after, will we be allowed to remain free?"

"You do this for the Elders and yes, you will be allowed to kill all the druids you wish, and I will personally give you the Valkyrie Stick so that you will be forever free. I will even have the druids at the Citadel rewrite the Valkyrie history so that you will be remembered as heroines, Warriors for the mortal's gods," he declared with a grand wave of his arm.

She looked over at her sisters and, as one, they nodded their acceptance.

"We will do this," she said, turning back to Odive.

"Now call in the others. We need all to fight the battles," Odive demanded.

Kianna looked at him for a long minute, then turned to the trees and let out an ear-piercing shriek and then settled into what sounded like a war cry. As her voice rang out, the mists rose in bellowing waves from the trees and, like the movement of the ocean, they rolled and crashed, becoming increasingly more violent as the storm of mist rushed towards where they stood. Then she went silent and the rolling mist slowly began to settle. Enormous stag-like creatures emerged from the trees and galloped in a cloud of mist towards them. Their antlers were copious full racks. Their thick boney spikes towered over the creature like malevolent crowns. As they coursed forward, the creatures became to shift forms. By the time they were close enough for Edme to see, they had transformed into females wearing either hide battle armor along with headdresses of large stag antlers or white robed beings. The warriors carried a variety of weapons—clubs, swords and bows. They looked dazed and glanced around as if they did not know where they were.

Edme turned to Odive with bewilderment which quickly turned to extreme outrage.

"You knew? That's the lost Sisterhood. No one knew where they had gone. We debated for hundreds of turns if the Eilibear had killed them off or if some twist of magic had cursed them into the void. But you knew all the while," he screamed. "It wasn't only the Valkyries that were locked inside this Meadhan, but the female druids also!"

"Of course. We couldn't just take away the six of them without taking the entire Sisterhood. The Elders knew there might be a time when they would be needed once more...and now is that time," Odive answered smugly.

Edme felt a cold shiver deep in his bones. He wondered if the Elders really had known about this all along, and even if they had, did they now realize what the ramifications of releasing them would be. One thing was for sure, he was very glad the Oak Triad of the druids had been disbanded. They had been the governing body for the fey, the mortals and the Eilibear. Those druids had sided with the Eilibear before the war, and afterwards their thinking was deemed traitorous. They had been supplanted by the fey Elders and a new Druid Council installed in their place. If any of them had known then that the new Druid Council had been responsible for the disappearance of all the females of their tribe, they may have not lost their power within the fey world. This whole situation would not end well if any of them were still taking breath.

CHAPTER 2 – Ivy

"Crud!" I said, as I peered at myself in the mirror. Really? A zit? I leaned closer, putting my tongue against the inside of my cheek to push it out and see it better. No way was I going out in public with this thing on my face. I glanced over my shoulder to see what Margo was doing. She was busy pulling on knee-high striped orange socks to go with her purple polka-dot capris and brightly flowered tee and somehow managing to dance while she did so. I smiled.

She had been a bubbling ball of energy since the first day I met her and even now that she knew that she was a Sprite, there wasn't that big of change in her. She was the epitome of a storybook fairy...all cuteness and butterfly wings and silliness. I wanted to hug her all the time, even when she decided that sitting on top of your head, holding on to bits of hair was the place to be. She was, inside and out, the sweetest person I had ever met and right now she wasn't paying any attention to me.

Turning back to the mirror, I felt for the tingle at the back of my throat, and then whispered. "Heal and go away." I watched as the stupid zit sank, changed from red to a normal flesh color and completely healed up. Next I needed to do something about the bags under my eyes. Granddad or Margo would be sure to comment on them. I looked worn out and, not that I wanted to admit it, a bit sickly. I rolled a bit more energy into the familiar tingle and gave myself a nice healthy glow. My eyes cleared and the puffiness faded as my skin smoothed itself out. I inspected my reflection again and was pleased with the results.

It was really cool. I loved being a fey with magic. I quickly finished applying what little make-up I wore and cleaned up the small mess I had made on the dressing table just as Margo came up and threw her arm around my shoulder.

"Today's the day," she chirped, and gifted me with a darling grin. "Excited?"

"No…not at all," I lied. What could I possibly be excited about? Just over a year ago I had been a normal teenager and had barely completed my sophomore year at high school. Then I had run away to Granddad's cabin and discovered I was anything but normal. I was a fey with unique powers that rolled off my tongue and vines that sprouted on my face in really cool spirals, and I could make things grow. Add to that, my best friend was a Sprite and I had a boyfriend who was a real catch, and a druid to boot.

I had given up on going back to high school and, with a little help from the Alltha Order, obtained my diploma and had started my freshman year at college. I was now a student at Southern Oregon State University—SOU—in Ashland. It was the same school that Zack had been attending. I loved it there and really enjoyed my classes, far more than I had at high school. I'd picked botany as my major. I knew that with my special ability to make plants grow, I needed to know more about the things. No way was I going to be the one who destroyed the world by growing some man-eating plant. I had all the time in the world, so I figured I'd keep taking all the courses I could and maybe become a Master Gardener along the way. Granddad thought my reasoning was cute…which annoyed me to no end.

My life had been going through flip-flops, yet my relationship with Zack was growing stronger every day. I was still trying to work it all out in my brain, but there was no doubt that my life had gone from a crappy nightmare to an enchanted daydream. It had been more than a year since I'd met both Margo and Zack, and they had been working on some big surprise for me in celebration. Nope…nothing to be excited about here.

"Right…like I'd believe that. You've been trying to get me to tell you what the surprise is for a month." Margo laughed at me, taking me by the hand and pulling me out of the room. "But tonight *is* the night," she finished as she made kissy faces at me.

I giggled and she leaned in close and winked at me. I really couldn't wait to see what these two had planned. Zack and Margo had been all secretive for the last few weeks and my anticipation had been growing daily.

"Are you feeling better today? You looked pretty ragged when you came in last night," she asked with concern.

"I'm feeling fine. I don't know why you all think I'm sick. I'm just tired from studying for exams is all. I really wish you, Granddad and Grandma Winnie would leave off. There is nothing wrong with me," I said as I stepped out of the room and into the hall.

I had been feeling run down for the last few months, and it was beginning to be a nuisance. It seemed whenever Zack and I spent any amount of time together I ended up exhausted. It was a pain, but I didn't want others to worry about it. Maybe I was going through some fey coming-of-age thing.

Margo gave me a worried look but didn't say anything more on the subject, and I was relieved. As I moved down the upstairs hall, I knew instantly that Granddad was cooking breakfast. I could smell bacon. He didn't need to; all of us could take care of ourselves. I had for almost a year, then Granddad had returned to my life, not dead, and we both regressed right back into the roles we had before he had disappeared—him, the adult and me, the child.

She linked arms with me as I reached the stairs and started making exaggerated smooching faces at me, then switched to a scrunched up face as Granddad's off-key singing hit us full blast.

"Sugar, aww honey honey, you are my candy girl..." came Granddad's gruff crooning. "Oooooh, pour a little sugar on it, ooooh yeah..."

"What *is* he singing?" Margo whispered, leaning over to me.

"I think it's supposed to be 'Sugar, Sugar' by the Archies," I replied with a grin.

"And who or what is the Archies and why would Granddad want to sing that?"

"It's a really cool story, actually. The Archies were characters in that comic book, remember? Archie, Jughead, Betty and Veronica?" Margo gave me a blank look with raised eyebrows. "Well it was a comic book until they made a cartoon out of it in the 60s. And they started a band and this was their big hit."

"The cartoon characters started a band and had a hit song?" The look on her face was pure disbelief, but I liked the story and the words were out before I could stop myself.

"Yeah, Archie was the singer, but some guy

named Ron Dante really sang it. I think it's horrible that his name isn't anywhere on the song. It was a big hit. I have it on my MP3 if you want to hear what it really sounds like," I offered. I did like the song and knew it would now be stuck in my head for the rest of the day.

"Please, I beg you, NO," she whispered with force, rolling her eyes at me.

I finished hopping down the last couple of steps into the kitchen, trying hard not to laugh, and came face to face with a banquet. It looked like Granddad had cooked for a large group of people.

The table was piled with heaps of hash brown potatoes, homemade biscuits, bacon and eggs fried in the bacon grease. It looked nauseating to me.

"There's my girls," he boomed when he saw us. Margo flitted around, grabbing a biscuit and filling a glass of water from the sink. "Sit down Margo, eat right. You too, Ivy. Grab a plate and eat something. You are both looking too thin," he said as he added more brown fried eggs to the pile.

"Someone joining us?" I asked as I sat and tried to figure out what of this mess I could eat.

"Eddie and Carmen are coming over. We've been called to a special meeting with the Alltha, only for the night," he said pointing to a couple of scrolls lying on the table. I was getting used to seeing these things. Communication between members of the Alltha Order was done by this really cool little bit of magic. A chime would sound when there was an incoming message and then a scroll would appear in front of the person the message was intended for. The members could also snap their fingers, calling on a blank scroll and quill if they needed to send one. A soft chime sounded just before they appeared too. Grandad could write his message, roll the scroll up, snap again and the scroll would be magically whisked away to whoever he was sending it to. So much for snail mail.

Granddad was still talking, so I pulled my eyes and thoughts away from the scrolls and tried to pay attention.

"You and Margo will be on your own and I wanted to make sure you ate decent before I had to leave," he explained, pulling something from the oven that looked like pancakes. Those I could eat. I waited until he put the plate down and then transferred one misshapen pancake to my plate.

"Sorry Granddad, but I promised Grandma Winnie that I'd help at the shop today since I don't have classes. In fact, I'm going to be late," Margo announced as she glanced at the wall clock. Another new addition to the house from Granddad...he was all about schedules and being on time now.

"I spoke with her this morning already. If you want, she said she could come back with you tonight to keep you company," he informed us, turning from the stove with a spatula in his hand, dripping grease all over.

Margo gave me a look that said it all as she grabbed a biscuit and hugged me. Whispering as low as possible she said, "Don't worry, I'll make sure Granny doesn't come." Then she kissed my head, swirled like a ballerina and blinked. She didn't need to spin first, but ever since she had discovered that she could blink out like Zack and me, she had been practicing different means for her exits. I liked this one the best.

The room grew very silent without her. Granddad sat down across from me and started to fill his own plate. I picked at the pancake and eyed the coffee pot. Granddad saw my look instantly.

"No.   There's milk in the fridge and I think there's some orange juice in there also."

"Really?" I whined. "I've been drinking mochas for years and you and Marmaw never said a word. Now I can't even have one cup of normal coffee in the mornings?" Geez, I felt like I was ten years old.

"That's enough.   Milk or juice and take your vitamins."

I huffed loudly as I got up and found the bottle of vitamins. I took two out and gulped them down dry, then grabbed the orange juice. I wasn't sure how I was going to get it through to Granddad that he didn't need to worry, that I was okay. I sat back down and poured a glass. I sipped it slowly. It was tangy and I had to admit, it tasted good.

"Granddad, Margo and I will be fine on our own," I said.

"I worry," he said as he continued to eat. I drank my juice and waited. He looked up at me finally and his eyes were filled with concern. "How are you really feeling? You've lost weight, I can see it. And even with the vitamins, you seem tired all the time."

"Well, I've grown taller so I do look a little thinner, but it's really nothing to worry about. And I'm tired because I'm in college and have a buttload of homework every night," I said, trying to shrug off his concerns.

"Language," he admonished looking at me closely.

"Sorry, but really, Granddad, I'm fine."

He picked up his coffee and took a drink, not

looking at me. "And how do you feel when you are around the druids…or with Zack? Tired, sick?"

That caught me off guard. I bristled, instantly on the defensive. "Of course not! I don't know what you are implying, but being with Zack does not wear me out. I have plenty of time to do my homework and get the chores around the house done," I said heatedly. Granddad tightened his lips and just looked at me, concerned.

"Maybe I better not go. Eddie and Carmen can tell me what's up when they come back," he mused aloud.

Crud, this wasn't going the way I wanted at all. I tried to stay calm as I ate the now foul-tasting pancake.

"Why would you want to do that? You are on the Alltha council now. Don't you vote on stuff? You really don't want the other Uncles and Aunts making decisions without you having a say, do you?" I knew I had said the right thing.

"Maybe you're right. But I don't feel good about leaving you alone right now."

"Granddad, I'm hardly alone. You have the whole forest filled with druids. Nothing would dare harm me with them around. Besides, Zack is here, and he can stay with us while you're gone, you know, as added protection."

"No," he bellowed as he stood up. The muscles in his jaw grew taunt as his face under his beard deepened to a bright red. "You need to keep your distance from him from now on. He's a druid, he's too old and…well there are things you don't know. You stay away from him, you hear me?"

His sudden explosion was unexpected. Not once

in the last few months had he told me to stay away from Zack.

"All of the sudden you don't want me spending time with Zack? He lives in the forest with us. I'd see him every day even if he wasn't my boyfriend," I said, fighting to keep my voice level.

"You're too young to be around boys his age."

"Granddad I'm in college now, remember? I'm around boys his age every day."

"That may be...but you are too young to have a boyfriend," he said faltering a bit with his logic.

"Too young to have a boyfriend? Granddad I'm, what, 120 years old? I think I'm old enough to decide for myself," I snapped at him, then instantly felt guilty. I wondered if he'd discovered that I'd been sneaking out a lot to spend most nights with Zack. I knew it was wrong, but we weren't doing anything other than making out. I knew I needed more time to sleep and to study, but still, I didn't like being told what to do.

"Don't give me lip. Maybe in fey years, but in my mind you've just turned seventeen and he's grown. He's too old." His face had changed to a bright purple and I was afraid he'd burst something soon. It wasn't worth it. He simply wasn't in the mood to see reason right now. He still thought of me as a little girl and until he came around to realize I had grown up all we were going to do was fight. I didn't want to do that now, and especially not today.

"Kay, Granddad, calm down. Sorry I snapped," I said. I wanted him to leave. I had plans for tonight. I knew that Zack was finally going to show me the *big surprise,* and I wasn't going to let Granddad ruin it for me.

"You should be. You don't go talking to me like Skyler used to. Don't you do that to me," he reprimanded with a clenched jaw.

That was a low blow. His overprotectiveness was in overdrive, and he needed to take a breath and calm down.

"That wasn't nice," I said as coolly as I could and waited for him to compose himself. It didn't take long. He ruffled his hair and paced for a time before he sat down next to me and took my hand.

"I'm sorry, Ivy. I didn't mean to say that," he said as his brows drew together. "It's just that something Eddie said a while back has been gnawing at me. I got to thinking over some of the conversations I used to have with Elsie and no matter how I connect the pieces, they do not fit," he said in a worried voice.

"About what? What did he say that made you think about Marmaw?" My curiosity was piqued since Granddad didn't mention Marmaw very often.

Granddad shook his head and tried to smile. "I'm not sure and I don't want to say anything until I have more information. But I've been thinking..." he let that hang in the air as he shoveled a forkful of greasy hash browns into his mouth.

"Thinking about what?" I pressed.

He put his fork down and looked at me with that serious Granddad look he had. "I think it would be best for us to get away for a time, away from these fey. Maybe you and Margo would like to travel for a while, go to Italy or France. I hear there are some wonderful exchange programs. You could study abroad for a time," he said, warming to the idea.

"Margo needs to help Winnie and we both just

started college. We can't just take off to another continent."

His face fell as his shoulders lowered in defeat.

"I know, but we need to do something. Make a change. Listen to me," he said as he gave my hand a little squeeze. "There are other things going on. Things are getting a bit heated at the counsel. I think we need to go out into the real world again, live in Alainn, close up the forest and stay away from the fey...*all fey* for a time." His tone was pleading and it tugged at my heart. He was worried. Not just about me and Zack, but the fey in general.

I started to shake my head, wanting to tell him that he was wrong, that I liked living in the forest. I could blink outside to the human world, Alainn, any time I wanted and still be part of it. Zack's dad seemed pleased with their being here, so I didn't understand why Granddad was so worried.

"Uncle Eddie doesn't seem to have a problem with me being around Zack or our living arrangements here in our forest. Have you asked him what's up?" Granddad and Zack's dad had been friends for more years than I knew. Surely, if he thought something was wrong, he'd tell Granddad.

"That's part of the reason I think something is wrong. Eddie is all about the Alltha Order and his calling of being a Warrior. His past actions tell me he should be concerned with training his son now and getting back to the fight against the Eilibear. But he's not. Instead he is here and encouraging the two of you to be together, as if that is the most important aspect of his life right now."

"He cares for his son is all," I said rather lamely.

I knew deep down that Granddad was right...it was odd. Uncle Eddie pushed the other druids relentlessly, but not Zack. If I showed up, he waved Zack off from training to be with me. I looked up at Granddad, considering what that might mean. "Have you asked him why?"

"He merely laughs and says something about young love and then changes the subject. I've seen him and other warriors at the council meetings share glances when I ask questions. I know that there's something they're not telling me," he said shaking his head in frustration. "I feel in my bones that everything is not what it seems. I think we made a mistake allowing the counsel and druids to have access to our Meadhan. The only way to get them out now, without creating a war with the fey, is to close up the forest."

"You never had a problem just pushing them out before, not that I want you to, but why is now any different?" I asked.

"Because *you* are the owner now. If I lock it, the fey will see the action as a breach of ownership protocol and will expect you to discipline me. If you tell me to lock it...or lock it yourself, we have another whole set of problems. Just believe me, it's complicated, especially since they still have concerns about you and...well let me worry about the fey," he replied and I was still at a loss about what his concern really was. We seemed to have switched topics. I had been the rightful owner my entire life, Granddad was the guardian in my stead until I was old enough. Now I was officially the owner, by the fey bylaws, so I couldn't see what the problem was.

"Can't I do anything I want with my Meadhan? You always have in the past and it doesn't seem like such a leap that I would act the same as you."

"I've tried to explain before about the fey. They are magical and unless they were raised as Alltha, they don't understand having a normal life like humans. They just pass time. That is what the fey do—they pass time and never do anything. The druids and the Alltha are productive, they have purpose...their lives have meaning. The other fey? Well I've never seen them do anything but make trouble. And I think trouble of some kind is brewing. This meeting today is with the fey leaders...again, which is odd that they are poking their heads in so often with matters of the Alltha. This makes the third time this year and with Eddie acting secretive, I'm even more concerned."

As he spoke my mind raced, trying to think of what the fey could be upset about and what Uncle Eddie might be up to. It made me wonder what would be happening now if I hadn't run away. What if I hadn't met Laven? He was the jerk who first told me that I was a fey and then tried to trick me into giving him my Meadhan. And what if I hadn't met Zack and Margo. Would Margo have discovered she was fey also, or would Zack still be in school and unknowingly waiting for his dad to tell him the truth? Would Laven and his bunch of friends have found a way to take the Meadhan from me if I hadn't met the other two?

When Granddad had first returned, he said things happened for a reason and he figured we three were meant to be together. Yet now he wanted to get me away from Zack. I didn't know what my life would look like without my dreadlock-wearing, Dywel-toting druid.

I wanted to stay here in the forest. I felt safe and at peace...well most of the time at least. We had lost the solitude of having it all to ourselves. But almost everything I needed was right here. I could blink outside to any place I wanted at any time. So could Granddad, Zack and Margo. The other fey had to have three of them together and then they could blink as we did. Were the fey upset now because I still wasn't acting like they expected a normal fey to act?

No way was I going to just hang out in a forest without a house to live in or dress the way they did. I didn't even know how they got their clothes...though Margo and I had discussed that a lot. She wanted to study fashion design and was fascinated by what Laven and the sisters had worn.

Granddad interrupted my inner dialogue by standing up and moving a couple of feet of away from me. With his back to me, he said, "I've decided that when I get back from this meeting, we're going to close up the forest. We're going back to the real world. You can finish college if you wish. You can pick where we go, the town and even the house we buy if you want. You don't have to stay at SOU, you know. There are other colleges that are more focused in what you want to study," Granddad finished, as he finally turned to look at me.

My body tensed. I wasn't mad, but I could feel tears starting to fill my eyes. I loved my forest and I felt I had finally found my true home. I didn't want to get another house or even consider changing schools. Out there, I had all the memories of being with Marmaw and my horrible year with Skyler. I needed time to process this and Granddad looking at me all compassionate-like wasn't helping. My tears started to fall freely down my cheeks and I wiped them away, embarrassed that I was losing it in front of him.

"I know I've sprung this on you rather suddenly, but we have discussed something like this before. Remember, I am still your Granddad. Something is off and until I can figure out what it is, we need to do this. I am sorry, but my decision is final," he said gently as he reached out and placed his hand on my head.

CHAPTER 3 – Zack

Zack opened his eyes to darkness. By the angle of the moon outside his tent's window, he knew it was close to four in the morning. His body needed more sleep, but he needed Ivy more. The last few months had been stressful. It was almost a compulsory need to be around her all the time. It wasn't fair to her since he knew he was making it hard for her to get her studying done and he *did* have other things he needed to do, too. He knew that he had been being an ass to her this last week. He had made her feel guilty for not sneaking out every night after her Granddad went to bed. He just wanted to hold her and be around her. It wasn't sexual...he just felt so much better, physically and mentally when he was near her.

He had been working on a surprise for her and finding the time for it had added even more stress to his life. His dad was being a bulldog about his training, though he did seem uncharacteristically understanding about letting him spend time with Ivy.

The man was impossible to figure out. At first, after the battle with the Eilibear, his dad had tried to convince him that he couldn't stay here, that he needed to start his training as a warrior. Then suddenly he had relented and become all cheerful about him and Ivy. It seemed like he had decided overnight that he was okay with Zack's decision not to leave the Hemlock forest, be with Ivy and continue his studies at SOU. It was the college he had picked, not the one his dad thought he should be going to, so that was something of a shock. It got even stranger when his dad had rearranged his own plans and rounded up all the young druids that needed training, too, and brought them back to the Hemlock forest.

It irked Zack. This was Ivy's forest; she was the owner of the Meadhan and the doorway and she hadn't wanted all of them here. Her Granddad had simply flexed his muscle as her guardian and she had yielded. She'd said it was her decision, but he didn't believe her. He had given up trying to convince her to tell them all no. She had lost her grandparents and then got her Granddad back, and she wasn't going to go against the man and risk losing him a different way. He did understand that.

Zack eventually found he didn't really mind having the other druids around. In fact, he had been missing other young men his age. And these guys really were his age, as in really old in mortal terms, but young for druids. They were each just learning about their Dywel's also, so it was cool to hang out with them. For a few days after they had shown up, all of them had worked together to clear out the undergrowth by the fallen tree where he and Ivy had fought the battle.

When it was cleared, his dad had them blink out of the forest and collect Army tents and a bunch of supplies he had left at the start of the path in Coos Bay. Zack thought they would just blink back with the stuff, but to his surprise, they were told to hike in. None of the other guys complained so Zack didn't say anything.

Zack figured that his dad must have thought the hike, while carrying a heavy load, would be good for them. Since he and Ivy had blinked from halfway up the path to the hollow where the doorway into Firinn was, he had never hiked the full path and wasn't opposed to doing it.

Besides, it was a nice change to hang out with guys who cussed, spit and peed wherever they wanted. The hike had taken no time at all and by the time they returned, Zack had a fresh arsenal of dirty jokes to chuckle about.

The only down side was that his dad had demanded that he move to the tent city with the guys and out of the house he had been sharing with Ivy. But again, he wasn't too upset; it was good to hang out with all of them. His dad had also set up a strenuous workout regimen for them. They might as well have been in the military. It was like boot camp on steroids, with his dad as the drill sergeant.

They did the normal running, sit-ups and push-ups, but concentrated more on the weight lifting, bodybuilding, and muscle toning. It took a lot of strength to not only hold onto the Dywel, but also to control it so it would work correctly. Dywels were swords and could be used like a normal everyday sword, but they had been created by magic to fight the Eilibear. And the only way to fight the demons was with the cords of flame that erupted from the swords' tip. Zack had discovered firsthand what it felt like, trying to control a strange sword formed out of his right arm as it shot out cords of flame that lassoed the Eilibear.

Eilibear didn't have a solid form. They were like a poisoned mist. Unless, of course, they had taken over something else's body. Then the cords would wrap around the fey or creature the Eilibears had contaminated and squeeze until the Eilibear let go. Sometimes the fey or creature survived, most times not.

Normally, Dywels only produced one cord, but Zack's had shot out multiple cords. After the battle, their lives had settled down, and Ivy and Zack had tried to figure out why his was so different. His dad thought it was because Ivy had powered him, but Zack and Ivy secretly thought it probably had more to do with the talisman he had placed in his right wristband. It had formed into part of the Dywel when it had suddenly appeared.

Zack had tried to tell his dad about it, but his father had stopped him, assuring him that it did not matter what had happened then. Now that he was with him, he would be trained properly.

The first time all of the druids had stood in formation and, one by one, attempted to call out their Dywel, Zack was the only one who was able to do it on the first try. He didn't feel right about it, and a few of the others seemed offended by his ability. It didn't help when they finally did get theirs to appear since his produced multiple cords of fire and theirs only brought one. At first all of them were impressed until his dad ruined everything by informing them that Zack was in line to be a Grand Warrior, something only one in a thousand druids could hope to achieve. It probably should have made him feel special, however he had never liked to be in the limelight and this was setting him apart from the group. That and his dad allowing him to have Ivy around all the time. Whatever chance he had of being friends with most of the group dissipated rapidly in the first few days.

For the first week, the group worked out and practiced calling their Dywel's every day. Ivy and Margo hung out, watching for the first few days, but they both had other things to do. Zack understood and having Ivy around was a bit distracting. The problems for him started after not seeing her for a couple of days. He found he had no energy to work out or produce the Dywel on command.

At first he had thought he really was only tired or coming down with a cold, but then he had sought out Ivy and felt right again, stronger even. Since then, he made sure he was around her as much as possible. Zack wasn't about to tell Ivy or his dad since really he thought it was all in his head. How degrading it would be for him if the other guys or his dad thought he was so lovelorn that he couldn't function unless he was around her.

Everything was better when he was with Ivy or at least had spent some time with her. Just being near her energized him, like he was only partially there until she was with him, completing him. Mentally, and physically, he felt better after only a few moments with her.

But whether he said something or not, his dad seemed to have figured it out since if Ivy happened to show up while they were training, his dad would call a halt and allow him to see her. Even more bizarre was that if he showed any signs of fatigue, his dad would tell him to take some time off and go find Ivy.

After about a month, his dad had started to attend the Alltha meetings again and he put one of the other young druids, Reed, in charge while he was gone. Reed was an ass, didn't seem to like him or Ivy at all, but the guy did the same thing. If Ivy showed up, he told him to spend time with her. It was confusing and, although they seemed to know more than he did, none of the guys would tell him what was going on.

And there were more and more meetings with the Order that both his dad and Uncle Milton went to, leaving him alone with the druids, making him more uneasy with them each time. It seemed that with each meeting, his dad came back agitated and more determined than ever that Zack should spend as much time with Ivy as possible.

Last week another warrior, Carmen, had showed up to help with the training. Now all his old man talked about was what they were going to do when they left the forest, as if it was a done deal and Zack would go along with it. He was very confused by his dad's love-hate thing towards Ivy and her forest. His dad acted as if he was waiting for something to happen and talked about when they could leave the Meadhan, but Zack had no clue what his dad was waiting for. Not that he wanted to leave, but fighting the Eilibears was what the training was for and that excited him. He hoped that whatever was going on with his health would clear up so that he would stop having this driving need to be around Ivy all the time.

Zack had fallen asleep the night before in his clothes, listening to his dad tell him where they were going first, Russia, the land of the Ice and Fire. Zack had shut him out, thinking instead of his plans with Ivy tomorrow night. He missed her. This last week had been hard on him as she was studying for finals and they had only spent a few hours together. His joints hurt and his head felt like it was going to explode from the headache behind his eyes. He *needed* to hold her.

He had finished stage one of his special surprise for her and there were just a few more last-minute items to transport and then everything would be ready. He had hidden them in the forest, on the other side of the massive fallen tree. His dad probably would have been okay with everything, but he didn't want him to know what he had been doing. It was for Ivy, Margo and himself only.

His dad's snoring came from the other side of the tent and Zack lay there measuring the breaths, making sure his dad was really still asleep. When he was satisfied, he quietly rolled out of his sleeping bag and crept out of the tent, hoping his dad wouldn't wake. There was a chill in the air, the only hint that winter was on its way.

The remains of several fires glowed dimly in the darkened forest, giving off just enough light to guide him. He stepped lightly, listening for any change around the glade. Suddenly a snap of a twig made him jerk his head around.

"Up early this morning. More stuff to move?" Telfer whispered from the shadows.

"You've been watching?" Zack asked, instantly on guard.

"Yeah, I took this time slot for guard duty knowing you needed some cover. Don't worry bro, I've got your back. She's pretty sweet, you're lucky," the tall blond said, chuckling softly.

"Thanks Tel, I owe you one."

"No problem. I'm getting sick of Reed's mouthing off and playing all buddy-buddy with your dad. He's out to get you, watch your back."

"Who? Reed or my dad," Zack asked, dead serious.

Another chuckle. "Sadly…probably both. Your dad seems to like her and we have all been told to allow you to spend as much time with her as you want. I'm betting that he thinks you'll have a hard time with the Gorffen and just wants it over soon. I know I would have problems with it... so I have to admit I don't understand why you aren't ruffled."

"Gorffen? What's that, the Welsh word for *finish,* right?"

"Yeah, they like to use old words. I find that annoying. But it's cool that at least one of us will reach full power and be a Grand Warrior. I'm just glad it won't be me that has to go through the whole Gorffen thing."

"Never heard of it," Zack said dismissing yet another oddity of being a fey warrior. He was only half listening and really wanted to get to work before his dad woke up.

"Yeah right. Well, you are taking it all in pretty calmly...I don't know how you do it. Some of the stuff about being a druid is sort of freaking me out," Telfer admitted.

Zack could only stare at his friend. He didn't know what to make of that statement. Since the guys had been here, he had never seen Telfer show fear towards having a Dywel or even knowing that their whole purpose in life seemed to be to fight the Eilibear. Telfer probably needed to talk it out with a friend, but this couldn't be a worse time. Telfer seemed the only one that really wanted to be his friend with no pretense. Zack felt a little shitty about not taking the hint to sit and talk, but not enough to stop him from leaving.

"Dude, we'll find time to talk it all out soon, promise," he said laying his hand on Telfer's shoulder. "But right now I've really got to run or I won't get this done before Dad's up. Catch you later." He hurried to where he had stashed the last of the items. He had already put them inside a large tarp, so it was one quick blink and he moved the items to the site. In another couple of minutes, he had everything put away and he was set. One way or another, he and Ivy were going to be alone for the full night.

He blinked back to where he had started, behind the tree. He stood as still as possible to hear if anyone else was up and about. No sounds came to him, so he inched forward and looked out at the glade. He could make out only Telfer's shape by one of the fire pits. He strolled over, not caring now if anyone saw him and sat down next to the large druid.

Telfer didn't see him coming and was up, starting to power his Dywel before he realized it was only Zack.

"Shit, that was quick," he cried out in a whisper. "You've got to teach me that trick of blinking with things." He relaxed and sat back down.

"It's no different than blinking yourself or another person," Zack replied casually, picking up a stick and poking at the fire.

"Uh, yeah it is. I don't know anyone who can blink more than their pack with them. Even blinking people, you need a minimum of three if you want to go any distance."

"That's just because of the barrier on this Meadhan."

"Zack, this Meadhan isn't normal, I'll give you that. But all fey need three to work any type of strong magic. That was like the first thing I was taught when I was told who and what I was."

"Then define strong magic," Zack countered. He was growing uneasy. This was a topic he had steered away from. He hadn't wanted to know what the other druids had been told, what was normal for a druid or what the training had been. Somehow, he had skipped past all that and really didn't think it mattered…but maybe   it   did.

"Well, like blinking any distance greater than a mile or two. There is a weight limit on items you can carry. I'm not sure what it is, but it's pretty low. You need three fey to blink or bring heavy stuff with you."

"No you don't," Zack said. He was sure Telfer just didn't know everything he could do yet. Maybe it was the way the adults controlled them.

"Yeah, you do."

"That's nuts. Ivy and I do it all the time."

"I wouldn't say that very loud, Zack. There's already some pretty weird rumors flying around about Ivy…don't add to them," Telfer whispered, looking around with a twinge of panic.

"What   are   you   talking   about? What rumors?" Zack asked, instantly on the defensive.

"Well, the most ridiculous one is that she blinked that house into the Meadhan by herself. I'm not sure who came up with that one," Telfer replied laughing nervously.

"That's not a rumor, it's true. I would have helped, but I needed help of a different kind at the time. She used the house to save Margo and me," Zack said growing irritated.

"Come   on,   Zack. That's   impossible. No fey…and I mean *no* fey…can blink something that big. I don't think a team of fey could do it together. It's impossible."

Zack looked at his friend in the dim light. He

was being serious; he really didn't think it was possible. Zack hadn't even thought about it. From the first time he and Ivy started to blink together, they were hauling items all over the place. He had brought in two full pallets of concrete for the foundation. He'd never told his dad or anyone else. It didn't seem important.

He wondered if it had something to do with the talisman. Once Margo had discovered she could blink also, she was always bringing stuff back from her home in Coos Bay. She brought back a huge antique armoire just the other day for her and Ivy's room.

The talisman seemed to provide a lot more for them than simply keys to get into the Meadhan. He wondered if Ivy's Granddad could blink stuff around also.

"Hey, it's okay. It's your story. Tell it how you want," Telfer said. "But I promise not to tell anyone your version." Before Zack could answer, a roar came from behind them and both vaulted out of their seats from shock.

"EVERYONE, UP AND OUT!"

Zack's dad stood directly behind them, his hands cupped around his mouth to make the yell more powerful. He grinned wickedly and then continued to yell, calling all the druids out of their beds and into the cold morning air. Zack and Telfer were the only ones fully dressed. The others were still pulling on pants and shirts.

Seven sleepy forms shuffled out of the tents and came to stand in front of his dad, Rōber Edsmond, Eddie to his friends, Uncle Eddie to some. The young druids called him Sir. Carmen strolled up after everyone else had taken their places and stood lazily off to the side.

Zack didn't trust the older druid. There was just something odd about the guy, like he was on edge all the time. His face was pitted with scars, and he spoke with a heavy Russian accent. Ivy said he sounded like a B-movie star, trying to act like a KGB agent.

"Listen up! We are going to start early this morning. A nice ten-mile run, then weights. I leave at 0700 for a meeting with the fey Elders. Reed, you will lead the team in swordplay for two hours. After that, you will have free time," he said as he looked over at Zack.

"Do with it what you will. Those of you who have classes at the college, go ahead, but be back and ready to break camp tomorrow morning. Word arrived this morning that a band of Eilibear have been spotted on one of the Kuril Islands.

"Carmen has been observing you and agreed with me that you are ready for your first encounter. We will be leaving as soon as I am back. Be packed and ready." His face, normally stern, was all smiles. Zack could tell he was looking forward to the fight...this was what his dad lived for. Now he understood why he had been talking about Russia last night, the islands were off the coast of mainland Russia, right above Japan.

Part of Zack really wanted to go, but he didn't want to leave Ivy. Conflicted, he readied himself for the run. At least he could spend his time with Ivy tonight. His body shivered with pleasure at the thought of being near her.

CHAPTER 4 – Ivy

Granddad and I finished our breakfast in heavy silence. When I couldn't take it anymore, I got up to wash my plate. Granddad was an okay cook but I knew why Marmaw never allowed him in her kitchen. He made one hell of a mess. I had the sink filled with soapy water and was collecting the dirty pots and pans to put in to soak when the front door burst open.

Uncle Eddie walked in followed by Uncle Carmen. It irked me that these men would come into my home unannounced whenever they wanted. Hadn't they heard of knocking first?

I watched them enter out of the corner of my eye as I started to wash the dishes. Zack's dad was a big man, tall and muscular like Zack, and they did look alike, but that's where the similarities ended. He was nice enough to me and Margo, but there was something off about the way he spoke to us. It was rather condescending and rubbed me the wrong way. My apprehension grew every time I came into contact with him.

I had just met Uncle Carmen and he was clearly worse. He was short and round, but I'd seen him on the practice field with the young druids. He was a powerhouse, like Zack's dad. I really, really, didn't like the man, and it wasn't because he was Russian. He seemed to be glaring at me all the time.

"You ready?" Uncle Eddie asked Granddad, giving me a curious sideways look.

Granddad turned to me. "Are we jake?" he asked.

His old fashioned way of asking if I was okay

was mildly comforting. "Sure, Granddad," I answered quietly.

"You stay around the house and spend some time cleaning up."

I nodded gloomily, knowing he meant that I should start getting ready for us to leave.

He saw my look and leaned down to kiss my forehead. "I'll be back tomorrow. It will be okay."

I forced a weak smile and he studied me for a moment before turning back to the men who were waiting for him. I watched as they gathered in a circle, linking their arms, and then blinked out as a group. I stood there for some time before I pulled myself together and finished clearing away the breakfast no one had eaten. There was too much food to keep, and I couldn't eat it all. I couldn't bring myself to throw it out. Instead I packed it up in plastic containers. The guys would like it, and maybe they'd be distracted enough to leave Zack and me alone.

The sun was just starting to rise, providing a bit of light, but no warmth as I walked down the path carrying the bag of food. I could hear the clang of swords echoing through the forest. My nice quiet paradise wasn't so quiet any longer. My MP3 player was in my front pocket and I turned it on and plugged one earbud in. The soft mellow music of the Everly Brothers merged with the sounds around me.

"Dream, Dream, Dream..." I sang softly along with the words. It was a good song to accompany my thoughts about Zack. It fit my mood and cheered me, making me eager to be near him. The forest that surrounded me was rich with life and I wished again that it was still just us—Zack, Margo and me in my Meadhan. It over a year since I had first met Zack on the bus, seen him at the bus stop, let him steal mustard for me and felt the beginnings of a friendship. It was on the same day that I had met Margo and we had celebrated the anniversary a few weeks ago with hot fudge sundaes at a little ice cream shop near the college, then a whole afternoon of clothes shopping. Zack had begged off, asking for me to be patient as he was working on something special for me. Margo knew what the surprise was, but wasn't going to be there since she didn't want to be a third wheel. Margo was, hands down, the best girlfriend I had ever had.

Birds erupted out of the trees above me as the reverberations of noises from the druids rang out. They were dueling again. I followed the thuds and clanks, which grew louder as I almost skipped up the path, humming along with the music. I wondered if tonight would be *the night*. Zack had been the perfect gentleman. Not that I was a prude, but I hadn't been ready for more yet. I wasn't sure if I was now even. Granddad and Marmaw had done a really good job on the moral issues with me; *that* was for after marriage...when you were older, ready to support yourself *and* a family. To do it before that was giving something special away that you could never get back...not ever. For months now, Zack and I had crept around the edges of it. I knew it sounded lame and hopelessly romantic, but I knew that we were part of one another...we were meant to be together.

The sounds of roughhousing and guys

skirmishing with swords intensified as I came near the end of the path. Their voices rose and fell with excitement and insults. Reed's voice rang out above the other, calling someone a wuss. I didn't really like Reed. He was the dumbest excuse for a young man I'd ever met. He seemed to think that cuss words were nouns, verbs and adjectives all rolled up in one. I thought it only made him sound like a buffoon.

The end of the path opened up into a small glade under the looming gigantic trees. I didn't like this one place in the forest and wished they had made their camp anywhere else. Still, it had changed quite a bit since all the icky Eilibear and frogs had taken it over and then killed Skyler. I couldn't see anything that remained of them now.

One of the damaged trees was regenerating rather nicely and I had to pat myself on the back for that. I had told it to heal and it had, and it had gained about twenty feet of new growth since then. The fallen trees created a solid, walled-in section that was now being utilized by the druids as the border for their ugly, green, army-tent city.

I looked at the tent I knew was Zack's and despised it. I missed having Zack in the house with me. Part of me loved having Granddad there, but I had changed during the time he had been gone and was starting to discover it wasn't easy going back to how life had been before. Sometimes it was amazing how the things you thought you wanted, like having Granddad back, could turn out so weird.

I rounded the corner and came face to face with Telfer. He looked about the same age as Zack, built the same at least. But there the similarities stopped. He had close-cropped, white-blond hair and a devilish smile that I was rewarded with now.

"Little Ivy, have you come to rescue Zack from us big bad warriors?" he bellowed out in a loud, brash laugh. As he spoke, he swirled around in a circle, a broad sword gripped in his hand, and then charged back into the fight. Adding Telfer to the mix, there were now four druids, all sporting some type of sword and battling it out in the center of the glade. The remaining five young men were either lying down on the forest floor, nursing their wounds or standing and shouting encouragements, slurs or a combination of the two at the few remaining in the practice fight.

Zack looked like he was taking a beating. His long dreadlocks were pulled away from his face and tied back in a knot on the back of his head. The long locks swung wildly, along with his pendants, as he spun to his left quickly and fought back Rush, a redheaded druid from Ireland. The sounds of laughter, grunts and curses grew, as each fought to prove who was the strongest of the druids.

Zack swung in another direction, caught sight of me, and paused to smile just as he was clobbered from behind with the handle of Reed's sword. Zack dropped to his knees and stayed there, panting. I knew better than to run up to him. He wasn't hurt…except for maybe his pride.

"Got you! That's three take-downs, I win! You all are a bunch of losers," Reed proclaimed, holding his sword up high and whooping for all his worth. The others stood down and wiped the sweat from their faces.

"He got you that time, doesn't happen very often," Telfer said to Zack as he held out his hand to help him up.

"I was distracted," Zack said, as he stood and beamed at me.

"In the battle of life, there are always distractions..." the blond declared, then tilted his head towards me. "Some nicer than others." That brought on laughter and a couple of raunchy comments from some of the other druids, which Zack ignored as he walked over to me.

I held up the large bag of containers I had brought with me. "Breakfast for the animals. Feeding time, come get it."

Keyair jogged over to me, slapping Zack on his back as he passed him. He came up, slinging sweat from his face as he stopped suddenly in front of me. I opened the large bag and let him look in it.

The beefy looking druid let out a whoop and then turned back to the others. "Hey there's bacon and taters and I think pancakes in here." Taking the bag that I offered, he ran back with it, holding it high while the others tried to get it from him. Their rowdy banter continued until they all sat down on the ground and started to pull containers out.

Zack came up and stood beside me, a smirk on his face. "Good idea...feed them to keep them quiet."

"Yeah, you can thank Granddad. He kind of overdid the cooking...again."

"They gone?" he whispered. I nodded with a little smirk. Zack quickly turned back to Telfer, glancing at the others that had gathered on the ground. They weren't paying any attention to us as they had emptied the bag and were eating out of the containers with their fingers.

"Hey, I'm taking off, Telfer. See you on campus," he said quietly. Telfer waved us off with a grin as he turned back to the group that had taken the bag of food. I could hear Telfer calling out to the others to save him some as we hurried back down the path.

"I need a shower," Zack proclaimed as he slung his arm over my shoulder.

"Yes you do, you stink big time," I agreed with him playfully. He smelled like a sweaty football player, and I liked it. Simply being around him was cheering, though for some reason I always felt drained of energy after only a few minutes. I figured it was just my hormones working in some weird way...he was just so yummy he made me lightheaded.

The sounds of the other druids dimmed as we walked, replaced with the sounds of birds and soothing nature all around us. The path had been widened since we had first made it, chasing the Eilibears. Now it was well trampled, clear of any low hanging branches and led straight to my private glade.

When we reached the house. Zack headed straight upstairs to the shower. Their tents didn't have heat, let alone running water. I heard the door open to the upstairs bathroom and the shower turn on. Before I had left to get Zack, I had started to pack a lunch for both of us to share between classes. I took a deep breath and pulled in some magic from my house to make the wooziness go away and then quickly finished making lunch.

The sounds of footsteps on the stairs made me turn. Zack was quickstepping down the stairs, shirtless, muscles bulging and my heart did a flip-flop. Crap, I bet there wasn't a teenage girl in the world who wouldn't have traded places with me in a heartbeat. Zack's long dreads were loose now, wet and wild looking. He was wearing his now-familiar pendants and wristbands, and a pair of faded jeans…which fit him very well, I should add. He had a flannel and sweatshirt in his hand. He must have left a stash of clean clothes in the little room that had been his for a short time. He was absolutely rippling with muscles and was the most magnificent looking guy I had ever seen.

"Hey," he smiled as he came over to me and leaned down to kiss me. I forced myself not to touch him. I wanted to…really wanted to. But I knew if I felt his bare chest, we would never get out of this house and the lightheaded feeling was already returning. I had to pull away as he tried to deepen the kiss. He sighed and opened his eyes to see why I had stopped him. Raising my eyebrows, I whispered, "exam today."

With a humph of acquiescence he moved back and pulled on his long sleeved flannel. He didn't need to do that. I might not have wanted to touch right then, but it didn't hurt to look. He saw my pout and made a face at me like *that's what you get.*

"Killjoy," I shot at him as I picked up the pack with the food. My backpack, filled with my school books and the homework I had slaved over last night, was ready except for the lunches. I quickly pushed them inside and zipped it closed.

"Brat," he answered jokingly, taking my pack.

"Jerk," I said as I walked past him on my way to the front door. He slapped me, none too lightly, on the butt.

"Ouch!" I cried out as I jumped, rubbing my behind. "Not nice…and you *want* to be nice to me," I teased, giving him a sly look.

"You asked for it. Besides, I'm always nice to you. I have to be or your Granddad will beat me to a pulp."

"Uh-huh," I said smiling and picked up my pack. It seemed like old times, us grabbing our backpacks and heading out. Only this time we knew that people would be looking for us if we didn't come back…someone would worry.

I went to open the door, but Zack reached out and took my shoulder.

"Part one of my surprise to you first, just a little gift," he said.

"Oh really and what would that be?" I asked as I turned. My heart was fluttering with excitement as he leaned in close and rubbed his nose against mine. His hair swung into my face and I reached up to brush it aside. My fingers touched his face and I felt a soft pulse of energy leave through my fingertip. It didn't hurt and I paid it no attention.

"I like your hair," I murmured into his chest. "But it can be annoying at times."

Unexpectedly he swooped me up in his arms and carried me over to the couch. Sitting, he arranged me so I was snuggly settled on his lap.

"I'm so glad I followed you off the bus," he admitted, starting to look all serious.

"Only because I smelled good," I had to joke. I still thought it was funny that that was the reason, at first anyway, that he had decided to follow me. He thought I smelled good. Like a man following the aromas of food, I guessed.

"You were just too darn cute and doing so many

outlandish things. I didn't have a choice, you know."

I had started to play with his hair. I remembered my first thought when I had seen him in the bus terminal. I had wondered if he really used pee to make the dreads and I had been turned off by them. Now, they *were* Zack. He wouldn't be the same if I had let the other fey cut his hair.

"I do really like your hair," I said simply. I felt Zack shift, reaching for something in his jeans pocket. I sat up to see what he was doing and saw the pocket knife.

"I want to give something to you…something that is part of me," he said with his eyes going to his arm. He picked up one of the locks and went to cut it, remembered and looked at me.

Yep, another one of my brilliant ideas. When the female fey had glamoured him, they wanted to cut off his hair, his protection. I had used my little voice magic on it and now it couldn't be cut. I leaned down and waited for the tingle in the back of my throat to come before I whispered, "you can be cut," then deciding to add, since it was his hair, "if Zack really, *really* needs to, and is thinking clearly."

Zack waited for me to finish and then cut off a couple of inches at the bottom. He closed his knife and put it back in his pocket, before handing me the piece of hair. He wasn't done yet though. He wore two really awesome wristbands. The one on his right arm held my family's talisman, and I had always wondered if the talisman becoming part of his Dywel played any part in how powerful it was. The talismans had been created by Granddad using the Sumair stone's magic, kind of like how I had gotten my magic. We had never told

Granddad, or his dad, about it being a part of the Dywel now. It hadn't seemed important. Maybe it was…something to think about.

Zack moved his various other bracelets off his other wristband, and undid the cords that held it on. This one was a lighter, tanned hide, with a line of small gemstones inlaid into it. I thought they were cool looking: yellow, blue and green. He laid the wristband flat on my knee, and unfolded it. I had no idea it was only a flat piece of hide, folded with the stones sewn on, along with the cords. There was a flattened piece of black hair already there along with a symbol drawn on the leather. It was a simple design, just a circle with a dot in the middle. It looked like it had been there for a very long time, along with the piece of hair. He took his lock of hair from me and laid it next to the other one. He started to fold it back up when I had to ask.

"Zack, what's that other piece of hair?"

While he finished putting it back together, he answered me quietly.

"Remember the old lady I told you about that made my dreads? She lived in Jamaica? I got to go back there with dad a few years ago. She was still there, old and wrinkled and happy to see me. She had been waiting for me. This wristband was already in a small box with my name on it. She said she had a vision about me and was driven to create it, with these stones and a lock of her own hair. It was my *blaze*, my way to always find the right way to go; the symbol was there to always show me the way. She blessed it and put it on me. I've never taken it off." He looked up at me thoughtfully, "I think she would like it if you wore it now."

He held it up, and I put my right arm out and I

watched as he put it on my wrist. I'd never worn something like this before, and didn't think it would fit. But Zack didn't seem worried in the least. He wrapped the main hide around my wrist; it overlapped some, but didn't cover up the stones. The cords he wrapped a couple of times before he knotted them tight and bit off the extra bits. It would take a while to get use to wearing it, I was sure. But it was soft and warm from Zack's skin. I put it up to my nose…it smelled like him.

"Cool stones, what are they?" I asked looking at them closely.

"She said the blue one is amethyst and holds magic, the yellow one is topaz and is supposed to attract power and the green one is something called moss agate. It's the stone of warriors and is supposed to balance power and energy," he said looking at them more closely. "You know I haven't thought about that in a long time. I guess this really was made for me."

"Maybe I shouldn't have it," I said, starting to take it off.

"No…you *should* have it. I definitely feel like you need it *and* I need you to have it," he said reflectively.

"Okay. Well, I do like it." I looked up at him. "Someday we need to go there, so I can meet her."

"I'm sure she would like to meet you also," he said with a quiet smile. "I like it on you. Keep it on when you shower. When it dries, it will mold to your arm better."

"I'll do that. But I think I can help make sure it is part of me." I could see he didn't understand, but I let him think about it while the tingle built and moved to my tongue. I held my wrist up and announced clearly, "you are part of me now, just as Zack is. You cannot come off." My arm tingled a little bit, but it didn't hurt as the band molded itself into my skin.

"Wow, that's what your talisman did to me," Zack said, looking from my wrist to me. "I think that just about seals us together." I wasn't given a chance to respond, as he leaned down and kissed me tenderly. The same odd little pulse of energy seemed to mingle between our lips.

"Okay, now we go to class," he said as he stood and almost dumped me on the floor.

"Nice move, Conan," I snarked as I righted myself and started to move towards the door.

"No, don't go out. If the guys think we're staying here, they won't look for us at the college."

I didn't think the druids were that dumb. One of them would be sure to check in Ashland, or come into the house to look for us, just in case. One of the reasons we were never alone much was because one of the other druids always seemed to turn up and it didn't matter where we were or what we were doing. It wasn't that they were trying to keep us apart, but more like they wanted to be part of our group, too.

Right," I said. "We blink from here."

He took my hand and together we blinked at the same time. When we opened our eyes, we were standing in a small outcropping of trees in Lithia Park near the college. I had placed a bubble barrier here when the three of us had started classes in the fall. It was a wonderful little space of privacy where the three of us could store our bikes, as well as come and go without anyone seeing us appear out of nowhere. Zack had found a small bike rack somewhere and we had installed it inside. We even had extra packs with spare clothes and some money. The three of us didn't ever want to be caught unaware or unprepared now. I wasn't really sure what we were worried about, but the feeling lingered for all of us that we needed an escape plan in place.

I hadn't told Granddad what I had done. He had gotten so weird about my powers that it was better not to mention it. Some things I didn't feel comfortable sharing with Granddad right now.

Taking my pack from Zack I pushed my arms into the straps and pulled my bike out of the rack between his and Margo's. Mine looked a bit dull next to theirs. Zack's was a high-tech, fancy mountain bike and Margo's was an endearing purple girl's bike with a basket on the front. She even had little lights on the spokes of the wheels that flickered purple and pink as she rode. I was into function when it came to bikes. It had to fit my short stature and not let me down...hence just a good ten-speed, painted a dark metallic green.

I did one quick scan of the area to make sure I could make my entrance into the real world without being seen. No one was around at this time of morning so I could safely leave the bubble I had created. I walked the bike across the grass to the paved walkway before getting on. I wasn't good at riding on anything other than something solid like a sidewalk.

Zack followed behind until we hit the main road up to the college. He blew me a kiss as he zoomed by. I wasn't into speed, which was a good thing since I couldn't have gone as fast as him anyway. The ride through the historic downtown of Ashland was pleasant and I made note of little shops I wanted to check out. Margo and I hadn't had the time to go into many yet.

I stopped at my favorite coffee shop with the little drive-through window for bike riders and walk-ups. The girl smiled as I pulled up and, without even asking me what I wanted, handed me a double white-chocolate mocha. Guess I did come here a bit too often. I paid with my swipe card and nestled my drink into my handy, dandy little cup holder and continued on my ride to the college.

When I got to the first bike rack with an empty slot in it, I locked my bike up and started walking. I strolled along leisurely. I felt like walking—not riding, not running, not blinking—just plain ole mundane walking. Normally I blinked almost everywhere. I blinked around the forest, to school and I'd blink to meet up with Margo or Zack. Most of the time we would blink some place to eat, then back to class and then back to the forest. It was a heck of a lot of blinking, but today I wanted to walk. I had a lot to think about.

If Granddad wanted to close up the forest, what did that mean for Zack and Margo? I knew we could blink to see each other, but we wouldn't be living together. I needed to decide if that was a good thing or not. And I needed to figure out what to say to Granddad if I did decide to go against him.

The sun was trying to shine, but it was nippy out…fall was in the air. The leaves on the trees were turning some absolutely spectacular colors. All around me, leaves were falling as bits of wind loosened them. They floated around me and blanketed the sidewalks and lawns with oranges and golds. I carried my mocha over to a bench that sat by the trunk of a large oak tree and sat down, leaning against the trunk. I wanted to enjoy my coffee and the peace and quiet before the exam today.

Closing my eyes, I lay back and enjoyed the feel of the tree caressing my magic. I could sense it rubbing its way into my store of enchantments and took some of it in, which seemed to make the tree happy. I pushed back a *thank you*, giving it some energy from the forest. The tree continued to share and other plants around me joined in with the game, the interaction completely undetected by any mortals walking around. My special power of being able to connect with nature was pretty cool at times, if rather odd. I had felt really good this morning, but just that little bit of time with Zack had left me with the need to lay down and sleep. The small bit of clean magic that the tree had shared with me made me feel energized again. I relaxed and allowed the natural magic around me to soak in.

A slight breeze blew against my skin, ruffling my hair. The air was cold and fresh. The breeze shifted slightly and an odor came to me on a wisp of air. My eyes popped open and I looked around, surprised. Students had begun to fill the walkways and bike paths; classes were about to begin. I didn't know where the smell had come from. It was vaguely familiar, yet I couldn't place it. It smelled like rotten meat, pungent and foul. As quick as it had come to me, it was gone.

I scanned the people walking by and they all looked like normal mortals. There was a group of Goth kids, dressed in black and covered with tats and piercings, but other than being misguided in their fashion choices, I couldn't detect anything off about them. I got up and started to walk to class, finishing my mocha and depositing the cup in a waste can along the way.

The campus wasn't too large, though it spanned several acres of land, all connected by walking and bike paths lined with flowers, trees and lawn. The yard-maintenance guys did a pretty good job keeping everything looking nice, and I had helped out a little bit at the start of the school term. There were only a few trees that needed some of my special magic to stay healthy and I kept the flowers blooming a little longer than normal for this time of year. The trees had become my friends now in a weird sort of way. I could hear them speaking to me, not in English of course. They had a language all of their own and just knowing that they were aware of me felt good. I pushed the thoughts of Granddad and the odd smell out of my mind. I had an exam to pass and nothing was going to get in the way of me doing that.

I returned waves and good mornings with a few students as I came toward the front of Cascade Hall. I quietly joined the crowd of undergraduates making their way into the building to take our first large exam of the term.

Two hours of reading and writing down my answers flew by and when I finally laid down my pen, I was feeling pretty good about life. I knew I had aced it and Granddad would be proud.

I was in a good mood as I starting walking towards the library. College was different than high school had been, yet in some ways still the same. Even here, there were the cliques of preppies, jocks and nerds. Friends of like minds hung out together, but unlike high school, no one really cared which group you aligned yourself with. Besides they all looked the same to me. There was a very interesting mix of students and people in general who lived in Ashland; you name the type and you would find it there.

As I neared the Hannon Library, I noticed the Goth kids were hanging around the entrance. I started to move through them towards the doors of the library. I didn't mind how anyone dressed or what type of makeup they wore...I could even handle their tats. More power to them. Geez I had vines growing on my face when I was in the forest and what looked like green henna swirls by my eyes out here in Alainn.

It was the piercings that creeped me out. I didn't understand why anyone would want to poke holes in themselves, and seeing them made me uncomfortable. Even in high school, if someone had more than a couple of earrings, I was repulsed by them. I'm sure they were nice people and all, but we all have our quirks and this was mine. I was really trying hard to divert my eyes from any sort of piercings on the members of the group I was moving through so I wouldn't end up shuddering or doing something else dumb that someone might take offence to. Stupid me...I ended up running into someone and I heard the sound of a book dropping at my feet.

"You dropped something," a rough voice said next to my ear. I was instantly physically nauseated and had to gulp down bile the that had started to build in my mouth. It was that smell again, only a lot stronger.

I looked up to see a girl about my age. Her hair was oily and black with deep shimmers of blue and it hung in her face. Her eyes were almost hidden behind all the black makeup. But it was the piercings that froze me. They were everywhere; her lips, nose, eyebrows, and her ears had lines of rings around the outside rims. Next to her right eye was a small tattoo. It was very simple so it stood out against all the other strong statements her makeup and piercings were making. It was a simple circle with a dot in the center. I stared at it, then at her and then gagged violently.

This was the most extreme reaction I had ever had to being close to people with piercings…there was a smell emitting from her that was gagging me. I was scared. Scared of her, and I wasn't sure why. Scared that I might spew right here on the steps of the library and petrified about what all of these people might do to me if I did. I wanted to run, or blink, but I was frozen to the spot and couldn't take my eyes off the girl.

"I said, you dropped something," she repeated slowly and forcefully, as if I was dumb and hadn't understood her, then she looked down. I followed her glance and saw a book at my feet. I had never seen it before.

"That's not mine," I managed to say and finally found my feet could move. I started to take a step around her.

She linked her arm tightly with mine and leaned close to me. "You dropped it, pick it up," she jeered.

I struggled to pull myself away and she held on even tighter, shoving me down towards the book. I gave up and looked at the book on the ground. It was a normal looking text book…but it wasn't mine. I picked it up anyway and held it out to her.

"Here, it's not mine. I think you dropped it," I said.

"Shit, are all fey as stupid as you? Take the damn book into the library and look inside it!" Shocked beyond belief, I tried to figure out how she knew I was fey as she dropped my arm and moved back into the crowd, disappearing from sight. I was left standing there, speechless and feeling even more terrified. At least when she had released my arm the need to puke had gone away.

I stood there for a minute more and finally decided that I should do as the odd girl had said. Go inside. I was shaking as I walked to the doors and opened them. The library was quiet and normal. It instantly calmed me. Making my way to the back of the rows of books, I found my favorite place to sit.

There was a little cubby at the far end of the room with an overstuffed chair and a small side table. I plopped myself down and set my backpack next to the chair. I was still holding onto the book and turned it over to see if there was anything special about the back cover. There wasn't.

I laid it on my lap and slowly opened it. It was just a text book—math. A subject I wasn't taking. I flipped through the pages and didn't see anything of interest...until I got to the middle of the book. There, tucked into the pages was a yellowed piece of paper. Pulling it out, I flipped it over and then dropped it as if it were burning my fingers.

It fluttered down and lay staring up at me. The words were written in a flowery detailed script.

Ivy, don't go back. Don't tell anyone. Run now. We will find you.

I read and reread the words over and over again. My mind registered that the writing was beautiful, however that wasn't something I needed to focus on. Questions filled my mind. Who was that girl? How did she know I was fey and how did she know my name? Run where? Don't go back where? Did it mean don't go outside the library, to class, or to my forest? Why shouldn't I tell anyone? Did I trust that girl and if I did run, did I really want her to find me somewhere? And just who was *we*?

I don't know how long I sat there looking at the note. I didn't take my eyes off of it until the sound of people coming close to where I sat made me look up and then at my watch. Crap, I was supposed to meet Zack in the quad ten minutes ago. I hurried to close the book with the note inside and shoved it into my pack.

I rushed through the library and out the doors. The sun was bright and blinded me for a second, but I noticed that all the Goth kids were gone. I sprinted down the pathway towards the Stevenson Union building. Zack and I always met up for lunch at the tables outside the little book store and usually ate there if we had brought a sack lunch. I could see him standing with a bunch of students by the tables. Telfer, Keyair and Reed were with him, along with the normal gaggle of hot coeds hanging on them. Seeing the girls fawn all over the guys always brought back to mind what Whisper and the other female fey had done to Zack.

I couldn't blame the girls. Zack and his friends looked like bodybuilders and their normal attire of tank tops and jeans did nothing to hide their bulging muscles. I had to take deep breaths myself at times so I wouldn't swoon in front of all of them. You'd think that being around a buttload of brawny druids all the time would get me used to seeing musclebound young men. It was different in the forest; we were all on a level playing field there.

But out here in the real world, I always found I was extremely intimidated by them. I *was* a normal girl, fey or mortal, it really didn't matter...these guys were just too hot to be real. I slowed my pace as I grew close and tried to get control of my breathing. By the time I reached Zack, I had a nice ordinary smile planted on my face.

"Hey," Zack said as I walked up. "How did the exam go?"

A stunning redhead was standing next to him and had been trying to grab his full attention. She turned to look at me and if looks could kill, I'd be toast.

I forgot all about the exam…and the note—thank you bitchy girl.

"Good, I think I passed," I replied as I took the hand he held out to me. Telfer said hi and I smiled to acknowledge him, trying to completely ignore the looks of hatred from the girls. Zack moved me away from them, over to a free table and we sat down. Out of the corner of my eye, I saw that the three druids had moved just far enough away to give us privacy, but remained close enough to keep an eye on us. I sighed in surrender to it…we seemed to have bodyguards, and there was no use trying to fight it.

I pulled out our lunches and we ate. Zack told me about his morning and some of the campus gossip. I let him do most of the talking and wondered if I should show him the note. Damn, I hated this. I had no clue what to do.

Both of us had one other class today so when we were done, he took off for his and I sat there staring off into space. I could leave now. Go get my emergency pack from the bubble and blink someplace. I could visit the Grand Canyon or go to Disneyland. Both sounded dumb. Was I really thinking of taking off without telling Zack? I guess I could for a few hours and he wouldn't know. Maybe whoever the *we* were would find me and tell me what the hell was going on.

That felt like the best plan. That way I wouldn't have to tell Zack. If it was something stupid, some prank by another fey, he wouldn't have to know I fell for it. That's when it dawned on me. Geez, I can be so stupid at times. The druids. They had to be the ones who did this. Probably Reed. That dumbass hated Zack, and what better way to hurt him than to scare me into taking off? They all knew my story, how I had run away and ended up at the cabin. He must have planned it all out and found the girl to hand the note off to me.

In a huff, I gathered my stuff and started to class. I wasn't going to fall for it...I almost had, but I'd never tell anyone. As I hurried across campus, I could feel eyes on me and smugly disregarded them. *Nice try, Reed,* I thought and then wondered who else might be in on it. Maybe I should tell Zack what they had tried to pull.

CHAPTER 5 – Ivy

"Close your eyes and keep them closed," Zack said to me.

We had finished classes for the day and had come back to the cabin. Margo was still at work, so this was a good time to take off. I was very glad I hadn't fallen for the dumb note and had not told Zack about it.

I had already taken a shower and changed into something more appropriate for camping, since that's what I thought Zack had planned. I was ready now for whatever he had schemed for tonight.

He placed his hand on my shoulder and I did as he asked with a silly smile plastered on my face. With my eyes closed, I could still tell when he blinked. Suddenly I could feel the wind and there was a sensation of swaying under my feet.

"Keep those eyes closed," Zack said as he moved away from me. I could hear him doing something, but couldn't place the sound. He had moved something on hinges, that much I knew.

"Okay, open them," he said cheerfully.

Oh my. I was standing in the center of a small octagon tower, there were eight sets of windows and that was what I had heard Zack doing. He had been opening all of them. I moved to the side and looked out at my favorite place in the entire world...the top canopy of my forest. I had discovered it when Zack and Margo had been glamoured by the fey and weren't talking to me. High up, at the top of the trees in my forest, was another world. Butterflies and birds mingled in the treetops creating the most awesome sight I had ever seen.

"Zack...I don't know what to say," I said as I turned back to his grinning face. "You built a tree house for us. Wow."

"Well this part at least, the other parts are still a work in progress. This part is called a Birds Nest Tower," he explained.

I liked the name. It did feel like a bird's nest at the top of the trees, and I could see for miles. I moved from one set of windows to the next, giddy with excitement. Zack was quiet as I made my way around the circle and when I finally ended up back next to him, he pointed at the center of the room. A large gray tarp covered something, and I was amazed that I hadn't noticed it until that moment.

I watched as he lifted the tarp off and revealed the grandest telescope I had ever seen. I was speechless.

"This was Margo's idea," he informed me and it did not surprise me at all. Margo always seemed to know the perfect thing that was needed for any situation. Going over to it, I felt overwhelmed, both with love for the two of them and with intimidation. I had no clue how to use the thing.

"I have the manuals for it. We can figure out how it works together," he said, knowing what I had been thinking. He knew me too well. He took my hand and pulled me over to one side. He opened a latch and the wall with the windows opened like a door. I went to the opening and looked out. There was a rope ladder that led down.

"Ladies first," he said as he motioned towards the opening. I smirked at him as I swung myself out onto the ladder and started down. The ladder hugged the large tree and was quite long. When I arrived at the bottom, I found myself standing on a deck. In front of me sat the beginnings of a treehouse. I moved inside through a roughed-in doorway and squeaked with delight. It was actually larger than Granddad's original cabin, oddly shaped, as it conformed to what the trees allowed. It wasn't even close to being finished. The frame was there for the walls and roof, and a couple of walls were up, but it made sense that Zack had focused on building the deck platform first.

I could feel Zack as he came in behind me, but I couldn't pull my eyes away from what he had created. There were a couple of steps up to another level and I had to move deeper into the tree's foliage to see where it led. It turned out to be a small room, maybe meant as a bedroom. I could see through it to the rest of the deck on the other side of the structure.

"What do you think? Of course it's not finished," he said from behind me.

I turned and jumped into his arms. "I love it," I murmured into his hair and hugged him tighter.

"The adults kind of took over our new house and I had been thinking of building a tree house ever since I first stepped foot into your forest," he said as he looked around the room proudly.

"I remember thinking at the time that you wanted to play Tarzan," I said.

"If I'm Tarzan, then you are my Jane," he announced as he picked me straight up off the floor and started to carry me towards the raised room. With my feet dangling and trying hard not to giggle, he walked with me up the stairs into the small room. He lowered me to the floor and then he stepped out onto another section of the platform.

Now I could really see how massive this deck was. It spanned outwards through several large trees. Numerous piles of outdoor furniture and large pots were scattered about and off to one side, there were stacks of large bags of potting soil. A card table had been set up and there was an ice chest sitting next to it.

"I was busy building, so I didn't really have time to bring the stuff in. Margo did my shopping and brought in the lumber for me. You can thank her for all the other stuff. She thought you might like to get some flowers growing…to make it more like your other home," he said pointing at the potting soil and pots.

"It's really perfect Zack. How did you do this? I know your dad was keeping you busy. How did you have time to find this place and build everything?" I asked as I started to pull the stack of outside furniture apart so we had something to sit on.

"I did that trick you used to spy on the boggarts. I blinked up to the highest tree, and from there just keep blinking until I knew no one could find me. After that I kept at it until I found the right trees and then, piece by piece, built parts and put them in place. It only took about four months," he said, trying to sound humble. He failed and I threw a seat cushion at him that he caught easily. "And just so you know, the guys all think I have a really bad bowel problem as I use the outhouse a lot. I'd go into it and blink from there, or wait until everyone was asleep at night. Lately I've been ditching my last class so you wouldn't know what I was doing," he said grinning.

"Not good. Don't skip classes for me. But geez, four months? You and Margo have been working on this for four months and somehow I never found out. You guys are wicked; you know that?" I said, trying not to be annoyed that I wasn't allowed to help. It was a really neat surprise.

"Well it was really about six months. We needed a couple of months to plan everything."

"Right…six months," I repeated after him. I went to the side rails and looked out into my forest. This is what I missed, the silent sounds of the forest. I could hear birds and the wind in the trees. It was green, full of wild life, yet void of others. Zack did understand me. The house Zack and I had found and brought into the Meadhan wasn't ours anymore. In fact, we had only been able to enjoy it by ourselves for a couple of days.

"This is our place," I said wistfully as he came up to stand behind me and wrapped his arms around my shoulders.

"Yes, it is. We are miles and miles from everyone and I would suggest you do your cool whammy thing and seal all the fey out."

I thought about what to say for a moment while I let the fire build in my throat before I spoke. "Seal this area two miles out in every direction. No one but Zack, Margo and me can see it, find it or come here. All magical creatures, good or bad, cannot see it, feel it, or even come near it. We are safe here," I said firmly, letting the power go out with my words.

"Our haven," Zack whispered into my ear.

Yes, I thought. This was our haven. "That's its name," I said as I turned and looked around the platform.

"What are you searching for," he asked quietly.

"Something to christen our new home with," I said looking up at him. He went over to the ice chest and brought out a bottle of strawberry soda.

"Will this work?" he asked holding it out to me. Grinning widely, I took it from him and unscrewed the cap. Taking his hand and placing it over mine on the bottle, I held it out over the rail.

"I christen this place Haven Nest," I declared formally as, together, we poured some of the soda out over the rail.

"I think for a christening you are supposed break the bottle," he said with a chuckle.

"I'm not going to have broken glass all over our new home. This will have to do," I replied and then took a drink of the remaining soda. I did like strawberry the best.

We spent the next few hours going through all the stuff Margo had brought and ended up with a nice little sitting area. Zack moved the pots around as I directed, filled them with the potting soil, and then handed me a large bag full of seed packets.

I planted wisteria, dozens of varieties of climbing roses and clematis along with a bunch of lavender and other small plants. Then, one-by-one, I talked to the seeds and told them to grow. I had always been able to make things grow but hadn't realized when I was young how special this ability was. I had been pretty dense before I had run away to the forest.

We stood back and watched as the frame of the deck and surrounding trees were covered with vines and flowers. The vines twisted their way up, blooming as they went in a wide array of color. Margo had been right. This did make it feel more like home.

As the sun started to set, we blinked down to the forest floor. A stream meandered through the trees, stopping briefly at a small dam to create a miniature pond. Zack built a fire next to it and we roasted hot dogs. This was what I liked—the simple things…and the quiet of the forest.

After we ate, I curled up next to him and we sat there talking. Zack had so many plans for the treehouse and I let him talk as much as he wanted to about it. Besides I had started to feel woozy and drained again. It took too much energy to talk. It must have been hard not being able to tell any of the other guys, or me, about what was going on in his head for the last few months. There was no doubt that he intended for this to be our new home. That worried me and I knew I needed to tell him what Granddad had planned. I was growing drowsy, but worked hard to stay awake and listen. When he finished telling me about the second treehouse Margo wanted him to build for her, I decided I needed to broach the subject before I fell asleep.

"Zack, I really love this…but do you really think Granddad would let us do this. What about your dad, what do you plan on telling him?"

"Well, I wasn't sure I'd tell him much of anything. Just that it's time for me to live my own life, I guess," he said.

"Granddad told me this morning that he's worried about the fey and wants to close up the forest. When he gets back he's decided we are leaving."

He bristled and moved me around so we were looking at each other. "Ivy, do you want to go back and simply pretend all this hasn't happened?"

"No. No I don't. What I want is for everyone to leave us alone and for us to find our own lives," I said. As I spoke the words, I knew how unrealistic that was.

What was our plan? Would Zack and Margo and I just move here and play house? Would we blink around outside to go to school, get food, clothes and catch a movie now and then...and then what?   Maybe this plan of Zack's wasn't sensible. Maybe it was too soon for Zack and me to do everything on our own.

"I know you don't want to hurt your Granddad, but it's time for us to stand up for ourselves," he said as he kissed me gently on the lips and then looked into my eyes. "We are meant to be together, Ivy. We both know it." He looked up into the trees above us towards the treehouse that was out of sight. "This is what I want, to be with you, and I know it's what you want, too."

"Zack, I don't think it's the right time. I'm really uncomfortable with this," I said. It dawned on me that for the last few months I hadn't stood up to anyone. If Granddad wanted to do something, I eventually always went along with it and if Margo or Zack—especially Zack—wanted something, I found a way to do that too. Somewhere along the way, I had lost me. I knew that I didn't want to live in a tree house, not now at least. It was a nice getaway place, but what I really wanted to do was to finish college and find a life for myself. I just always thought Margo and Zack would be part of that life.

"You're clearly confused right now. It will be alright in the end, I promise you," he said, looking back at me. And then he leaned forward to kiss me again. We needed to talk this out, but I didn't pull away and the kiss deepened. We lay back and our kissing intensified. When he touched me, everything melted away—all my fears and doubts and dreams. Right now, as he kissed me, all I wanted to do was live in the moment and not have to think about what would happen tomorrow.

"Ivy, I love you so damn much it hurts. Forever, we belong together forever," he mumbled as he kissed me deeply again.

"Forever," I tried to say back, but he kept kissing me, making it hard to talk. It seemed like my senses were in overdrive. I could feel everything, from his emotions to the air around us. I worked hard to take all of the feelings in, wrap myself in the moment of Zack being all mine. I could feel his fingers working the buttons on my shirt, and it wasn't long before I felt our skin touching.

Just moments ago, I was sure that I would leave with Granddad tomorrow, lock the forest, and have a normal life. Now Zack was all I could think about. I really wanted to please him. Deep down I felt that was wrong—something was off kilter in my mind, but the more he kissed me, the less I thought about it.

I could sense everything around me. The trees stirring slightly as a soft breeze touched them, the small creatures scurrying amongst the foliage and even the cushion of litterfall beneath my back felt stimulated by the sexual tension we were creating. But as Zack became more aggressive, I started to feel smothered and couldn't catch my breath. I was exhausted, my sight had grown blurry, as had my mind and I just wanted to sleep. I tried to ease away, but my body was sluggish and I realized that I was very low on magic. I pulled some from the closest tree and my mind cleared for a moment. I felt a deep need to get away from Zack. I pushed hard against him, trying to sit up, but he acted like I was playing and shoved me back down.

He started to kiss me harder, forcing his lips

against mine. It didn't feel like a kiss as much as... My thoughts started to fog up again and I knew my energy was draining again. I placed one hand on the ground and pulled energy up into me. This time since I was focusing hard on keeping the energy inside myself, I could feel Zack undeniably extracting it from me. It was just like when we fought the Eilibear and I had to keep him charged with magic, only this time he was pulling it from me without my permission. I fought at resisting, but his pull was overwhelming and I couldn't stop him. I put my other hand to the ground and this time, with both hands, I drew forcefully, pulling as much energy into myself as I could hold.

Before he had a chance to drain it out, I pushed with both hands against him and fought to move my head away from him. Finally, I was able to break the contact of our lips. To my shock, Zack grabbed my hair and slammed my head violently against the ground. I connected roughly with the sharp edge of a rock and the pain was almost unbearable. He grabbed my neck with his other hand and brutally squeezed it, keeping me from moving. My head spun and I couldn't focus my eyes. He smashed his lips back to mine and I could feel my energy draining even faster than before.

In a full-blown panic, I struggled underneath him and started to hit him as hard as I could with my fists. He didn't even seem to notice and kept his hold on my neck and hair, forcing me to stay connected to him. I continued to thrash around beneath him. This wasn't my Zack...I didn't know what was happening, but he wasn't in control of himself. I had an endless source of magic from the forest, however I didn't see how allowing him to pull that energy from me would help either of us. He was just getting stronger and more forceful, while I continued to wither.

I tried to force the tingle of magic at the back of my throat so I could push him away with my powers. But there was no magic left to use and even if there had been, I couldn't speak with his lips against mine. I began to cry silently as my body started to go limp. My arms slipped off his back, I didn't have the strength to even try to hit him.

He was draining me, and soon I'd be nothing but an empty shell. This was one of the few ways a fey could die, having their life force taken, and Zack was doing it to me. I had no willpower to stop him; my body felt wilted, almost used up. I scratched my fingernails into the ground and tried to pull again, but I barely had enough energy to try.

There was a tingling in my fingers which then moved up my arms as the forest gave up its power to me. I was done playing nice. I kept one hand flat on the ground, continuing to pull and as soon as I had enough strength to raise my other arm I slammed it into Zack's neck and dug my fingernails into his skin as hard as I could.

He screamed as he pulled away, looked at me with such a look of disgust that it almost paralyzed me and then slapped me so hard that I was sure he had broken my jaw. My true will returned with that blow. Skyler and her boyfriends used to hit me like that, and back then I didn't know I had the power to fight them. Now I knew I could.

"Get the hell away from me!" I screamed out and knew the tingle of magic in my throat had mingled with my spoken words.

Like a giant's hand had reached down and plucked him off me, he soared up into the air and then flew backwards a good twenty feet until he slammed against a huge tree. Vines started to twist around his frame, securing him to the trunk. He roared with anger and fought ferociously against the restraints. The vines wrapped themselves around his arms, legs and neck and within seconds, he was imprisoned by them. He screamed obscenities at me as I sat staring at him in shock. I was shaking uncontrollably as tears ran down my face. I couldn't bring myself to move or look at him.

"Let me go! You know you want this!" he screamed at me. "We are meant to be together. I love you Ivy. This is what is meant to happen, YOU KNOW IT!" He fought against the restraints and as he did, his face and tone of voice became more dark and angry. "YOU HAVE NO RIGHT! I AM A WARRIOR DRUID!"

My ears started to ring from the intensity of his bellowing. I was terrified, but as his screams at me continued, I became furious. Not really at Zack, but at who this frightening person was and what he had almost done. Somehow I started to disconnect *my* Zack from *this* Zack.

"WHEN I GET LOOSE, YOU WILL REGRET THIS!" he bellowed, then he became even more chilling when he lowered his voice again. "Please, Ivy, I'm sorry. I didn't mean to scare you. Just let me loose and everything will be fine. Come on, just come over here and let me touch you," he begged.

There was no way I was moving an inch closer to him. He pleaded with his eyes and I stared at him. I was sure he knew I had no intention of doing as he asked when his eyes narrowed again and he all but snarled at me.

"YOU BITCH! IT IS MY RIGHT! HOW DARE YOU CONDEMN ALL OTHERS TO DEATH BECAUSE OF YOUR SELFISHNESS!"

I have to admit, that one got to me. I didn't want anyone to die because of me, but for the life of me, I couldn't see how not wanting him to kill me had anything to do with others dying. I took one tentative step forward.

"Why would anyone die because of me?"

"They will all die because I won't be strong enough as a warrior to save them. Everyone will die because of you," he snarled and then looked me up and down with contempt. "You think you are this wonderful person, this over-the-top powerful fey. You are nothing compared to me," he hissed through gritted teeth.

Well that did it. This macho, I'm-all-great-and-you're-nothing crap was over the top, even for a normal guy. I stepped back and started to turn around. I couldn't look at him anymore.

"WHERE THE HELL DO YOU THINK YOU'RE GOING? DO YOU REALLY THINK A STUPID FRÍTH FEY CAN STAND UP TO A WARRIOR DRUID? YOU ARE NOTHING ...NOTHING!

I didn't turn back around. Instead I moved a few more steps away and sat down on the wet grass. I could still see him out of the corner of my eye as he continued to scream at me. I let him rant as I sung my favorite songs in my head to drown him out.

After about half an hour, he switched to telling me I was killing him, that he needed to be near me, begging my forgiveness and pleading with me to release him...and on it went. The few times I managed to look in his direction, I regretted it. His eyes were bloodshot and glazed over and, more disgustingly, there was drool dripping from the corners of his mouth. He looked like a rabid dog.

The forest must have grown tired of his screams also, as the vines eventually started to grow again and twist around his head until his mouth was covered. The new quiet was eerie and the night sounds around me seemed out of place. I was cold and wanted to leave, but something held me to the spot. The fire was nothing but embers now, and I decided I needed to build it back up. As I went around gathering firewood, I kept watch on him, scared that somehow he would get loose. His bloodshot eyes followed me everywhere, eyes that radiated hatred at me.

My face, neck and head hurt horribly. I reached up to gingerly feel the areas and knew that I must have some nasty bruises. It felt swollen around my jawline and the skin was painful to touch where Zack's hand had squeezed my neck. I reached up to touch a bump on the back of my head and when I brought my hand away, it was covered in sticky blood.

He had really done a job on me. I thought about leaving to find Granddad, but then remembered that he was gone for the night. I could get Margo, but she wouldn't have a clue what to do any more than I did. I could simply heal myself, but then no one would believe me about what had happened. I worked at taking the pain away and that helped. Until I had some idea what to do, I'd leave everything as it was.

So I built up the fire, watched, waited and thought. I tried to remember when it was that I had started to feel tired all the time. It must have been only a few days after Zack's dad had showed up with the other druids. At the time, I'd thought I was coming down with a cold and then Granddad had started getting on me about looking worn out. That's when he began giving me vitamins and making me eat more. Had he known that this was going to happen?

What *had* happened?

I was pretty sure it had to do with the druids, or the fact that Zack was a druid. His screams about him being a Warrior Druid and me just a Frìth fey seemed to lead to that assumption. Was this something else that no one thought to tell us? Uncle Eddie was always making sure we spent time together. Did he know this would happen?

There were too many questions that I didn't have the answers to.

My body and mind were exhausted, but in the normal way. My eyes kept closing on their own and when the moon hit its crescent, I fell into a restless sleep. Dark nightmares plagued me. Ones of Skyler beating the shit out of me, only to have the dream shift to Zack being the one doing the beating. I knew I was shaking with cold and fear, but could not escape from the dreams. Sometime during the night, the cold was replaced by peaceful warmth and finally I slept undisturbed.

Sunlight on my face woke me to the cheery sounds of birds singing and the bubbling of the stream beside me. It took me a moment to remember why I was here and what had happened. I looked over to Zack and saw he was still secured to the tree. His head had loped to one side and his eyes were closed. If he still looked scary when he woke, I decided I would go wait for

Granddad to get home and then bring him here. As I went to sit up, I discovered I was covered with a thick layer of soft moss.

Bryophyte…the correct name for moss popped into my head and I had to smirk at myself for remembering that cute little fact from class.

The forest must have decided to keep me warm, or maybe I had done it with my own magic and not realized it at the time. Either way, I had been cozy. I pushed it back like a blanket and pulled myself out from under it. It gently fell back to the ground and molded in with the forest floor.

I looked around for my backpack and saw it was where I had dropped it last night, when we had first made our little camp. Going over to it, I snatched it up and opened one of the outside pockets. I usually kept power bars in there for snacks between classes. There were a few left and I pulled one out. I ripped off the edge of paper with my teeth as I swung my pack over one shoulder.

I had almost finished it when I chanced a look at Zack. His eyes were open, watching me. He wasn't moving and his eyes weren't bloodshot anymore. In fact, he looked frozen with fright. I slowly made my way over to him and stopped when I was about five feet away.

"Are you *you* now?" I asked and waited.

He couldn't respond, but he tried to wiggle and I think he was nodding. I took a deep breath and then let the tingle build.

"Release his mouth so he can talk," I called, letting the magic roll out.

The vines receded and he sputtered and worked at

moving his mouth and jaw. Then he looked up at me.

"What the hell, Ivy?" he cried out.

"You tried to kill me."

"No I didn't, I was kissing you."

"You were draining me, sucking all my energy away. You *were* close to killing me, Zack," I screamed at him.

"No I wasn't, I was..." He stopped talking. I could see he was trying to figure it out. He looked confused, just like he had when I had brought the house in to shock him out of the fey enchantments.

I took a couple of steps closer and his face changed. His eyes focused on me and grew bright. He ran his tongue over his lips and I could see him taking deep breaths. When he started to speak again, his lilt had altered and now there was a condescending undertone to it.

"It was just your imagination. I would never hurt you. Come on, get these off me and we can work it all out." His voice was silky and he was seriously creeping me out. I took a few steps backwards, watching his expression as I did. Like he was coming out of a fog, he shook his head and looked at me with scared eyes. I was terrified all over again.

"There is something seriously wrong with you. Look at my face. Do you see the bruises? Look here," I said turning my head so he could see my neck and the back of my head. "You did this to me. You were a monster, and you were not going to stop. You were bound and determined to kill me," I shouted at him as I started to cry.

"I don't know what is happening to me. I have this need to be near you all the time or I feel wrong," he said mournfully, and I was disgusted with him. He didn't sound sorry for what he did to me at all and seemed more concerned for himself.

"Well that's just peachy, isn't it?" I said sarcastically as I worked at getting my emotions under control. "I think you have been draining me ever since the battle. I've felt tired all the time and whenever we touch, there are little pulses of energy that pass from me to you. I don't know if I did this by powering you for the battle or if it's some sick druid thing, but you are not going to come close to me again or be alone with me again until I figure this out," I said. I worked hard at keeping my voice level, but it broke several times as I had to choke back tears. I had started to shake again and wanted so much not to be here.

"So what, you're really going to leave me here?" he said, narrowing his eyes at me. "Let me loose Ivy, right now!" He was angry and started to thrash violently against the vines. I took another step back and glared at him, all feelings of compassion gone.

"Don't you dare get all enraged with me!" I was losing it completely. "You listen to me, Zack, and this time, really listen. YOU TRIED TO KILL ME!" Yep I had lost it. "And what would have happened if you had, huh? Answer me that. One, I'd be dead so you could never be 'near me' again. Two, Granddad would have killed you. Three, if you did find any way to get away from Granddad, you would never be able to rest. He would track you forever...forever Zack, and when he finally found you, he would kill you. And four...damn it I WOULD BE DEAD! Are you listening to me, do you understand my words? Knock- knock, are you there Zack?"

He was silent for a long while, which gave me time to catch my breath. Being furious with Zack was exhausting. He hung there and stared at me. He had relaxed and maybe it had finally gotten through his thick head what he had almost done.

"So let me go, so I can find Dad and see if he knows what is happening to me," he said in a low voice. He still hadn't said he was sorry, but I couldn't just leave him here.

I thought hard about what to say that would protect me, and as I looked at the vines that held him, an idea came to me. I let the tingle build to as much strength as I could before I spoke. I whispered the words, choking back tears.

"Vines release him, but make sure he cannot reach if he means me harm in any way," I said, letting the magic roll out.

The vines started to recede, taking most of his shirt with them. The cloth ripped and was yanked from him and I could tell it wasn't a pleasant experience for him. As soon as he could move, he staggered out from the tree and pulled vines away from his legs and chest. One persistent vine had wrapped itself around his left forearm and angled up towards his left ear. It was a small, dainty vine with tiny variegated green leaves, but no matter how much he yanked at it, he could not get it off. He heaved himself away from the tree trunk and the vine snapped off. He was left with the end of the vine still attached to his arm and neck. He pulled and scratched at it, but even I could see that it had molded itself into his skin. There was no way that was coming off.

He looked over at me with an irritated sneer.

"Tell it to come off, Ivy. It won't budge," he said and held his arm out towards me. I inspected his torso. He had bulked up...again. His muscles rippled and bulged as he moved. I was so freaking stupid. All summer long, I had noticed that he was looking very fit and every time we were together, he seemed to look even more so. I thought it came from working out, bodybuilding and the like. Not. The damn druid had to have been using me to obtain his ripped physique. No steroids needed; he had me instead.

I pulled my eyes away from his muscles and looked at him steadily.

"No," I said.

His expression turned to anger again and he bolted towards me. I stumbled backwards even though I was pretty sure he couldn't get to me. I was right. As soon as he was within arms-reach of me, the vine on his arm started to grow rapidly and twisted around his neck. He fell to the ground with his hands clutching his neck, pulling franticly at the vine. His body twisted in pain as the vine tightened. I blinked backwards about ten feet and then waited.

He sat up sputtering and gasping for air. The vine loosened and started to recede back to his arm.

"You will never be able to come close to me again if you intend to do me physical harm," I said grimly. "Please go, Zack. If you get it figured out, come back and we'll see what happens."

His eyes were glazed over...then cleared for a moment...then glazed over again. It was rapid and creepy to watch his features go from those of *my* Zack to those of a crazed fiend. Like a light switch being turned on and off. I watched and waited.

Off, on, off, on…
"Zack!"
Nothing.
Off, on, off, on…
"Zack!"
Recognition for the briefest of moments.
Off, on, off, on…
"Fight, damn it!"
Fear.
Off, on…off, on….
"Fight it!"

I could see his inward struggles as his chest heaved. He threw back his head and a deep rolling growl of anger and anguish erupted from him. The sound ripped through the forest, vibrating against the trees, and echoed for miles.

He looked at me then…on…
"Ivy, get out of here!"
I blinked.

CHAPTER 6 – Milton

Milton opened his eyes and discovered he wasn't where he expected to be. This wasn't the Alltha headquarters in New York. He knew this place. One time, many years ago, he had come here with Eddie.

He stood in the vestibule of the Citadel, the domicile once home to the Oak Triad and the headquarters of the Druids. The vestibule was wide, with oak columns holding up long beams of roughhewn oak trunks. It encircled the Citadel with multiple doors leading into the main chamber, outside or to various other parts of the compound. He looked over at Eddie to ask what was up, but his friend had a stunned look plastered on his face. Milton knew then that it was Carmen who had brought them here and he had no idea why. Two thoughts entered his mind; either this was about Ivy again or something was wrong.

Suddenly a chime sounded, then a small winged person appeared and dropped a scroll into Carmen's hand. The little hummingbird-like creature fluttered to Carmen's shoulder and sat there quite matter-of-factly, as if this was the most normal thing in the world.

"It seems there is a delay. We are being asked to wait in the outer corridor until we are summoned," Carmen said as he read the scroll. Milton barely heard him as he was concentrating on the little person on Carmen's shoulder.

"Is that a Sprite?" Milton asked, unable to stop looking at the small fey. It was a female with red curly hair and tiny pink-veined wings. She looked at him and smiled widely.

"Of course, who else would bring a communiqué?" Carmen asked in a condescending tone.

"That's how the scrolls come to me? I never saw a Sprite, other than Margo."

"A well-trained Sprite would only show itself to its owner. The half-breed Sprite you allow to live with you is abnormal and I do not understand why, once discovered, it was allowed to live," Carmen said with disdain.

"Enough Carmen!" Eddie exclaimed reproachfully.

With unbridled contempt, Carmen glared at him. "I tire of this. We are Warrior Druids, not nursemaids! The time has come for us to take our rightful place and do our duty. I understand your need to allow your son to complete the Gorffen, but there is plenty of time. I do not see what the hurry is, other than to have the pest gone."

"Carmen, I warn you. This is not the time or place," Eddie cried heatedly. Carmen glared at him, glancing once at Milton before exiting the vestibule to the outer corridor.

Eddie and Milton followed, and Milton could see Carmen's back as he strode off down the length of the corridor and out of sight.

"Mind telling me what all that was about?" Milton asked.

"He's just in a foul mood since we are being made to wait. I'm hungry, let's get some food," he said, changing the subject.

He went to the inside wall and pulled on a cord three times, then stepped back. An elegant table laden with food appeared. Eddie went over to it and started to fill a tankard with ale from a barrel, then proceeded to fill a plate with food. He was acting as if what Carmen had said wasn't important, but Milton wasn't fooled. He wanted to know what the Gorffen was and what the *nursemaid* business was about.

When Eddie was done, he found a small side table with some chairs near it and sat down with his plate. Milton wandered over to a large clear bubble-glass window and looked outside to the courtyard.

This was where Eddie had brought him when he was initiated into the Alltha Order. It had been a rather uneventful and anticlimactic ceremony. He had enjoyed the experience of seeing first-hand where the original Druids, the heroic vanguards of the fey, had made their first home in Alainn. Then and now he was impressed that they had the courage and valor to leave their home in Firinn and relocate to Alainn for the betterment of all the realms. For a long while, they had been outcasts and were not allowed back into Firinn, but at some point in history that had changed. What remained of the non-Warrior Druids still resided here and their appearance and countenance reminded him of human monks.

On his first visit, after the short initiation ceremony, he had been permitted to wander the compound to his heart's content. It was here that he had first heard about the now defunct Oak Triad. He had seen a few murals that literally told the story of their inception and the work the Druids did on behalf of the fey and humans. He had wanted to know more, but none of the druids or Alltha would speak of them, saying their religion had been discredited. Much of the war with the Eilibear was blamed on them and he could not find any that spoke kindly about them.

He had tried several times throughout the years to locate information on them, but to no avail. It was his wife Elsie who finally found the information he had been looking for. Her fey friend Elizabeth had provided the names of several libraries around the world that held writings about them. Elsie had been fascinated and continued to gather material, while he had lost interest.

After all these years and now with Elsie gone, here he stood once more. He longed to wander the grounds again and went to one of the outside doors. It was locked and would not open for him. He returned to the window and gazed out, remembering what it had been like to walk the gardens and halls of the compound.

On the exterior, outside the walls, it looked like the ruins of a nondescript minor castle, and even if a human walked along the insides of the ruins, they would only see the same rubble as on the outside. He remembered being confused at first but Eddie had taught him how to switch his view from human to fey, like changing the lens on a camera, and suddenly there was magic in the air.

The fey Citadel compound was extraordinary. In America it was popular to put on Renaissance fairs, dress up and pretend to be back in the time of kings, queens, royal jesters and the like, but here time had stopped. The world had moved on, but in this one little spot, disguised by the fey, time was held stationary. There were hundreds of acres of lush green meadows and small woods brimming with every sort of fey one could imagine. The rhythm of time stood still and gave the fey a safe haven outside of the fey realm and the Meadhans to conduct their business.

The Citadel stood in the middle, a towering stone castle the likes of which no human eye had ever seen. He had assumed it was magic that made the Citadel, however he had discovered it was just the opposite. In Firinn, it was the magic that held that realm together. Here it was a human place, only obscured by magic to give the fey their safeguard, the same as the Meadhans were.

Behind him he heard Eddie get up and refill his plate from the table. He needed to broach the subject that had been nagging at him. He turned and went back over to where Eddie was sitting down with another plate piled high with food.

"Eddie, we have been friends too long for me not to know when you are keeping something from me. Carmen clearly has some idea what is happening, which means you do also. What is the Gorffen?"

His friend picked up a drumstick from his plate and took a bite from it before he answered.

"It's a druid rite of passage. Like when you were initiated into the Alltha Order. Zack is close to the time when he will be ready. It's rather personal and very much a Warrior Druid thing. You have to understand, our friendship is...not ordinary," he said searching for the right words. "Carmen and others of the Warrior clan cannot really comprehend it. They find my actions beneath my rank."

"I've always understood that. And I understand that the Gorffen is a personal thing for druids. However, am I right that Ivy somehow plays a part in it?"

Eddie was quiet for a moment and stared down at his plate. When he looked up, Milton knew his friend was troubled.

"Yes, but only because of her affection for Zack. It will be fine; neither will come to harm. It's not an easy thing for Zack to endure, however he has Ivy to support him and I trust her. She will be able to help him through," he said as a muscle in his jaw twitched.

"I guess I have no choice but to believe that you and Zack wouldn't do anything to harm Ivy. So let me ask instead, what are we doing here?" He waved his arm out towards the Citadel.

"The Eilibear have broken through another sealed doorway. They have massive numbers and all fey are concerned. We do not have enough warriors to defeat them, or be in all the places they are at one time. The only positive point is that the area where they came in is not highly populated. The doorway was near Magadan on the coast of Russia, and now the Eilibear have spilled out to every bit of land that surrounds the Sea of Okhotsk. We need a battle plan and we need it fast."

Milton pondered his friend's words. He wasn't familiar with the area, but even the battle the kids had fought in the Hemlock forest took four, five if you counted Margo, to defeat the demons. He didn't know the Warrior Druids full numbers, but he knew it wasn't more than thirty. And the young men in his forest were not battle trained. Yes, he could see how this would be a difficulty.

"Thank you for sharing what is clearly a druid matter, Eddie. I do understand your concerns now. But tell me, why was *I* brought here if this is a Warrior Druid matter?" he inquired.

There was a long pause and Eddie sighed deeply before he spoke. "I don't know. We were told to."

They sat there in silence, each lost in his own

thoughts. The time dragged on, but they could not leave until the summons came. After a time, Eddie produced a chess board from one of the side console tables, and they lost count of the number of games they played to pass the time.

Milton grew restless and started to pace the corridor. This was not an area where he had ever spent time. As he moved closer to one expanse of bare wall on the inner side, words started to appear on the wall in a glowing blue script.

We call on the three to weave the balance,
We give thanks to the circle three for their restoring might,
We bow to the balance derived from the three.

As he moved from in front of the wall, the words dissolved. He stepped back and the scribbling appeared again, but with different wording.

Hail the Oak Triad and their Scepters three,
That gives fire to the Orb and sets us free,
Hail to the Balance that gives us life,
That pours out blessings from the realms trice.

Again he moved away until the words vanished and then moved forward once more.

We bind unto our brethren,
The magics from the Sunstone,
Rays of glory shining,
Rays of light illumining,
Rays of power unending,
We bind unto our brethren to the three.

He moved away and then back several more times. Each time, a new poem appeared. He turned and hurried back to where Eddie had lain down on a settee.

"Eddie, writing is appearing on the walls. What

is that?" he asked, pointing to the place where the words had been.

"Oh...I had forgotten about those. When the Citadel was built, there was an alliance with the Eilibear...that whole Oak Triad matter. Those are remnants of the magic the Eilibear provided. It's the old chants and prayers that were used in the Oak Triad Rimwalk."

"Why are they still here if the druids have abandoned the ceremonies?"

"They couldn't be removed, we tried. If you are interested in all that shit, just walk around the corridor. There are many on the walls and I think some carvings that go with them," he said in a bored tone and closed his eyes in dismissal.

Milton thought that finding information about the Oak Triad *was* interesting. He left Eddie to his nap and started walking the corridor. He found six spots where the wall was blank until he came close to it. The scripting always appeared with blue glowing flames. The writing was in a flowing cursive that he had only seen in older manuscripts. The first five sets had six chants in rotation. The last one only displayed a single chant:

> *Pure balance of the flowing tides on you,*
> *pure balance of the quiet wind on you,*
> *pure balance of the spinning worlds on you.*
> *We three of the Oak Triad do bless and greet you.*

On the wall next to the flaming words was a carving, filled in like a painting. It depicted the Sunstone and the table that encircled it. Three people were standing on the table, holding up maces. Flames like lightening were shooting out from the maces up to a ball.

The ball resembled a small glowing sun and from the bottom of it, a braid of all three flames twisted together and shot down towards the Sunstone. Underneath the image, two words had been carved into the stone of the wall, *Sunstone Rimwalk.*

He continued walking, passing Eddie a number of times. He was still sleeping and Milton left him to it. He never came across Carmen and had no clue where the fey had gone off to and really didn't care. With each full walk of the circle around the Citadel, he noticed something new. A carving of a creature he'd never seen before or small empty bowls jutting out from the wall— he had no idea of their purpose. There were statues and busts that lined the corridor, along with many paintings on the walls. As he inspected them closely, he realized that he could distinguish the fey and druid fey from each other, along with the druid fey from the Alltha fey. But there was another he couldn't recognize, similar to both races, fey and mortal, yet different and he wondered if those were the Eilibear before the war occurred.

He finally grew tired from his walk and sat down next to Eddie. As the day dragged into night, Milton lay down on a bench near Eddie and slept.

Eddie and Milton were awakened abruptly by the sound of a bell tolling. It had the deep sound of a thick church bell and after each ring, the sound lingered for a count of five before another clanged. At the end of three, Eddie stood.

"That's us."

Together they made their way to one of the large double doors that allowed entry into the Citadel's main chamber and waited.

When the doors finally swung open Milton

moved forward, and as he had been on his first visit here years ago, he was awed by his surroundings.

He looked around, overwhelmed once again by the grandeur of the chamber. It was enormous and put all the cathedrals he had ever seen to shame. The chamber's walls and ceiling were supported by giant oak trunks that had been carved with images that were so detailed he knew it must have taken years to do just a small portion of one illustration.

There were four massive fireplaces set evenly around the room and they were so large they were small rooms all by themselves. Fires blazed in all and provided enough light that no other was needed. Each fireplace was flanked by sculptures of what could only be fey, impressive ones with long flowing beards holding scrolls and others with serious expressions, their arms raised outward with their palms up as if in prayer or maybe casting an enchantment.

He pulled his gaze away from them and looked up to the ceiling. A mural covered the immense space. Many of the pictures depicted images unknown to him, of places that he was sure no human had laid eyes on.

The sound of a chair scraping across the marbled floor pulled his attention to the center of the room. A large table, sat in the middle of the chamber. It was round and at least thirty feet across. In the epicenter of the table, the tip of a massive gemstone could be seen. He was sure was a diamond. The stone looked like it had been there since the dawning of time, large and uneven. Eddie had told him that the gem was enormous and this was only a tip that poked out of the ground. He wondered just how deep into the earth it went.

The table had been constructed around its edges

and it was a good thing the tip was somewhat flat or when one was seated at the table, it would be impossible to see over the stone to the other side. The stone gem had seen better days as a crack had formed, making a jagged line from one side to the other. He had asked numerous druids about the crack in the stone, but none would speak of it.

Now, after reading the poems on the wall outside and seeing the carving, he realized why the chairs looked so out of place. That wasn't a table with a gem in the center. That was the Sunstone and the table was where the Oak Triad had once stood for the Rimwalk.

He wondered absently what could have happened that would have led the druids to abandon their beliefs so thoroughly. Suddenly the room was freezing and he could see his breath before him. He wondered if he had violated some law by thinking of such things.

Looking over at the fireplaces, he could see that the fires still roared brightly, but he was cold to the core. He looked over to the table again. There were fey seated and he saw that Carmen was one of them. They all stood as they became aware of his and Eddie's presence, giving the newcomers unnerving glares.

Suddenly chimes rang out, a gentle jingling as if a breeze had blown through crystal wind chimes in his Hemlock forest. The sound reverberated throughout the chamber and as the sweet sound began to dissipate, it sounded again and then again. After the third chime had silenced, Milton realized that the chamber itself had grown still. Seconds dragged to minutes until the swish of a door opening turned all heads towards the sound.

Two fey wearing long flowing white mantles exited from the door and walked purposely toward the head of the table. He had met both before. One was Edme, the Elders' Minister. He was one of the fey that he had kicked out of the Hemlock forest at the very beginning of his tenure as the Woodsman. There was no love lost between him and this fey and not once in all these years had they spoken.

The second one he had never had dealings with. He had seen him only twice before and Eddie had made sure that they both kept their distance from him. Odive, the head of the Druid Counsel. If he had met him on a street in any city in Alainn, he would not have thought *fey*. The man was shorter than most fey, scrawny with a horrible comb-over, trying unsuccessfully to hide his baldness. He looked like an aging accountant. All that was missing was a pair of thick, outdated glasses.

All the Alltha Order's fey were afraid of him and if they had to speak of him, it was in hushed worried whispers. From what he had heard, this was one fey that no one wanted to deal with. Word was, he could squelch another fey's powers and immobilize them in seconds. The power seemed to work on humans also, somehow stifling their life force until there was no life left. One very dangerous fey.

Odive turned his gaze towards them, focusing on Milton for a moment before he motioned to a line of benches off to the side. Eddie took his arm and pulled him over to it. He wasn't sure what was going on, but this did not bode well. He looked at Eddie, but his friend would not meet his eyes. Milton allowed himself to be placed before the bench, but did not sit. Eddie took a place next to him. Milton glanced at his friend, then turned to Odive who was staring directly at him.

"You are the Woodsman," Odive said plainly as

he looked Milton over. "I expected something more impressive." Snickers sounded around the room, and Milton was instantly on guard.

"What is going..." Milton started to speak and found his words were gone. No sound would come from his lips.

"Shifted mortals do not speak unless they are asked to do so. It is insulting enough that we found it necessary to have you in our presence," Odive said, giving Milton a look of disgust before turning his attention to the assembled group.

"The Elders have stayed out of this matter of the Alltha. We expect you to be able to handle little annoyances as they arise. You have been remiss in your actions and we find it necessary to step in. Sit, your rudeness displeases me," Odive said with irritation as he sat down himself and casually straightened his robes.

This fey's demeanor was intimidating and Milton knew that somehow he had been careless in not locking down the Hemlock forest and telling all the fey to be gone as he had years ago. Milton looked at each of the fey seated around the edges of the table. He knew a number of them as friend and all had always been on his side when it came to matters of him and Ivy.

A dull tingling sounded and Milton looked over at Odive just as the fey set a small brass hand bell down on the table. Edme produced a scroll and laid it out in front of Odive. He glanced down at it and then slowly lifted his head to look around at the assembly.

"This tribunal has been called due to the numerous communiqués from various Alltha members. The Elders are tired of your inability to handle these issues yourself and *I* find this whole situation unacceptable," he declared, looking directly at each of the fey seated until he or she lowered their eyes in humility. Finally, his glance came around again to rest on Milton. They locked eyes and when Milton did not look away, a small smile started to play at the corners of Odive's mouth.

"Woodsman. I find that an interesting moniker. Tell me, *Woodsman,* have you unleashed the Eilibear onto the fey by keeping a demon-mutant fey as a pet?"

Milton felt a tingle at the back of his throat and knew his ability to speak had returned. He took a moment to feel the sensation of magic that this Odive had used. It was unknown to him, but one he believed his unique powers could find a way to counter if given enough time.

"Speak, Woodsman," Odive said and that same taste of magic hit Milton again. He focused on it and discovered that he could weave it around and control it. It wouldn't be good for this fey to know of his ability and instead he decided to play along.

"I have no demon pet," he answered, keeping his face and voice void of emotion.

"Well, I'm told that you named it Ivy," he replied pointing towards the scroll. "Do you have a pet named such?" The fey smiled maliciously at him and Milton wondered what game he was playing at with this farce. Milton decided he wasn't going to take the bait; it would be no help to Ivy if he lost his temper.

"I do not," he replied coldly. "Ivy is a Frith fey by birth. Everyone is aware of that fact. I am her guardian and have raised her as my own. She is the rightful owner of the Hemlock Forest." He wanted out of here and wondered if he blinked into the forest, if he would have time to lock it down.

"Yes, I have been informed of that. Edme here has spoken of his adventures with you and the Meadhan you took from the fey," he said as he absently started to tap his fingernails on the table. His eyes never left Milton's, and the two stared at each other, neither giving in. Finally, Odive seemed to come to some conclusion, raised his hands good naturedly and smiled at him.

"Well, all that is behind us now, isn't it? The fey Ivy is of age and, as you pointed out, is the owner of the Meadhan," he said casually, but there was a hint of cynicism in his tone. "I resolve this topic. The Frith fey, so named Ivy, has found Favor with the Elders and *is* the rightful owner of the Hemlock Forest Meadhan. However, the Elders' only concern is that she has not been properly trained on what her duties are. We do not believe that being raised by a shifted mortal, no matter how well meaning he may be, could instill within her the pride and honor of her station. She will come to Firinn, to the seminary there-in, for said training and to be acclimated with what it means to be fey."

Milton started to protest, and Odive flicked his hand out towards him and once more he could not speak. He had to watch in forced silence as Edme handed Odive a quill and, with a flourish, he made a large check mark on the scroll. When done he looked around the room and smiled coldly. "That situation is now resolved. On to the next."

Milton was enraged. Since the time of his shifting into fey, in one manner or another, the fey had fought against him and his family. He knew something was wrong, but had never even thought that the Elders would try to take her again. That hadn't worked out very well for them the first time. He wondered what they thought was different now. There had been no mention of the Sumair stone, so maybe that was finally a dead topic.

He had to get out of here and get Ivy somewhere safe. Maybe they would need to lock down the forest with them inside for a time. Ivy wouldn't like not being able to go to college, but he thought she would not like the idea of being hauled off into Firinn with the fey any better.

"Rōber Edsmond, I am told that you broke the fey decree and traveled into a Fearainn Eadar," Odive stated. Milton looked over at Eddie. He had no clue what or where this Fearainn was and wasn't sure even when Eddie could have had time to travel in the last year.

Eddie cleared his throat as he looked straight ahead. His body had grown ridged and Milton could feel fear radiating from him.

"I did travel into a Fearainn Eadar, with the Alltha Order's permission," Eddie said with a shaking voice.

"I see, so we should not be holding you accountable, but the whole of the Alltha Order?"

"That's not what I meant. The decree states that no fey is to seek out a Fearainn Eadar for any reason…other than to save another fey. One of ours was taken. We tracked the Eilibear to a newly re-opened doorway and followed them in."

"So one of *ours* was taken? This is what you claim?" Odive sneered unpleasantly. He looked down at the scroll that Edme had lain out on the table before him and started to read silently to himself, using his finger to keep his place. When he looked up again, he locked eyes with Milton.

"Woodsman. You are shifted, are you not?" he asked coldly.

Milton wasn't sure what this question really meant. All fey who knew of him also knew that he had been shifted by the Sumair Stone. He felt the tingle and knew his voice had returned. He wanted to scream at this vile fey that he wasn't going to get his slimy hands on Ivy, but the look of desperation in Eddie's eyes made him concentrate on this new line of discussion instead. Taking a deep breath, he answered the question.

"Yes, that is common knowledge."

"Do you consider yourself fey, mortal or something else?"

"I am fey via the shifting."

"Fair answer. And your mate...one Elsie Glenwood is fey via shifting also?"

"She was. The Eilibear killed her," Milton said, trying to keep his voice level.

"Ah, well that is indeed sad. So you, along with this fey, Rōber Edsmond, traveled into a Fearainn Eadar to attempt to save her...and you failed," Odive said, glaring at him.

"I don't know what a Fearainn Eadar is. We followed the Eilibear into Ifrinn after they took my wife."

"Well now I can see that we have an issue with semantics here and I must say, *Woodsman*, you are showing your ignorance very blazingly. Allow me to educate you, since it seems your friend here has neglected to do so. Just as we have Meadhans that act as the *between* for Firinn and Alainn, there exist other *betweens* called Fearainn Eadar. This is the space that connects Ifrinn with Alainn and in some places with Firinn. We sealed all the doorways and there was a reason that we did this. By some manner, the Eilibear have found a way to unseal them, as they did when they took your mate."

Milton glanced over at Eddie to clarify this new information and his friend nodded forlornly.

"Crap," Milton mumbled as he glared at Eddie.

"Your friend here should have informed you of this, or someone else should have," he said glancing around the table with distaste. "I will ignore this oversight if you can answer this correctly fey Edsmond. At any time, did you enter into Ifrinn?"

"No," Eddie replied forcefully.

"Did you at any time leave *that* Fearainn Eadar for another?"

"No, we stayed inside that one," Eddie said hesitantly.

Milton watched Odive's body language. The fey seemed to have a strong need to make sure they hadn't left that one place and Milton wondered why that was.

"Did you seal the doorways into the Fearainn Eadar up once more?"

"Yes, a group of other Alltha helped me. We sealed and barred them with the strongest enchantments available.

"Good, all is as it should be. This issue is now closed. I have resolved this topic. The fey, Rōber Edsmond, did not dishonor the Elder's decree and is freed from any discredit," he declared casually. Once more, he picked up the quill. With the same flourish as before, he checked something off.

Edme rolled up the scroll from the table and laid

it off to the side. Out of his cloak, he pulled another larger scroll and laid it out in front of Odive. It was very thick and long compared to any Milton had seen before. This was much older—the parchment was yellowed from age and the rollers had elaborate etching on them.

Odive took his time looking over the writ, rolling it out several times, while Edme worked at rolling up the other end so it would not fall from the table. Milton wondered just how large this scroll was. Finally, Odive placed his finger on one point on the document and looked up at the assembly.

Milton looked around and knew that no one was paying any attention to him since all eyes were glued on Odive. He decided that this was as good a time as any to get the hell out of here. He needed to make sure Ivy was safe and lock the damn forest down so none of these fey could get inside. He blinked…and nothing happened. He tried again and remembered that as long as an Alltha meeting was in progress, they were all in lock-down.

He turned to Eddie in frustration, but went still when he saw his face. Eddie had gone ashen. Milton had never seen his friend scared, but he was clearly petrified now. He was staring at the scroll that Odive had been reading, and it was apparent that he knew what it was.

"Eddie?" Milton whispered out of the corner of his mouth.

Eddie turned to him, eyes wide with fright, and shook his head.

"We need to get out of here, now," Milton hissed at him.

His friend only shook his head more fervently and looked back to Odive.

"It is known that the Eilibear have indeed found a

means to unseal the doors. We do not know how they have unwoven our enchantments, however the doorway that fey Edsmond discovered open was just the first of many. For a time, we were able to seal them once more, but they are being opened in greater numbers now and the Eilibear are gaining presence in Alainn in record numbers. The fear is that Alainn will be overrun with the demons and they will find their way into Firinn again. This threat is at the forefront of the Elders' concerns, and they believe they have found a means to neutralize this vulnerability."

Odive whispered something to Edme who then walked over to a side door, opened it and waved at someone to come in. Edme came back to stand beside Odive as five female fey filed into the chamber and stood in a line against the far wall. Eddie made a choking sound and Milton looked over at him. His friend looked like he was about to faint.

Milton looked back to the females, wondering what could be so unsettling to Eddie. They were five of the most striking females he had ever seen; it almost hurt to look upon them. They were garbed in skins and leather armor that barely obscured their bodies and it looked like the clothing was more to carry their weapons than as coverings. Huge glimmering swords hung on their backs and a variety of daggers hung from leather around their waists. One smiled brightly at him with an impish look, and he felt himself getting pulled into her heart-melting eyes.

She moved away from the others and came to stand between Odive and Edme. Her posture spoke of royalty, and the air about her simmered with power. The fey haughtily bowed her head to Odive before positioning herself firmly next to him.

"Ah, here is the Elders' answer to our dilemma," Odive said cheerfully. The room had a paralyzed feel to it, the tension and fear could almost be seen in the air. Not a sound could be heard. Milton pulled his eyes away from the females to look at the other fey. They looked as shocked as Eddie.

"May I introduce..." Odive began, only to be interrupted.

"Kianna! You released the demon Valkyries?" Eddie bellowed as he jolted forward. The spell was broken and a few others followed suit, crying out their alarm and disapproval.

"Silence!" Odive roared out. "We deliberated long and hard and, as we all know, the druids need help. You have to admit you have been barely making a dent in the invasion of the Eilibear. It has become apparent that the Warrior Druids are not equipped to handle their task as their numbers have dwindled. We allowed the Alltha's decision to keep the current young Warrior Druids away from their heritage for some time now and do not see the results that we were told would come about. There has not even been an increase in births from the druids that might bring forth more warriors. It seems like you, druid, have almost stopped taking part in the acts that produce children.

"Seeing how the Eilibear have found ways to gain increasing access into Alainn and in at least one case, into Firinn, the Elders feel more drastic measures are needed. Our very existence is at stake and you have not fulfilled your duties," he declared as he turned and pointed at Eddie.

"You, Master Warrior Druid, have hidden away

your own offspring from us and I believe we would never have known of his powers if not for your brother Warrior Carmen informing us that he has almost completed the Gorffen and is close to full powers.

"The Elders are done allowing you to go unchecked. The time is right to release the Valkyries and allow them to once more join with the fight,"

"But you can't. They will kill us all," Eddie screamed out in panic. Milton wasn't sure what was going on. He had never heard of the Valkyries.

"Fey Edsmond, you took part in casting the enchantment that led to the creation of Valkyries and all druids have had to live with the consequences. *You* should have been punished after the affair and not these dear sweet fey. *I* have found a means to reverse the curse you laid on them. They are no longer true Valkyries. We use that term now only in reference to these particular females. They are now willing and able to once more take their rightful place on the battlefield.

"I reiterate; the Valkyries are no threat to you. There are only five now. They are released from the Valkyrie curse and have reverted to their original Sisterhood. They can help…they *will* help," he said, lowering his voice to a steady forceful tempo. "Fey Edsmond, you will gather your young druids and, together with the Valkyries, start to put down the threat in Russia."

Kianna stood straighter and tilted her head arrogantly at Eddie. Milton sensed she was daring Eddie to make a move towards her. Milton watched the silent exchange and looked again at the other females who still stood in a line against the wall. They looked anything but harmless.

He looked back at Eddie and saw his stare leave the woman, Kianna, and focus instead on the female at the end of the line. Eddie's eyes locked with hers and Milton could see hatred etched onto his face. Milton looked hard at the female. She looked no different than the others and he couldn't fathom why his friend would hold such dislike for this one.

"Druids...you *will* accept the help we have provided and do all you can to put down the Eilibear," Odive roared, the threat very apparent.

The female, Kianna, moved from her position next to Odive and walked gracefully towards Eddie. She stopped when she was standing directly in front of him. Eddie ignored her.

"Fey Edsmond...it has been a long interval since we have been one on the battlefield. I look forward to this season of war against our enemy, the Eilibear." So saying she held out her hand in the gesture of friendship. Eddie finally looked at her, then down at her hand before looking up with concern at Odive. Milton could see that Odive was watching him with steel in his eyes. Eddie took a deep breath, then reached out and clasped the girl's wrist, as she did the same to him.

"Together we battle," he announced stonily. Kianna smiled and bowed gracefully, moving aside to stand next to him.

Eddie looked over to the other female again.

"Akneeta," he said loud enough for all to hear. "I will lay my reservations aside and welcome you...and your sisterhood's help defeating the enemy."

"That is very intelligent of you, dear father...and I look forward to shedding the blood of my enemies once more," she replied with velvet smoothness.

Milton looked from the female named Akneeta back to Eddie. He had a daughter? Damnations, this was news to him.

Odive clapped his hands together in mock happiness. "There now. See, we are all a happy family again.". "But there are more glad tidings! I have great and miraculous news. While researching the method to release the Valkyries and reverse the curse placed on them, the Elders have made a shocking discovery. All fey have long worried over the sudden disappearance of the Druid Sisterhood. We are pleased to announce that they have been found!"

Shocked gasps rippled throughout the group and their questions echoed in the chamber so loudly that their words were lost in the clamor.

Milton leaned over to Carmen since Eddie looked like he was about to pass out.

"What is the Sisterhood?"

Carmen turned to him, eyes wide with excitement. "It's the female druids. All of them vanished and could not be located, even by magic."

"They have been reinstated in their home at Aforne and once this threat of the Eilibears is put down for good, we will celebrate their return. Valkyries, you are dismissed to ready yourselves for battle," Odive said.

With devious smiles aimed at Eddie, the Valkyries sauntered back out the door they had entered. When the door closed behind them, Edme picked up the scroll and tucked it into the folds of his mantle.

"Warrior Druids you are to gather your ranks and meet on the battlefield as soon as you are able this day," Odive said, looking over to Milton.

Milton tried to blink, hoping that at last the

enchantment was off. He still could not. Odive smirked as if he knew what he had tried to do and slowly ambled over to where he stood with Eddie.

"Myself and Minister Edme will go with the Woodsman and fey Edsmond to complete our business on that end," Odive stood in front of Milton and slapped his hand onto his shoulder. Milton wanted to shake it off, but before he could do so, he felt Eddie's hand on his other shoulder and they blinked.

CHAPTER 7 – Ivy

I blinked into my bedroom and stood frozen. When I finally snapped out of it, I started to shake violently. What a crappy surprise this had turned out to be, I thought dejectedly. I loved the tree house, the concept of it at least. But from the start, it had been depressing to know that Zack and I were not on the same page concerning it. Then all the horrible stuff that happened last night and this morning.

I had shackled Zack. He had to detest me for that, but really, what else could I have done? And I hated to admit it, but maybe this was the real Zack. He was as clueless as I had been about being fey, but maybe when he'd discovered that he was a Warrior Druid, his true self had been released. Geez, that was just too depressing to even think about.

I sat down on the bed and closed my eyes.

"Ivy?" Margo whispered. I jumped as I opened my eyes to stare at her. She was standing in the doorway.

"Granddad just got back and there are fey with him who I don't know, and everyone is really angry," she said in a rush. "Where's Zack?"

"He's not here," I said. She all but ran over to me and grabbed my hand, yanking me up.

"Come on," she said again, then saw my face. I still hadn't healed it.

"What happened, did you fall?" she screeched.

"Zack happened. He went all animal-weird on me and tried to drain me of my powers...kill me. When I tried to stop him, he did this to me."

"Noooo," she said in shock.

"I'm afraid so."

"Was he enchanted again or something? Can you heal yourself so Granddad doesn't go all bat shit crazy?"

"I guess," I said. Somehow I didn't think Margo really comprehended what I had just told her. I used the tingle to tell myself to heal. It took only a second and then Margo blinked with me.

I opened my eyes to find myself mid-way down the stairs. We could have just walked, I thought, and then I heard the voices. I let the tingle build and whispered, "They can't see us." I inched quietly down the stairs until I was on the first step with Margo right behind me.

Granddad looked like he was going to explode. His face was bright red and he was barely holding his temper in check as he watched a strange, undersized fey wander around our house, looking at things. Each time the guy picked something up, he would hold it out for another fey to see. Both were not talking, but making sounds like they found everything peculiar and comical.

I was sure the guy was a fey, but he didn't look like a fey. He looked like my old math teacher from high school. He wore the same look as old Mr. Patters always did…boredom.

"Woodsman, I had heard so much about your curious home in the Hemlock forest. I'm glad I have had this opportunity to see it firsthand." His voice dripped with malice, and I felt the hairs on the back of my neck prickle. "I do like this abode of yours. Very interesting…and very mortal. Never have I seen fey with a home such as this inside a Meadhan. I'm told that the house was *brought in*…by Ivy. Is that really true? Surely you built this structure yourself and simply allowed her to take the credit, to build up her status with the fey," he said in such a condescending tone that I wanted to rush down the stairs and slug him.

"Believe what you will, Odive," Granddad answered.

"Fey Edsmond, do you have knowledge on the truth to this matter?"

I hadn't realized that Uncle Eddie was down there also. Margo tapped me on the shoulder and when I looked at her, she put her finger to her lips to tell me to be quiet and then converted to her smaller size. She blinked and I figured she had found some place where she could see better.

"It was here prior to me and the Woodsman returning from our mission," he answered with a shrug. He looked as ill at ease as Granddad did.

"Interesting. Well, it doesn't matter. Oh my, is that your famous axe I see being displayed so proudly?" he asked with excitement. His cheerfulness didn't really fit the circumstances and Ivy watched as he walked over to the wall and took hold of the axe. Granddad didn't make a move to stop him, but she could see his hands balling into fists.

He swung it absently once, then raised it with both hands and swung it down next to Granddad's feet, stopping just short of burying it in the wood floor, then laughed as if it was a funny joke. Granddad didn't move, but I could see a twitch around his eyes.

"I don't find anything special about it. Why is that? Surely the renowned axe of the *Woodsman* would be exceptional…but this is just wood and iron," he said sarcastically.

"It is just an axe...my axe," Granddad replied quietly.

"Yes...yes, it is."

He continued to look around the room, swinging the axe carelessly, indifferent about the possibility of hitting the walls or furniture. He was destroying my home and Granddad was just letting him do it. But still, I kept myself cloaked. I was sure that Granddad had a reason for showing restraint. The fey wandered over to the door to the old cabin and tried the handle. I was sure it wouldn't open and gasped when it did. The fey moved inside the small hallway and then disappeared for a moment. When he came back, he seemed as blasé as before.

Abruptly the air altered and Zack appeared in the room. Carmen was only seconds behind him. Looking around quickly to get his bearings, he spotted the other two fey and froze with an expression of alarm. I backed up a step and quickly threw up a protective barrier around myself. I really didn't want Zack to know I was here.

Zack quickly scanned the room until his eyes landed on his dad.

"What the hell did you do to me?" he screamed as he rushed over to him and grabbed him by the front of his shirt. "I hurt Ivy, dad. I almost drained her! What is happening to me?"

"Get him out of here," Uncle Eddie yelled at Carmen and at the same time, Granddad came to life.

"You hurt Ivy? Where is she?"

"Get him out of here now!" Uncle Eddie yelled again.

Carmen seized Zack in a chokehold and blinked,

taking Zack with him. Granddad looked like he was going to tear someone's head off.

"Where is Ivy and what did Zack do to her?" he bellowed as he moved around the furniture to where Uncle Eddie stood. Uncle Eddie backed up as he came close.

"Carmen and I have to get the druids ready. Ivy is not *hurt*...not really," Uncle Eddie said solemnly.

"What the hell does that mean? Granddad roared at him.

"This is a druid affair and does not concern you," Uncle Eddie said darkly.

"Anything that has to do with my family concerns me, you asshole!" Granddad boomed as he slammed his fist into Uncle Eddie's face. I watched in fascination as Uncle Eddie went sailing across the room and hit the wall so hard the house shook. My eyes went wide as I stared at Granddad with newfound respect. The man had some wild skills. That was down and out awesome.

"You have a war to fight. Be gone," the odd fey said. I had forgotten about him. He looked bored with the whole affair. He flicked his hand out towards Uncle Eddie and he was indeed gone.

"Odive, I don't have time for you right now. I have to find Ivy and make sure she's okay," Granddad said as he looked franticly around the room. I knew he didn't know where to look for me, so he must really have been in a serious panic-mode. Damn Zack for letting Granddad know.

"We have plenty of time and you have no say right now. It is the Elder's decision and it will happen," the fey, Odive, told Granddad. I had a name for him now and it suited him. It sounded like something that smelled foul and this guy was certainly that.

"She isn't here, and I don't know where she is," Granddad said firmly. Edme leaned close to Odive and whispered something I couldn't hear. Odive's lips twisted into a smirk.

"She is near," he declared and then rotated himself around the room until he was staring at the stairs.

"Fey Ivy, please show yourself," he said pleasantly. He was still holding Granddad's axe and I looked from it to his face. This fey was not to be trusted…but then were any fey?

"I only wish to meet you. We both, Edme and myself, are representatives of the fey Elders. We are here to confirm your status as owner of this Meadhan. Once we make it official, you and your guardian will be left in peace."

I was petrified. He moved closer to the stairs and the other fey moved to stand beside him. They couldn't possibly see me, could they? I didn't want to have anything to do with these fey and their nearness made me want to bolt out of there. I knew that was what Granddad would want me to do, but I *was* the owner of the Meadhan. Allowing these fey to meet me and give me formal rights would be a good thing.

"I told you, she is not here. I will send you a message when she is ready to receive you," Granddad said firmly.

"Be still, she is with us," Odive said softly in response. He never took his gaze away from the stairwell, but I saw his hand flutter slightly.

He knew I was here and pretending I wasn't would not help this situation. I was the rightful owner and I was fey. It was time to meet these guys and show them I wasn't scared of them. Taking a deep breath for courage, I released my protective field and then the cloak.

His eyes sparkled as I appeared and he clapped his hands jubilantly, like a child receiving a special treat. I didn't look at Granddad. I could feel his fear from where I stood. I straightened my shoulders and walked as confidently as I could down the stairs and stopped a few feet from him.

We stood looking at each other, our eyes locked. I knew that even though he was looking right at my eyes, he was still inspecting me. Maybe I should have changed before I showed myself. I was in the same jeans and shirt that I had been wearing when Zack and I had fought and then I had slept in them. Chances were pretty good that I looked like something the cat had dragged in.

"I am Ivy," I said, trying hard to keep my voice level. "What is your purpose with me and my guardian?"

"Oh my, isn't she charming!" Odive said cheerfully, looking at Edme. Instantly he was standing next to me and I felt a cold shift of air on my other side and knew Edme was there. I looked over at Granddad for some sort of direction on what to do now and gasped. Granddad was struggling wildly. I could see the faint outlines of a snake that had coiled itself around his body and the lower half of his face. The fey had somehow bound him with magic. He looked up at me and we shared a look of sheer terror as I felt hands on my shoulders and then knew only darkness.

CHAPTER 8 - Milton

The magic that had bound Milton dissipated as soon as Odive left. He struggled and fell to the floor. Odive had gotten what he had come for...Ivy. Milton felt foolish for not realizing the scope of the power this fey possessed. He should have been able to stop it, warn Ivy and get them both away. But Odive had taken control from the moment he had entered their home and, damn it, he had just let him do it. He should have known that Ivy would stand up; he had been telling her over and over again how important her new role was. He hadn't had the time to mentally process that Ivy *was* there, let alone get her away, before he had been bound.

It was his fault. If he had only kept the Meadhan locked down, then no fey could have come in. He thought that by letting Eddie bring the druids in and allowing some fey to come and go, he could dispel all the rumors and thereby keep Ivy and himself safe. Whoever that devil Odive was, he was completely in control now. Milton wondered what the damn fey were up to.

The Elders had to be behind this and in spite of what he knew about fey, he feared for Ivy's safety. If they had really taken her into Firinn, she should be somewhat protected. True fey would not hurt one another. They may like to make trouble, even cause chaos worse than the Eilibear could dream up, but it went against their very nature to harm each other. But that wouldn't stop them from keeping her away from him or the forest.

He laughed mournfully. There was no getting

around it; it was his fault. He should never have let his guard down or tried to make friends again with the fey. If he had just stayed with the Alltha Order, locked the forest again and taken Ivy away, none of this would have happened. He missed Elsie. She was the one that always told him the truth when he was messing things up. He hadn't always listened to her, but she had always been right.

He slowly stood and looked around. All the furniture was in tatters, very little was left on the walls and the entire kitchen had been pulled apart while he had just stood there and watched.

"Bloody hell," he said under his breath as he kicked debris out of his way. He moved purposefully towards the door that led to the older cabin.

"Granddad?"

Margo stood by the fireplace. Dread and concern were written on her face.

"Stay there Margo, give me a moment," he said softly, giving her a weak smile. His body felt like he had been in a boxing match...and lost. Whatever the magic that had bound him, it had been very strong.

He opened the door that led to old cabin and took the couple of steps to the second door. Putting his hand against it, he could feel the enchantment was still intact. Odive might have powers, but Granddad had some nice ones of his own. His illusion enchantment had held. Even Odive's magic hadn't detected it or broke through it, though Milton had been worried.

He put his hand on the door and told it to open, leaving the enchantment whole. A solid *click* rang out, echoing through the hall and out into the larger room. Without hesitating, he opened the real door and walked over to the stove. He reached behind and pulled out an axe.

"There you are. I knew it was best not to display you," he said aloud. He looked up at where the stone was embedded in the wall. Ivy had done a very good job painting it. No one would ever be able to tell that it was anything other than a river rock just by looking at it.

He steeled himself and then slapped his hand down firmly on the stone's face. The power of the Sumair stone tore through him, filling his very pores with magic. Pain engulfed him as it permeated his physical form. When he was sure he was saturated once more with the stone's stored magic, he pulled his hand away and picked up his axe.

The stone continued to try to connect with him, shooting out little rays of magic.

"That's enough for now. Sleep," he told it.

He left the little cabin, locking the door behind him, and walked back into the main room. Margo looked up at him and then at the axe in his hand, her eyes wide with fear. He didn't pause, walking straight to the door that led outside, opened it and went though.

What he needed to do took just a few spoken words and then he went back inside. Margo hadn't moved.

"Where did they take Ivy?" she said as he entered the room. She sounded hysterical and Granddad understood the feeling.

"Into Firinn, I think. Odive and Edme work for the fey Elders. Today I was told that they thought Ivy needed instruction on how to be the owner of a Meadhan. I didn't have time to warn Ivy or stop them," he said as he tried to control his own emotions. "I should have locked down the forest days ago...too late now, but that's what I just did. We are safe here."

"But is Ivy safe? How long did they say they would keep her?" she asked and then shook her head as if to clear it. "Screw that, how do we get her back?" She stomped towards him. "Do we use the doorway?"

"It's not as simple as that. We can't go inside without a full fey with us. Neither of us can enter," he said as he ruffled his gray hair in frustration.

"So?"

"We need Zack," he started to say, but Margo was already gone and it wasn't hard for him to figure out that she had taken off to see if Zack was still at the druid camp. He had little hope that anyone was left in the forest with them.

She was back in only a few minutes, with her face scrunched up woefully.

"They are all gone. Even the tents."

"I figured that was the case. I didn't feel any fey when I did the enchantment. Like I started to say, I think we do need Zack. Any willing fey would work, but the only close friend that *would have* helped in a time of need was Eddie. I know he will not help now, and I doubt any in the Alltha Order would either. Besides, I don't trust any of them. Zack is our only hope and I believe he will do anything to keep Ivy safe," Granddad said as he started to pace around the room, kicking out at debris with frustration.

"I think Ivy and Zack got into a pretty serious fight last night...she had nasty bruises on her face and neck," she said cautiously.

"I knew Eddie was holding something back. Zack has never hurt Ivy before...has he?" he asked spinning around to look at her.

Margo shook her head. "He's like the most calm and collected guy I've ever met. Even when all the stuff happened to us, he was the one…when we weren't glamoured by the fey…that always kept his composure. He has always been more concerned about Ivy and me than about himself. Ivy said she thought he was draining her and might have been glamoured in some way…I just know he wouldn't have done it purposefully."

"I think that's the key here; being glamoured, enchanted or something else that is unique only to the druids. I knew Eddie was keeping something from me, and with Ivy looking so worn out all the time and then Eddie saying it was 'a druid thing,' like it wasn't a worry."

"Zack didn't sound too happy about it, so maybe he really didn't know," she offered.

"No, you're right. He probably didn't know about…whatever it was. I'm pretty sure that Eddie will make it impossible for me to get to Zack now. I don't think he wants me to know about whatever it is he's hiding," he paused speaking as he continued to pace.

"Margo, how far can you blink?" he asked suddenly, turning to face her again.

"You mean like miles? I don't know. Ivy, Zack and I go everywhere and don't have any problems. We just need to have been there before so we know where to blink," she said with a shrug, then added sheepishly, "or have seen a current picture of someplace."

"You figured that out, did you?" he said with a weak chuckle.

"Yeah, we saw a notice on the internet for a band we all liked that was going to be performing in Puerto

Vallarta. We looked up the hotel they were staying at and then blinked there to hear them play."

"You know that ability isn't normal don't you? I thought I was the only one that could."

"We all sort of gathered that in the last few months," she replied awkwardly.

Granddad looked at her and knew he had been blind about so many things. He needed to start trusting the young people—they were not stupid or naïve. He had known all along that they probably had the same type of powers that he had, but he simply hadn't wanted to admit it.

"Zack is supposed to be on an island north of Japan. I don't know which one. If I did, I would go there myself and not involve you. I think since you can fly you might be able to find the island. If you can get to Japan, then you can blink north until you find what you can't see."

Margo looked at him and repeated the words he'd just said under her breath and then scrunched up her nose with irritation. "I need to find what I can't see?"

"The fey will have secured and hid the island...there *are* Eilibear on it. Do you have a laptop stashed away upstairs?"

Margo twisted up her face and then nodded yes. Granddad knew the girls were breaking some of the rules he had laid out, and right now he was glad they had.

"Go get it and let's see if we can find a current picture for you to lock onto."

Margo blinked out and then blinked back in seconds. She sat down at the table and booted up her little pink computer. She tapped purposefully for a few moments and then leaned back and pointed at the screen.

"There, this is a live webcam of the Rainbow Bridge in Tokyo. I could blink there very easily."

"Pull up a map of Japan," he directed as he laid the axe down on the table and waited as she tapped the keys a few more times. As much as he hated to admit it, he really needed to learn to use one of those things.

When the map was on the screen, he had her zoom in to the northern tip of the island country. There at the top he pointed out the long strip of islands that hemmed in the Sea of Okhotsk. It ran from the tip of Japan to the tip of Russia. One of those islands was where he knew Zack would be.

"Tokyo is in the middle of Japan, look for a city or town in the north, closer to the line of islands."

Margo did as he asked and together they scanned the map and decided that the town of Shari would be closest to the point where she needed to start. She looked over the most current pictures the internet had and decided a sightseeing dock that reached out into a marsh would be a good place to blink.

"It will be cold there, possibly snowing. Can you bring up the weather?" Granddad asked and watched as she quickly did. The screen showed that it was in the forties with rain.

"Jeepers, it is cold there. I'll need to go and get the right clothes," Margo said with a grimace.

She left the map up so he could look at it some more and showed him how to zoom in and out on the screen, then she blinked out. He played around with the computer and found that it was rather easy to use, though he didn't know how to type so it took him some time to search out new information.

Margo was back by the time he had found a page

on the islands and had made some notes with information he thought she should have. She was dressed in polka dot ski pants with a hot pink thermal top. Over that, she wore a neon green vest that sported a fur-lined hood. Both her boots and gloves were purple and she looked like she would be able to stay warm in sub-zero temperatures.

"You had ski clothes at home?" he asked, shocked that she'd had the perfect garments.

"Uh…no, but I knew where to go to get them," she answered, shuffling her feet uneasily. He didn't want to know what that meant, but could guess that she'd blinked into a ski shop to do some quick shopping. At this point, it didn't matter how she got them, and he let it drop.

He told her what he had overheard about the island from Eddie and what she would need to do when she found Zack. Margo listened attentively and then together they formulated a strategy. When they had covered every detail he could think of the young Sprite hurried upstairs to retrieve a pack. He wasn't a bit surprised when she returned with a child's small knapsack decorated with large bright flowers. Together they gathered some apples and power bars, along with a flashlight and a simple camping kit just in case.

"Remember, you won't be able to see where they are. Eddie told me once that when they are in a battle, they put up a containment field so they are undetected. It's magic so you should be able to feel it. Do you know how to do that?" he asked, worried that he might be asking too much of this young girl. She made a frown and shook her head no.

"It's easy. See that bowl by the sink? Reach out

your hand and *feel* for it," he directed.

She scrunched her nose, unsure of what he meant, but did as he asked.

"I didn't feel anything," she said after a moment of trying.

"That's okay. That bowl doesn't have magic. Now do the same towards my axe."

He watched her face as she reached out her hand towards it and her face lit up with a smile.

"I could feel it!" she cried out, looking up at him. "I can't describe it, but I really could tell it had magic."

"All magic has a *feel* to it, sometimes very strong. I think the one you are looking for will be extremely strong. Do you think you are ready?"

"Yes. I have everything I need and if I get in trouble, I can always blink back," she announced with confidence.

He gave her a hug and when she moved away, she gave him a thumbs up and then blinked out…without doing her normal spin.

Milton sat there quietly for a moment, wishing he could do more. He couldn't fly and it would be useless for him to blink around blindly to islands. He couldn't figure out how he could find something he couldn't see if he couldn't even get near it. It was pointless to try, but still it grated on him how inadequate his powers were to help. Part of him was galled that little Margo had powers that surpassed his own, but at the same time was glad she did. He looked around the room and sighed. If nothing else, he could put this place back together and be ready when she returned with the young druid.

CHAPTER 9 – Ivy

I came to in whiteness. As my head cleared, I realized that I was lying on a stone floor. Looking around, I could see that I was in a bare room. There was one door and a tiny window. The space was white...no that was wrong. White was normally nice looking, clean and pure. This place didn't look like that; it was white, as in void of color. Cold rough-cut stones, drab and lackluster, shrouded in a weird white haze. In fact, the whole room was hazy, and I could barely see.

My first thought was that I wanted Zack, but then I remembered what had happened between us. Where the hell was I, and what had happened to Granddad? Blinking myself someplace was confusing enough, as it always took a minute for my brain to process where I had landed. Having someone else blink me muddled my brain even more.

I decided I was getting tired of all this blinking stuff. When I got out of this mess, I was going to sign off blinking for a long while. I lay there, letting my thoughts clear until I realized I was cold.

That's when I discovered that I was only wearing my panties. I hardly ever wore a bra and now rethought that decision. I reached up to my neck and felt for my necklace with the talisman. It was still there, as was the wristband Zack had given me. I had locked these onto myself so I should have known they couldn't be taken. They may have taken my clothes, but they didn't get the most important items.

I glanced around the room, trying to focus my

eyes and finally spotted a pile in the far corner. I hurried over to it and discovered it was indeed my clothes. My shoes were not with them and a quick glance around the room told me they were missing, as was my backpack.

I quickly pulled the jeans on and pushed my arms into my shirt. Most of the buttons were gone. I ended up tying it together at the bottom. Not my best look, but at least I had something on. I didn't want to think about why I had been undressed…or who had undressed me.

The only light in the room was coming from the tiny window. I moved over to it and had to stand on my tip-toes to see out. For as far as I could see, there was nothing. No trees, no grass, no hills, no buildings and no people. Just a heavy white haze. It didn't even look like a desert. This place was the pits.

I felt for the tingle in the back of my throat, so I could roll some magic and blink back home. Nothing happened. There was no tingle. I put my hand up and felt outward, testing the surroundings for anything. There was no magic in this place, nothing to pull magic from. I decided I really, *really* didn't like this place.

I speculated that I must be in Firinn, but if this were Firinn I didn't see why any fey would want to live here. I was scared and mad. My magic was gone, my battery not drained but not working. And I couldn't pull magic from anywhere, so that left one option. I went over to the door and started to pound on it.

"Hey, let me out of here," I screamed at the top of my lungs…and kept on screaming. This I had energy for, until my voice gave out. I was determined to get someone to hear me. I banged and yelled for almost an hour. My arms grew tired, but I didn't stop until I heard the unmistakable sound of footsteps.

I moved back at the sound of a key being put into the lock. There was a strange old-fashioned clanking sound and then the door was pushed inward. Edme was standing outside the door. I thought about putting my hands around his pale neck and squeezing. I wanted to, but I didn't think that was the best way to deal with these guys. Besides I couldn't get the image of that snake coiling around Granddad out of my mind. I wasn't sure I wanted to piss them off when I didn't have my powers to use against them.

"We are not scared of you, hellion," he said, eyeing me scornfully.

"Fine, whatever. Where I am, and why am I here?" I asked.

"You were brought here so we can regain what you have stolen from us," he replied coldly.

"I haven't stolen anything from you. I don't even know you...or want to for that matter. Tell me which way to go and I'll go home, thank you very much." And I started to walk forward.

Edme put up his hand, palm out and I felt my breath being sucked away. I narrowed my eyes at him and put my own hand up toward his and pushed back with my will. It worked. Whatever he was doing stopped. His pale fishy eyes opened wide with fear, and he backed up. I took that as permission to leave this ugly room and started out the door.

"Edme, you surely should know better than to give her a chance to take energy from you," a harsh voice I recognized said. Odive was suddenly standing behind Edme and without thinking, I hurled myself at him. Bad mistake as my vision went flat and I was flung to the floor. I hit my head and it hurt like hell.

"Just pick her up and bring her. The Elders wish to interrogate her."

I was lifted and could do nothing about it. My world had gone cloudy and images of hallways and closed doors came and went as Edme carried me like a sack of potatoes. When I was finally unceremoniously dumped onto a cold stone floor, I had no choice but to lie there, my limbs leaden. I didn't know who the fey surrounding me were—they *could* have been the fey Elders. But fey didn't harm fey, right? Then I remembered what Laven and his family of fey had done to me and my forest. Fey didn't hurt other fey unless it was in their best interest to do so. My mind raced to grapple with the thought that these may be the very same Elders who had tried to take me away from Granddad and Marmaw when I was little. But I was the rightful owner of the Meadhan, and I was grown now. Shouldn't that mean something?

"Is it alive?" I heard a whiny voice ask.

A hard kick to my side produced a silent cry from my lips and my anger grew.

"Yes, it appears so," came the voice of Edme, and I hated him even more for kicking me.

"Well good. Let it go, Odive. Let's see what it has to give us," the whiny voice declared. As suddenly as my strength had drained away, it came back, thinly, but enough for me to open my eyes and look around. The asshole Odive was standing behind me and Edme was next to him. Odive had a look of pleasure on his face. He was enjoying this.

Whoever, or whatever he was, this fey was not my friend; he hated me. I didn't know what I had done to make him dislike me, but I only thought of it for a moment as my present dilemma took precedence.

I was in a huge gray-white room, as large as my old school's gym. Tall columns held it up and I was reminded of Disney movies with kings and queens and beautiful princesses. It was void of anything, just like the room where I had woken. I found that odd; even fey needed to have a place to sit.

A shuffle from my left made me jerk my head in that direction. Three large, ornate thrones sat in a row on a raised platform. Okay, they did have places to sit. I guess these three were the important ones, but they looked ridiculous. The thrones were so huge the fey sitting in them seemed tiny and shrunken. Or maybe they *were* tiny and shrunken; my brain was not doing so well. One fey was holding a fancy golden club with a huge diamond at the top. Gold ribbons wound around the handle, encasing the gem at the top. The gold twisted into a tiny tree at the tip. The fey was waving it around wildly.

"Stand, Alltha hellion," the whiny one demanded. I didn't move. Rough hands grabbed me under the arms and almost threw me in the air, forcing me to get up. I caught myself from falling and stood, wobbling on weak legs. I didn't want to look weak, but I was sure feeling it.

"Who are you?" I managed to croak out. My throat felt dry and it hurt to speak.

The whiny one had fuzzy white hair; the one to his right was smaller in size and someone must have used a bowl to trim his thin gray hair, making him look absurd. The one on whiny's left side was larger in mass, with a bald, pock-marked head. They were a creepy version of Larry, Moe and Curly. Images of the three stooges came to me, and I imagined that at any moment Curly was going to say woo-woo-woo and Moe was going to poke Larry in the eyes. Only Shemp was missing. I loved the three stooges...but I instantly hated these guys.

Moe stood and walked...glided...to me. As he came close, he stretched out his hand toward me. "There's magic there, but I can't pull it," he stated as he lifted one thinning, gray eyebrow on his ugly wrinkled face.

Curly joined him and did the same, reaching out his hand to me. "She is hiding it; it is shielded."

"She is wearing items we could not remove." Edme stepped forward offering up the information. He grabbed my wrist before I could stop him and held it up for them to see. The two stooges stepped closer and inspected it.

"Well?" Larry asked from his throne.

"It looks to be part of her skin. There is magic in it," Moe said gleefully, turning back to the fuzzy-haired one.

"There is this also," Edme announced, reaching out to pull down the neck of my shirt. I was ready this time and bit his arm as it came close. I'd learned that trick from Skyler. She had given me a nasty bite right before I had run away. The fey screamed in pain and jumped back. I was quite pleased with myself until I was hit on the back of the head and fainted dead away.

I came to in a messy heap on the floor. This was getting old. The fey were all talking around me. Moe wanted Edme to take my necklace off, Larry was telling Moe to do it himself, while Curly was inspecting my wristband and jumped back as my eyes opened.

"It's awake again," he said to the others. They all backed away.

"Odive, bind her again," Larry said unemotionally from his place on his silly-looking throne. My body lost its strength...again. Weird magic, this guy had. It was annoying how easily he seemed to be able to do it.

"*Now* Edme, take the necklace and bracelet off and bring them to me. They must be her source of magic."

I watched as Edme came over to me and attempted to take my necklace off. I couldn't do anything to stop him. He was getting frustrated and I could feel his yucky fingernails digging into my neck. Moe glided toward me and I saw that a trail of haze lingered after them. I'd seen something like that before, but my brain was too foggy to place it. He took my arm and started scratching at the edges of the wristband. Both gave up their attempts, but left my neck and arm bloodied.

"They are fused into her skin. Neither will move," Moe announced with irritation.

"So cut them out," the fey answered aloofly. "Odive, get the Woodsman's axe and summon Derl."

I lay there, paralyzed as much from Odive's spell as from fear. They couldn't be serious; they just couldn't be. Footsteps walked away and I lay there immobile and terrified.

The three stooges spoke in hushed whispers, along with Edme, and kept glancing back at me. I couldn't move, even to give them a dirty look. I tried though; my eyes were shooting daggers at them.

Moments later, there were footsteps again and I

heard Odive's voice telling someone to put *it* there. A thud to my right made me attempt to move my eyes to see what it was. If I could shake, I'd be doing it. A chopping block, a friggin wooden chopping block. They were serious. Two unidentified feet came within my sight and the edge of Granddad's axe.

"Where is Derl? I need some now," Moe screeched like a spoiled bratty kid.

I heard someone snap his fingers, like Granddad did when he was calling for a scroll and pen. A tiny bell chimed and I looked up as far as I could to see what was happening. There was a delicate little butterfly hovering above me. What was a butterfly doing in here? Before I really had time to focus, it whooshed out of my line of sight. *Butterflies don't move that fast,* I thought to myself.

The three old fey started to make sickening moaning sounds and I forgot all about the butterfly. The sounds were nasty and when at last they stopped, I was extremely glad.

"Pick it up," Larry suddenly demanded and I tried again to see what they were doing, but still couldn't move my head. Footsteps came close to me and I felt someone put their hands under my arms. I was lifted up, only to be dumped abruptly next to the chopping block.

Odive leaned down and smiled cruelly at me as he lifted my arm with the wristband and placed it on top of the block. I tried to move, I tried to scream, but couldn't.

"Cut it off, then we will see if it works for us," Larry declared icily.

Someone positioned themselves next to me. It might have been Odive or even Edme, but I couldn't see.

I heard the swoosh of the axe being raised and swung.

"I love you, Zack. No matter what you did, I still love you," I whispered to myself, as tears started to fill my eyes. I was grateful that I couldn't see at all now, and waited dully for the axe to come down.

CHAPTER 10 – Zack

Zack didn't know where he was. The last memory he had was of yelling at Dad and then of someone grabbing him from behind.

Now he was standing at the top of a hill that slopped down to a meager village. Small fishing boats dotted the beachline and one pier jutted out into the water. The village looked destitute and poverty-stricken. Inland, amongst the trees and looking completely out of place, were huge rounded metal structures with canvased trucks parked in front of them. The Quonset huts and trucks reminded him of military bases he had seen. Zack thought back to what his dad had been telling them about where the Eilibear had shown up—a fish processing island, complete with factories, that the Russians had taken away from Japan.

Crap, he mumbled, this is *not* where he wanted to be. He tried to blink back to the forest. Nothing happened and he was stuck in the desolate place.

When Ivy had blinked out of their special part of the forest, it had taken a few minutes before he was sure his head was clear. Everything about last night was a blur. He remembered starting the fire and roasting hot dogs and then nothing until he woke up tied to that tree. At first he had been more scared for Ivy, terrified that she had been hurt, but then there she was safe and sound and he'd figured out that she was the reason he was tied to a tree. It got really weird after that. His mind had split, and he could see and feel himself becoming furious with her for daring to keep him from getting what he needed from her. It was his right, his due for being a Warrior Druid. He shuttered as he vividly remembered his thoughts, none pleasant, towards Ivy. He had felt hatred and anger and if he could have gotten his hands on her, he knew he meant to kill her.

He looked down at his arm. The ivy vine was now a dark green tattoo that innocently wrapped around his upper arm. Any other time, he would have thought it the coolest tatt he had ever seen…but now? He was just glad that Ivy was strong enough to resist whatever magic was driving him. He closed his eyes and took a deep breath and really tried to think back to what his mind had been doing. The only true thing he could remember was that he *needed* it, he *deserved* it and it was his *right* to take it from her; she wasn't supposed to oppose him.

The air shifted next to him and he felt a presence. He turned to see his dad standing nearby, looking at him.

"What the hell happened to me?" Zack ran to his father, grabbed the front of his shirt like before and roughly lifted him off the ground.

His dad's shirt started to rip and Zack released him with a shove, throwing him violently backwards. Eddie was able to steady himself enough to keep from falling and then marched up to Zack and leaned in close, looking with anticipation into his son's eyes, and then moved back, shaking his head.

"So you weren't able to complete it," his dad said with a sober voice.

"What the hell are you talking about?"

"The Gorffen. The damn Gorffen, Zack. You were so close, and every day you've been getting closer. I had hoped that you would pull enough last night to finish it and I was so sure that Ivy was powerful enough to handle it," he said clearly upset. "I was hopeful that maybe, for the first time since Dywel's were formed into our arms, that it could be completed without the normal outcome."

"Dad, what the hell are you talking about? What *is* the Gorffen?" Zack said, feeling his face flush with anger.

"It's how Warrior Druids come to full power. If it doesn't occur, the Dywel will eventually start drawing from our own life force and we will die, just fade away. It's our curse, Zack. Magic gave us this exceptional weapon to overcome the Eilibear, but in return Magic extracts a sacrifice from us. We are required to take the life energy from the one we love the most. You would have had to have drained her completely for the Gorffen to finish."

Zack stared at his dad with revulsion. "You knew I was doing that to Ivy, and you didn't tell me?" His dad looked at him with a mixture of pity and scorn.

"You are a Warrior Druid! I tried to tell you about what our heritage entailed and you didn't *want* to hear. I told you that you would hurt her. I told you that her acting as some sort of conduit when your Dywel came into being *was not* the way our powers worked. Did you listen to me at all? This is who we are, how we gain our energy to fight the Eilibear. All fey know this. I had hoped that Ivy would be strong enough to let you complete it or somehow take the need away from you."

"You asshole, Ivy didn't know...I didn't know. I still don't know what you're talking about. What I do understand is that you knew I'd hurt Ivy, and you let it happen," Zack accused heatedly. He watched the emotions play across his dad's face and knew the truth.

Dad had *wanted* it to happen.

His hands balled into fists and without another thought, he reared back his arm and then let loose a punch to his dad's face. He felt crunching as his fist connected and knew he had broken his dad's nose. This time his dad couldn't keep himself from falling back and he lay on the ground dazed. As Zack brought his arm down, he saw it was covered with his dad's blood and felt satisfied.

"I had hoped she would be powerful enough to let it happen and then revive herself," his dad whispered.

"I hate to rain on your parade, *Dad,* but Ivy *was* powerful enough. She was powerful enough to stop me and make sure I would never do it to her again. I hurt her and she is scared shitless of me now. Maybe if you had told us, we could have found a way to work around it...or at the very least I would have known that I needed to stay away from her," he said sarcastically as he stood over him.

His dad reached up and touched his nose, then pinched it tight and yanked it straight again. Wiping the blood off his face with his sleeve, he looked up at Zack. "That's the second time today that I've been sucker punched. Glenwood did the same," he said with a mocking chuckle.

"Good for him. I take it you didn't tell him either."

"Didn't dare. He's my friend, the best damn friend I've ever had. I was sure that it would work out for both you and Ivy, and then he wouldn't need to know."

"Some friend...and father you turned out to be," Zac sneered with contempt.

"Zack, you just don't get it. We *are* Warriors.

That is our reason for being and nothing you do can halt the attraction to battle. Can't you smell them? The Eilibear are all around us," he said, gesturing out to the view in front of them.

Zack wanted to slug his dad again, pound him into pulp until he was unable to speak. But he found he couldn't resist looking out to where his dad was pointing.

He did smell something, something other than the salty air and dead fish. Down the hill, he could see that Telfer and the others had arrived also and were running forward, their Dywels beginning to form. With them were close to fifty female fey, swords drawn, running wildly alongside the males. The battle with the Eilibear was about to begin.

"Who are they?" he asked pointing out towards them.

"The female Paladins have returned to us, along with others that are joining the battle."

He continued to stare out at the fey who were racing forward, and his arm started to burn as his senses connected with the threat of the demons. He closed his eyes as the Dywel throbbed within his arm, but then flung them open again when a deafening wail tore through the air. He wrenched his head to the right, toward the sound.

Five of the most beautiful young women he had ever laid eyes on stood in a line a short distance away. They wore thin leather straps around their breasts and more tied around their privates. It barely covered them, leaving no detail of their forms to the imagination. Rough cut pieces of hide wrapped around their shoulders and backs, holstering gleaming swords, and all five were howling a high-pitched banshee wail.

One of the women saw him watching them and halted her cry to smile at him instead. Without hesitation, she then sprinted over to where he stood and stopped just short of running into him. Taking the arm that the Dywel had started to form in, she sniffed at it, then looked up into his eyes and smiled brightly. He tried to shake her off and when she wouldn't let go, he shoved her away roughly.

To his amazement, the woman only smiled wider at him and then sauntered back to the others, swaying her hips seductively and throwing little glances back at him as she went. When she was back in line, she seemed to forget about him. She pulled her sword out and raised it in unison with the other four. They shrieked wildly again and the sound penetrated his soul. It did something to him...he was immediately electrified and felt the need to have the full power of his Dywel in his hand. Turning back to his dad, the look on his face must have spoken his questions for him.

"It's the cry of the Valkyries. They have the power to pull the Eilibear to them. Can you feel it, son? The power, the energy?"

He watched as his dad faced the battle below, stretching out his arm to allow his Dywel to form. Zack couldn't take his eyes from his dad's sword as it emerged. He felt his own burning to be set free. The shriek from the women continued and seemed to stimulate his Dywel even more. He extended his arm to give it freedom, and it shot out of his hand in all its glory.

The battle was calling to him...he could smell the blood and the fire. He wanted to fight, to kill. He moved forward, heeding the call of his heritage. Together, he and his dad, followed by five women, raced down the hill to the thick of the combat. He gave no thought to anyone else, not caring if they were safe or not. His only thought was of the Dywel he held and killing Eilibear, forgetting all about the women, his dad…and Ivy.

The battle raged for most of the day. As the Eilibear were driven from their hosts, their life force rose up in clouds of thick, sickly green mist, which the ribbons of power from the Dywel caught hold of and extinguished. Zack thought of nothing other than combatting the demons who continued to appear. Every time the battlefield would start to clear of the things, one or more of the Valkyries would scream again, enticing more demons to show themselves.

Each time Zack would reach out towards one of the green mists, his Dywel would shoot out the ribbons of power and easily twist itself around the Eilibear, squeezing the life out of it. It became repetitive. Locate, shoot, concentrate, kill.

The voices of the veteran Warriors could be heard shouting commands to the new druids he had trained with, working in sets of three. But Zack found he did better when he fought alone. His Dywel's three ribbons of power effortlessly found their target and put down the enemy without much loss of life from the unwilling host.

As the sun moved lower in the western sky, Zack could feel his sane thoughts returning. Memories of the war he and Ivy had fought against the Eilibear entered his mind and as he stepped over yet another dead human, he cringed inside. He had discovered the first time he had come up against the Eilibear that if he lassoed the victim, he could force the Eilibear out and the victim might live. He wasn't sure if he had been doing that all along, as his mind seemed clouded by the blood lust of the fight, but he hoped he had. Now he consciously worked at doing so. The other Warriors, though, were not as sympathetic for the victims the Eilibear had found to enter. Animals, mortals and a few unlucky fey had been and were being slaughtered all around him.

He was covered with green muck and gore and as a bull overtaken by a demon lumbered up to him, he absently reached out his Dywel. One ribbon tightened around the beast, the other two waved and twisted in long cords above. As soon as the Eilibear pulled out of the bull, the ribbons snared the demon and quickly ended its existence. He watched as the bull struggled to keep upright. It snored and shook its head, then bellowed as if to say *what the hell just happened?* Within a few moments, it had gathered its thoughts and lumbered off into the forest. Zack watched its process and hoped the Eilibear wouldn't take it again.

Without giving it thought, he allowed his Dywel to power down. He didn't want to be here, nor did he really wish to fight. It all seemed so mindless. Bitterness welled up inside him as he stepped back and looked around him. He was on a dirt road that led from the forest down to the beach. Pockets of fighting surrounded him. To his left were a number of older Warriors and a few of the younger druids. They were slashing out at a herd of goats. It looked comical.

He pulled his eyes away and looked down the road. There were about ten of the female warriors, swords in hand, battling with a couple of mortals who had been taken by the Eilibear. He felt sorry for them.

All the female warriors could do was kill them, thereby releasing the Eilibears. Their swords were useless against the demons and their only goal seemed to be to kill anything living so the Eilibear would not have access to a host body.

His peripheral vision caught a glimpse of one of the Valkyries. She was fighting to keep a demon-riddled horse away from her. There was no doubt she was having problems as the horse was rearing and pawing the air over her head. She had her sword in her hand, but seemed to be reluctant to use it on the steed. He moved closer as he reached out his arm and allowed the Dywel to escape him. Quickly he shot out the ribbons of power towards the animal and encircled its body. He pulled against the power of his Dywel and the ribbons squeezed the horse's frame until the poor creature's knees buckled and it dropped to the ground. As soon as it did, the green mist of the demon shot out from its nostrils. He quickly angled the ribbons towards the mist and within seconds it had been killed.

Dispassionately, he looked over at the Valkyrie. She had dropped her sword in the dust and stood watching as the horse worked at recovering. When it finally rose to its feet, she looked over at Zack.

"I cannot do this again," she said in a flat tone, then turned from Zack and slowly began walking down to the beach.

A shrill wail exploded from behind, making him flinch and spin around. Another of the Valkyries was screaming the call to the Eilibear. He waited, his soul numb from this carnage around him, but knew he could not do as the Valkyrie had done. He couldn't leave his friends, or his dad, to fight this battle alone. He rejoined his band of Warriors and they continued to battle the demons until no more Eilibear responded to the Valkyrie's call.

When it was over, bits of goats and cattle lay all around them, mixed in with unlucky mortals and fey. The population of the island had shrunk to only the druids, the five Valkyries and maybe twenty of the other female warriors.

The stark metal and stone buildings built by the Russians sat empty, depressingly so. Gore covered everything and by the time Zack's Dywel powered down and shrank once more into his arm, he was a sticky gruesome mess.

He stood there in the middle of a parking lot, feeling drained and woozy. All around him, he could hear shouts of victory from the other druids. A couple of the Valkyries hadn't ceased hacking up what bodies remained, even though everything was quite dead. He watched as his dad and Uncle Carmen rushed over to the women, attempting to halt their continued butchery.

"That's disgusting. Those Valkyries really are barbarous," a voice said from behind him. He turned to see Telfer. His friend was covered in as much muck as he was. Something red and slimy was dripping down his face and he watched as Telfer absently wiped it away.

Turning back to the scene, he asked, "What are they? I've heard the name before, like in video games. Some sort of female warrior?"

There was a long pause of silence for a moment as Telfer moved to his side and looked at him hard. "You really don't know?"

"Know what?" Zack asked, looking at the muscular druid beside him.

"The story of the Valkyries? They are like the female version of us, or at least they were meant to be."

Zack croaked out a gruff laugh. "Right, if you say so. And the other women that were fighting, are they Valkyries also? I've never heard of any female warriors."

"Only because they all vanished. I was told that if a druid happened to have a child, it's always a male. Personally, I think that if a girl child is born, it's likely killed and then they try again. The fey don't seem to want any female druids around, so I don't know what changed or why they are back now," Telfer answered.

Zack recoiled from shock and took a step away from his friend.

"Your dad really hasn't told you anything, has he?" He took Zack's arm and pulled him around. "Come on, let's go find someplace where we can talk before they come looking for us. There is power here that is untamed and unholy; I feel that we are going to be called to fight more than just the Eilibear." With those cryptic words, he pulled Zack across the field.

Zack allowed himself to be led down to the beach. An old wooden pier jutted out into the sea on battered pilings. Several fishing boats that had seen better days were tied up and bobbing wildly as the waves hit. The ocean spread out from them, lazy clouds sitting low on the horizon. The breeze was cold and smelled of seaweed, while the waves drowned out all sound other than the birds flying overhead.

A water faucet with a thick, black hose attached stood at the start of the pier and Telfer lost no time turning it on and holding the hose over his head. Zack did the same, washing his hands and face as best he could. The water was cold, but it was a good way to clear his head.

Too much, too fast. Being with Ivy, almost killing her, then all the drama in the forest and *then* being pulled away to a bloody battle—his brain hadn't caught up yet. This new information that druids probably killed female babies was over the top, and his brain couldn't process it.

"Here, drink this." Telfer said holding out a small silver flask before he walked out onto the pier and found a place to sit, hanging his legs off. Zack took it without hesitation, followed his friend and sat down next to him before he upended the flask. Whiskey. It burned going down and he coughed until his eyes watered. Telfer patted him on the back without saying anything until the coughing subsided. Zack took another swig and then handed it back before leaning against the low railing wearily.

Telfer lost no time taking a drink himself, then both sat there looking at the waves as they crashed underneath them into the pilings. The pier swayed as each wave hit.

"Someone needs to tell you...your dad should have," he stated reflectively. "A lot about siring druid children was changed because of the Valkyries."

"How? Why?" Zack asked, really not needing more bizarre information right now but knowing it was his own disregarding of the lessons his dad had tried to push on him that had led to him hurting Ivy.

"There are two versions of the story. Both start with the Valkyrie curse. Back before even the druids were recording history, there were these six she-devils. They would materialize on white demon horses and kill everything in sight whenever there was a fight of any sort. If you even *saw* them appear, you were as good as dead. The druids stepped in and somehow canceled the curse and locked it away. It was called a Mystery. The druids have always been the Keepers of the Mysteries, my dad said. So then, as one version tells it, years later when the war with the Eilibear started, there were awesome female warriors like us, just minus Dywels. They had the knack for being bitchin warriors. All of them, along with the rest of the female druids were moved to one estate and the Sisterhood was formed. I don't know if everyone forgot about the Valkyrie curse or what, but these six girls somehow joined their powers, or it just happened on its own and the curse was activated again. These six started appearing, like the original ones had, whenever there was a battle; mortals or Eilibear, it didn't matter. They would show up on the same horses as the original Valkyries had and just kill everything.

"The second version is a little different. Some say six female druids were chosen or volunteered and the locked Mystery of the Valkyrie curse was used on them purposely. I guess someone thought bringing them back would wipe out the Eilibear threat. Whichever version is correct, the end result was the same—the Valkyrie curse should never have been reactivated," Telfer said, finally out of breath. He took another long draw from his flask before he continued.

"My dad said no one knows for sure how it all came about. There's no written history and the regular druids, the ones that aren't Warriors, won't talk about it. Anyway, somehow all of the girls were captured and locked away. To be honest, I thought it was just another fantastic story my dad and some of the uncles had made up...until I saw them today."

"I counted only five females...and none of them had horses," Zack said, finally finding his voice.

"Something must have happened to one. That may have broken the curse. Either way, since that time, no females have been born and an Uncle whispered to me that he thought if one was born, it was killed. My guess is that it was so no more Valkyries would be created."

"You're shittin me," Zack said, almost choking.

"No, I'm not. I was told of this when my sire informed me about who I really was. It was part of my 'coming out' party. Told me all the dirty details of our lives and duties." The last word he spat out with disgust. "Until the Valkyries, Warrior Druids had normal lives...though they did run around trying to kill any Eilibear that showed up. They got married and had kids if they wanted to," he paused to take another drink and then almost gagged as he started to speak again. "Oh, I know what I forgot. The Gorffen stuff started about that time, too. The story goes that the Eilibear were winning, since there was not a good way to kill the things. The Warrior Druids evolved somehow and were given the Dywels. The swords are really powerful and end up sucking away all of a Warrior's life energy. Some bright Warrior discovered that it was possible to find a fey that would instinctively give up their own power, thereby allowing the druid to reach their real potential without being killed. Down side was that the female died when they gave their last bit of magic to the Warrior. I was told that it had to be a fey that we really loved for it to work. Being a Warrior Druid or in love with one has some serious drawbacks now...and supposedly it's all because of the Valkyries."

"Dad said that I am close to completing it," Zack said softly.

"Wow. I'm sorry, I really liked Ivy," Telfer said, looking down at the bottle in his hand and then taking another drink.

"She's not dead. Somehow she was able to stop me, thank goodness for that. There is no way I'm going to go near her now. I don't want to kill her simply to save my own hide and be able to fight."

"Really? That's good, I guess," Telfer said in a tone that suggested he doubted it.

"Someone should have told me. I didn't know what I was doing to her, and it's a miracle she survived it," Zack said looking at his friend accusingly.

"What? Don't go blaming me. I thought you knew."

Zack recognized that Telfer was innocent. It was his dad that had kept the information from him.

"It's a no-win for us druids. If we find someone we really love and connect with, we end up killing them and if we happen to have a female baby along the way prior to them dying, she has to be killed, too. Pretty crappy situation if you ask me."

"But they released the Valkyries. Does this mean that it's all over, that the stupid rule is cancelled?"

"I doubt it. But at least you might get to finally meet your sister. I guess that's a nice plus…though I doubt she's the touchy-feely type. She'll probably want to hack you to pieces along with the rest of the druids for locking her up all these years."

"Wait, is one of those females my sister?" Zack all but yelled. He turned and looked back where they had come from. From here he couldn't see anyone else, but knew they were there, somewhere in the empty town, merrily chopping up the remaining bodies the Eilibear had taken. Sick. He could hear shouts and voices being carried on the wind.

"Yeah, I think so. I was told she was one of the six…but there are only five now. One might be her."

"I don't have a sister, I couldn't have. Mom died shortly after I was born." Zack said, then paused. "Wait, like really, a sister? Dad said I was an only child. Why would he tell me that if it wasn't true? And he told me Mom died from complications from childbirth. So if I understand all this right, Dad drained Mom and killed her?"

"Don't know, probably because your sister was gone and no one knew where or if she would ever come back, so you were an only child at the time. As for your mom, I don't know. What I do know is that every older Warrior Druid out there is still around because they drained someone. My dad said I had a choice to make: take the chance of falling in love with a fey and then decide what to do, or never take the chance and stay away from female fey altogether. You can see why there aren't too many Warrior Druids left. Dad said that at one time, there were hundreds of us and now there are less than fifty," he said taking one last swig from the flask. "Come on, let's get back. I'm sure someone will be looking for us, and maybe someone will know if one of the women is your sister." Telfer stood and reached out his hand to help Zack up.

Pieces of their conversation started to come together and Zack stopped in shock. "Hold up a minute. If we drain any person that is close to us, how do we have children at all?" He was worried he knew the answer and anger at his dad grew to a new level.

"I guess the key is coming to full power by killing our first love and then finding someone else to have kids with," Telfer said without turning back. "Like I said, being a druid has some serious drawbacks."

Together they walked from the pier onto the sand, then up to the unpaved road. They followed the sounds of others until they found a group of Druid Warriors standing just outside of the town on a small grassy hill. Zack's mind was whirling; chances were, his dad had killed his mom...and somewhere here, he had a sister. A sister who could help fight the Eilibear. He didn't know what other powers she might have or how being locked away would have affected her. Maybe she wouldn't hate him. He didn't care what she thought of Dad; right now he wasn't fond enough of the man to give a shit.

He wanted to talk to Ivy. Tell her that he knew what had happened and why. Now that he knew, maybe they could figure out a way to control it together. He wanted to tell her that he might have a sister. He thought she would be as excited as he felt about both developments. Cheered now, he walked along with Telfer, going over the list of things he wanted to share with her.

As they drew closer, the stench of death was propelled by the breeze towards them. Zack felt a tingle in his arm, taking his attention away from thoughts of Ivy. His Dywel could sense the Eilibears, even in death. Shaking his arm to calm the thing, he continued to walk towards the group of druids standing with his father.

Mixed emotions of hatred welled up almost choking him as he came close to his dad, and he had to spit to get the foulness out of his mouth. How could his father not have told him? How could he have killed his own wife and locked up his own daughter, or at least allowed her to be locked up? He looked around for the Valkyries and found them back in seemingly normal form, standing off to the side. They were covered with blood, but at least they weren't still hacking up bodies and animals.

One of the women caught his eye and he found himself folding into her gaze. His body grew weak as he continued to stare at her and felt his jaw drop as he, for the first time, really saw her. She was breathtaking. Sexy Barbie meets Lady Gaga…times five, he thought as he pulled his eyes away from the one to look at the other four also. He wasn't sure which one of them was his sister since, except for slight variations in their faces, they were all the same. He felt a stirring of desire and thought of Ivy as he tried to fight it. It didn't work; his brain kicked off and other parts ignited. It pulled on him and the harder he tried to fight it, the more intense it became. He was sickened by his body's reaction—one of those women might be his sister.

"Wowzers, will you look at those knockers," Telfer said from beside him. He had to agree, the females were hot. He could only stare until he felt others come up beside him.

"Kind of puts your little girlfriend to shame, eh," Trone's deep growl of a voice came from behind him. He turned to see Trone and Keyair standing there, ogling the Valkyries also. He couldn't bring himself to defend Ivy…she was his ten, but these creatures were closer to a hundred. He took a deep breath and closing his eyes he tried to regain some composure. When he at last opened them, he found the females standing not more than five feet away, the shock of seeing them so close forced him to take a step backwards. He found himself speechless.

"Sisters, I believe they are happy to meet us," the silver-haired leader said as she pointedly looked down at the druid's privates.

Her voice was a chime of splendor to his ears. Zack felt his knees grow weak at her exquisiteness and couldn't help himself from inspecting her from head to toe. His mouth went dry.

She moved toward him, reached out with one bloodied hand and brushed her finger down his cheek, leaving a line of wet redness. His eyes only saw the blood as her hand came close, and part of his mind wondered when it had appeared there.

"You are Zaccheus," she declared, coming closer still. He could feel her breath on his skin and goosebumps erupted from his flesh. No words formed as he stood as still as a statue, staring dumbly at her. The way she spoke his name opened up visions of knights and ladies in flowing gowns. She reached out and played with one of his dreadlocks, holding it out as she turned to look at the ones she called *sisters*. They were radiating magic; he could feel it seeking to swathe his thoughts in desire. He pushed against it, laboring at retaining control.

Another of the Valkyries moved close to him and he wondered what the other druids were doing. He couldn't see them, as this one with matching silver hair and a body of a goddess came closer.

"Brother...we meet," she said with a controlled smile. "I am Akneeta." He recognized her. She was the one he had helped with the horse. She moved until she had replaced the other in front of him and leaned in, kissing his cheeks softly. He was glad that his body didn't have the same reaction to her as it did to the others; either she wasn't emitting any sexual vibes towards him or discerning that she was his sister had stifled it.

"Enough! Power down the charming this instant!" The sound of his dad's voice broke the spell and Zack shook himself and moved back, away from the females. The glamouring evaporated and his body relaxed. Now that his mind was not fighting against their powers, he could see them clearly; magically enhanced, captivating beauty, but no more so than his Ivy. Only females now…with killer boobs and wearing little…but still just young women with silver hair and covered in blood.

"Rōber, we were told this would happen." Uncle Carmen had appeared beside Dad and gripped Dad's arm.

"I don't care. I don't like them using this part of their magic," his dad hissed back, while the rest of them watched the two adult fey argue. Carmen leaned in close and heatedly whispered into his dad's ear. After a moment, Dad visibly relaxed, his face producing a smile that didn't reach to his eyes.

Dad's Adam's apple bobbed as he swallowed hard. He turned to one of the women.

"Forgive me, Kianna. I did not mean to be gruff, only to caution you that if you are to work with the Warrior Druids, you must create a friendship of truth, not magic." Eloquent words coming from the beefy older druid, and Zack wasn't sure he understood what game his father was playing at. He glanced over at his sister, and caught the same glimmer of thought run across her face as she glared with hatred toward their father.

He wondered what she was thinking as she turned and their eyes met. He gave her a brittle smile and a nod of acknowledgement before he turned and started to walk way.

"Zack, wait. You go with the other druids to where we will set up camp. Ready the tents first for the Valkyries and the Sisterhood," his dad's voice called out. Zack stopped and looked back over his shoulder at him. He looked no different than before, except covered with splatters of blood. He started to tell him he was leaving…to go back to Ivy. Then as the cluster of druids closed in around him, he decided to bide his time. Ivy was safe with her Granddad…and he really wanted to learn more about his sister and the Valkyries as a whole.

Telfer stayed with him as they followed the more energetic of the druids down to a cove out of sight of the town. A large supply of camping equipment was piled in disarray on the rocks above the beach. All of their packs, abandoned when they'd arrived, had been gathered up and were heaped haphazardly on the sand. He spotted his own that dad or Carmen must have prepared for him and brought along. He was mildly grateful.

It was nightfall by the time all the tents were erected and a bonfire was blazing on the beach. Zack kept to himself, watching. The adults stayed close to the young druids, while walking a wide berth around the Valkyries. Zack couldn't help but wonder what Carmen's comment to his dad had meant: *we were told this would happen.* He found it difficult to believe his dad had just magically changed his mind about what the Valkyries had been doing; his dad never changed his mind about anything.

The darkness grew around the encampment and

Zack found a place back in the shadows where he could sit on a large tree washed up by the waves. Getting back to Ivy was in the forefront of his mind, but he wanted to find out more about the new fey. Maybe they knew how to stop the Gorffen from happening.

He could hear them talking, all of them, the druids and the Valkyries, about common things—the weather, their weapons, the battle and what to eat for dinner. Everyone had cleaned up, washing in the freezing ocean. Even the Valkyries were now clean and dressed somewhat more appropriately. All of them were wearing flowing dresses that reminded him of renaissance fairs and medieval times. Kianna's was the most baroque, with yards of heavy rich fabric swaying around her as she walked and a very low-cut bodice, made even more so by the leather waist corset, showing off all the attributes of her cleavage. The others wore garments of a simpler nature, more tavern-wench style, but just as revealing. Overall, the group looked more normal than they had in their battle gear and could pass for ordinary people in Alainn…especially if they were in Ashland near the college. Ashland was legendary for its Shakespeare Festival and the women would not even be looked at oddly if they were walking down the main street. Ivy would be rolling her eyes at how the druids, even without glamouring, were fawning all over them.

He did laugh out loud when he caught sight of Akneeta though, as she was having none of it. She had found a pair of jeans, slightly too large, that she had hacked off the bottoms to just under her knees and cinched tight around her waist with a rope. A red long-sleeved hooded sweatshirt, sporting SOU on the front and tennis shoes completed her look.

She kept herself apart and spoke sparingly with the other Valkyries and druids, seeming to have another purpose in mind. She tended to move when his dad moved, staying far enough away so that she could hear his words, but not be noticed. Zack could tell she was up to something, but what it was, he couldn't figure out.

"So you are all alone. Want some company?" A silky voice whispered from close by. Zack looked up at the one called Kianna, the one that had sniffed at his arm when he had first arrived. Something about her put him instantly on guard...as if she knew something he didn't and found it amusing.

"No, not really," he answered, dismissingly as he looked back at the group around the bonfire. She wasn't the one he wished to speak with.

"Good, I'll take that as a yes," she said as she planted herself down next to him. He paid her no mind, hoping she would get the hint and go away.

"So the other druids tell me you have a girlfriend...a **Frith** fey. What does she change into?"

Zack looked over at her without answering. His face must have relayed his feelings as she shifted uncomfortably.

"Not a topic you wish to discuss. I will respect that. How about talking about past glories?" Zack made no response to her.

Of the five, watching her interact with the other druids, he could tell that she was a sexual being and used that on all the males in the camp. Zack was not going to go down that path again. Apparently she wasn't used to being ignored by men, which Zack found to be ironically funny since she and the others had been locked up for so many years. Maybe they just missed male companionship.

Keeping her voice low, she began to talk, and Zack tried hard not to look over at her.

"I never got to see the aftermath of a battle, not like this. When we were allowed to fight before, it was usually cut and slash and then back to our home. We always wanted more, to be a real part of the fey fighting the Eilibear. It was our mothers who stopped it from being so; they worried about us. They wanted us to be proper fey… gentle, spending our time weaving pleasant magic for the benefit of all," she relayed softly.

Zack could hear the resentment in her words. His voice came as a shock even to himself, the question out before he could stop himself.

"What was it like…when you fought before?" Turning her body slightly so she was facing him, he could feel her eyes on him…inspecting him.

"Your hair is like nothing I've seen before. Nor are your skin markings. Do they have special meaning or bring you special powers?"

Zack did not answer but was beginning to feel very ill at ease with her scrutiny of his person and wished he had put a long-sleeved shirt on over his tank top. He had asked the question because he really wanted to know, but there was no doubt her mind was on other things.

"You have strong features, very much like your sire. And I find I like your hair. It is wild and fresh," she said, then went quiet for a time. When she spoke next, she changed subjects again and finally answered his question. Zack was relieved.

"In my day, the mortals left us alone, wallowing in their immaturity. The fey were powerful and abundant… here in Alainn and Firinn. The Eilibear were the clear enemy…and then it all changed," she mused almost to herself.

"What happened?" he asked quietly, not wanting to speak with her but wanting more information at the same time.

"We were called to battle the greatest of all battles. Against the protest of our mothers, we were taken and propelled into the thick of it. It should have been the end of the Eilibear, the greatest victory ever achieved. But we were once again pulled away before we finished the battle."

Zack wasn't sure what game she was playing at, her voice was begging for pity and Zack felt none. What she said might be the truth, but he didn't see how it really mattered.

He could hear the movement of people nearby and knew without looking up that they had been joined by others.

"That is a fascinating version of the events, Kianna. I would beg to differ with you though on the order of them, along with the reason for the outcome. But then you have your reasons, do you not?" A new voice asked, breaking whatever mood Kianna was attempting to spin around him. Zack looked up to see they had been joined by Telfer and a couple of the other Valkyries including Akneeta, the one who had spoken. Zack watched her face closely as she glared at Kianna, daring her to say something.

Kianna frowned back at Akneeta and then let her eyes roam down the woman's frame.

"What are you wearing?" she asked with disdain.

"Why do you care? They are comfortable and

warm, and personally I find them very appealing," Akneeta answered looking down at herself.

"You look ridiculous. Go change into garments more befitting your position," Kianna snapped at her.

"I am fine dressed the way I am," Akneeta replied with a crooked smirk. "I would think that we would want to adapt into this Alainn's times and so be free of the constraints from when we were last here, do you not agree?" Akneeta was clearly baiting her.

Kianna's eyes narrowed threateningly as Akneeta smirked back at her. The two glared at each other and the air grew tight with tension. Zack wondered if we were in for an old fashioned down-and-out cat fight.

Kianna was the first to lower her eyes and relax her body. Akneeta allowed a true smile to creep across her face, clearly the winner in this odd battle.

"Enough Akneeta…we do not wish to hear any more of your notions. Go…you bore us," Kianna proclaimed and waved her hand as if dismissing a server.

"Kianna, you are not the leader now as there is nothing to lead. Even in battle, it is not you who is the most powerful. It is now Bertelle. You hold no power over me or any of us. Do not pretend that you do." With that Akneeta turned and marched happily into the shadows.

Kianna rose and yelled for Akneeta to return and put out her hand and yanked it back in the air as if she was actually pulling Akneeta back. Nothing happened except for Akneeta's voice coming through the darkness.

"Told you, doesn't work now." Akneeta's voice floated to them and then she laughed delightedly.

Kianna screamed in frustration, while the other Valkyrie's faces went pale and they glanced worriedly at each other. Quickly they all started to back away, pulling the confused druids with them. Zack found himself once more alone with the woman and couldn't help but watch with fascination at the emotions that were playing across her face.

Her face had twisted up, quite unbecomingly, with rage and she was actually snorting with fury. Zack was sure he had seen a hint of fear flicker though her eyes when whatever magic she had been trying to use on Akneeta hadn't worked.

She glanced around in a frenzy, looking for someone else to throw her wrath onto. He was very glad that the others had known to leave…this woman was pissed. Ultimately, she looked up at him and grew still, as if she realized there was a witness to her anger. She visibly worked at bringing her temper under control as she sat herself back down as if nothing had happened.

"Well, leave it to that one to bring us all down," Kianna said sullenly. "I don't know about you, but I'm a bit cold." She looked up at him expectantly. Her voice had grown husky and she was trying to be sexy he was sure, but it sounded like whining to Zack. She inched closer, almost climbing into his lap. Zack was repulsed by her.

He stood suddenly, and watched her almost topple over, a shocked look on her face. He chuckled to himself as he walked away.

"The manners of druids has certainly changed over the years…" he heard her grumble as he passed the fire pit, and headed towards the tent he was sharing with Telfer. He ducked inside and grabbed his flannel and then proceeded to leave the camp. He pulled the flannel on as he continued to walk until he was at the water's edge. The night was silent by the water, with only the sound of the pounding surf. He stood there, watching the waves and thinking about Ivy. He really missed her, as well as Margo and the forest. He wasn't sure he really wanted to even be a warrior, though it was cool to be a fey and to have powers and such. But he'd give it all back in a second if he didn't have to fight battles or have the Dywel or any of the shit that went along with having it.

Zack was pulled from his inner thoughts when Telfer strolled past him to the wet sand of a receding wave. He looked out into the darkness for a long moment, then turned and walked back to where Zack stood.

"Been looking for you. Should have known you'd be down here. I think the victory celebration is in full swing right now. Your dad and Carmen produced some barrels of beer... or maybe its mead, but it's good. The Valkyries were dancing around the bon fire when I left. You really should have come with us when Kianna had her little tantrum. That gal is...distasteful," Telfer said.

"Yes, that's a nice way to put it. Did the others say what was going on?"

"Yeah. Turns out that Kianna is a **Shifter** and she had the strongest power of all of them. When they were..." he broke off and looked back towards the camp. "You know none of them will talk about where they were. I don't know if it's because they don't know or because it was such a horrible experience that they don't want to relive it by talking about it. Anyway, when they were wherever they were, Kianna became their leader due to her powers. She could call them and force them to heed her whenever she wanted. I guess that part of their time away was not the most enjoyable. **Bertelle** said that when they were released, Kianna's power over them was released also. I think we just saw what Akneeta thought of being under the bitch's thumb. I think that it wasn't only Akneeta that ticked her off, but you also."

"Me?" Zack raised a brow.

"She stomped up to **Bertelle and Vada,** having a real hissy fit about you. She is a major drama queen. I hightailed it out of there real fast, but caught the gist of what she was pissed about. I guess she has a thing for you and was infuriated that you didn't respond to her."

"Right, like that's going to happen," Zack scowled.

"That one needs to be sent back. It's not ready for polite company," Telfer said stonily.

Zack looked over at him, lifting one eyebrow, and they both broke out in laughter.

"Did Akneeta come back? Is she partying with the others now?"

"Nope and Kianna never said a word about it, at least while I was there," Telfer replied.

"I'm going back to the forest. You want to come with or stay here?" Zack asked looking at his friend expectantly.

"Yeah, I'll go with you. I'm not sure I like this battle stuff. It's like I forgot about everything but killing, like I lost myself…going all mindless, you know?"

"Yep, I understand," Zack said.

"We need three to blink out, should I go ask one of the others?"

"No. I don't need three to blink long distances; I do it all the time."

Telfer gave him a scrutinizing look, but didn't say

anything. Zack put his hand on his friend's shoulder and blinked. Nothing happened.

"Won't work. Odive put a containment enchantment around the island," Akneeta said startling both of them.

"We're locked here?" Zack asked crossly.

"I think the fey Odive likes containments. I believe it was him who locked us away...and possibly the one who created the Valkyrie Warriors in the first place," she said dryly.

"Who is Odive?" Zack and Telfer asked in unison.

She glanced back towards the camp and then motioned for them to follow her. They took positions on either side of her and walked down the beach silently for a time. When they came to a patch of large driftwood, Akneeta started to gather wood for a fire and they did the same. It didn't take long before a fire was blazing, but it gave off little warmth as the wind blowing off the ocean was freezing.

Akneeta sat with her back against a large tree that had been washed up by the tide, and motioned for them to sit also. They sat across from her and waited, watching her as she watched them. The wind wasn't as bad low to the ground, but it still could be felt and was bitter cold as it hit their backs.

After a few moments of silence, she raised her arm and swung it in a wide arch over her head, and instantly the wind stopped. Zack looked at her with raised eyebrows but she only held her hands out to the fire and paid them no mind. It wasn't long before Zack started to feel quite warm, like he was inside a tent with a heater.

"I've been watching you," she announced and then smiled at him.

CHAPTER 11 - Ivy

Terror is a strange thing. Not like the terror from watching a scary movie, but terror like when you are *in* the movie and the star of the show. I could see everything, hear everything and feel everything almost in slow motion. Maybe I had gone into shock...I'd taken a first aid course once and aced the exam. I wasn't sure how, but I could see the red first aid manual lying open to the page dealing with shock.

Shock may result from a severe trauma; the skin may be cool and clammy, the pulse weak and rapid, breathing may be shallow and blood pressure may be low. Sometimes the pupils are dilated.

Yes, I believe I probably had all of the classic signs.

If you think that someone is going into shock, call 911 and keep the person warm and comfortable.

That is what I needed to do...call 911. Were there phones in Firinn? My brain wasn't working.

Zack? Zack, where are you? I screamed in silence as the axe came down toward my arm.

I couldn't look away. It might be the last time I saw that arm and I'd miss it...I tried to wiggle my fingers...just one last time, but I was frozen. They wouldn't move.

Zack? Granddad?

The axe hit...

I'd hit my thumb once, with one of Granddad's hammers. I'd been helping him in his workshop, getting in his way mostly. He had found a piece of wood and pounded in a couple of large nails and told me to finish hammering them. I knew he was just giving me something to do...but it was still fun...until I hit my thumb. It hurt like hell. I had screamed and jumped around and shook it and looked accusingly at Granddad, like it was his fault.

He should have told me hammers might do that. I'd never forget his reaction. *"Hurts huh?"* I had nodded as I sucked on it with tears welling up in my eyes. *"Ruth dear, if that's all the hurt you ever have to know, consider yourself lucky. You'll be okay, go ask Marmaw for a cookie."* He had hugged me, and soon it was all better and even turned pretty shades of green and blue.

The axe hitting my arm hurt just like that, like when I'd hit my thumb with the hammer. Only I couldn't hop around and there was no one here to give me a cookie. But I could inwardly smile. Just like the hammer, the axe hit, hurt like hell, then bounced upwards and smacked the fey who held it hard. I saw blood start to drip down his torso. Oh, that made me happy. I had to force myself to look at my arm, lying across the chopping block. I couldn't talk or scream...and really didn't need to. The fey were doing it for me.

"It did not cut!" one cried out.

"Look at that, her arm is the same as it was before."

"It must be the stone's magic. She can't be indestructible. Cut it off. Get me that magic. Try again, cut it off!" Curly screamed from his throne.

Zack, you will not believe this one, I thought to myself. I was going to have one hell of a bruise, but my arm was still attached. There wasn't even a mark to show where the axe had struck. The horrible fey who had wielded it was wobbling still, a nice pool of pink fairy blood at his feet. He had dropped the axe, or it had slipped out of his fingers. The blade side was shiny and clean, the blunt side was covered with pink blood and sticky stuff. I wished I could look up to see what the fey looked like, but only his lower half was in my view.

I watched as one of his knees buckled, then the other, and the fey fell in a heap next to me. It wasn't Odive or Edme. It was some fey I had never seen before. He was large and beefy looking. Their executioner? Did fey have executioners? Duh, of course they did since that's what this guy had to have been. But I had always been told that fey couldn't die...wrong again, buckos. Why would they have need for someone like him? My brain was misfiring; nothing made sense.

There was blood. It wasn't mine. Thought fey couldn't die? This guy's face was smashed in...cool. Wish all of them here were in the same condition.

"Get the axe and hit her again! I want that band!"

"He's dead," Edme yelled out. "She killed him."

"More reason to get the magic from her, you fool!" Larry wheezed.

"Odive, do it yourself. You can hit her harder. Sharpen it with magic first."

"Hit closer to the band..."

"No, you might hurt the band. Go up to her elbow." The fey yelled out as one, all giving different directions on how to get the band off my arm. I, frankly, didn't like any of the suggestions. *Eat shit and die*, would have been mine. As their suggestions continued, their voices merged into nothing more than high-pitched noise.

A bell sounded again and suddenly everything went still.

"I'm needed on the battlefield," Odive said, breaking the silence. I forced my eyes to look over at him. I couldn't see much, but I did see the edge of a scroll.

"No! You stay here and get us that magic!" Moe shrieked.

"Please forgive me, your Excellences, but this cannot wait. Edme is more than capable of overseeing this matter for you." There was a slight fold in the air and I knew that Odive had left us.

"Edme, take care of this," Moe yelled at him. I didn't think Edme had the stomach for it as he took his time moving the fallen fey out of the way and positioning himself next to me. I was numb and in shock for sure. Everything happened in slow motion.

I could hear the sound of footsteps on my other side, outside of my field of vision, and knew Edme was going to give it a go. A bit of robe appeared and I could tell he was moving gingerly around the blood to retrieve the axe and position himself where the other fey had been.

I heard the axe being raised again and then the swoosh as it cut through the air. I watched my arm this time, fascinated, as the axe came down hard. Again it hurt like a bugger but bounced off. Edme tried to get out of the way, but he wasn't fast enough. His hands must have twisted as it bounced around and slammed into his side. I heard a grunt, then a multitude of screams and shouts—anger and frustration from all the witnesses to the torture. The injured fey wasn't saying much at all. I smiled. Edme was wounded, not as severely as the other had been, but he was in no shape to swing the axe again.

The older fey had started to yell at Edme, offended that he had not accomplished the deed. I turned to look at them and it hit me, harder than the axe had. I could move. Odive was gone and he was the one who had put the enchantment on me and now it had loosened somewhat. I didn't think the others in the chamber realized that Odive's enchantment had relaxed on me.

I felt inside myself…yes…I could move, well my head at least. I was back. I reached out mentally for anything, some tiny crumb of magic I could pull in to free myself completely. There was a morsel …something …yes, the blood from the prone fey. It held a miniscule amount, but it might be enough. I pulled it in, then pulled some more. I kept searching, reaching. I found more from Edme and pulled hard. It felt gross, like sucking from a straw. The tingle was back in my throat, I rolled it…not much. What to do with it? Think…think. My biggest problem, I thought, was Edme. He might be able to call Odive back to bind me again. I wanted out of here and I couldn't do that unless I could move.

I wet my lips as I moved the magic from my throat to my tongue. It was weak, but might work…it had to or they would keep torturing me. I mouthed the words rather than speaking them aloud and let the magic roll out. *"Break the bonds of the enchantment Odive wove."* The magic hung in the air, congealed like a ball of jelly and slowly loosened into tiny spirals. One floated upwards, but the remainder spread out and wrapped itself around my form. Weird that I could see it.

Then it was gone, I had used it all. Once more, I was empty…but not helpless.

I moved my head slightly to one side and could see them…the stooges. They were arguing with each other, mainly about what to try next on me to take my arm off. One was still waving the club around in the air as if to punctuate his point of view. I peeked over to Edme and he wasn't doing well. He had managed to move over to a wall and was using it to stay upright. His skin looked pasty, but I didn't care. I pulled again, harder than the last time. I wasn't going to leave him with anything.

The taste of his magic was like soured milk. It was so gross that I couldn't accept it all and a small amount of the magic stopped its journey towards me. I had to let it go or I was going to throw up. It did not recede back into Edme, but instead, like smoke, it spiraled up towards the ceiling. It was fascinating.

I watched as it rose, holding the magic I had drawn in the back of my throat. I rolled a small bit out and allowed it to rest on the tip of my tongue. I needed to be ready. I had training in this…thank you Skyler. My body was accustomed to having to function around pain. Zack had provided a refresher course, so I knew I could do it. I glanced over to the asswipes still arguing with each other. None were looking at me, so I had to do it now.

Gingerly, I tried moving my arm. Oh geez it hurt…like someone had hit me with a sledge hammer. I wiggled my fingers and had to hold in a scream as fire ripped up my arm. But it moved. The arm would be useless for a while. I didn't dare waste the magic on healing it. Sucking in my breath, I moved the arm off of the block and rested it on my lap, as I worked at pulling my legs in close so I could stand up.

One, two, three...I counted to myself, then stood and faced the thrones. Edme saw me first and cried out. The other three turned toward me with astonishment. I expected them to come after me, or throw magic at me, or at the very least yell for help. They did none of those things. I didn't have enough magic to try to blink out or I would have right then. They watched me with curiosity more than anything else. I looked over at Edme. He looked like he was going to pee his pants.

"I'm going home." I announced, daring them to stop me. They didn't say anything as I turned and started walking to the only door I could see in the chamber. Harsh, angry whispers echoed around me as I neared it, but I didn't turn around and I didn't stop. It was hard to move my feet at first, every movement sent a rip of agony through my arm. *Mind over matter* was my saying of the day, as I quickened my steps, unsure where I was headed.

"Stop her!" one of the old fey finally screamed. I didn't know which one and really didn't care.

"I can't. I don't have enough magic left," Edme cried back at them.

I must have taken quite a bit from him and it served him right for what he and Odive had done to me. What happened next was peculiar...I could feel magic in the room. Little tantalizing bits, and my mouth watered for them.

I couldn't stop myself. I swung around and regretted it instantly. My body quivered with pain and my legs wobbled underneath me. Curly had his hand up and was pushing magic out towards Edme, I assumed so he could stop me. As the magic hit Edme, his eyes rolled up and I could see him sucking it in. I stood there, transfixed, watching as the pulse of magic moved through the air.

Edme was making a horrible, revolting face, like he was slurping the magic in and I was sure it was because he was trying to heal himself. It was disgusting and I had to look away.

"Enough!" Curly yelled with just a hint of panic. I looked over at him. He had put his hand down, but the line of magic was still being drawn out from him by Edme.

Larry put his hand up and started to draw magic out of Edme, then Curly started to do the same to Larry. Moe joined in and it was bizarre. Magic was shooting from all of them, then reversing and going into them, then out, then in. They were fighting each other over the magic.

Edme seemed to be winning the strange battle. He was visibly growing stronger. Moe screamed and he folded in half with his arms outstretched. The other two kept trying to pull magic back out of Edme, but Edme looked like he didn't even know what he was doing. Maybe the will to survive at all costs had kicked in for him, too. Ivy could understand that, but the results were nauseating to watch. Edme looked like he was in the middle of some perverse form of ecstasy.

Edme let out an ear-piercing howl as he held both arms straight out with his palms angled toward the fey. His eyes were closed and he kept extracting from Moe until the fey was a hollow shell, dried and brown like a dead leaf. The club dropped to the floor and rolled out of sight behind the thrones.

I thought I was going to be sick. That's what could have happened to me if Zack had continued drawing from me last night. I wanted to turn and not see this, but I couldn't pull my eyes away.

The other two fey, Larry and Curly, started to squeal like stuck pigs as Edme's pull jumped from the remains of Moe and branched out to them. In seconds, they were just like Moe, folded in half and then shriveled into brown skeletons. The tiniest bits of magic were still being pulled from the remains, creating little whirlwinds as Edme pulled it towards himself. When the last little bit was absorbed by Edme, the air stilled.

He opened his eyes with a deep sigh of pleasure, and then looked around the room. When his eyes fell onto what was left of the other fey, he screamed and his face was contorted with horror and disbelief. He jerked his gaze away...it *was* pretty revolting, and then he looked at me. Like a dope, I was still standing right where he could see me.

"You did this to us! You killed the Elders!" he screeched at me. "You are a demon!"

I started to yell back that it was his fault, not mine, when I felt the pull from him. Damn that stupid fey if he wasn't still determined to kill me, too. He had stretched out his arm toward me and again I could see the line of magic bursting out from my body and shooting towards him.

I pulled back and drew some of the power to my tongue. Stupid me, when I had used my power before, I should have made sure I couldn't be drained again. There was very little and Edme was a fey with a purpose. I kept heaving back, but his drag was hard, almost as hard as Zack's had been and I didn't have the forest to help replenish me. I yelled out for him to stop, letting the tiny bit of magic roll off my tongue.

I kept pulling back and couldn't stop, even when he no longer fought me. I needed the magic, I needed the power. He screamed and collapsed, but I kept pulling. I knew I was losing control and fought against myself to call a halt to it. I didn't realize how hard it would be to stop draining a fey once you had started. It was rather creepy and I now knew how it might have felt for Zack. Once the power started to pour in, it became a thirst that was extremely hard to resist. It took all the focus I could manage to close my fingers and relax my arms. Ultimately, I was able to close the connection between us.

I looked over to where Edme lay. He was still alive...barely. His body was a crumpled heap and I could see he was gasping for air. I turned and ran.

CHAPTER 12 – Odive

Odive blinked into the center of the tent city. He hadn't wanted to leave the palace. It was very enjoyable to watch his Elders find ways to torture the abnormal fey. It galled him that Edme was going to be the one who got to see the final outcome.

He was annoyed and irritated and downright fuming. It didn't help his mood, discovering that it was growing late in the day on this side of Alainn. The sun had set on the horizon and darkness was descending. It always annoyed him that Alainn wasn't equalized enough to keep its time level.

A druid was building up a fire and others were loitering near the tents with three of the Valkyries. He glanced over toward the shoreline and saw a lone figure standing on the beach and knew it to be Rōber Edmonds' offspring by his ghastly hair.

He turned back to the druid by the fire and stomped over to him. The druid looked up at the fey and stood. Odive puffed out his chest, sure that the druid had recognized him to be an important fey. Odive sneered at him.

"Bring Kianna to me...now," he demanded firmly.

The beefy druid turned and ran, stumbling in his haste, righted himself and continued out of sight. More druids emerged from their tents and stood looking at him, anticipation written on their faces. Shouts could be heard and a commotion behind the tents. More and more of the druids appeared, all talking in hushed tones as they stared at the Troika who stood in the middle of the camp.

Kianna came from between the make-shift shelters, hesitated a brief moment when she laid eyes on him and then walked forward. Three of the other women fell in line behind her, but kept their distance as she continued moving toward him.

"Odive," she said in acknowledgment and bowed her head slightly to him.

"What happened here?" he raged at her.

"We battled the Eilibear. I was just with the Master Warriors going over the plans for the next attack. What is it you need?" she asked in a calm tone that grated on his nerves.

"Need? What do I need?" he spat with impatience. "I need you to tell me why you didn't kill *all* of them!"

From around him, he heard gasps and looked up. They were being watched and these damn druids were listening to every word he said. This would not do. He reached out and placed his hand on her shoulder and blinked them to a more private location deep in the woods. When they appeared, he didn't hesitate.

"I was pulled away from something very important because of *you*. You failed at calling in all the Eilibear, you failed at killing all the druids. Why do you think I released you? For you to kill a few of the Eilibear shades and call it a day? I spent many turns working on a strategy and then looking for the right place for the final battle. I found this disgusting rock within the water for you to do what Valkyries do best...*kill, slaughter everything, exterminate them!*" he screamed, spraying her with spit.

She calmly pulled out a handkerchief and wiped

her face, then glared at him.

"That is not what you told us to do. You said you wanted us to battle alongside the druids. You told me to keep the druid with the long hair occupied. That is what you said and that is what we have done," she pointed out.

"Damn it! You are Valkyries and you kill everything! That's why I locked you up, and that's what I expected you to do again when I released you."

"Then you should have made that clear. You broke the curse when you took Gunilla's life, taking away our ability to slaughter all in sight. Maybe you should not have killed her," she said scornfully.

Odive's brain felt muddled. He looked at her with wide eyes and then started to pace and mumble under his breath. He had worked it all out, he knew he had. Find a location that was isolated, fill it with Eilibear, bring all of the druids to it under the pretense of fighting the demons and then release the Valkyries to fight with them and the end result should have been that everyone was dead. Then he only had to get rid of the Valkyries again. Of all the Valkyries, it was the Seer that worried him the most. He was sure she would have a vision and know his plans. It had made sense to get rid of her.

Nowhere in the scrolls did it say that if one of the Valkyries died that the full effect of the curse would be broken. It only spoke of how to bind them and control them. Damn, damn, damn. He should have known when the stallions had disappeared. How could he have been so inane! When was this going to stop happening to him? It should have been so simple. He wanted to go back to his sanctuary and be alone again. That had worked all the other times he botched an enchantment.

He could curl up in front of a fire and have a cup of tea…maybe some headcheese and biscuits. He licked his lips at the thought. No, maybe blood pudding or that lovely casu marzu cheese he had recently discovered would be better.

"Uh hum."

He looked up to see that Kianna was watching him with a raised brow. He had to pull himself together and fix this.

Squaring his shoulders, he marched back up to her and then slowed as he noticed something was different about her.

"What's wrong with your hair?" he whispered nervously.

"My hair?" she repeated as she picked up a few strands and pulled it around so she could see. She gasped and looked at him uneasily.

"You're reverting to your normal form…No!" he screamed and stamped around in a circle. When he was facing the Valkyrie once more, he flung his hand out towards her. "Go gather the others. I want to see if it is happening to them also."

She vanished immediately. His eyes darted back and forth as he franticly tried to figure out what to do now. Nothing came to him. He needed to study the scrolls again. There had to be something.

The air shifted and four of the five women appeared before him. One by one, he looked them over and could see that each of them were indeed changing in appearance. Vada and Kianna were the only ones to retain what could be called true beauty. Bertelle's face was growing wider and her lips thinner. Her brows had bushed out and grown tighter together, while her form had thickened. He was disgusted. Inger seemed to have shrunk, and he knew it wouldn't be long before she resembled the little mousy fey he had seen when he had first gathered them. He stood back and stared at them, then counted and the hairs on the back of his neck stood up.

"Where is the fifth?"

"I couldn't find her. Bertelle saw her walking toward the beach and after that, no one has laid eyes on her," Kianna said cautiously.

"We need to find her and..." A notion entered his mind, "Do all of you still have your shared powers?" he asked taking another step back to study them.

"I am still a Siren, but the connection with my sisters has gone away. By the end of the battle, I was the only one who could call the Eilibear," Vada said woefully.

"My powers to heal do work, but I had to use them on my sisters as they could not join with me to do the restoring themselves," Inger whispered.

"It's like that with all of you? The bond of sharing your powers is now absent?" He watched in shock as the other two nodded agreement.

"So if Inger doesn't heal you, the Eilibear shades could take your life force," he mused out loud and instantly saw the stunned look on their faces. He flapped his hand out dismissively, "That would never happen, I'm sure."

This was very interesting. An idea started to form as he stood there looking at them. Kianna could still shapeshift, he supposed, and that might be useful. The others could still battle with the druids so even though he wouldn't be able to be rid of the Warriors, yet anyway, he would just have to use what was at hand. The loss of the other was unfortunate as he had hoped that she would get rid of her sire and brother. But on the other hand, she was a shield, which meant she could provide protection during battle for everyone and that would not be good. He hoped that she had simply run off into the woods and was hiding. She couldn't get out of the containment enchantment he had cast so she had to be here someplace.

His mind raced, recounting all the enchantments and artifacts he had at his disposal...and then he remembered. He still had the clock. If he used it now it wouldn't matter if the Valkyries killed everyone. He could do it himself *and* get rid of the Valkyries at the same time. He should have thought of this before releasing them, but no matter now. A smile started to creep up around the corners of his mouth and he looked up at the foursome of women in good humor.

"All of you go back. You three," he said pointing to Vada, Bertelle and Inger, "do what you can to glamour the druids and battle alongside them. Kianna, I think you should stay shifted to your Valkyrie form and keep working on the young Edsmond druid," he announced feeling quite proud of himself. He didn't know why he had been so upset—the clock would take care of everything.

CHAPTER 13 – Ivy

I had no clue where I was going. I ran until I couldn't run anymore. The hallway I had run into was blank and blurry, like everything else. It was wide and seemed endlessly long. My arm was throbbing and it hurt horrendously. My battery of magic wasn't anywhere near full. Edme hadn't had much magic, only what he had pulled from the Elders and it all had that sour taste to it. It felt watered down, tainted and I wasn't sure if it was even strong enough to heal me or to blink. I weighed my options and decided getting out of here was my first point of action.

I tried to blink and it didn't work. I wandered down halls and into chamber after chamber. My bare feet burned from the freezing cold floor. The pain in my arm had dulled somewhat or maybe my body just couldn't handle the additional pain from my feet. Either way, I wasn't going to waste the magic on healing. I had started to shiver and couldn't stop my teeth from chattering. My head throbbed and all I could think of was that I needed to get out before Edme found a way to come after me or Odive came back.

There were no doors leading out and no furnishings of any kind. The ornate thrones the Elders had sat in seemed to be the only pieces of furniture in this place. I found a few more small windows, but none that I could fit through.

Every once in a while, I'd feel a cool breeze swoosh by my face but could find nothing that would have created it. I kept walking, kept searching, long after my feet had gone numb.

After a while, I was hopelessly confused. This place seemed to be a large maze, a labyrinth of blurry whiteness. I went up and down a wide assortment of stairs. Some were wide, lavish staircases, others just basic steps that led to more empty corridors and even more empty rooms. Hours went by and I had almost given up finding anything when I opened yet another door. There was a bit of color in the far corner of the room. I staggered over to it and cried out in joy. It was my backpack. Someone had pulled everything out into a messy pile. I guess my stuff didn't hold any interest for whoever had done this and I was glad. My shoes were still nowhere to be seen.

I picked up my sweatshirt and pulled it over my head, gingerly forcing my arm into a sleeve. I had to grit my teeth not to cry out, but I got it on. Getting the other arm in was easier and it was with a relief that I was able to put the hurt one into the front large pocket of the sweatshirt and use it as a sling.

I hadn't had much in the pack, since before Zack and I left, I had taken out most of my school books. I kept power bars and my MP3 player in the small front pockets and they were still there. Sitting on the cold floor, I tore open one of the power bars with my teeth and hungrily devoured it.

Since I only had one hand to use, I had to wait until I had shoved the last of the power bar into my mouth before I pulled out my player. It didn't look damaged, even the cord with the ear buds was still in one piece. Almost reverently, I put an ear plug in and pushed the *on* button. The last song I had been listening to bombarded me...

"We gotta keep searchin', searchin', find a place to hide...'"

Thank you Del Shannon. I agree with you, I gotta keep searching, I thought as I switched it back off and tucked the player inside the pocket with my bad arm. My fingers could move a little bit without causing me pain and I discovered I could hit the buttons to turn it on and off. That cheered me. I switched it back on and turned the volume down so it was only a nice hum of melody in my ear.

I felt revitalized by the music, finding my pack and eating the power bar. I could do this. These damn fey had brought me here, tried to chop my arm off, gotten into a magic pissing match with each other and somehow I was the one being blamed for hurting all of them. This had really turned into one crappy week, but I could and would get out of here and find a way back home. Granddad had to be looking for me, I was sure of it.

What I needed was a plan. If I couldn't find a way out, then I needed to find a place to hide. I figured that aimlessly wandering around wasn't exactly helpful since I couldn't tell where I had been...though I had found my backpack. I stood still and looked around me. The rooms with windows had to be on the outside walls, and none of these rooms had windows. I had just come up a wide staircase which probably meant there wouldn't be a door leading outside on this level.

I needed to go down and stay on the floor that had the windows. That decided, I backtracked the way I had come until I found the stairs and went down. I continued in that manner until I found a large room which looked like it might be an entry hall. Unfortunately, there was no door, but there were a couple of small windows. They were up too high to look out, but I could see white haze out through them. That could be sky...or not, but at least it was something.

I sat down on the stairs and my body seemed to melt with weariness. I couldn't keep this up. I sat there and stared at the haze as I pondered my options. Maybe I could use the magic to blast a hole in the wall to escape, but did I have enough to do it? That seemed rather over the top anyway. Odive had left, he had blinked. Maybe here there was no need for doors if you could blink anywhere you wanted. But how did they blink without magic? My battery seemed to be draining just by walking, which made no sense. It was now so low it was but a flicker, and I had felt the other fey in the chamber. They held no magic. My body was shutting down, I needed food and rest...and Zack.

I was so tired and I wanted Granddad or Zack to hurry up and come save me. The tears came on their own, filling my eyes and dripping down my face. My nose stuffed up, like it always did when I cried. Silent sobs wracked my body. I let it all out...what had happened last night with Zack, what he had done to me and me to him. I was worried for Granddad and, to top it off, these crazy fey had really been trying to cut my arm off.

I pulled a Kleenex out of my pack and blew my nose. That's when I felt it again, a bit of coolness drifting across my face, with it the hint of magic. There was a faint rich smell that reminded me of my forest.

"Hello, is someone there?" I whispered as I looked around myself. The space was unchanged, yet...something was different and I felt no malice from it.

"Hello?" I called out again and had a flash memory of calling out to fey in my forest and having them not answer. "Hello, please is anyone there?"

"Hello," a charming little voice said from the handrail on the stairs. Out of the corner of my eye, I could see him. A tiny little man, with wings like oak leaves, perched daintily on the rail. His hair was brown and pulled back in a smart ponytail. His skin was tanned a golden brown and his only item of clothing was loose fitting shorts. Even his little feet were bare. I knew what he was, though I had only seen and met one other such as him. He was a Sprite, like Margo, and rather handsome in a small, little fairy way.

"You are fey, but not *fey*. You smell like a forest, but not my forest," he said displaying an enchanting smile. "I saw you. You are very brave." He announced cheerfully, and then his voice took on a serious tone. "We need to leave. Odive is sure to come back and Edme will throw the blame on you for breaking the enchantments."

Ivy's heart skipped a beat. Had she really found a friend in this appalling place?

"Do you know a way out?" she asked, hope starting to grow. "Wait, just what enchantments did I break?"

"It's a secret and I was bound not to tell," he looked around as if scared that someone would overhear, then whispered with joyful glee, "You broke the connection between my master and me. You freed me."

The little guy was so excited that he quivered blissfully, his tiny wings pulsating like a hummingbird's, making a buzzing sound. With his eyes bright, he regarded me with pure adoration.

"I'm very happy I did that for you, but I don't know how I did it. Odive was your master so you were like, what, a slave?" I asked uncertainly.

"Not a slave, but I am a Sprite," he answered with a sweet smile, as if that explained everything.

"I figured you were a Sprite. I have a friend who is one, but you are the only other one I've ever seen."

His face dropped into a sad pout. "Oh...I was hoping that you could be my new master, but if you already have a Sprite, I am unneeded." He looked so forlorn it was almost comical, but my heart skipped a beat with the thought that he might take off and not help me.

"I need you! I need you so very much," I cried out.

"But fey only have one Sprite who serves them," he said, tilting his head. The little guy looked very perplexed.

"I don't *have* Margo. She doesn't *serve* me. She's my friend. Can't you be my friend also?" I asked, confused as much as he seemed to be.

"You freed her also? You are a fey like no other," he gushed with admiration.

"No, I didn't free her," I said. I was trying hard to understand this line of discussion, but he was making my head hurt. We needed to get back on topic and get out of here. "I'm sorry, but can't you just be my friend and help me find a way out?"

"Oh yes, I would enjoy being your friend," he went still and stood straight. With great ceremony, he bowed formally to me. "I am Derl, from the Llover Meadhan, home of the clan of Kapok."

I had to work very hard not to laugh. He was

delightful. I stood and did a slight bow back to him. "I am Ivy, from the Hemlock forest...um I mean the Hemlock Meadhan, home of the clan of Glenwood," I said, trying to match his formality. I was rather pleased with myself that I was able to do it. "Oh and I guess I should tell you, I am the owner of the Meadhan, too."

There was no possible way for his eyes to get wider. The look of surprise on his face was rather alarming and I thought the little guy was going to faint. Suddenly he zoomed up into the air and before I had time to stop him, he zipped down the long corridor. I started to scream for him not to leave me, but before the words left my lips, he was back, hovering right in front of me.

"Chief Ivy, we need to go now!"

"That's what I've been trying to do and can't find a way out!" I said, exasperated that we both knew we had to leave and yet were not doing it. "Oh and I'm not a chief, I'm only Ivy," I said, not really liking the idea of being chief of the Glenwood clan. If anyone was that, it was Granddad.

"Only Ivy..." Derl said, correcting his title for me.

I gave up the fight, I figured it didn't matter what he called me as long as he helped me.

"I have heard of you, and Odive wishes to do to you what he did to the Elders. He cannot find you here," Derl said, finishing his thought.

"What did he do to the Elders?" I asked cautiously.

"He did a *bad* enchantment," he said, emphasizing the word *bad*. "It didn't work the way he hoped and the Elders were caught in the backlash...he destroyed them by taking all their magic. The bad, unspeakable enchantment sucked all the magic from this part of Firinn. Odive was hysterical for a time and I did not like being his Sprite. Then he attempted another *bad* enchantment and reawakened the Elders," he fluttered closer and whispered his next words. "But it was *not* them, they are…were…different, very scary and their minds not right. Odive didn't care. He had them back, so no one would know what he had done. But keeping the Not Elders animated takes *a lot* of magic. That was my duty. I travel back and forth from Meadhans to collect clean magic to supply the Not Elders. I did not like my duty," he finished with a grimace. His expressions and words were a bit exaggerated, but I got his point.

"So he wants to kill me and then bring me back?" I screamed in terror.

Derl tensed and put a finger to his lips as he looked around nervously.

"You need to speak lower Only Ivy. Sound travels within these walls. He wants to take your magic, but I do not think he means to bring you back. You were almost all that the Not Elders and Odive talked of in the last few years. They say you have very strong magic…unending magic. The Not Elders craved it and Odive desires it. There is no telling what he might do to you to try to take it from you. And you will be *dead*-dead."

Well, I didn't want to be *dead*-dead and I certainly didn't want to meet up with Odive again.

"Can we leave now…please," I said. Just standing here was giving me the creeps.

"Yes, that would be good. There is no clean magic in this place and only the three servants of the

Elders, the Troika, had the ability to blink. I could also when I was connected to them, but now I have lost that talent. I know of only one way out for us. It will not be pleasant for either of us, I'm afraid," he said mournfully.

"I can't think of anything that would be more unpleasant than having someone try to chop my arm off," I said as I moved my bad arm slightly. He looked at it and frowned.

"That was bad," he said, summing up my feelings exactly. He looked up at me, gave me an encouraging smile and then motioned solemnly for me to follow him.

At first, he zoomed down the hallway and then had to wait for me to catch up. That got a bit tiring for the both of us and soon I found myself with a cute Sprite sitting on my shoulder, telling me which way to go.

It turned out that my plan to just keep going down had been correct. He told me as I power-walked down the corridors and hopped down the multiple staircases that we needed to go to the lowest level...what he called the crypt. That, in itself, didn't sound like a place I wanted to go to, but what choice did I have? Visions of mummies and zombies coming out of coffins filled my thoughts and by the time we opened the last door to head down to it, I was close to having a major panic attack.

Derl poked me on the cheek when I hesitated at the door.

"It is the only way I know of, Only Ivy," he said.

I opened the door and looked down the narrow stairs. It looked the same as every other part of this place. Not scary at all. I started down and even before I left the staircase, I could see that the room was massive, with huge white pillars every ten feet or so. It reminded me of the basement at our house in San Diego. There, we had rough wood columns that held the crossbeams up, supporting the house.

"Is this it, the crypt?" I asked, feeling a lot calmer now.

"Yes. We need to go to the far end, see that place where the walls do not look pure?" he said, pointing off to our right.

I could see where he meant and hopped down the last few steps and hurried over to the spot. I had been cold for most of the time I had been here, but as I moved closer, the air felt like it was growing heavy and warm. It felt so good that I didn't care if this seemed to be the only place in this structure that had little light. It grew increasingly darker and when Derl started to glow a soft shade of yellow, I wasn't shocked at all. It was dark, he was a fey and we all seemed to have quirky powers of one sort or another

"It's there," he said, pointing towards the wall.

I went closer and saw it was only a wall. A dirty wall, with black mold covering it. It was rather gross looking.

"Where's the way out?" I asked twisting my head to look down at him.

"See the small crack...there?" he said pointing. I couldn't see anything but mold. He left my shoulder and fluttered close to the wall.

"It is here. I can get through it, but you are too big. Can you make yourself smaller?" he asked, giving me that little tilt of his head when he asked questions.

"No, I can't get smaller," I cried with annoyance. "This is the only way out and you knew this whole time that I might not be able to fit through it? Well crap, crap, crap!" I said stomping my foot.

CHAPTER 14 – Ivy

"Only Ivy, you have some magic. It's the tainted magic from the Not Elders and Edme, but it's still magic. You will want to get it out of you as soon as possible anyway. Just do an Open-spell. Put your finger here on the tiny crack and see if you have enough power to open it to allow you in," he said in a calm tone. He looked at me and waited for me to do as he'd said.

The little guy was right. I had magic and I had saved it for getting out. It didn't matter that I didn't know how to cast the kind of spell he was talking about. Casting spells must be something normal fey knew how to do, but I had other ways.

I put my finger where he directed and scrunched up my nose in revulsion. The mold was sticky and gross. Something slimy wiggled against my finger and I choked down a scream as I worked at letting the magic build on my tongue.

"Open to allow me in," I told the crack. The magic that rolled out felt greasy and as gross as the mold did.

The magic connected with the wall and suddenly I could see a crack. It widened and then widened some more. We stood, waiting, hoping that I had used enough magic to do the deed. It was creepy to see the mold moving as the crack stretched itself like a deformed mouth, opening. All that was missing was a set of decayed teeth and the picture would be perfect for a horror film.

When it stopped moving, there was an odd angled

opening about three feet long and two feet wide, more than enough room for me to go through. Derl flew into the darkness first. His soft yellow glow was clouded, making his form hazy and what light he emitted did little to illuminate the space. Yet I could see that it was a tunnel of sorts. I had to bend and push in sideways after him and as soon as my feet touched the ground on the other side, they started to sink into gooey mud. I was really missing my shoes right now.

"Can you close it back up so Odive will not know we came this way?" he asked, his voice echoing slightly in the space.

It was hard work to turn around as my feet were sticking in the mud. I twisted and pulled one foot free and rotated myself. There wasn't much magic left, surely not enough to heal myself. I let it build until I knew all of it would be used up and told the wall to close. The magic rolled out once more and as the rest of it left my body, I felt much better. My headache faded and I didn't feel quite so achy. Now that I knew that the magic was tainted, I was glad to have it out. The wall was doing as it had been told, and as it closed tightly, all the light from the large room was shut out.

I pulled my foot up again and rotated myself until I could see Derl. He hovered a few feet down the tunnel and was patiently waiting for me to follow. I had to trust that he knew where he was going and was really a friend to me. I didn't want to think about the possibility that he was leading me somewhere even scarier than what I had just left. Right now, any other place was a good place to be.

I started to walk and found that pulling my feet out from the squishy mud was a chore. My first few steps were a struggle and I was extremely glad when the mud changed to hard-packed dirt. A thought occurred to me then...I am on dirt. I could pull magic from dirt. I twisted my toes down firmly and tried to pull. Nothing came to me. Disappointed, I started to follow Derl again.

The tunnel was a tight fit and I felt like it was closing in on me. I had never felt claustrophobic before, but then again, I had never felt inclined to crawl into holes or roam around in caves before either. I could see Derl up ahead; he kept to a slow pace for my sake, providing light to show me where to go.

I had begun to count my steps soon after we started walking so I'd have some idea how far we had gone and to keep my mind occupied. When I reached sixty-one, the tunnel started to angle downwards.

Little rivers of water ran down the dirt walls and had made ruts in the ground as it followed the slope of the tunnel downward. I stopped counting since I had to start concentrating on not slipping instead. Derl's glow provided just enough light to see, but not enough to *really* see. I was glad of that. Water dripped from the ceiling and I knew there had to be worms and bugs everywhere. I worked at thinking of the Entomologist who had lectured a few weeks ago. One of the things she had said had stuck with me: *worms are good, worms are a botanist's best friend.* I repeated it to myself whenever my toes connected with something that wiggled.

The air had grown thick, with a peculiar taste and smell to it. It was a strange combination of a closed-up room, fish left out too long and overly fragrant flowers. It became stronger with each step and I had to start breathing through my mouth so I wouldn't gag.

Derl finally stopped his forward progress and

came back to hover in front of me.

"The passageway ends soon. There is a drop into a large cavern and the exit we need is about halfway across on the right. You will need to climb down and make your way there on foot. It will not be pleasant. I need to check to make sure the opening is still where it was."

Before I could reply he took off, zooming out ahead to provide me with the yellow glow once more. I was not looking forward to having to climb down anything, but I would do it no matter how much my arm hurt. He was right, that would not be pleasant.

I started forward and the angle of the tunnel grew steeper. The little ruts with water changed to slick mud. I slipped a couple of times, putting my good hand out to the wall each time to catch myself.

Without warning the light up ahead disappeared, and I was engulfed in complete darkness. I yelled out for Derl, but there was no response. I took a tentative step forward and then another. Abruptly my left foot went out from under me. I stretched out my arm and there was no wall to help catch my fall this time. I hit the ground hard and then started to slide down the remainder of the tunnel. A wave of hot, foul-smelling air hit me as I was finally able to dig my nails into the ground and stop my downward slide. I sat up, reaching out with both arms to see if I could find the side of the tunnel. There was nothing there.

Standing was out of the question. I screamed for Derl again and was met with only silence. I squirmed myself up to my hands and knees and started to crawl, yelling for him as I moved. Unexpectedly the ground beneath me gave way and I found myself sliding downward again, this time face forward. My bad arm connected with rocks and I screamed. Then I started to tumble, rolling down the steep slope, loosening rocks and dirt along the way.

Mud and water rained down on me as I landed face first in something mushy. I pulled my face out of whatever it was and started to gag uncontrollably. Dry heaves racked my body and I decided it had been a good thing that I hadn't had much to eat today. I forced myself to roll sideways to get away from it and, to my horror, tumbled over an edge.

This time I rolled downward, but the rocks had been replaced with something softer, though still uneven and bumpy. I really hoped it was just some type of friendly moss that simply smelled really bad. I landed with a squish onto more mushy softness. The smell was even more nauseating and I started to gag again. I really didn't care at this point, at least whatever the stuff was, it had cushioned my fall.

I lay there, trying to catch my breath when the familiar soft yellow glow started to shine off to my right. Derl finally reappeared, hovering overhead and looking down at me with concern.

"Are you alright? I thought you would wait for me to come back before you made the climb down," he said in his little singsong voice, and I felt an insane desire to laugh. That's what he had meant with he said he needed to check to see if the opening was still there. He was going to leave me and make sure. I felt a little stupid.

"I didn't mean to, but I'm down now. Is it safe to move out of this stuff?" I asked, hoping he would say yes.

"We are in the main cavern now. You will not fall again," he replied, but really didn't answer my question. I hauled myself into a sitting position before leaning forward to use my hands to push myself up. Whatever the stuff was I had fallen into was soft and pliable. I didn't weigh much, but still I sank into it. I was finally able to stand, but had to work hard not to slip and fall again into the slimy mass under my feet. Once I was sure my footing was sound, I started to move awkwardly forward.

"What is this stuff I'm walking on?" I asked. No matter where I put my foot, it was met with the same uneven mushy stuff. It was hard to keep my balance.

He came close, fluttering in front of me. "Only Ivy, you do not want to know."

My heart skipped a beat. I did not like his tone, but I had to know.

"Yes I do, Derl. What is this stuff? And why does the air feel so heavy and smell so foul?"

He hesitated, making a facial expression like he didn't think this was a good idea and then floated down to the ground near my foot. I followed his little flight as his glow started to illuminate the ground. My eyes grew wide as my body started to shake. As more was revealed, I couldn't contain myself and started to scream with terror.

Faces. Faces stared up at me. Arms, legs, bodies, shoulders, heads…people. I looked down at my feet and saw I was standing on someone's head. I screamed even louder and jumped off, only to lose my balance and fall backwards. Derl came close and when I turned my head, a lifeless face was gawking back at me.

"Only Ivy, I told you that you wouldn't want to

know and that it would be unpleasant," Derl said wretchedly.

Okay, understatement of the year! my brain screamed.

"Lay still for a moment, Only Ivy. They cannot hurt you, nor can you hurt them."

I gulped deep breaths of the foul air and tried to calm myself. I had to tell myself that I could do this. I had been through a lot in my life and I could handle this if it was the only way for me to get home. I closed my eyes and tried to relax my body, breathing in and out as I worked at finding some resemblance of calm. Where were those Yoga instructors when you needed them? Geez, I really needed some Zen right now.

When I found the courage to open my eyes again, I looked up to see Derl waiting and quietly studying me.

"Who are they? What happened to them?" I asked in a whisper.

"They are the results of Odive's bad enchantment. They are Eilibear."

"Eilibear?" I focused again at the face next to me and was more confused than ever. It looked like the normal face of someone I would see back home. "These aren't Eilibear, I've battled them. They are horrible lines of green slime that take over other things; they are demons."

"That is result of Odive's mistake. He wished to make an end to the race of Eilibear, but he made an error and cast a corrupted enchantment. First the spell was supposed to pull all of the Eilibear into this **Fearainn Eadar** and take their magic. It did that and more. I was here with Odive and saw. It pulled the Fearainn Eadar out of its place in time and put it in the ground under

Firinn and *then* took the magic. The second part of the enchantment was to destroy the Eilibear. Odive meant to end their lives, but instead their spirits were merely extracted from their bodies, leaving these, their empty shells behind. *Bad* Enchantment," he said shaking his head woefully.

"So the first part is what killed the Elders?"

"Oh yes. And he didn't discover the damaging consequences until we went back up to the palace. All the space above the Fearainn Eadar, in Firinn, had its magic ripped from it also. I do not know the number of other fey that were affected and died, but it was a great number."

That was a lot of information to process. I tried to organize it better than when Lavin had first told me about me being a fey. That had thrown me for such a loop that my brain had shut down. I was fey, I told myself, and being a fey meant that there was a lot of odd shit that I knew nothing about.

"So this place is called Fearainn Eadar?" I asked, pulling this first easy question out of the mix.

My mind had resolved itself that what was underneath me couldn't hurt me. The tension in my body started to relax. I did find it interesting that I was having this informative discussion while lying on top of Eilibear. Kind of disturbing.

"It is not Fearainn Eadar, it is *a* Fearainn Eadar…a land between."

"A land between what?"

"You are not educated in this, Only Ivy?" he asked tilting his head slightly at me.

"I was raised in Alainn…as an Alltha and only last year was told I was fey. I know practically nothing,"

I admitted.

He scrunched up his little face as he digested this fact about me. He looked so cute with his brow furrowed and his nose all crunched up. Margo needed to meet him—they would get along wonderfully. He fluttered down and sat on the head next to me, completely unconcerned with what he was perched on.

"A Fearainn Eadar is the land between Alainn and Ifrinn. It's like our Meadhans that connect Firinn and Alainn. The Eilibear's betweens allow access from Ifrinn to Alainn. I never had the opportunity to travel into them, however, many fey did when the realms were allies and worked as one."

"Are you telling me that the Eilibear used to be friends of the fey and mortals?" I said with a huff of skepticism.

"Of course. It was Odive that did all this," he motioned out to the expanse. "We were not at war with them until he stole their physical forms. They were upset, you see, and wanted them back."

Another colossal understatement. If Odive had stolen my body, I'd surely be pissed off and want it back. I'd fight like hell...just as the Eilibear were doing.

"If they find this place, can they..." I hesitated as I sought to find the right words. "...fill them up again and be whole?"

"Oh yes and that is what they want to do. Odive sealed this Fearainn Eadar and cloaked it. Only one other besides myself and Odive found out about what happened and Odive made sure that fey would never speak of it."

"How did he do that?" I asked, not sure if I really wanted to know.

"He used another *bad* enchantment and made it impossible for him to speak."

Derl relayed this so casually that it was almost as disquieting as what he was telling me. I just couldn't think about Odive. He was a horrible, creepy little fey and I did not want to come into contact with him again.

I needed to get away from this place. There was no telling what he would do to me or Derl now that he had revealed these secrets to me.

"Let's talk while we walk," I said as I pushed myself up. All this talking had been interesting and enlightening, and I found that I wasn't as grossed out by what was under my feet now.

"Which way?" I asked when I was upright once more.

"Follow me," he said as he flew up and waited for me to start forward.

I started to walk and discovered that I had to climb mounds of the bodies. Once on the other side, I tried to walk but slid more than anything else, then climbed up again. There was no way I could talk and make the trek across this ocean of still forms and I put all my concentration into just moving forward and following where Derl led.

At first I noticed the forms more. The Eilibear looked like normal people, their skin tones had a wide range just like mortals and fey, and their bodies were all shapes and sizes. They were only another race of beings. There were male and females, young and old. The most disturbing to me was when I came across babies. Unsettling small forms with soft features that, when alive, were probably very sweet. It wasn't right that Odive had done this to them. It was the vilest of all evils, a full blown genocide. What could they have possibly done to make him want to exterminate a whole race of people?

I lost count of the mountains of Eilibear I walked over. I stepped on arms and hands, and used heads and feet to steady myself. They stopped being body parts after a time and were just things I needed to get over. The odor was overpowering and I worked at breathing through my mouth. I don't know when I grew used to it, but the odor settled on my senses until it was only the smell of flowers that assaulted me. I had always loved the fragrance of Jasmine or a bouquet of Gardenias and worked at isolating those aromas from the nauseating assortment of smells.

As I labored at navigating over the bodies, Derl informed me that there were millions of them in this Fearainn Eadar, close to ninety-eight percent of the Eilibear that had been either in Alainn or one of their Fearainn Eadars when Odive had cast the enchantment.

I pondered what happened to the ones who had escaped the slaughter. Where were they? Had they also been robbed of their bodies? Could they have been locked inside the other Fearainn Eadar's when Odive sealed them or were they still in their world?

My heart went out to them and, as odd as it sounded, even to me, I discovered I was now on the side of the Eilibear. When I got out of here, I was going to tell the Eilibear...didn't know quite how I would go about doing that, but I would. It was the right thing to do.

CHAPTER 15 – Ivy

I walked, crawled and slid for hours. I was becoming accustomed to the odor around me and I think my arm had gone numb. I felt no pain, but was extremely tired. It had been the longest day I'd ever had to endure.

We came to a dirt wall that had the forms piled up against it. Mold covered the dirt and the bodies and this time I was sickened that the bodies were so ill kept. If the Eilibear got their physical forms back, I didn't think they would like finding out they were covered with nasty fungus. Which I knew was kind of moronic since I had been walking on hundreds of them.

"Okay, Derl, where do we go from here?" I asked.

"The opening is high above us. It is very small. When I used it before I could barely get through," he replied as he looked up.

"And what is your plan?" I asked, following his gaze up. I was sure he had one as he seemed like one smart little Sprite.

"You may not like it, but I do know it will work. I will fly up there and go through the opening which leads into Firinn. From there, I will fly to the nearest Meadhan and gather clean magic. I will come back, give the magic to you and I am hopeful that you will be able to use it to get up to the opening, enlarge it and finally escape," he said without faltering. I could tell he had really thought this out, and it did seem like a good plan.

I considered how I could use my powers to do

what was needed. I had never tried to fly and didn't think it was possible without wings. I guess I could use the magic he brought back to try to shape myself into something with wings. I'd never tried to shift before, but I was a Frìth fey and that's the magic that would be normal for me to have. But what if I did turn into something and still couldn't fly? Or worse yet, what if I couldn't figure out how to shift back to me? Nope, that was a dumb idea. What I needed was a way up and the means to enlarge the opening. I could climb if I had something to climb. Or maybe I could blink.

"Derl you will be able to blink back here when you have magic again, right?"

"Yes, I will be able to do that, after I pass through the Meadhan doorway," he answered with a little tilt of his head.

"Once I have magic, will I be able to blink also?"

"Maybe, but only to the doorway of the Meadhan. If there is not enough, you will need to walk the distance."

"Well, let's tackle one thing at a time. I need a way to climb up and enlarge that opening," I said. "Can you bring back a piece of vine? Any vine will do, but if there is a bit of root or a leaf on the stem, it would work best for me."

He squinted his eyes at me, considering why I would want such a thing, but didn't say a word. Instead he nodded once at me.

"It will be dark when I leave. You are safe unless Odive comes back and figures out where you have gone. I will return as soon as I can," he said and then was gone.

I had been feeling pretty confident up until the point when Derl had mentioned Odive again. I had all but forgotten that the fey would be searching for me when he returned and found me gone.

I nestled in amongst the still-silent forms of the Eilibear and closed my eyes. It was better being in the dark if I didn't have to *see* that I was in the dark. And then I waited. Sleep overcame me eventually and, amazingly enough, it was a very nice, restful sleep, with wonderful dreams of rolling plains of soft yellow grasses.

"Only Ivy?"

Derl's soft voice roused me and I turned towards it. When I opened my eyes, the little Sprite was sitting on the big toe of a foot sticking out partway from the pile. He held a small piece of a Lianas vine. Again, I was very pleased that I had chosen Botany as my course of study. I knew this vine. It was infamous for being one of the fastest-growing climbing plants known and to make it even better, it had wonderful thick, woody vines like tree trunks.

I took the bit of vine from him gleefully.

"Are you ready?" he asked. I nodded and closed my eyes. I could feel when he started to give the magic to me. It felt so marvelous and I almost moaned out loud from the bliss of feeling it inside me again. I wanted all he had to give, but forced restraint on myself. I would not pull from him…he had to give it freely to me. No way in hell was I going to do the same thing to him that Zack had almost done to me and I had watched Edme do to the Not Elders.

I kept my eyes closed long after Derl stopped pushing the magic out to me. I just wanted to savor it for a while before I had to use it up again. When I did open my eyes, I could see Derl watching me with a delightful smile.

"Clean magic feels nice," he said with a wide grin.

"Oh yes, it does," I replied. "Let's see if my power will work now." I took the little vine and set it at the top of the pile next to the wall. I let the magic roll around on my tongue, enjoying the feel of it, before I spoke.

"Grow tall and strong, twist up to the little opening and force your way into it, break it open, wide enough for me to fit through. Grow," I said forcing the magic out to the vine with the strongest push I had.

Derl started to clap merrily as the little bit of vine began to twist and creep along the wall. Roots spouted out from the bottom and pushed their way down through the bodies to gain a tight foothold. At the same time the vine picked up speed as it grew a couple of feet a second, twisting itself into intricate lattice as it worked its way upwards. It wasn't long before the top of the vine was out of sight and I could only hope that it continued its mission. What I could see of the vine continued to expand and mature into thick tree-like trunks.

A breath of air made me look away from the vine to catch the quick movement from Derl as he rocketed up to see what the top of the vine was doing.

"Only Ivy, start climbing!" he called down to me and his voice echoed out into the void of the cavern. I pulled myself up over the bodies, grabbed hold of the vine and started to climb. The vine had created wonderful foot and handholds for me and even with my bad arm, it was an easy ascent. I could see Derl's yellow glow high above and kept that as my focal point. As I neared the top, I could see that the vine had sprouted multiple leaves and it was like climbing a normal tree.

Branches of the vine had shot out and twisted around itself over and over again to create a nest of vines and leaves. I moved through it, keeping close to the wall and was to the opening before I expected to be. The vine had done what I asked of it and widened the opening to almost a two-foot circle. I pushed my way through it and popped out of the ground into the white haze of Firinn.

It was very disorientation to have been climbing up the side of a wall, only to emerge through the wall and find oneself coming out of a hole in the ground. I looked back in, but couldn't see through the vines and leaves. Derl appeared, fluttering in the white haze next to me.

"Do you have enough to close it now?" he asked. I detected a bit of worry in his voice and didn't know if it was due to the opening I had created or something else.

Quickly I pulled the last of the magic onto my tongue. "Thank you vine, pull back from the opening so the opening can close...close," I said touching the edge of the hole.

Both Derl and I waited with baited breath to see if I had enough magic to make it happen. The vine did start to recede and very, very slowly the hole began to close in on itself. When it was done, there was still an opening large enough to put my hand through. It had to be enough.

I finally turned and surveyed the area. The place was dead and blurred. The air was damp and felt tainted...sick and very thin. The landscape was barren, with only a boxy structure in the far distance.

"Is that where we came from?"

"Before Odive, it was magnificent. The fey were very proud of the home of the Elders, as we all gave of our magic to help construct it," he responded quietly as he gazed over at it. "Very sad now, very sad," he said shaking his head.

It was sad and I wished I could have seen Firinn when it was still healthy and full of magic. I was sure that it would have been exquisite. Now there was only that lone, desolate structure to break the emptiness.

"The Meadhan is that way. I do not know if they will let you in, but we can try," he said pointing off into the distance.

I could feel a wave of panic rising in me. The aura of this place was suffocating me and I didn't know how long I could stand it. Nor did I want to be captured again by Odive. Derl moved to my shoulder and I tried to blink...but nothing happened.

"I don't have any left," I admitted with dread. My inner battery was almost dead and I could feel what tiny bit I had left slowly ebbing away. "I'll have to do it the old-fashioned way and run."

I started to race in the direction that Derl had pointed and didn't look back. When I had run as far as I could, I stopped to catch my breath. The air was sucking away what physical energy I had. It must be residue from the bad enchantment Odive had cast. I was stumbling with fatigue by the time we reached a rise in the ground and a strange shimmering wall.

"That part there," Derl said, rising from my shoulder and flying over to a section my eyes hadn't seen.

"What's this other stuff?" I asked, huffing.

"Firinn ends here." He replied as he hovered near the doorway to his Meadhan.

"Firinn has an end? I didn't know that, I thought it was like Meadhans or Alainn, that it just kept going and going." I managed to get out between deep exhausted breaths.

He looked at me strangely, but didn't comment. I looked back the way we had come and wondered how Granddad or Zack were going to find me. I needed to leave a trail for them, if they were indeed looking for me in this terrible place. I had no magic so I searched around, trying to find something I could leave here that they would recognize. I couldn't think of anything, my mind felt as blurry as my surroundings.

"I'll go in and ask permission for you. I'm not sure what the fey will say, but I'll be back," Derl said, biting at his lip, and then disappeared through the shimmering. I touched the doorway after he left, just to see if I could go through. It was solid. There was nothing I could do but wait.

I had started to shake. It was cold and growing colder by the minute. I wasn't sure if it was me, without any magic, or Firinn, but it scared me. I crossed my arms and started to hop from foot to foot to try to stay warm and conscious. I turned back to look behind me, surveying the landscape. I could barely make out the small shape of the palace from here. Other than that, it was just the hazy barren land. The air vibrated slightly and my ears popped painfully. I jerked around to see Derl in the doorway.

"They will allow you through," he announced with a wide smile.

Whatever the drag was on me was increasing; it took everything I had to move toward the doorway. The weird feeling of passing through maple syrup came and went as I pushed forward, and then I stepped out into a jungle. It was a tangled mass of trees, vines and vegetation, so very different from my own forest that it intimidated me. Out of the corner of my eye, I caught the blur Derl made as he whooshed down the path in front of me.

Turning around, I looked back at this side of the doorway. It looked like the mouth of a dark cave pushed into the side of a mountain. My eyes followed the edges, seeing the outlines of what had to be the original wall that guarded the area. Now it was crumbling, pulled down by the strangling vines, or covered with them and moss, joining up with the trees to make an impressive structure of greens. On both sides of the doorway, there were etchings, words maybe, in some language I had never seen before.

I wanted to go home. I wanted Zack and Granddad and Margo. I wanted to make use of a bathroom, in fact right now would be a good time for that. Looking at the ground, I squished one foot into the leaves until I hit bare dirt. A surge of a peculiar magic welled up inside me and I felt revitalized. I tried to blink, but instead I had the feeling that a massive hand had reached down and taken hold of my head. I felt the magic drawn back out of me and then the world seemed to spin. When my mind cleared, I tried again, but no matter what I did, I couldn't hold the magic inside me now. Guess the magic here wasn't free for the taking.

"Crap!" I screamed at the top of my lungs, only to scare a large number of birds out of the trees above me. They startled me into silence. I decided I'd better remain a bit quieter; I started forward, following the path that wove its way through the dense jungle vegetation. I hoped this was the way Derl had gone, as there was no sign of him. I walked until I came to a crumbling stone wall covered with vines.

I climbed over it, lost my footing, and tumbled down the other side. I landed hard, knocking the air out of myself. When I was able to stand, I discovered that I had fallen into an ancient ruin. Large blackened stones rose through the foliage, giving hints to what the structure must have looked like long ago.

"Wow, *The Jungle Book* could have been filmed here," I muttered as I surveyed the place. At any moment, King Louie and a bunch of apes would start singing "I wanna be like you, hoo hoo". The silliness of it made me want to laugh.

I was surrounded by towering mahogany trees, enormous palms and vines intertwined with everything. The smells and sounds threatened to overpower me; monkeys, that I couldn't see, were screaming amongst the trees, brightly colored macaws and toucans called from the high branches and a distant roar made me jump in alarm. Way too real for me. I wanted to go home but didn't know how to get there if I couldn't blink.

My feet had started to tingle, like just waking up after falling asleep. I glanced down and saw I was sinking in a marsh of decomposing leaves. Pulling one foot loose, it made a sucking noise, then a mushy splat as I put it down again. It instantly sunk in and the tingle came again. I tried a tentative pull and it resisted. I didn't like this place…but so far it was better than Firinn.

Derl had disappeared on me and I didn't want to start screaming for him. I didn't know what else might decide to come get me. I tried to light step out of the marsh, sinking more with each step I took. I really did not want to move farther into the ruins, but I was being left without a choice. When I finally mucked my way over to moss-covered pile of stones, a chill ran down my spine as a thick tentacle of a creeper purposefully shifted places beside me. I felt something on my shoulder and jerked to push whatever it was away. A long vine hung down from the tangled masses of branches above. It moved and touched me again.

I followed its shape up to the greenery above, trying to see what tree it was part of. It was a good thing I did as more vines had begun to push down from the trees towards me. Soon there was no escaping and I was completely surrounded by them. This was so completely insane. I forced myself not to panic. I was in a Meadhan, which meant magic was involved. I tried to move away from them, but the darn things were persistent and more lowered themselves to block my escape.

"Derl!" I screamed as I wiggled out of the way of more of the vines. One vine snaked itself under one of my arms and tried to wrap itself around me. As I struggled, I yelled as loud as I could. "Derl where are you?"

The jungle seemed to come alive with sounds. Loud chirping, monkeys screaming franticly in the underbrush and birds flapping out from the trees overhead. Still I was alone with ugly, touchy vines.

"Stop touching me," I yelled at the vine. At home, plants always minded me...here I think they were laughing at me instead. My good arm was tangled completely and the vine was attempting to lift me off the ground by it; another vine attached itself to my leg and pulled it out from under me. I lost my composure completely at that point and started to scream at the top of my lungs, fighting against the advancing creepers. It seemed that the more I struggled, the more they fought back.

One vine twisted its way around my body and within seconds, I was ten feet off the ground, one arm pulled out straight and the other locked firmly against my body. My legs were completed entangled and twisted in a very uncomfortable position. A tentacle of vine pushed into the front pocket of my sweatshirt and I could feel my player being pushed out. When the vine emerged from the other side of the open-ended pocket, the player went with it. I heard it hit with a thud below.

"Derl!" I screamed again. I was mad as hell that I was tangled in this mess and that it had probably destroyed my MP3 player. I loved that little device. "Derl, where are you?"

"Only Ivy."

Faintly, I heard my name being called from beneath me. I wiggled around as best I could when he fluttered into my line of vision.

"I am sorry. The owner of the Meadhan changed his mind and does not want you here. He is worried that Odive will come looking for you. I am sorry I should not have mentioned his name. I did not know. The owner is going to put you out, I hope to a safe place, inside Alainn," he relayed in a whisper.

"I certainly understand his not wanting Odive to come here, but really? I hate the guy too. I just want to go home!" I shrieked at him. One of the thicker vines was beginning to creep around my head—not a calming feeling, I can assure you.

"Only Ivy, the fey are watching," he whispered, his eyes darting around. "If you wish this situation to conclude differently, now might be a good time to do something."

I stopped my thrashing and glared at him. "Really, Derl? Have you seen where I am? Don't you think I would have done something if I could have?"

The vines abruptly released me...I fell onto the soft goopy ground. Within seconds I was soaked, muddy and covered with dead vegetation. I had to squirm around to right myself and when I looked up, there was a multitude of angry fey staring at me.

"I wouldn't make any sudden moves, Only Ivy," Derl advised, looking none too comfortable himself.

"No shit, Sherlock," I snapped back at him.

One of the fey grunted sternly at me as he moved closer. When he held out his arm towards me, I cringed away. He grunted again and chortled, looking around at the others with him. They chuckled along with the first guy. He turned back to me and reached down, poking me with a bony finger, and then pushed me out of the Meadhan.

CHAPTER 16 – Ivy

I was suddenly lying on soft, tall grass staring up at the sky. The sun beat down on me with bright cheerful warmth. I breathed in deeply and let the clean air fill my lungs. I could smell the fresh earth and foliage around me. It was delicious. I took another deep breath and silently thanked the angry fey for sending me here…wherever *here* was.

My ears started to crackle, like they were trying to pop. I yawned wide and allowed my eardrums to open. Sounds erupted around me as my ears cleared. There was the splashing of water nearby and I sat up. It was a waterfall and it was breathtakingly beautiful. I'd never seen such a spectacular waterfall before. My little one in the Hemlock forest was quaint compared to this one. The water was a clear turquoise color; it shimmered in the rays of sunlight that found their way through the vines hanging from the trees. It was a magical place, and invited me to dive in, clothes and all. The mortals that lived in Alainn did not know how good they had it.

I lay back again and looked up. The sky was deep blue with not one cloud to mar its expanse. The ground beneath me was so soft and warm and I wanted to curl up and sleep. I flung my arms out wide, forgetting for a moment that my one arm was sore. I moaned and squeezed my eyes tight until the pain receded.

This was Alainn, I didn't know where, but it was most definitely somewhere in the mortal realm. I could pull power from here. I lay my hand flat to the ground and pulled the fresh power up into my body and allowed it to heal me from head to toe. It felt like taking a hot bubble bath, all cozy and refreshing. I savored the feeling and then started to pull more into me so I could blink home.

"Not wise pickney," a voice advised. I stopped what I was doing and turned in the direction it had come from.

The voice was ancient, had an odd accent and came from the undergrowth to my right. I opened my eyes and jumped up. A small woman was standing there, looking at me intensely. She cocked her head to the right, then to the left. Her face was deep black, blacker than I had ever seen before and she resembled a raisin that had been left in the sun way too long.

It was her hair that first caught my attention—dreadlocks. They hung to her knees, which wasn't hard since she was bent over, holding on to a twisted wood walking stick. The dreads were so thick and black that they looked like ropes.

"Well, sweetie, I knew you be coming, the Seer done saw it," she said, through blackened, wrinkled lips. I couldn't help but look into her eyes. They were mostly yellow and bloodshot, with huge black pupils the size of dimes.

She started to hobble closer to me, sniffing the air until she was only a foot away from where I lay.

"Aw yes...you be the fey," she said with a wide grin that showed yellowed, crooked teeth. I couldn't help but flinch when she reached out to touch the vine on my face. Her fingers were swollen and twisted, with long yellowish, chipped fingernails. I was assaulted by the smell of her skin, a strange combination of sandalwood and jasmine. When I pulled back, she stopped and gave me a long hard unreadable look.

"Who…What are you?" I asked when I found my voice again. Watching her warily, I got to my feet.

"Why, I am Mother Vondra. Think, pickney, do you not know of me?"

"No. I've never seen you before. How would I know you?" I stammered.

"You wear the band I created for the other. It holds a piece of my soul. Feel for it pickney, it will not harm you." My mind started to spin. What the hell was she talking about? Then a feeling of recognition washed over me and I looked down at my arm, still sporting the band that Zack had put on me. He said that the old Jamaican woman who had made his dreadlocks had given it to him. My head jerked up in shock.

"You…you are the woman Zack was talking about?" My voice cracked as I spoke, barely able to get the words out. "Am I in Jamaica?"

"Yes, pickney. Long story; no time now. The evil one surely will come and we need to be out of his reach."

"What?"

"You heard her. We need to leave, like right now," a rough voice proclaimed next to my ear, startling me. Suddenly my arm was linked with another's. The grip was strong and I looked over to find a girl I had seen yesterday. It was the girl from campus. I don't think I'd ever forget what she looked like or how all her piercings had made me feel. She was the one who had forced that note on me.

"I see you remember me. Too bad you didn't read the damn thing and do what we told you to do. We went to a lot of trouble to get that message to you and you discarded it, didn't you? I would gather that the last few days have been unpleasant for you."

Why did everyone keep describing things with the word *unpleasant*? Unpleasant meant it rained a bit when you were having a picnic or had a flat tire on your bike. It most definitely did not describe all the horrible crap that had been happening to me.

I wasn't sure it would still be there, but I reached into my pocket and was relieved when my fingers touched it. Smugly I pulled out the note and held it up for her to see.

"You should have told me what it was that I needed to run *from*. I thought the druids were playing a trick on me," I retorted reproachfully.

"You are really dense then," she said, snatching the note from my hand.

I wasn't being assaulted with the same horrible smell as I had been the first time we came into contact; now I smelled only the sandalwood and jasmine of the old lady. But just one look at her piercings made me feel the need to puke. I couldn't help myself, I had to pull away. She wouldn't let me though, keeping my arm in a vice-like grip.

I looked down at her hand so I could remove it and saw it was covered with tattoos also, spirals of black intermingled with unusual symbols.

I jerked away with all the strength I had and this time she let me go, laughing as if it were funny.

"There now, Rave. Leave off, you be scaring her," the old lady said, coming to my defense. "We really must leave now. You have no choice but to come with us, pickney. It's the way it has to be."

"Where would you go anyway, huh? Your home

is the first place they will look. At least no one would ever think to look for your skinny ass here. You aren't safe anywhere but with us," the girl, Rave, said in a rather friendly, though still sarcastic manner.

"Bring her along, Rave. Don't be using no magic here, little pickney. Just like the movie shows where detectives always be tracing cell phones, your magic be unique to you. Whoever it is that is after you would be able to find you."

That scared me. I had already used some magic to heal myself. Was that enough for Odive to hone in on my location? The panic started to rise inside me and I struggled to keep myself from shaking.

"Can I ask where you are taking me?" I really did want to get somewhere safe and I did not feel safe right now.

"Somewhere shielded ...I be hoping," she said. I glanced over at Rave and she shot me a dark look.

"Where am I?"

"Jamaica, mon," the girl answered in a heavy Jamaican accent. The old lady chuckled merrily and took my hand.

"I figured that," I snapped at Rave and then turned to the old lady. "I meant why did the fey in the Meadhan send me here? Are you Alltha fey like me?"

"We are the closest point in Alainn to their Meadhan. Come, we have lots to speak of, pickney. Be at peace."

Still confused but somewhat calmer now, when she tugged on my hand, I went with her. I allowed her to guide me to a path shrouded by tall bamboo. Who were these fey? I looked back at the girl following behind us on the path. She puckered her lips and sent an exaggerated kiss at me.   Embarrassed, I turned back around. I could hear her chuckling behind me.

We followed a trail through a thicket of bamboo. I had no idea that bamboo grew in Jamaica. It was dense and prevented much of the sunlight from reaching us. When we finally reached the end of the trail, it was blocked by a very old school bus painted with bright colors. We had to force our way between the bus and the bamboo until we reached the road.

I could see the tops of buildings through the trees and I started to crave the chance for shade. It was sweltering hot on the dirt road and my feet were kicking up dust as we walked, making little dust devils that swirled around my legs. We walked downhill for a time and when we went around a bend in the road, the beginnings of a town appeared. Small, humble houses lined the road. Some were made of wood, others bits of tin sheets and cast-off pieces. Chickens clucked about and happy children with wide, white, toothy grins played. I'd never stood out because of the color of my skin before, but I seemed to here. At least people weren't staring at me because of my purple and red hair. Everyone looked happy and alive with a vibrancy that had nothing to do with their flamboyant clothes.

We walked down the road and people waved or shouted out greetings to Mother Vondra or the girl.

"Morning, Mother."

"Hey Rave, come over tonight for a party."

"Can you send Silver to fix my roof?"

"Mother, my pickney is well now, the tea did its job," one mother called out as we passed by, patting a baby in a sling against her chest.

Light bulbs went off in my head when I heard the

mother speak. I had been wondering why Mother kept calling me pickney. Now I knew it meant child...or maybe baby.

The greetings continued and were all varied and happy. These two were well known and apparently well thought of. I started to relax, feeling safe, safer than I had since the fey had kidnapped me.

Old dusty cars and tour buses passed us, sending up clouds of dust. There was no scariness here, no evil fey trying to kill me, no hint of malice from anyone. The town took me by surprise. One minute we were in another time, and then the real world caught up with us. The makeshift homes were replaced with modest wood and stucco houses. Over the treetops, I could see the blue-green ocean and a soft white beach. Tall hotels dotted the shoreline, and I really hoped that was our destination.

"What town is this?" I asked, taking in the sight.

"Manchioneal," Rave said as she walked out ahead of us, waving at someone who honked his horn as he drove past.

Manchioneal looked like a town, a real town, that I could have come across on the Oregon coast. There were of course the run-down tin structures and clapboard homes, but there were also shops and fancy cars and people who looked like they had just too much money. There were wide gates with ornate signs naming resorts I had never heard of. I stopped to look down one long driveway to gawk at the lavishness of the place. Mother and Rave had continued on and when Rave realized I had stopped, she ran back and pulled me away. With one last look of longing, I went with her.

We passed several other resorts and then moved

into what must have been the town proper. I followed Mother as she moved from the dirt road onto a thin sidewalk, and we stayed on it as we moved deeper into the town. Mother eventually turned onto a paved walkway between two buildings. Sounds of music and laughter assaulted me as we exited from between the buildings into a marketplace. It was quite clear that I was in a tourist town as I looked at the variety of stalls and shopkeepers displaying their wares to tourists.

The vacationers were working hard at blending in with the locals. But rich white tourists looked like rich white tourists, no matter what they wore. It wasn't their skin color as much as the way they walked and spoke. The way they picked items up in the market, inspected them and smiled what they thought was a nice smile. I only saw, "Yuck, like I would buy that!" on their faces. Chickens mingled underfoot and as we neared the outdoor market stalls, the sounds and smells intensified.

I watched as Rave stopped at one stall and dug through a pile of used clothing. It looked like an outdoor thrift store. Margo would love this place. Rave picked up a couple of items, spoke with the man behind the stall and they shared a laugh, both looking over at me.

Looking down, I saw that I was covered in dried mud. I must look a mess.

"Here," Rave said as she came over. She tossed a pair of shorts and a flamboyant yellow tank top into my hands before she turned and started walking away swiftly. In just moments, I lost sight of her.

"Thanks!" I called out after her.

"Come dear; let's get you home so you can change," the old lady said laughing joyfully. I was starting to think of her as *Mother*, the name everyone kept calling her. It did seem to fit. She seemed to know everyone and care about everyone.

Making our way along the road, I had to stop myself from wanting to linger and look at each of the stalls and shops. They seemed filled with laughter and bright colors. It drew me, life... a happy, real life. I couldn't help but feel better.

Mother turned down a side street filled with little shops with perky signs gracing the windows. Most were hand painted, very charming and all described what wares were to be found inside. We turned yet another corner onto a lane that looked less traveled. The buildings were taller and blocked out most of the sunlight. Signs advertising palm readings or spiritual cleansings captured my eye and when we stopped before a red door that read *Voodoo and Fortune Telling,* I wasn't surprised.

She opened the door and went in with me following curiously. Rave was behind a counter with a young man. His skin was a delicious chocolate color. He grinned widely at me, showing the whitest teeth I had ever seen.

"You found her, Mother," he said, as if finding me was a great prize.

I had to stop and look around. It was a real voodoo shop. Shelves held mason jars filled with herbs and incense. Cool shaped bottles held oils with little labels indicating what they were for. Another shelf was filled with candles and little books tied up with ribbons. Voodoo dolls and little mojo bags lay on a table in the middle, mixed in with an odd assortment of feathered jewelry. *Spells of all kinds,* the little sign stated. I thought it should have said *Smells of all kinds* as the shop was packed with merchandize that emitted exotic scents. Incense burned on in a little dish on the counter, sending up spirals of smoke. It was a heavy, earthy potpourri of aromas and I started to feel faint. I wondered if this was the place where Zack had his dreads put in.

"Come, pickney, you need to wash up and change," Mother said, taking my hand as she clucked her tongue at me. I followed her through a doorway strung with beads into a back room filled with boxes of inventory. A small flight of stairs led up and another down. She chose the one going up, and I trailed behind.

A door at the top of the stairs opened into a little apartment. The walls were white washed and the furniture was an eccentric mixture of mismatched items. Everything had seen better days, but all of it was clean, bright and cheerful.

"There, child…" Mother said pointing to a closed door. I nodded and went over to it, opening it gingerly. A bathroom; just a normal bathroom with a cracked pink toilet and a claw foot tub. Looking back at her I smiled, grateful, and went in and closed the door behind me.

I took a shower, standing under the lukewarm water for as long as I could, washing my hair and body thoroughly.

A big, fluffy towel had been laid out on the sink for me, along with some undergarments that hadn't been there when I'd gotten into the shower. I figured that Mother must have brought them in for me. I dried myself off and fingered my hair out before I held up the panties. They were thongs and I really hoped that Mother didn't wear this type. Not a sight I wanted to think about on the old, wrinkled lady. I pulled them on, then the shorts. They were a really tight squeeze, but they fit none the less. The wild shirt was lightweight and bright yellow with large pink flowers on it. I pulled it over my head and looked at myself in the mirror. I didn't look too bad.

There was toothpaste lying on the counter, along with a toothbrush. I quickly brushed my teeth. It felt good to have clean teeth again. Now I was ready to deal with whatever was going to happen next.

When I emerged from the bathroom, the apartment was empty. I took my time inspecting it. There were no personal pictures, but lots of hanging objects. Feathers and bits of wood with strange writing on them hung from hooks in the ceiling. Handmade afghans covered the old furniture, and more of them were being used as curtains.

The kitchen held little more than the basics. The refrigerator was a small one, and the stove was just a hot plate. Sitting on the counter was a paper plate with a sandwich and some fruit. Hoping it was meant for me, I took it and sat at the metal dining table. It looked like it had been recovered from the 50s, something that Marmaw would have liked. I smiled at the memory of her and ate the sandwich quickly, then found a cup and filled it with water from the sink.

I thought of home and considered blinking back to my forest just to see what was happening and let them know I was okay. Then I remembered I shouldn't use magic right now and pushed the thought aside. When I was done eating, I cleaned up after myself and then went down the stairs to the shop below.

Rave and the young man looked up when I came in. A couple of customers were just leaving and Rave was quick to follow them to the door. She locked it after them and turned a sign in the window around to *closed*.

"Come, Mother is waiting," she said as she finished her task and started to walk past me. The young man did the same, smiling broadly at me. I followed as they went into the back room and took the stairs down.

CHAPTER 17 – Ivy

As I entered the room, I was met with a strange sight. I had expected to find a dark room, maybe an altar with blood and some ghastly rite being conducted. Instead Mother Vondra sat in a rocking chair…knitting. Around her, seated on a bunch of mismatched sofas and old overstuffed chairs was a group of young people.

Rave had already sat down and patted the spot next to her.

Going over, I sat down and pulled my legs up. The sofa was old, but clean and extremely comfy. The group looked like maybe a youth group having a meeting. Every one of them was wearing clean, cheerful clothing, like they had just spent the day in the sun. Girls and guys; some sporting dreads like Zack's; some blonds and some red-heads; clean-cut or Goth. They were just normal-looking kids you would find on any college campus.

One looked like he had been surfing most of his life, his tan so dark I didn't know where he might have originated. There was only one thing similar about them. All had tattoos next to their eyes that matched Rave's. A circle with a dot in the center.

I realized as I inspected them that they were doing the same to me with barely concealed anticipation. The guy with the tan held up his hand when I looked at him.

"Hi, I'm Silver."

The girl next to him looked like she had left a prep school to come to this party.

"I'm Cinder." Around the room, one by one, they introduced themselves. Silver, Cinder, Bran, Chara, Darcy, Coco, Talon and Adar. Rave sneered at me, daring me to make her speak her name. I let it go. I'd never remember them all anyway.

A microwave dinged and the one named Bran got up and hurried over to it. When he opened the door, the smell of popcorn filled the room. He pulled out a bag and, munching it, sat down again. He saw me looking and held it out in offering. I shook my head and looked instead at the old lady.

"So, pickney...there is someone that wishes to speak with you," Mother said, rocking back and forth. I waited silently. No one in the room spoke, but I saw the younger members of the group glancing at each other as if they were worried.

The rocking stopped as she leaned forward. "It might be a bit of a surprise to you, so we would like to prepare you for it first," she said as she relaxed back into the chair and started to rock again.

"You see, this be my family," she said motioning around the room at the young people. "We are all that is left. We have kept ourselves apart from the world, living quiet lives...while we wait for the balance to return."

She spoke very quietly and I knew what she was saying somehow meant a lot to her and her *family*. Most of them did not look like they could be blood relations, but I did understand that a person's family was not just about blood ties. What I didn't understand was her saying that they kept themselves apart and were waiting for a balance to return. Everyone we passed in the town seemed to know them and were very friendly towards them.

"Mother, is this really necessary?" Rave asked from beside me. "Ivy's a big girl, aren't you?" she asked, glancing at me. She didn't give me time to answer. "Let's stop with all the secrecy and just get on with it. I'm uncomfortable having her out here in the open."

"If you think it best," Mother replied in her calm voice. But then Mother started to cough, a deep hacking cough that sounded like it must hurt dreadfully. The girl called Cinder hurried over to the microwave. We all waited in silence while Cinder made a cup of tea and brought it over to her. Mother sipped it and when her coughing had subsided, she handed the cup back to Cinder.

"Come, Pickney," Mother said as she labored to stand, using her cane to steady herself. Silver moved in front of her and hurried to pull aside a curtain at the back of the room. Behind it was a faded wooden door. He opened it to reveal smooth blackness. What was odd was that the light from the outer room did not even begin to penetrate past the doorframe.

I got up and took a couple of steps closer. I couldn't see anything other than the black. It could be a small closet or a huge room—I couldn't tell.

She hobbled into the darkness and disappeared. I looked around the room and everyone had stood and formed a line, with Rave directly behind me. She put her hand on my back and pushed me forward. Once my foot had been touched by the black, she shoved and I found myself stumbling forward.

Rave pushed me again and I twisted around to tell her to knock it off, but she only pushed me again.

"You need to move out of the way so everyone can come in," she said as she moved around me and kept going. My eyes followed her and I saw that I was in a large white space. There were columns set throughout, providing a sense of division from various rooms. It was a very modern bit of architecture. I hurried to catch up with her, taking in the contemporary furnishings with nothing short of wonder. It was night and day from the basement we had just left.

"What is this place?" I asked Rave.

"It's our safe house. We live here. Out there is just for show. Normally we transport in, but we did not want to take the chance of using magic with you around," she explained as she came to the entrance of a large round nook and motioned for me to go in first. With a sense of surprise, I realized I needed to rethink my first impressions of these fey.

"Is this a cave, underground?" I asked looking around.

"Yep."

It was the coolest cave ever. The ceiling was well over fifty feet high, but unlike most caves the ceiling was bare of any irregularities of stalagmites. It was rounded and smooth, as were the walls and multiple columns that peppered the open area. In fact, everything was curved in some manner and chalk white. There were numerous curved fireplaces set in walls and all had cheery fires crackling in them. Scattered around the expanse were various seating areas. Soft curved sofas, chairs and lounges were arranged either in front of the fireplaces or in loose circles with round low tables in the middle. All of the furnishings were in soft pale hues of pink, blue and green. I was astounded at how beautiful it all was, even though it was so unadorned.

"How do you protect it? Is it like a Meadhan?" I asked, hoping she would answer.

"Coco put a protective barrier around the outside of it. One of her unique talents. Nothing can get through it, not even magic," she answered in her normal patronizing voice.

Just then, Cinder walked past us and up to one of the columns. I watched as the girl leaned down and reached her hands into what looked like an outgrowth on the side of a tree...a *burl* I thought to myself. They were not uncommon on trees in Oregon. She cupped her hands and brought them up to her face. Sparkling water glistened from her fingers as she splashed it over herself. As she stepped back, she started to hum and the air around her shimmered.

Silver and the others formed a line behind her and when she was finished, each in turn did the same.

"Purifying Ritual," Rave said at my ear. "You will need to do it also. I will teach you the melody." I twisted my lips considering this, but then figured why not, what could it hurt?

We waited our turn and I tried to listen carefully to what each was humming. It was a sound like none I had ever heard before. It resonated in a drifting sound, then seemed to cascade downward for a few seconds and ended with a gentle splash.

Rave took her turn and then moved out of the way for me to step forward. I looked down and could see that the burl was like a bowl attached to the column. It was filled with water that swayed and glittered...I wondered if it was alive.

"Cup your hands, gather some Varese and spread it over your face," she instructed me.

"This isn't water?" I asked, looking down at the liquid again.

"Similar, it's called Varese."

When in Rome, I thought and put my hands into the Varese. It was warm and seemed to soak into my hands, making them tingle. I cupped my hands and leaned down to do as I had seen the others do. When I touched my face with it, the tingles built until my whole body was covered with goose bumps.

"Now look at the pillar and hum what you see."

I looked up. My vision was a bit obstructed by the Varese in my eyes, but to my surprise, I could read what was written. I started to hum, understanding exactly what was required. The goose bumps dissolved into pure pleasure and I took a deep breath as I completed the hum.

"Wow, that was…" I didn't have the words for it.

"I know," Rave said with a snicker. "Damn, she was right."

"Who?"

"You will see, come on."

Still feeling the effects of the Varese, I followed Rave through the space. Several times we came close to the walls and lines of writing appeared as we passed by.

"What is that?"

"Trillas. Our prayers, I guess," Rave responded in a bored tone.

We continued walking through a maze of rooms until she finally stopped at a large alcove and gestured for me to go in.

There was a grouping of curved aqua loveseats. Mother was sitting facing me and another person was sitting with her back to me. The person stood and turned to face me. My head started to spin and I was sure I was going to faint. I wobbled and Rave took hold of my arm.

"You can do this, Ivy," Rave said from behind.

I inhaled. I couldn't move, couldn't speak. I was frozen with shock.

There in front of me stood Marmaw.

She had started to cry, and tears ran down her face. She took a step towards me and I jerked backwards and bumped into Rave.

"Suck it up, sweet pea," she put her hand on my back and pushed me gently forward.

It wasn't my Marmaw. It couldn't be. Marmaw was dead, delivered up to the Eilibear by Skyler and then killed by them. I never even got to say goodbye to her.

She continued toward me and reached her arms out. A squeak of fear escaped before I could stop it and I turned my eyes away from her.

"Ivy? Oh Ivy, it is me. I'm so sorry, my dear."

I couldn't look up, I didn't dare. If I did, I would start to have hope that it was Marmaw and I couldn't allow that hope to grow. She was dead. Granddad had brought her body back and she was buried in the garden. I started to sob and then to hiccup uncontrollably. My darn nose started to run and I wiped the snot away with the back of my hand.

A hand appeared with a handkerchief. It was dainty with yellow and purple pansies in the corners. Marmaw's handkerchief. I remember watching her when she embroidered the flowers onto it.

"Wipe your nose, Ivy. You were always such a mess when you cried," the woman who looked like Marmaw said. I wouldn't look at her, I just couldn't.

But I did look up at Mother and whisper, "Why

are you torturing me?"

"Ruth, really dear, you are a sight. Look at me!" Marmaw demanded. My head jerked up automatically. She had used the name she had given me when she'd found me. I knew that tone of voice. I never disobeyed Marmaw when she spoke like that.

She took hold of my hands and hers were warm.

"There now, that's better. Oh my, you have grown tall," she said smiling. I was eye-level with her and when I had last seen her, I had only reached her shoulder. Hope began to grow and I pushed it down.

"It is really me, Ivy. You must have figured out from my writings that I had powers also, just like you and Milton. I knew what Skyler was going to do before she did it, so I sought help from some new friends. It was to protect not only myself, but you and Milton as well."

"But..." I didn't know where to start. She had known what Skyler would do to me, and she'd let it happen? She had known that I would be all alone and have to find out about being a fey on my own?

"Ivy, I did leave you with the writings. I did what I could," she said, answering my unspoken questions. "Besides you have so many untapped powers. I knew all you had to do was logically think it out and you could do anything you needed to do."

I gulped and really looked at her. It looked like Marmaw. It spoke like Marmaw and acted like Marmaw, but how could I truly be sure?

"Do you remember my tomato plants? You were the best little gardener in the world," she said with a smug grin.

Only Marmaw knew about that. It was our secret

and not even Granddad knew that I had always told the little plants to grow.

"Oh geez, it *is* really you!" I cried and flung my arms around her.

"Yes, dear. It really is," she said and hugged me tight. "There is so much I need to tell you and I want to know everything that has happened since I left."

I nodded agreement against her shoulder, but did not release her. I didn't want to let her go ever again.

CHAPTER 18 – Zack

Zack wasn't too shocked by Akneeta's declaration that she had been watching him, as he had been watching her also. It was her next words that gave him pause.

"I like Ivy and would like to meet her someday. You have led a very exciting life as an Alltha," she said.

"How?" Zack asked, leaning forward to watch her face.

"Gunilla, the one Odive killed…"

"This Odive killed someone?" Telfer growled, instantly on guard.

Zack put up his hand to stop Telfer from asking more questions. He wanted to know how he had been watched.

"Gunilla was a Seer. We had little to do in our confinement. At first she gave us news of the battles and what was happening with the druids and fey at large. After a time, we, I, lost interest in such matters. I was more concerned about what was transpiring with my parents. Father had already submitted himself to the enchantments and had been transformed into the new version of a druid, a warrior to replace what we were to have been.

"I volunteered to be enchanted to join the fight and it did not go as planned. Mum was distraught at my disappearance, but no more distraught than she had been when I was transformed into a Valkyrie. Father was not as upset for the loss of me. He came to see me as only a monster and was relieved at the Valkyries removal from

Alainn. I knew when Mum grew heavy with child…you, and was told when you were born. It broke my heart that I could not be there with my family," she said solemnly.

"Gunilla told you all this?"

"At first, but then we discovered that if she laid her hand on the Valkyrie stone, the barrier would show her the outside world. Gunilla became very adept at manipulating these images and finding events through time, or even specific people. It was like the televisions the mortals created that tell stories with people…" she leaned closer and looked at Zack excitedly. "I very much want to see one of these."

Telfer and Zack looked at each other with amazement, both trying hard not to chuckle at her enthusiasm. Akneeta looked mildly embarrassed at her confession and, red-faced, continued with her tale.

"You were born and then Mum paid the price for father's new power. She allowed it to happen, didn't fight it and was seemingly not even upset about it. Father showed no remorse, from what I could see, and my hatred for him has festered every moment since," she cried and shook her head. "But now…it's different, my hatred is fading, as is the enchantment."

"So you know of the Gorffen?"

She looked up at Zack with tear-filled eyes. "Yes, I know of it. It is the cost the magic of the Dywel demands of the Warrior Druid. You fought it and still fight against it and your friend, Ivy, fought against it as well. Gunilla was very excited to tell me of what happened. It was the last vision she shared with me before she was killed," she said lowering her voice solemnly. When she looked up, her eyes moved to Zack's arm. "Can I see it? The vine of power Ivy created?"

Zack shrugged and took off his flannel. He leaned over so she could see it better. She reached out and ran her hands over it.

"This Ivy is very powerful. I've never heard of anyone who could cast an enchantment such as this, nor one that would halt the Gorffen."

"So there's really no way to stop it?" Zack asked gravely.

She shook her head solemnly and sighed. Zack could feel his heart start to race. What if he was never able to stop this? The thought that he would have to stay away from Ivy forever was very scary...and forever was a very long time.

"So, who is Odive?" Telfer inquired, effectively changing the subject.

"Odive works with the fey Elders. He is a hideous fey. **Gunilla** spoke of him much during the first days of our internment. We had little contact with any from the Citadel prior to our transformation. A call for volunteers from the Sisterhood was made. Many did so, but only six were chosen. I had never met the others until the day we all gathered for the special ceremony. We went into the Citadel chamber with one druid whose face was hidden with a hooded cloak. He told us to place our hands on the Sunstone and close our eyes. The druid cast the enchantment and then we were the Valkyries. I now believe the druid with us was Odive.

"He is the one who released us this morn and I do not think he knows that all of the bonds we possessed as Valkyries have started to fade. Like Kianna's power over the other Valkyries or our shared powers or the manifestations of our physical forms," she said as she touched her hair.

Zack had somehow forgotten that she was a Valkyrie. Before, she had looked almost indistinguishable from the others. Their matching hair had been long, straight tresses of silver and all had deep cobalt blue eyes. It had been hard to tell them apart. He saw that Akneeta's hair was no longer pure silver, but was shot with sandy brown strands, the same color as his, and starting to form waves. Her features had softened and her eyes had slanted slightly and had a hint of green in them. Zack knew that she was beginning to look like him.

"I believe I am reverting to my natural form. I used to resemble Mum," she said softly.

"I'm sorry, guys, but I want to know more about this Odive character. Is he short and thin, with a serious superiority complex?" Telfer interjected.

"I don't know what a superiority complex is, but Odive is short and does not resemble a normal fior-ghlan fey."

"Fior-ghlan?" Zack asked, working hard to pronounce the unknown word.

"A pure blood, a fey that has not altered form after leaving Firinn. All druids are fior-ghlan," she explained patiently.

"I think that guy is at the camp. I saw him talking with Kianna, and I swear he was ripping her a new one and then he vanished with her."

"Ripping her a new what?" Akneeta asked innocently. Zack had to cough to cover a laugh that started to erupt and shot Telfer an annoyed look.

"Sorry, wrong choice of words. He was mad at her about something," Telfer explained.

"Probably mad that she had failed to seduce my brother. That was part of the mission she agreed to."

"Seduce me? Why?" Zack asked.

"I do not know. However, he made it very clear when he released us that he wanted you distracted and kept away from your friend Ivy," she informed him. "My only thought was if I were to be released, I would find a way to gain retribution from father for what he did to Mum. But as soon as we arrived here, my thoughts began to clear and by the time the battle was over, I discovered that I was not mad at Father...and did not wish to fight this war any longer. I know Kianna and the others enjoy their role as warriors, but I do not. I want to explore the new Alainn and form a different life." She stopped, waiting for him to respond.

Zack chuckled to himself. His sister's words seemed to mirror his own feelings. He studied her features. She had continued altering as they had sat talking. Her hair was almost completely sandy blond now and had developed tight ringlets of curls.

"You overheard us?" Telfer asked, surprised.

"Yes. You tried to leave and could not. Zack you have very strong magic, but I think we should try with the three of us since it did not work for you."

Zack agreed. He moved over beside her and waited for Telfer to do the same, then together they attempted to blink. Again, nothing happened.

"Odive's containment enchantment is too strong," Akneeta said when they opened their eyes.

"We will just have to wait until he decides it's time to move to another location, I guess," Telfer said as he stood. "Let's get back. I need some shuteye."

"Are you coming?" Zack inquired of Akneeta.

"No, I will stay here, hidden. I do not wish to be with the others. If you come back to this place, you will not see me. Call out my name and I will know you are seeking me," she said decisively.

She waved her arm in an arch and the full impact of the wind hit them. Zack looked down at his sister and she smiled softly back at him. Telfer had started walking back up the beach and after a moment, Zack followed. When he looked back, both the fire and Akneeta had vanished from sight.

CHAPTER 19 – Zack

Zack caught up with Telfer as he entered the camp. The bonfire had died down and the camp was quiet. Zack had been hoping that his dad would still be around so he could pull him off to the side and maybe, for once, have a truthful conversation with him.

Shit, he mumbled to himself. No one was about, but there were soft giggles and whispers coming from a number of the tents. It seemed that the other druids were not opposed to being on friendly terms with the Valkyries or the other female druids. He wondered what the other Valkyries really looked like in their original forms. The druids might be in for quite a shock when they woke up tomorrow next to someone that looked different.

Telfer aimed towards their line of tents, but Zack hesitated. His friend turned to look at him curiously. Zack made a snap decision and changed directions heading toward the larger shelters set up behind the others.

"Where are you going?" Telfer whispered at his back.

"To see Dad. I need to get back to Ivy and, one way or another, I will," he replied without stopping.

Telfer sprinted over to him and blocked his way.

"Zack, stop. You can't just wake him up now. He'll be in a foul mood and you'll just end up in a fight that wakes everyone."

"Don't care. I need some answers," he said between clenched teeth.

Telfer moved out of his way, but didn't leave. Instead, he started to walk with him. Zack circled the druid's tents until he could see the one he was looking for. No lights showed from within and as he reached out to grab the tent flap, Telfer's hand stopped him.

"Don't do it, Zack," he implored in a harsh whisper.

"Why? Dad has lots of explaining to do. About the Gorffen, about my sister and about my mom. I don't know about you, but I am sick and tired of druids, our *grand purpose* and this"—he waved his arm around as if to encompass everything— "whole freaking mess. I don't want to fight the Eilibear, I don't want to have my life dictated by him or the druids or anyone." He had to stop to breathe. He was still whispering, though he wanted to yell. His throat felt raw.

"Everything you said is true and I acknowledge you know your dad better than I do, but do you really think he's just going to let you rant at him or answer any of your questions? Or for that matter, just let you leave? He's the most stringent of any of the Warrior Druids I've met. He lives for this shit. What do you think he will do when his own son tells him he wants nothing to do with it?"

Zack stopped and looked at Telfer. He was making valid points and Zack knew it. He felt deflated. He closed his eyes and did the meditation exercise Ivy had taught him. He arched his back and rolled his head side to side, letting his neck crack. He had to release the tension and anger that had been driving him. He couldn't make stupid mistakes. When he opened his eyes a few moments later, he felt calmer but no less determined.

"Fine. I'll not wake the beast just to fight a losing

battle...but I can't sleep. There is too much going on inside my head," he said as he started walking back towards the center of the camp. He motioned over to the remains of the bonfire and together they maneuvered around tent posts in the dark to find a place to sit.

Unaware of anything but his own inner turmoil, he picked up a stick and started to poke around in the fire. Small embers glowed as he turned the charred bits of wood. It wasn't long before he had a small blaze glowing before them. Pulling a piece of log closer to the fire, he sat down, staring blankly into the flames. Telfer had found a soft bit of sand and had already nodded off. His snores and the sound of the distant waves joined in rhythm. Zack barely noticed.

The night had grown cold, crickets and other night creatures were singing their songs, along with the sound of crashing waves. He thought about Ivy; what she was doing right now and if she had forgiven him. He fingered the lines of vine that wrapped around his arm and was glad that she had given it to him. It was a constant reminder that he wasn't in control of himself and he needed to get that control back.

The sound of footfalls nearby caused him to look up. Kianna stood just behind him. She had thrown a long hooded cape over her dress and Zack couldn't stop himself from thinking of little red riding hood. Her facial features hadn't altered like Akneeta's had, but her hair was now more blond than silver. She smiled sweetly at him and he looked away without responding in kind.

"Looks like your friend isn't much company," she said softly, her voice silky. He paid her no mind as she sat down beside him. "I'm sure I can be better company than him." She purred as she inched closer to him.

"Where is the rest of your gang?" he asked as he stood to pick up a small log and lay it on top of the fire. When he sat back down, he made sure he was further away.

"Oh, they have all found nice warm beds to sleep in. How about you, would you like some help falling asleep?" The wave of her magic seemed to roll over him. He knew what it was and, frankly, he was in no mood for games. He absently pushed the magic back and turned his head to look straight at her.

"No, I would not and please drop the glamour. You are wasting your magic."

"Well, aren't you the strong druid. You are the first who could do that, you know. I'm sorry, old habit and all, but you are different and I like different," she sighed wistfully, and reached out to touch a lock of his long hair.

Zack pulled his head away, out of her reach and moved to the far edge of the log.

"You don't have to be rude." Her voice had taken on an edge and he tried to inspect her face in the flickering of the fire. She might have been pouting; he'd seen other girls who didn't get their way make that weird face. Then it struck him.

"You said you were locked away for a very long time, right?"

"Yes. A very long time...it was boring and lonely. Oh so very lonely."

"Right. But your speech is like everyone else's. You don't even have much of an accent. Why?"

That seemed to catch her off guard. She leaned in slightly and Zack felt the air around him being drawn towards her. He heaved the air back and knew he had achieved success when the tightness in his chest receded. She grimaced and then sat back in a huff. She pulled her cloak tighter around her body, and then spoke in a cavalier tone, as if nothing had happened.

"I'm a highborn druid, from the purest of true blood fey, as all my sisters are. We are the fíor-ghlan fey. I can speak in any manner I wish or need to. What do you want? Vis antique loqui? Vis audire verba mea nativitate? Along with her voice and the language she spoke, her physical form changed also. She morphed into a dark-skinned woman with short curly hair.

"Or maybe wouldth thou prefer I spake as mine mother wouldth?" Her accent went heavy and old, and with the words a power seemed to radiate out. Old and strong, menacing…and it startled him as she morphed again, this time to a red-haired voluminous woman.

"Or maybe it's the women of your day that you prefer." And she morphed yet again into a famous model.

Zack felt chills run down his spine as he watched her continue, morphing into other women. At last she sighed disappointedly and gave him a knowing look.

"I know what it is you like," she cooed and she morphed into a version of Ivy. She was mocking him, and still trying to move closer so she could touch him.

"You are fíor-ghlan." She leaned in and sniffed the air around him, then looked up at him with a wicked smirk on Ivy's face. "Oh you are definitely fíor-ghlan, you have the fragrance of pure fey…and a hint of something more. Combined, we would be formidable…so very strong…we would rule over all." A glimmer of fiendish delight sparkled in Ivy's eyes and she licked her lips as she leaned in even closer.

"Where did you obtain this strong magic, Zaccheus? It's pure...and ancient. I would like to feel it..." and she reached out to take hold of him suddenly.

He jolted up and backed away, looking at her with disdain. She instantly changed back to her normal self and watched him.

"Whatever it is you want from me; you cannot have it. I didn't understand half of what you said, and really don't care to. Keep your distance from me," he spat as he backed away.

She reacted like a normal girl whose advances had been rejected. She jumped up and gave him a condescending look.

"You stupid fey...you stupid male fey. All of you are alike, small minded, rooted in your honor and fears. I'll not stay away. You will come to me...they all do." She bent forward, her face twisted in rage. "You have no choice, you know," she hissed at him. In the glow from the fire, her face contorted with anger.

"I always have a choice. And I choose to have nothing to do with you," he said as he stepped backward until he felt Telfer, still asleep on the ground. He nudged him, none too gently, with his foot.

"Wake up, let's get to our tent."

Telfer sat up, rubbing sleep out of his eyes and immediately saw Kianna. The look on her face shocked him awake and he rose quickly, keeping his eyes on her.

"Yeah, let's go." Then out of the corner of his mouth, "what the hell happened? She looks like she wants to rip you to shreds."

"I know."

Together they made their way over to the small tent they had left their packs in and ducked inside. Zack looked back once to see the Valkyrie still standing there, her fury visibly raging around her, manifested by red sparks of fire. Her nostrils flared and her eyes narrowed to slits as she glared at him. He could feel the magic she was attempting to throw at him. It buzzed around his head like a gnat and he pushed it away with contempt and just a little fear.

The woman definitely had a personal agenda that he was messing up by not playing along and he did not want to find out what it was.

CHAPTER 20 - Margo

Margo appeared, hovering over the rail of the dock she had seen the picture of. It was early morning and no one was around. She landed on the rail and looked out over the marsh. It was framed by snow-capped hills and the water had a thin layer of ice on it. It was freezing and she was glad she had gone to the store to get the thermal clothes.

Removing her pack, she got out the little compass Granddad had given her and held it up. She needed to go north and waited until the compass showed her the way. Making sure she had her bearings right, she put the compass in her vest pocket and zipped it up. It was starting to rain with soft slushy droplets. She pulled out a pair of ski googles and put them in place, then put her pack back on.

Taking a deep breath, she focused on the farthest point she could see, in the direction she needed to go, and blinked.

Blink and focus, blink and focus, rest, eat an apple from her pack, blink and focus, blink and focus; it became a game for her. How far could she go, how strongly did she have to focus on something? It was noon by the time she reached the first island. There wasn't any evidence of the Eilibear and she couldn't feel any magic around her. She really hoped that Granddad had the right information on where the druids had gone. Uncle Carmen and the others could have been lying. There was always that possibility, though she didn't want to think about it. She blinked from island to island until she ended up at a place called Baykovo. She knew she had gone too far since she surely was in Russia now. It was starting to get dark, making the search even more difficult.

She started back, this time flying out over the sea, weaving from east to west, looking for smaller islands she might have missed. It wasn't feeling magic that told her she had found it, but a weird sense that she didn't want to go that way. In her mind, a small voice started to tell her danger was ahead and to go back. It was an odd sensation and she knew it had to be a spell to keep people away.

Pushing against the peculiar intrusion into her mind, she forced herself to keep moving in that direction. She kept one hand out in front of her, testing the air for the feel of magic, like Granddad had taught her. When she thought she felt something, she angled downward.

She wasn't sure if this was the right place or not until she hit the barrier. She slammed into it hard and started to fall in a daze, sliding down the sloped side of the barrier. She caught herself before she hit the water and had to shake herself in midair as she rose back up and inspected the invisible wall. It was smooth and soft and all magic. There was a little light from the stars and she couldn't see anything but water. The island had to be inside. She started to fly around the perimeter of the barrier and had almost given up hope when she saw something out of place. The end of a wooden pier rose out of the water, cut off on one side like a cleaver had come down on it. It was only a couple of feet long, but enough for her to land on. Whoever had made the enchantment had made it just a bit too small and missed enclosing the pier within its boundaries.

Zack had to be inside, he just had to. But how to get in through this thing? She edged up to the side of the barrier and leaned against it. It was solid and smooth and hummed with magic. She wondered if this was what the barrier that Granddad had put up around the private glade was like to everyone else. Maybe he would know how to get through it…but she didn't want to leave and go ask. She sat cross-legged on the pier rail, staring at it, with the sound of the waves all around her. After a time, she looked down at the water and the waves that rolled beneath her and then kept looking, something didn't look right, but she couldn't figure out what it was.

The darkness didn't help, but she couldn't shake the feeling that something about the waves was odd. Bits of seaweed rode the waves in tangled masses, swirling as the breakers moved. She had spent a lot of time on the beach in Coos Bay and these waves looked like the waves when the tide was coming in. They were strong, throwing their spray up at her and rolled forward into what looked like the open ocean. *It's an illusion,* she realized suddenly.

She leaned against the barrier as she watched, tapping it with her fingers…until a thought occurred to her. She fluttered up and out over the water and then up to the barrier. Keeping her hand on it, she allowed herself to sink, taking a deep breath and holding it in as she entered the freezing water.

The water was cold, bitter cold. Her little wings felt like they had frozen and she was worried they would break. She held her breath and allowed the wave to push her forward, hoping she would be propelled through. And she was, hitting the sandy bottom and fighting to rise up out of the water. Her wings were useless, so she shifted and found herself rolling over and over again under the violence of the waves. With strong strokes, she swam upward and broke the surface gasping for air. She caught sight of the beach and, with the help of the waves pushing her, swam towards land.

When she could feel sand under her feet, she stood up, trying to keep upright as the waves hit against her back. It didn't take long for her to reach the shore. She was freezing, but she had found the way through the barrier. She did a little dance of joy before she shifted once more into a Sprite, only to discover she couldn't fly with wet wings. With a sigh, she shifted back and started to run up the beach, hoping to find some sign of where Zack was.

It didn't take long. She could see the glow from a bonfire set back from the beach and angled towards it. The camp came into sight and she shifted into her small form so as not to be seen, just in case any of the druids were around. Her wings were still soggy, but flappable and she slowly moved toward the fire. The fire was small, mostly just embers, but she could feel heat radiating from it. No one was around, so she got as close to one of the embers as she could. She warmed herself and allowed herself to dry out before she looked around.

It was late and it looked like everyone had gone into their tents to sleep. She could hear snores and tried to decide what the best way to find Zack would be. She didn't think there was a way she could *feel* for him, so she was left with having to go into each tent to look for him. At least his hair was different enough that he would be easy to see in the dark.

She rose up and started to fly toward the first tent. Forms appeared and she rose higher as she came close.

Two female fey she didn't know were standing next to the tent, whispering in hushed tones. One seemed really upset about something and the other was attempting to calm her. Margo didn't have time to stop and eavesdrop, though she was curious. She stayed away from them; instead she went to the front of the tent and found a small opening and flew inside. A couple of druids were asleep, one not alone. Another female fey, this one naked as a jaybird, was curled beside him, her hair in disarray across his naked form. She was grateful to see it wasn't Zack and quickly flew out the small opening and back into the night air.

She went into each tent, one by one, finding many druids but no Zack.

As she neared the seventh tent, she thought she heard Zack's voice. If he was talking with someone, she hoped it was Telfer. He was the nicest of the druids that had come into the forest and the only one who had ever spoken to her. The others treated her like she was not worth noticing, like she was beneath them.

The tent had been zipped, but she was able to inch through at the very bottom. The interior was dark, but she could see the shape of Zack sitting cross-legged against the back of the tent, and another form lying flat on his back with only his underwear on.

"I think you need to watch yourself around her," Telfer whispered.

"You don't have to tell me. I just want to get out of this place," Zack scowled.

"Well, we can't do anything until morning. I'm bushed," Telfer said with a groan as he rolled onto his side and pulled the sleeping bag up over his face.

"Zack?" Margo whispered. "Zack, its Margo."

She quickly changed shape.

"Margo? It is really you?" Zack cried out as she appeared in front of him. He got up and took a couple of steps towards her and pulled her into a hug.

"How'd you get here? Is Ivy here, also? Is she outside?" he asked excitedly as he looked towards the tent flap. He let her loose and reached around her to unzip the tent.

"Stop, Zack. She's not here. In fact, we aren't sure where she is. That is why I've been hunting all over these islands for you," she said taking his arm and looking up at him.

"What are you talking about? She's back at the cabin with Granddad...isn't she?" he asked as his expression dulled.

"No, she's not. The fey who came back with Granddad and your father tricked her and then blinked out with her. Granddad said the fey's name is Odive and he works for the fey Elders. They wanted to take her to give her special training to be the owner of a Meadhan. Granddad is scared that she is in danger with them. He thinks they took her into Firinn and we can't go in to look for her without a full-blooded fey. You need to come back with me right now," she explained in a rush.

"You guys need to keep it down. We don't want to wake the camp." They looked over and Telfer had sat up and started to pull on a t-shirt. "Odive again. His name keeps coming up, doesn't it? Hi Margo. You sure get around, for a bug."

Margo made a face at him and he snickered.

"I've been trying to blink back to the forest. Both of us have and we can't. How did you get here?"

"Granddad told me where your dad said the battle

would be, and he knew it would have an enchantment hiding the island. We figured out a way for me to search for you and when I found a place of magic I couldn't see; I knew I had found you. There is no way in or out with magic. I swam under the barrier out in the ocean. It was really cold."

"Damn girl, you are awesome," Telfer said as he stood and picked up his pants. She couldn't help but watch as he started to bend over to pull his pants on and when he caught her staring at him, she blushed with embarrassment.

"So we can't blink out?" Zack asked.

"Not from here, but if we duck under the barrier we can blink from the other side."

"I'm ready," Telfer proclaimed. He had pulled on his pants and a coat and stood, holding his pack.

"We should get Akneeta also," Zack added.

"Who's Akneeta?"

"Um, my sister," Zack informed her.

"Really? I've got to meet her. Is she like you, does she have dreads, how old is she, where has she been, did you know you had a sister, does Ivy know?" The questions flew out from her and he put up his hand to stop her.

"Let's just get out of this place and worry about finding Ivy."

"Right," she agreed and changed into her Sprite form. Zack unzipped the flap and waited for her to fly out first. They followed her quietly down to the beach and then she changed back into her normal form.

"Where's your sister?"

"Down by the pier, near that large driftwood pile or at least she was when we left her earlier tonight," Zack said, pointing.

"That works. Let's go get her and then we can use the pier so we don't have to swim out to the edge," Margo said as she worked out a plan.

They started walking down the beach and when they came to the pile of driftwood, Zack called out her name. Margo looked around, expecting her to come from behind the debris, and cried out with shock when a small fire appeared in front of them.

"Zack, why are you back? Who is this?" she asked, moving her focus to Margo.

Margo inspected her while she spoke. She resembled Zack a little bit, but was older and more mature looking. The woman looked over at her and Margo held her gaze.

"Who is this?" she asked.

"I'm Margo, Zack's friend," Margo said before Zack answered.

"She found a way in. Odive took my girlfriend into Firinn, and I need to find her," Zack informed her.

"A Sprite? A Sprite found a way to get though the enchantment?" Akneeta said doubtfully as Margo hovered in front of her.

Margo shifted into her normal form and smiled sweetly at the woman.

"I didn't find a way through the magic, I found a way under it," she answered proudly.

Akneeta stumbled backward when Margo shifted and she quickly looked Margo up and down before turning to Zack. "A shifted mortal?" she screeched in outrage.

Margo wasn't intimidated at all. She smiled sweetly and said, "No, I'm a Halfling."

"That's...that's just impossible," she stammered.

"Apparently not," Telfer said as he playfully ruffled Margo's hair.

"Not that, well it is sort of...I've never heard of a Sprite shifting to full form. But I meant that she found a way in. Containment fields are normally full ones, there is no *under*. I wonder why Odive cast it that way?"

"Who cares? Maybe he made a mistake, his bad, our good luck. We need to get going. We really need to get back to Granddad. He's genuinely worried," Margo said. She turned and started to walk towards the pier. She stopped and looked back to make sure they were following. Telfer was, but Akneeta hesitated long enough to put out the fire and Zack was waiting for her. When all three had caught up with her, she continued on to the pier and walked down to its end with them right behind her.

When she reached the edge of the barrier, she pointed down to the white-capped, rolling water.

"If we jump in here and swim underwater in that direction, we will be able to get outside the barrier."

Without waiting for the others, Akneeta dove into the water with Zack and Telfer following. Margo jumped into the freezing spray and then dove deep, swimming after them. She was the last to surface on the other side. All four of them had to struggle to stay afloat as the icy water heaved around them.

"Granddad locked the forest to only those of us with a talisman. Telfer and your sister need to be touching you to blink in now," Margo yelled at Zack over the sounds of the water. When she was sure he had heard, she blinked and hoped they would follow.

CHAPTER 21 – Odive

Odive blinked back to the Meadhan he used for coming to and from Firinn and quickly entered back into the fey realm. From there, it was an easy matter to blink back into the main hall of the Elder's palace.

He wasn't sure what he expected to see; maybe Ivy chopped into pieces or sunk into brown goo or the Elders still trying to get the items from her person. He had hoped that she would still be alive so he could test some of the more non-traditional enchantments on her.

As soon as he opened his eyes, he knew none of what he had surmised had happened. Instead his world seemed to tilt beneath him. The Elders were no more. Granted, he had killed the contemptible old fey first, but he had at least found a way to bring them back. Now they were gone for good. What was left of their carcasses had started to dissolve into a brown slushy stew. If he had gotten back any later, all evidence of them would have vanished and he would have been left not knowing where they were.

He pulled his eyes from the disgusting scene and looked around the room. The mock fey he had formed to provide services was still lying close to the chopping block. It had mildly shocked him when the axe had recoiled up into the thing's face and taken it down. He had created it from the hair of a mortal fused with a fey. It was mindless and had served him well for many turns. He hadn't known that the mock fey could be killed so easily. The thing's head had been smashed in to the point that his brains had spilled out onto the floor. Odive found the sight fascinating.

A moan from the other side of the chamber drew his attention away and he spied Edme. The fey was lying prone, wilted like a dead plant. If he hadn't moaned, Odive would have thought him gone also. He moved towards him, keeping clear of the gore from the other and stopped a few feet away from him.

He looked down with disgust at the fey. It was just one little chore, and Edme had failed spectacularly. He moved closer and kicked him hard on the side. Edme's eyes fluttered open and when he saw Odive standing over him, he struggled to raise one arm out towards him as if pleading for help.

Odive stepped back and watched with revulsion as the fey tried to talk, opening and closing his mouth like a fish.

"Where is the girl?" he snarled.

Edme just gurgled.

"Shite," he mumbled looking around. "Derl!" he yelled out and waited. Minutes seemed to tick by and he called for the Sprite again with the same results.

"Well, you have certainly mishandled this, Edme, haven't you? You let the girl loose, allowed the Elders to be killed and got yourself all drained in the process, and it seems you have lost my Sprite. You are one very useless fey," he sneered at Edme with contempt.

Edme gurgled again.

"Oh, shut up," Odive said and reached out his hand to drain the rest of the life from him. Edme shriveled up beside him as he considered the possibilities. Neither the Sprite, nor the girl, could get out of the palace. It was locked to all but him now since the other two members of the Troika were dead. No one could come or go without him. So they had to be here someplace. He had no idea how the Sprite had been unbound, but magic always seemed to be unpredictable...exceedingly so when it was his. He sighed and then spoke the words of the enchantment to draw Ivy and the Sprite to him....and waited.

When nothing happened, he started to walk the halls, casting the enchantment over and over again with the same results. He finally ended up back where he started in the main chamber. Fear was growing within him. The vile little Sprite knew too much of what he had done over the span of time and if the full enchantment to bind him as a servant had been severed, that meant the little pest could talk. And that meant that the Alltha girl was as much of a problem now as the Sprite.

He had abducted her under false pretenses, and with the regenerated Elders gone, there was no way to use them to cover for his actions.

The two couldn't blink out, nor could they break through the palace walls...*Shite!* his mind screamed. There *was* one place that might allow access to the outside. He hadn't been down there since he had sealed it up. He gulped with dread and blinked.

He appeared in the lowest bowels of the palace. The air was heavy and his breathing became shallow as he forced himself to move toward the deepest corner. The walls were covered with a heavy black fungus and the odor it emitted was the one he hated the most...Eilibear.

It was a place he had hoped never to visit again. The location of where he had cast the disastrous enchantment that had led him on the path to even more failures. The damn enchantment was supposed to kill the

Eilibear, not suck one of its **Fearainn Eadar** into Firinn and plant it under the Elder's palace.

In retrospect, it probably hadn't been the best idea to cast the enchantment from here. But he hadn't wanted to do it in Alainn where the Eilibear might find out and try to stop him. He had sealed up the hole that the magic had blown into the wall and figured it was as good a place as any for the Eilibear's last resting place. Of course he hadn't known then that the Eilibear hadn't been killed and had instead only been separated from their bodies. He had botched the spell so horrendously that at the time he was more worried about the fey finding out how inept he was at enchantments, than what they would do to him when they found out the ensuing war was his fault.

He moved to the place he remembered the hole to have been and held his breath as he moved in close to inspect it. There was no opening, however the fungus was thinner and there was the distinct residue of recently expelled magic emitting from the wall.

The question now was had the hole reopened by itself …or had they opened it and then resealed it? Either way, it meant that the Sprite remembered knowing about it and what it led to and now the Alltha fey knew his secret, too. Alarms were going off in his head. He couldn't catch his breath and he really thought he was going to faint.

A howl of exasperation and terror ripped from his lungs and reverberated through the chamber.

He had to find her. He had to find her immediately and he knew of only one way to do that. He blinked back to the doorway that lead into the Meadhan. The moment he went through its doorway, he blinked straight to his private place.

As soon as he opened his eyes to his surroundings, he felt a calmness envelop him. He loved this sanctuary he had created. He let his eyes roam the familiar surroundings and felt at peace. He had come across this exquisite space within days of entering the druid academy. It was a tidy little chamber, unused and forgotten, that he had taken as his own.

The space was filled with discarded furniture and morsels of treasures that he had decided were better with him than with the original owners. Bit by bit, he had pilfered the most ancient of scrolls and memorized the little-used enchantments he had found. He had been able to learn to create his wonderful containment barriers and peculiar minor spells that, when used together, allowed him to do create all manner of amusing events. As time went on, he grew bolder and found the means to steal away a few of the Mysteries that were stored at the Citadel. Only a few that he thought would never be missed, as they were never used.

He looked around the chamber now and smiled to himself. There was no doubt he had lost control of his willpower when it came to collecting. The space was piled high with scrolls and books and objects that he had hoarded away. He looked longingly at his cozy chair by the fireplace but knew he had to keep his focus and find the girl.

Striding purposefully through the clutter, he stopped at a low shelf and started to dig though the small artifacts he had stored there. On the middle shelf, he found what he was looking for, a jar with a large eyeball floating inside. He carried it to a table and found a tea saucer to use as the base. Flipping it upside down, he opened the jar and pulled out the repulsive eye.

He had come across the giant many turns ago. The mutant fey had the unconventional power of finding anyone it looked for. The giant had informed him that the energy seemed to come from his eye, which Odive had found just too enticing to pass up. He had killed the giant and taken the eye. If this item had been in his possession when the Eilibear counsel had survived and then went into hiding, he would have been able to find them. Where ever they were now seemed to be outside of the item's reach.

Placing the eye on the saucer, he spun it like a top and whispered *Find Ivy.*

The eye halted immediately and projected an image into the air. He found himself looking at fields of ivy. "Gar," he said in frustration. He spun it again.

"Find fey Ivy!" he called out. The eye displayed a little mortal child. She carried a lunch pail that had a name printed on it...Fey Ivy. "Shite," he screamed out and spun the eye again.

He tried several more ways to describe the girl and grew increasingly more frustrated with each failed attempt.

"Find Ivy Glenwood!" he called out. The eye continued to spin and he was sure this was the right combination of words. He left it to its spinning and went to make some lunch.

CHAPTER 22 – Milton

Milton stood when Margo suddenly appeared. He started to ask about Zack when the young druid and Telfer and one he didn't know materialized right after her. All four were dripping wet and shivering.

"Who is she?" he asked, looking from Margo to Zack. Without taking his eyes off of them, he reached out and picked up his axe. The woman looked down at his axe and then gave him an appraising look.

"It's okay, Milton. She's my sister," Zack said, but before he could explain, the woman took a step forward inspecting her surroundings.

"What is this place? It feels like a Meadhan, but there is a pulsing that shouldn't be here." she announced, and then turned her gaze back to Milton, still holding tightly onto his axe. "I know you. I saw you at the Citadel."

Before Milton could answer, Grandma Winnie's voice came from the stairs. "Akneeta? Is that really you? You may not remember me, I'm…"

Everyone turned to look at her. She came down the stairs in a rush and hurried over to where the newcomer stood frozen, a look of shock on her face.

"Mother Winifred?" the woman cried and threw her arms around Winnie. Winnie enfolded her in her arms, patting her back and stroking her hair. Granddad could see that the young woman was crying.

"Could someone please explain what is going on?" he asked in frustration. There wasn't time for this, they needed to get into Firinn and find Ivy.

"This is Eddie and Elizabeth's first child. She was one of the first to volunteer to fight the Eilibear and then was transformed and...well, many things went wrong and she vanished. Elizabeth was beside herself and there was nothing any of us could do. But you're back now," Winnie said as she stroked the woman's face tenderly.

Milton looked from Winnie to the woman in confusion. He had only just learned that Eddie had a daughter...at the Citadel...and she was one of the Valkyries. But this woman didn't look like the women he had seen there. He stared at the woman and she must have seen his bewilderment as she stepped forward to stand in front of him.

"I saw you with Father at the Citadel. We had been newly released and the Valkyrie enchantment was still binding us. The bonds started to recede during the battle today, and I was glad it was happening. I am free now and do not wish to return to that life. You should know that they are looking for me and will continue to do so. Our leader, Kianna, does not take what she sees as a betrayal on my part lightly, nor will Odive. I seek safety and beg your protection," she said standing before him, waiting for him to respond.

He looked at the faces around him. All of them were waiting for him to say something. That fey Odive had a lot of irons in the fire and the fires seemed to keep landing on his doorstep. He focused on the woman again. She looked like Elizabeth. He wished he could tell Elsie about this development. Looking over at Winnie, he wondered just how old this shifted mortal was. If she had known Elizabeth before the Valkyries were created, then she had been around for a hell of a long time. It was just too incomprehensible for his mind to digest. He finally shrugged and relaxed the arm holding the axe. Akneeta's eyes followed the movement as he set the axe down on the floor and leaned on it like a cane.

"You are safe here. I'm sure that there is a lot I don't know, but if Winnie vouches for you, then I'll not send you away," he said with a sigh of resignation.

"Woodsman...you are the Woodsman, are you not?" she asked and he nodded. "I am not safe anywhere. They will eventually be able to find me."

"Not here. I've locked the Meadhan. No one can come or go unless they have a talisman. You and Telfer were only able to enter because both Zack and Margo do. There is no way for Odive or any other fey to get in and you will not be able to leave unless one of us takes you out," he replied firmly. "Is this okay with you? Being locked inside the forest?" he asked.

She smiled for the first time and nodded. Winnie pulled her into a loose hug and gave him an approving look.

"Okay, that's settled...I guess," he turned to Margo. "Good job, honey, you found him."

Margo blushed at his praise and then self-consciously looked down.

"You are all wet and look cold. Go get changed. I have everything ready for our venture into Firinn. Telfer, you and Akneeta will have to stay here with Winnie."

"I'm fine with that, unless you think you will need my help to find Ivy," Telfer said.

"I would not ask you to put yourself in danger for my family, Telfer," Milton answered thoughtfully. He hadn't considered bringing others, since he didn't think any others would want to join in on an adventure that was sure to make the fey Elders angry. It would be wise to have greater numbers, though.

"Hey, the way I understand it, Ivy didn't want to go, so these fey kidnapped her. I'm willing to go to battle against anyone to get her back," Telfer declared firmly. "I've been inside Firinn once, for a few hours, so I know I can go in and out."

"I will come also," Akneeta stated as she moved closer to Zack.

Milton gaped at her with surprise and some suspicion.

"Why would you wish to come?" he asked with wariness.

"I'm told Odive is behind this. Odive is not to be trusted. He is the one that cast the enchantment on me and my friends, telling us it would make us great warriors. Instead we became monsters...and then his prisoners. I would not wish what happened to me to happen to any other fey, even if she were not a close friend of my brother's," she replied laying her hand on Zack's shoulder.

"Milton, she is more familiar with this Odive than we are. And I've never been to Firinn. She told me she spent many years in that realm before her transformation. If I have any say in the matter, I vote we allow her to come with us," Zack said.

Milton considered this. What both Akneeta and Zack said made sense. He studied the young woman and couldn't help but see his and Elsie's friend Elizabeth's features and manners in her. In the last few months, he might have come to distrust Eddie, but in the long years before that, Eddie had shown himself to be an honorable and a true friend. He couldn't dismiss the fact that Akneeta might be of the same material as the rest of her family. That theory brought another thought to mind, though. Margo said that Zack had hurt Ivy and he had heard Zack, himself, say the same thing before Carmen had whisked him away.

He moved his focus to Zack.

"Did you hurt Ivy?" Best to be blunt about the matter, he decided.

Zack looked uncomfortable and all three of the young people turned to look at him expectantly.

"Yes," Zack finally confessed. "Dad didn't tell me about the Gorffen and how it meant I would hurt...kill...the one I most cared about. I, she, figured out that I must have been draining her energy for months and the damn thing came on full force when we were alone and I had no control. Ivy was able to stop me and she did this to me," he said as he removed his wet flannel. He pointed to a line of vines that wrapped around his upper arm. Milton could see that it resembled the vines on Ivy's face.

"Wow, cool," Margo said as she moved closer to inspect it. No one paid her any mind.

"After she put this on me, she tested it. I tried to attack her again and the plant came to life and wrapped around my neck, choking me. I couldn't...*I can't* get close to her if I mean her harm. Believe me, *I* would never intentionally hurt Ivy," Zack said forcefully.

Milton looked from the vine up to Zack's eyes and held his gaze. Zack was a good kid and he was a good kid who was really, truly in love with his Ivy, he knew that. He also knew that this was what Eddie had been keeping from him, and he was sure now he had been keeping it from Zack also. Someday he would get ahold of his friend and exact payback for what he had allowed to happen.

"Really, you know I would never hurt Ivy on my own," he pleaded.

"I know. Damn the fey and damn their magic," he cursed. "Thank goodness Ivy is stronger than most of us and *was* able to stop you…" he paused to look at Zack's arm, "in a very interesting manner."

The room went silent as Milton stood and scrutinized them. *What an odd alliance*, he thought and wished for the umpteenth time that Elsie was here. She would be able to weave a marvelous story out of this whole fiasco…and she would give it a happy ending. He hoped that really would be the outcome.

"Fine, all of you can come," he said. "Go find some dry clothes and I'll get a couple more packs ready." He waved them away and started toward the door to his old cabin. When the young people had disappeared up the stairs, he turned to look over at Winnie.

"Is there anything you need to tell me?" he asked and she turned toward him with a cheerful smile.

"No, don't think so," she answered smugly and went into the kitchen and started to finish putting together sandwiches for them to take along.

He shook his head and mumbled, "Women." He heard Winnie chuckle lightly as he went into his room to finish preparing.

When he emerged from the old cabin, the young people were seated around the table, eating sandwiches that Winnie had provided. Akneeta was wearing clothing he recognized as Margo's, —a pair of jeans with a purple t-shirt. There was a picture of a fluffy white kitten hanging from a branch on the front of the shirt. Under the kitten were the words *Hang in there baby!* Very appropriate for the quest they were about to take, he thought. They were a little snug on her, but would do.

Winnie looked up when he came in and motioned to some bags she had piled at the end of the table.

"There are sandwiches and other items that should keep you for a few days. I hope it won't take you that long to find her and bring her home," she said as she pointed to a plate on the table filled with even more of them. "Eat something now before you leave."

He grabbed a sandwich and picked up one of the bags and put it inside his pack. The others did the same and donned their packs. Milton retrieved his axe and went toward the door, the others following.

"You be safe. Margo, you and Akneeta stay with the boys, and boys you watch out for them," Winnie called out as they left.

They followed him as he walked up the path that led to the doorway. The forest had come alive, seeming to enjoy the druids leaving the area. Overnight it had returned to its normal state, as it had been prior to the Eilibear invasion. Milton had to maneuver around tall elephant ferns and creepers that were now threatening to take over the path. The air was thick with energy and magic; it literally seethed with it. A breeze was blowing and the deep smell of dark earth and pine trees filled the air. Hundreds of birds fluttered in the branches overhead, cheerfully scolding them for trespassing in their forest. It was how the forest had felt when he had first brought his family there and he wondered why he had waited so long to lock it down again.

When he reached the doorway, he stopped and

waited for the others to catch up. Akneeta was looking around gleefully, taking deep breaths as if to fill her lungs with the bounty of magic. When he caught her eye, she grinned at him.

"Never have I felt this much magic in one place. Your Meadhan is amazing," she sighed. Milton looked around at his home and could only agree with her. This Meadhan was indeed amazing.

He turned and walked toward the massive tree trunks that formed the doorway into Firinn. Looking back, he could see that all of them were now holding their breath in anticipation of him opening the door. He held up the axe and a shimmering film appeared between the front two roots.

"That's the iuchair. It's the key the Woodsman uses to open the doorway here," he heard Margo explain to Akneeta.

"Except for the Meadhan they imprisoned us in, I've never heard of another Meadhan having a key," she whispered back to Margo.

Milton turned and looked at the group. "Are you ready? I'm going to seal it after us, so if you get separated from me, you'll have to find another Meadhan to enter back into Alainn. Telfer, you and Akneeta won't be able to get back into our Meadhan without one of us."

"Got it," confirmed Telfer.

Akneeta nodded her understanding and declared, "Woodsman, I will not leave your side," she paused and then asked. "What should I call you, I've heard many names."

"Milton is my name, Woodsman I guess is my fey title, and Ivy and Margo call me Granddad. Whichever feels right is fine with me," he said as he heaved the axe to his shoulder and started into the film of the doorway. The others followed in a line behind. Milton felt an odd sensation of cracking, like he was breaking out of an egg shell and his ears popped painfully. Once out, he stood, looking around him with shock. He heard gasps from the others as they came through behind him.

Before them was a wide, dead meadow covered in a thick white haze. It was different than the fog that rolled in from the ocean, denser and heavier. There was no wetness to it. The group spread out, surveying their surroundings.

"This is Firinn?" Margo asked, hopping down the incline to where Telfer stood. "It looks like someone put a blur filter on a camera."

"Yeah, it sure didn't look like this when I came through last spring. Of course, I wasn't in this part of Firinn. I came through the Baltimore doorway with a group of Alltha youth from the college. We wanted to see what it was like. We found it wasn't anything special and got out before anyone saw us," Telfer replied as he tried to focus his eyes into the haze.

Milton stood, transfixed by the change in the landscape since he and Eddie had come through just over a year ago. This was not right. When Akneeta moved past him, down the small incline, he snapped out of it and realized he still needed to seal the door. He hurried to do so and then shouldered his axe and joined them as they moved down the hill.

"This is not the Firinn I know. It should be full of energy...I feel little magic in the air," Akneeta said perplexed.

"It's deader than when I came through with

Eddie. Rootmire looks like it has completely died," Milton reflected as he took in the dry meadow and dead forest of trees.

"Personally, I don't care whether Firinn has issues or not. We need to find Ivy. Which way?" Zack asked looking out at the expanse.

"Winnie gave me a map," Milton said as he lowered the axe before kneeling down and unfolding the heavy paper on the ground.

"That's Grandma's way of making a map, alright. See look at that, that's her little note that means a road," Margo said as she peered down at the pen-drawn map. "Does it look like a bunny to you?" she asked, looking at it from different angles.

When Margo said it, Milton could see what she meant. It did look like an outline of a floppy-eared rabbit.

"So where are we on this thing?" Zack asked.

Telfer came over and glanced down at it, then pointed to the rabbit's left cheek. "I think we are here. See the drawing of a tree root."

"When the Elders first started talking about wanting to train Ivy, I was told it would be at a seminary in Firinn. And the only seminary I've ever heard of was one Elsie learned of when she was researching the Oak Triad. It was in a small village named Niksek, which is…here." Milton pointed to the start of the right ear. "So it's that way." He stood up straight and extended his hand toward the dead forest of small trees. He collected the map, folding it neatly before pushing it into the pocket of his jeans. He retrieved the axe and heaved it up on his shoulder.

"I've been to Niksek, traveled through it on one

occasion. I believe I can transport us there," Akneeta offered to the group.

"That would save us the time of having to walk there or doing multiple blinks," Milton said, grateful now that he had allowed her to come along.

They put a hand on each other's shoulders until they were standing almost in a circle. When Akneeta blinked Milton added his strength to it. Unlike transporting place to place in Alainn, Milton could feel them making the move. The magic was sluggish and the void they moved through was thick and made the action of blinking slow.

They all seemed to stagger when they reappeared.

"Damn, that was weird. It felt like I was moving in slow motion. What is wrong with this place?" Zack asked no one in particular.

"Yeah I thought this was the fairy realm. It doesn't look anything like a fairyland to me," Margo added with a pout.

They were in a dense forest standing on a little-used path that skirted the ridge of a deep valley. All they could see when they looked down was the billowing white top of a cloud bank.

"At least the mist isn't as heavy here as it was at Rootmire, and the air feels...fresher," Zack said as he looked around.

"Niksek is down there, in the valley. I remember it being quite beautiful, but this was the only place I could remember with enough detail to blink to," Akneeta relayed as way of an apology.

"This is fine Akneeta. We are here far quicker than I had anticipated. Let's go," Milton said. Without stopping to see if they followed he started down the path.

They trailed silently after him in single file. The path was narrow and hugged the side of a cliff as it descended to the valley floor. There were several times that they blinked ahead, to save time or avoid a dangerously steep part of the trail or most often, when the path disappeared altogether.

At the halfway point, they entered the fog bank. It was thick and wet and shrouded everything in an unnerving white darkness. Milton edged his way along slowly from then on. He could still see his feet and Akneeta directly behind him. But Telfer and Zack were hidden by the fog. Margo he didn't have to worry about as she had taken up post in his front pocket. He inched along, tentatively taking one step at a time, testing whether there was still ground for his foot to rest on before he shifted his weight.

"I don't remember it being this far when I came with Mum." Akneeta's voice came out of the fog behind him.

"Did you walk it then?" Milton asked as he paused to catch his breath.

"No, we blinked up to the ridge so we could have a full view," she confessed.

"Bloody hell, can we keep moving? I want out of this," Telfer's voice rang out and echoed about them.

It was a couple of hours of slow moving before the fog started to loosen and then a few more steps until all of them were clear of it. Milton heard Margo gasp and looked up to see the full effect of the scene before them. Niksek shimmered in the distance. Elaborate white stone structures with towers and steeples, wound up the far end of the valley. Multiple waterfalls plunged from the cliff above, creating iridescent rainbows of color. The colors reflected off the white of the buildings, producing even more hues of the vibrant colors that bathed the area richly. A forest of flat-topped trees framed the city and where there weren't buildings, foliage flourished in vivid shades of lush greens.

The path leveled and widened as they grew closer to the city. The air was bursting with magic and felt fresh as they breathed it in. They were all tired and hungry by the time they reached the first building. It was round and lavishly decorated with diamonds and opals.

"Where is everyone?" Milton whispered to Akneeta.

"Hiding, I assume. We are strangers and probably smell very different than what they are used to."

They continued to walk up the main path, passing over little bridges that spanned ponds filled with neon pink and yellow water lilies. Small pink fish swam in the cobalt blue waters and none of them could resist stopping to look at all the wonders. Statues were everywhere, each unusual and unique. All were carved from diverse shades of marble and encrusted with gems. The buildings were as varied as the statues, large and small, all ornate and rich with their own unique design and decorations.

After a time, they came to a courtyard. In the center loomed a large circular fountain that sprayed out shades of blue water into a shallow pond below. They stood as a group, silent, reverently watching the water fall before them.

"Are you here to pay the tithe?" a silky voice asked from behind them. Milton jerked and turned to see who had spoken.

A tall fey in a long, flowing red robe stood there looking inquisitively at them.

"If you are here to pay the tithe, you might not have bothered. We can't get in to him and he stopped asking, so we stopped giving."

"Get in to whom?" Telfer asked before anyone else thought to.

"Give what?" Akneeta asked at the same time.

The fey looked from Telfer to Akneeta and then shifted his gaze to Zack, studying the druid for a long moment.

"Our city Elder. We gave a tithe of magic to him and in turn he kept us safe from the mist. But then he decided he wished no more to speak with us and locked himself in his home and sealed the door. No one can get in," he relayed in a beautiful, low voice. Smooth and delicate, it seemed to glide through the air towards them. "But as you can see, the shield enchantment he created has kept us safe from the mist and the draining of the Eilibear."

"There are Eilibear here?" Zack asked as he looked around.

"We have not seen them, but who else but the Eilibear would be doing such a thing? They have been finding ways to drain us for many years. Our Elder did not know how to stop it, only how to protect us from it."

As he spoke, fey started to appear around them, silent, elegant, composed fey who all looked at them like they were a curiosity.

"How do you live? We see no food growing or smoke from fires," Milton asked, looking around at the crowd that had assembled.

"What do we care for food, we are not

mortal. We have no need for fires," he answered, looking at Milton strangely.

"What do you do then?" Zack asked, becoming irritated at the fey's quietness.

"Do? We do not *do*, we are fey," he answered, tilting his head slightly as he looked at Zack.

"Zack, don't try to understand," Milton interjected. "Friend fey, we are to meet a colleague at the seminary here in your city. Could you direct us there?" Milton asked politely.

"There be no *seminary* in Niksek. There used to be place named the Hall of Learning, however that is where our Elder lives and, as I said, he has locked himself in and no fey has seen him for many turns," the fey answered in his silky voice.

"Fine, take us to that place if you could…please," Milton replied flatly.

CHAPTER 23 - Ivy

Marmaw pulled me over to the sofa and I sat down next to her. Rave followed us in. We sat facing Mother, while Rave lay down on one of the side loveseats and closed her eyes. I didn't care what anyone did, I couldn't bring myself stop looking at Marmaw.

"Rave?" Mother's thin voice resounded from the end of the room.

"Yeah, she is too."

I looked over at her lying there and wondered just what that meant. *I was too*, what?

"Ivy, look at me," Marmaw said. "So much to tell you, but where to start?"

"Just rip off that band aid and get it over with," Rave said lazily.

"The beginning might be best," Mother interjected.

Rave snorted, "She's a big girl, she can handle it,"

I looked over and curled my lip at her. She still had her eyes closed so my brilliantly snarky face was wasted. I turned back to Marmaw. I thought I knew what they were going to say, some of it at least.

"Marmaw if you are going to tell me that you are the Seer they have been talking about, I already figured that out," I said patting her hand.

"Oh Ivy, there is so much more. It would take me years to tell you all of it, so I'm just going to come to the main point. I knew Skyler was being driven to give me to the Eilibear shades, so I contacted some friends," she said, motioning to Mother. "You see, there was no one who could save me unless it was those who were set on taking me," she finished and waited for me to catch up.

I repeated what she'd said to myself a couple of times and when I finally thought I understood, I found I wasn't shocked at all. I turned to look at Rave who hadn't moved. I got up and went over to her. I leaned down and sniffed. Sandalwood, Jasmine and Gardenias! I had been sensing it all along and just hadn't connected the dots.

Rave opened her eyes and looked up at me with a smug look.

"You are Eilibear who still have bodies," I announced, very pleased with myself.

"Takes one to know one," she sniggered.

"What?" I jerked back and looked at Marmaw.

"I guess Rave was correct that you could handle the news," she said, but not what I wanted her to say.

"What did that crack mean?" I said looking from Marmaw down to Rave, who continued to look smugly up at me. She twisted herself and sat up.

"It seems that the lovely Sumair stone did a bit more than simply shift Elsie into fey," she smirked and leaned forward to take my arm. "It's okay, we won't make you get any tattoos or nose-rings." She stood up and winked at me, then sauntered out of the room, leaving me gaping after her.

"Ivy, you seem to have handled the news that our new friends here are Eilibear a tiny bit better than I thought you would. Is Rave correct in that you have already figured out about the Sumair stone?" Marmaw asked as she studied me.

I looked at her with uncertainty.

"Uh no…what does the Sumair stone have to do with anything? I already knew about the Eilibear shades looking for their bodies because I just spent hours crawling over them."

Marmaw's jaw dropped and she stared at me with wide eyes.

"Rave!" Mother screamed startling me. I jerked my head to look at her and for an old lady she moved quickly, jumping to her feet as she continued to scream. "Rave!"

The room grew noisy as Rave came running back in, followed closely by the other youth group members all asking what the problem was. I couldn't bring myself to call them anything else. Rave was yelling, asking if Mother was all right, and Mother was repeating what I'd just said and then it seemed that everyone was shouting at the same time. I couldn't tell if they were mad or excited as Mother had recited my words exactly.

I sat down next to Marmaw and waited for them all to quiet down. Guess I could have phrased that a little better.

"Explain dear," Marmaw said as she put her hand out to stop Rave from yanking me out of my seat. When Rave finally stepped back, she folded her arms and started tapping her foot, glaring at me. I needed to hurry or she was sure to start thrashing on me.

"Odive kidnapped me and the Elders wanted my magic so they tried to chop my arm off and a whole bunch of other shit. I got away and then a Sprite appeared and he knew a way out and it was, in his words, not pleasant. I guess the fey Odive did a *bad* enchantment, that's what Derl, that's the Sprite, called it and it was supposed to kill you all, but instead it just pulled you out of your bodies. Which is better than being killed, I guess. Anyway, Derl, said that for some reason the enchantment pulled one of your between places into Firinn and buried it under the Elder's palace there. That's where all the bodies are."

"No freaking shit?" Rave blurted and several of the others chuckled.

"There is no way for us to enter into Firinn. How do we get them back?" Cinder asked.

"I don't think you do, not right now anyway," Marmaw answered. "We've had this same conversation ever since I came to stay with you. You can't go home because the **Fearainn Eadars** are sealed off on this side and probably out of alignment on the other. There is no connection right now with Ifrinn. So the main issue has never been if the physical forms of the Eilibear shades still exist, but how to bring the realms back into balance. It's fantastic that now we do know that they still exist and where the Fearainn Eadar is. We also know now that Odive is indeed the one behind it all. But does this knowledge help us solve the prophecy?"

"Three is always the key," Mother said.

"The balance key is the three, who are the three who know the key, to restore the balance three," Cinder chanted.

I looked from one to the other, completely baffled. "Is that some sort of riddle?"

"Yes and we might be one step closer to solving it now. We need to speak with this Sprite. Silver, can you take care of that please?" Mother asked, turning to him. Silver nodded and left the room.

Rave waved her hand and blue flaming words started to appear on the far wall, as if an invisible hand was writing them in flowing cursive. If this was Rave's handwriting, then I now knew who had written the note to me.

"The balance key is the three, who are the three who know the key, to restore the balance three," I read out loud.

"Ivy, do you know any of the history of what else happened when our brethren's bodies were taken?" Mother asked and I shook my head.

"Talon, Adar, history lesson time. You're up," Rave announced in a huff. She stomped over to where Chara and Darcy were sitting. They instantly stood up and gave the loveseat back to her. She lay down once more and closed her eyes. The girls moved to where Talon and Adar had been, as the two young men moved to stand in front of where the words had appeared.

Talon took the stage first and started in on a long explanation of druids and something called the Oak Triad who met in a place called the Citadel and a Sunstone and tons of philosophies and government stuff that meant nothing to me. I started to lose interest.

Then Adar took his turn. He told me about a druid called Guyye and how he was a member of the Oak Triad like their Eilibear Sovereign was. He said Odive decided he hated the Eilibear and starting casting minor enchantments that affected the Oak Triad. They always suspected he was the one who destroyed the Eilibear and cracked the Sunstone. Which in turn ripped the realms apart from each other and ruined the *balance*. The Sunstone cracked while the Eilibear counsel was holding a meeting in the Citadel and killed most of them, only Mother survived. The druid Guyye had gotten them out and Mother had given up a bunch of her life force and brought the rest of them back from the void of death. I guess that meant she had put life back into them and they weren't dead anymore. Then Guyye snuck them out and they ended up here, in this safe house underground. Guyye threw a ton of enchantments on it and they added more and have been hiding from Odive ever since.

Their information ran together in a muddied wave of words. My brain was mush by the time they were done. I sifted through all of the information and found I did have some questions, which I hated to ask. I was worried that Talon would be the one to answer and I'd fall asleep before he had got to the point.

I slumped against Marmaw and held up my hand weakly.

"It's not school, Ivy. What?"

"Mother gave her life force to keep you all alive, or bring you back to life, is that right?"

"Yep, that's why she looks like a winkled prune and we don't," Rave answered and Mother actually laughed. Rave was so not house-trained.

"So, Mother did the same for Marmaw?"

"Yep, added some more wrinkles, that one did." I disregarded Rave's uncouth manner of providing the information and glanced over at Mother.

"Mother, thank you for saving Marmaw and I'm really impressed you did that for all of your family," I said as I shot a dark look at Rave.

"It was my honor and duty to do so. Do not feel impressed as it is my calling. I am Mother. But you are very welcome. Elsie is a wonderful addition to our family…as I'm sure you will be," she responded sweetly.

"Um, about that. You think that Marmaw and I are Eilibear or at least related to you somehow? Don't get me wrong, I have nothing against you, though I really didn't like the shades. I'm not Eilibear."

"Tell her, Elsie," Rave ordered.

I turned to Marmaw and she put her arm around me. She had that look on her face that she got whenever she had given me bad news in the past...like my goldfish had died or my favorite dress had shrunk in the wash. I steeled myself for what she was getting set to tell me.

"You see, dear, we think that the Sumair stone carried Eilibear magic within it and when it shot its energy out and hit Milton's axe, the fey magic intermingled with the Eilibear magic and struck him and then me. It passed through my arm and then hit you." She pulled up her sleeve and showed me a nasty scar on the front and back of her upper arm.

I grimaced and shook my head. "Okay, but how can you be sure? This is just theory, right?"

"The Varese. Only Eilibear are affected by the Varese and can see the trillas that appears on the column or vocalize them. You passed all three tests, the same as Elsie. Welcome to the family, sis," Rave snorted.

"Ivy, there is something else you need to know. When the power shot through my arm into you, you received some of my essence also. You were given part of me, so you are part mortal as well."

I looked up at Marmaw and couldn't help it, I started to cry. I mean really cry, like bawling like a baby. I didn't care what anyone thought of me. Between my normal crying hiccups, I whispered to her, "I'm part of you." It was the best news, next to finding out she was still alive, that I had ever been given.

Marmaw must be rubbing off on Rave because she handed me a Kleenex and told me to wipe the snot that was dripping from my nose. I cried even more.

CHAPTER 24 – Milton

The fey blinked before Milton or the others knew he had agreed to do so. They found themselves standing at the base of a wide set of marble stairs leading up to a huge rambling structure built into the cliff's side. Compared to many of the other buildings, this one was elegant in its simplicity. There were no embellishments or statues, only pure white marble walls with ribbons of violet running through them. Stairs wove in and out, like an eccentric maze, among the various levels.

"The Hall of Learning," the fey announced proudly.

"Let's hope that Ivy is in there. How do we get inside friend fey, which stairs do we take?" Milton asked looking up at the building.

The fey turned and started up the stairs. They followed as he climbed one set of stairs then turned to go up another set, then turned to go back down yet another. By the time they reached a large unadorned door, none of them knew for sure where they were on the structure.

The door stood in the center of the wall. No windows were apparent on this side, not that any of them could see. Zack hurried up to the door and attempted to open it. The handle moved, but the door did not open.

"As I said, he sealed the door," the fey stated, looking at us with interest.

"Have you been inside?" Telfer asked.

"Yes," he replied, with just a hint of a smile at the corner of his mouth.

"Blink us in then," Zack demanded.

"I would do so, but we still have not discussed my compensation."

"Compensation?" Milton repeated. "Compensation for what exactly?"

"Why, for putting myself in harm's way by speaking with strangers. For answering your questions…and for bringing you to the place you sought, of course," he said unpleasantly.

"What sort of *compensation* are you seeking?" Milton asked, narrowing his eyes at the fey.

"There are only two things a fey desires. One is of course magic and the other…" he let his eyes roam from Milton's face to where Margo's head peeked out from his pocket. "Is our own personal bearer," he announced. "A bearer of my own would be my payment. I'm sure that travelers as influential as yourselves would have ample opportunities to acquire another one, where I do not. I wish to have your servant."

"Do you mean Margo?" Milton asked.

"That one. If its name is Margo, then yes, that is what I want," he replied sweetly.

"Margo isn't an *it* or a bearer or a *servant*. She is our friend and no way in hell are we giving her to you," Zack yelled at the fey, clenching his hands into fists.

"If you wish to go inside, those are my terms. It's only a Sprite, a small one at that, but I believe I could make use of it," he stated smugly, looking at Margo who was still in Milton's pocket.

It wouldn't serve any purpose to get in fights with this or any other fey. Not until they found Ivy at least. But Milton knew the fey had crossed the line with what Margo would put up with after his last declaration. She rocketed out of his pocket and zoomed out toward the fey.

When she was barely a foot from him, she suddenly shifted back to her normal form and slapped his face for all she was worth.

"How dare you think I'd be your servant, you pig-eyed jerk!" she screamed at him as she poked her finger at his face. The fey jumped back in confusion. "You are damn right I'm small, but I can kick your ass...and don't you forget it!" With every word, she took another step forward and poked him in the chest with her finger. He kept backing up, his face twisted into terror.

"Get it away from me!" he screamed. "What is that? That's not a Sprite!" He started to turn, looking like he was going to bolt on them, but never got the chance. Margo grabbed his arm and held on.

"No you don't. You are going to take us inside, and we will decide what the proper payment will be. And it won't be me!'"

He looked down at her hand clamped onto his arm, then at the young girl yelling at him.

"What are you?"

"I'm a Sprite," she said, still glaring up at him.

"You can't be. Sprites can't shapeshift in Firinn; they are ...Sprites."

"Okay, well maybe I'm only part Sprite...you don't have to rub it in," she admitted without letting his arm loose.

"A mongrel?" he said, looking at Zack and Telfer. "You keep company with a mongrel? They are not allowed into Firinn, no Meadhan guard would let one through," he cried as he continued to pull his arm loose from her grip.

"Don't you be calling me names, you weasel," she said in a low, threatening voice. She released him then and he started to lose his balance on the stairs, flailing his arms out, trying to retain it. Milton watched coldly as the fey started to fall backwards…and then blinked out of sight.

"I wondered when he was going to remember he could blink," Milton said with a chuckle.

"What a jerk!" Margo declared stomping her foot.

Suddenly the sound of robust clapping made all of them jerk around and look back toward the door.

A stately looking fey with a long braided beard stood, clapping his hands and laughing joyfully. He was dressed in a simple cream robe, tied at the waist with a length of rope. The door was open behind him and an orange fluffy tabby rubbed up against his legs, purring merrily.

"Oh that was wonderful, my dear. I do love a Sprite that stands up for itself. And you are a clever one," he glanced around the group and let his eyes fall on Akneeta and then at her shirt. He chuckled. "And a female druid who likes cats. So nice to know you all have returned to us."

He turned his attention toward Milton and studied him for a moment before he focused on the axe that he carried. "And Woodsman, I've always wanted to meet you." Lastly, he looked at Zack and then Telfer. "Warrior druids…my, my my," he said with a bit of awe. "Really, I've been expecting the Woodsman, but not this wonderful assortment of visitors. Come in, come in," he motioned for them to enter.

The five travelers had stood there gawking at him as he spoke, not knowing what to make of him.

Margo came to her senses first and clapped delightfully back at the fey, then she noticed the cat. "You have a kitty. Can I hold her?" she chirped as she ran up and bent down to pet the animal.

"His name is Furball and I'm sure you would be most welcome to pay him some attention," he answered good naturedly. "Come, we must get in. It is not safe for any of us to be unprotected.

Margo picked up Furball, hugged him to her and gleefully strolled inside. Milton glanced at the others and motioned for them to follow. He waited until the three were in and then walked up to where the fey was still standing, waiting for him.

"You know of me?" he asked quietly.

"Oh yes, and your mate. Do come inside Woodsman, there is much to speak of," he replied softly with deep compassion in his eyes.

"Is Ivy with you?" he asked hoping against all odds that the answer would be yes.

"I'm sorry, no. But be a peace, all is well with her. Let's not tarry any longer. Come inside so I can put the protections back in place."

Milton was crestfallen, but not overly surprised. It was Elsie who had led him to this city and he knew there had to be a reason why.

He walked through the door and then stopped, looking around the entry with amazement. The others of the group had spread out and each was holding a cat. There were cats everywhere, roaming the floors, sitting on the stairs and every piece of furniture. Something rubbed up against his leg and he looked down to find a sleek Siamese. He looked around to see the fey standing at the now-closed door, with his eyes closed, mumbling.

Milton waited until the fey had finished and turned around to smile at him.

"There, the protections are back in place," the old fey announced. He glanced around the room and his face lit up. "I see they have met Furball's brethren. They do seem to multiply, I think that one there is new," he said pointing to a striped kitten sitting on top of a small table. He caught Milton's look of incredulity and chuckled. "Forgive this old fey his eccentricities, I've been sequestered in this place for many long turns."

He clapped and threw out his hands and all the cats disappeared, except for the one Margo was still holding.

"Come," he bade as he turned and walked into a room that resembled a study. A deep fireplace blazed at the far end of the room, and there were a number of soft sofas and chairs that fanned out around it. A small man stood as they came in. He was dressed very proper, in tweed trousers and a waistcoat, very British looking. He was missing his right arm just above the elbow and the right side of his face was slack and horribly scarred.

"May I introduce my friend Pert," he said. The man bowed to us.

The older fey took a seat in the chair next to the fire. Pert moved to stand next to him and waited for us to sit.

When everyone had found seats, Pert snapped his fingers and refreshments appeared on the small center table.

"Enjoy," the other said gesturing towards the food. "You have many questions and there is a reason you are here. Let me start by introducing myself. I am Hueil," he said and then pointed up to the portraits that hung over the mantle of the fireplace. There were two and both seemed to be of him.

"I am the brother of Master Keeper Guyye of the Druid Citadel. My brother was a member of the Oak Triad when they were the voice of the fey in Alainn."

"The Oak Triad? You are twins?" Milton asked, inspecting the portraits.

"Yes, identical twins in fact. A rarity among the fey. My friend Pert was his Bearer, or that is what he was called then. Now fey seem to think of the Sprites as servants, which is not true. Sprites have unique powers and have always considered being the bearers of communiqués for the fey a very noble calling. The fey have come to abuse them and take them for granted over time."

"You're a Sprite? Like me?" Margo chirped.

"Very, though I am not much of a Sprite now, as I cannot fly. When I change, I am without one wing," he informed them sadly.

"I'm sorry," she said, looking like she might cry.

"It is as it is," he replied solemnly.

"I don't want to be rude, but we are looking for Ivy. A fey named Odive took her and we need to find her as soon as possible," Zack interjected.

"I understand your needs. Ivy is safe and with friends and will remain there until I provide you with the knowledge you need to move forward."

Zack jumped up threateningly. "You take us to her immediately. You have no right to hold her," he yelled.

"Warrior Druid, you cannot be near her right now, you know that," Hueil told him quietly. "Sit, be at peace."

Zack was agitated and looked around for the others to take his side. Milton motioned for him to sit and Margo looked down at the cat in her lap, clearly ill-at-ease. He sat, but his pose and features said he was not thrilled to do so.

"I will try to relay the information quickly, I can assure you of that," he directed at Zack and then turned his attention back towards Milton.

"My friend Pert was the sole contact I had with my brother when he went forth into Alainn to take the calling of a druid. At that time, any fey that dared to leave Firinn was considered to be a traitor or worse. They lost their standing as a fior-ghlan, a pure blood fey."

"Is that why fey in Alainn are called the Wild Ones, the Alltha?" Zack asked begrudgingly.

"It is indeed. Though the druids proved their theories correct and over time the relationship between the druids and the fey in Firinn was mended," he said and motioned for them to take some of the food.

Margo picked up a cookie and started to eat. Telfer took a couple of the miniature sandwiches and shoved them into his mouth. The others kept their attention glued to Hueil and Pert.

"Pert came and went, bringing communiques between my brother and me, even during the time this was not allowed. This provided me knowledge of the happenings at the Citadel at a very personal level. When serious events ensued, some very corrupt and immoral, Guyye sent Pert to me with many items that were unsafe to be kept in Alainn. I have quite a collection, if not almost the complete collection, of the works called the Mysteries."

"I have heard of these. Aren't those the essence of the knowledge the druids possess?"

"Yes, to a point. It is *all* the knowledge...of all things. Math, philosophy, physics, sciences...all of it, hundreds of millions of times more than has already been released into Alainn. But it is also the full knowledge of the fey. Our beginnings, our magic, our enchantments, our powers. The Mysteries are the knowledge of everything."

"Woooow," marveled Margo loudly. Hueil smiled at her tenderly and then turned to Milton.

"There has not been *new* knowledge or magic discovered since time began, until you Woodsman."

"Me?"

"Yes. The druids were aware of the Sumair stone when the Boggarts first created it. When it was stolen and taken into the Hemlock Meadhan, it became common knowledge among all fey. How you and your family and the little Frith fey were affected caused great concern with the fey Elders, for reasons you may not be aware of. When the Sumair stone was stolen and the fey who stole it ran through his clan's Meadhan in Scotland, many fey were damaged or killed, far more than in your own Meadhan. It was discovered that the powers the Sumair stone emitted were of three different types of magic: pure magic from Alainn, fey magic and Eilibear magic. The stone had been drawing all three and, when given the chance, it released them back out, one type at a time, it was discovered. That first Meadhan was in complete chaos with having numerous fey, mortals and nature as a whole, being converted with either fey, Alainn or Eilibear magic. You can only imagine the pandemonium that ensued, mainly due to the Eilibear magic.

"Many dhà ann an aon…Two in One…were formed. There were fey that now had both their own magic and Eilibear magic also. This was not a great concern as the original Eilibear and their magic was not and is not evil…just different. It had occurred before through interbreeding."

"Wait, are you saying that fey used to interbreed with Eilibear?" Telfer scoffed with disgust.

"The Eilibears are only another race, very similar to fey and mortal. They were our allies, part of the Oak Triad. And I assure you, they are a wonderful race of persons. What the Warrior Druids fight are Eilibear shades. Eilibear that have lost their forms and want them back and will fight until their bodies have been returned," he explained. "Your friend Margo is considered a dhà ann an aon as she is both mortal and fey."

"That's different," Telfer said.

"How? Many fey consider any dhà ann an aon to be a mongrel, like the fey you met outside. He was correct that dhà ann an aon's are not allowed inside Firinn," he said, then once again turned his attention back to Milton. "You are different, you are not a dhà ann an aon and I surmise it was due to your weapon there." He pointed to the axe.

"I'm a shifted mortal, so if I understand you, that would make me this dhà ann an aon also."

"The powers you display have the elements of both fey *and* Eilibear magic and it's our belief, my friends' and mine, that you are something never heard of before, a trì ann an aon…three magics in one person."

Margo squeaked with surprise and Furball leaped

off of her lap, appalled at being disturbed and strutted over to Hueil. It jumped up onto the fey's lap and, nesting himself comfortably into a ball once more.

"I know this may come as a surprise and maybe not a likable one, but I do have a theory. Your tale has always been that the Sumair stone hit your weapon first, then you and Elsie. Elsie still bears the scar where the powers went through her arm and struck the fey child. I believe that your weapon acted as a channel for the Sumair stone, collecting both fey and Eilibear magic and then propelling it into all three of you. My brother Guyye has described this happening with another item."

"And my natural child Skyler?"

"I do not believe so as she could only shift her form with fey magic."

"And Ivy?" Milton asked hesitantly. "She was already fey."

"Again, this is only my theory, but I believe the essence of Elsie, her mortality, was sent, in a manner, into Ivy. Thus she would be a trì ann an aon. Our friends are preforming what tests they can to assay my theory."

Milton was speechless…but it did explain a lot.

"You are to have us believe that Milton is Eilibear? And Ivy is part mortal *and* that his wife, Elsie, was part Eilibear also?" Zack said with a sardonic laugh.

"No, you have it wrong," Hueil answered firmly.

"I have what wrong?" Zack snapped.

"All three are part Eilibear—the Woodsman, Elsie the Seer, and your Ivy. We believe they are all *still* part Eilibear."

The room was silent as they worked at figuring out what he meant by that when Pert stepped forward.

"Let me help Hueil with this, if you will," he

asked with a nod towards them. "Elsie, as I'm sure at least a few of you already know, is a very powerful Seer."

"Was. Ivy, Margo and I figured that out. Maybe not that she was a seer, but that she knew things that were going to happen before they did," Zack informed them.

Pert continued as if Zack had not interrupted him.

"Elsie had a vision of great concern. It involved her and the Eilibear. She was so concerned that she sent out communiques asking for help to find any remaining members of the Oak Triad. One of those communiques found its way to me. I, in turn, gave it to friends I believed could help her. Her vision was very simple: A new enemy would betray her. She would then be taken by the Eilibear, killed by the Eilibear and then saved by the Eilibear. She knew that the Eilibear were once our allies and that if any knew whether or not those allies still existed, it would be someone of the Oak Triad."

"So the enemy was Skyler, they kidnapped her and then killed her. Those parts I think we all understand. Am I right, Milton?" Zack said looking over at him.

Milton was confused, but at the same time, pieces were starting to snap into place, pieces that had made no sense before now. He disregarded Zack and looked at Pert.

"Skyler wasn't the enemy, was she?"

"No, she was but a useful pawn. The fey Odive is the enemy. It was he who hated the Eilibear with such depth that he sought to destroy them. I do not know how, but he was somehow involved when the Eilibear were ripped from their bodies, the Sunstone was cracked and the realms spun out of balance...hence the war between us and the Eilibear was of his creation."

"Odive again," Telfer growled.

"So Odive set it up for Skyler to do what she did and Elsie knew this?"

"Yes, she was aware of it, not that the shifted mortal Skyler was not also to blame also. Elsie was taken by the Eilibear shades and her life taken, however my friends still retained their magic and they were able to breathe new life into her and bring her back quickly. She has been with them since that time. She is safe and well hidden from Odive. He does not know she survived."

"Wait, just wait," Margo said as she waved her hands around in confusion. "I find it hard to believe the Eilibear are anything but those horrible things Ivy, Zack and I had to fight, but..." she paused to shake her head, "but...if Eilibear were once like us, good and all, does all this mean that Elsie, Ivy's Marmaw, is really alive? That's not possible. I *know* Marmaw is dead. I was there when we buried her in the glade. She has a wonderful resting place by the roses," she said looking from Hueil to Granddad.

"I was there, too. I helped dig the grave and we had a service for her," Zack added and looked toward Milton. "Is Elsie dead or isn't she?"

Milton held Zack's gaze for a moment and then shrugged his shoulders. He wasn't sure what to tell the kids, but now seemed to be the time to come clean.

Zack's eyes went wide. "You aren't sure? So who'd we bury?"

Milton took a deep breath. This was a secret he had kept since he and Eddie had come back home.

"I don't know."

Margo and Zack both gasped and stared at him. Milton didn't have a choice but to continue. "The body we found wore one of Elsie's dresses. I'd know my Elsie no matter what condition her body was in and that wasn't her. I hoped she was still alive, somewhere, but she has never contacted me."

"Okay, so why not just say that it wasn't her body and leave it at that?" Zack demanded.

"Because she obviously wanted everyone to think she was dead, so I had no choice but to play along," he replied with a plea for understanding.

"So where is she?" Margo asked, shooting Milton a look of exasperation.

"She's with the Eilibear. The good Eilibear, isn't she?" Akneeta spoke up for the first time.

"She is indeed with my friends...as is Ivy now," Pert said with a nod and stepped back, placing his one hand on Hueil's shoulder. The fey reached up and patted his hand and then picked up an empty goblet. It filled with a deep golden liquid as he brought it to his mouth and took a drink.

"That's cool," Margo gasped, forgetting everything as she watched what Hueil had done. She picked up a goblet herself and it filled with chocolate milk. She tittered and took a drink, leaving a brown mustache on her upper lip. She smiled as she licked it off.

"So Marmaw...Elsie...is alive and has been this whole time, living with the Eilibear, and Ivy is with them now also. Am I really meant to believe this?" Zack snapped with irritation.

"Believe it or not. It is your choice, but it is the truth. Sprites do not lie," Hueil replied as he took yet another sip from his goblet.

Telfer and Akneeta had also picked up empty goblets and were enjoying their favorite beverages from them. Zack looked over at Telfer with annoyance.

"I'm thirsty," Telfer shrugged back.

"Fine, let's say I believe you. Just why would Odive want Elsie dead?" Zack asked Hueil, turning away from Telfer.

"I believe it is because he had figured out also that she was a trì ann an aon, which meant that the prophecy could be fulfilled," Hueil informed him as he set his goblet down on the table.

"What prophecy?" Margo asked between slurps from her goblet.

"Is í an eochair iarmhéid na trí, cé hiad na trí cinn a fhios ag an eochair, an t-iarmhéid na trí ais, it means…"

"The balance key is the three," Akneeta started to translate but then Milton cut her off.

"Who are the three who know the key, to restore the balance three," he finished for her, his voice shaking. When he was done, he stared, gaping, at Hueil.

"How'd you know that, Granddad," Margo asked with a puzzled look.

"Elsie. She started chanting it years ago, under her breath and it didn't seem like she even knew she was doing it. I remember it because I thought it was a poem or maybe a riddle."

"The prophecy appeared soon after the Sunstone cracked and the Eilibear were devastated, spoken by Seers in both Firinn and in Alainn. It is a riddle—the balance key is the three, who are the three who know the key, to restore the balance three. It was a great mystery and no one could figure it out…until the Sumair stone appeared."

A smile appeared on Milton's lips and he leaned forward.

"Are you saying that the key is the Sumair stone, and Ivy, Elsie and I are the three?"

"I am, or at least that is what Pert here and I have concluded. We think Odive is of the same mind. That is why, we think, he wanted one of you killed and Elsie was the easiest target. It is likely that he thinks that since there are now two of you, the prophecy cannot be fulfilled."

"I'm kind of slow at times," Margo butted in, "but what is this prophecy about?"

"I apologize…we have been pondering and searching for the answers to this riddle for so many turns that we forget others do not share our knowledge," Pert said, with a slight bow to her. "There was a wave effect, one event leading to another and another…someday we may know how it came to be, but for now we only know the results. Bear with me please. The Eilibear were pulled from their bodies, the Sunstone cracked and the three realms slid out of balance. That led to the war with the Eilibear shades and the need for special warriors to fight the shades. First the Warrior Druids with their special weapon, the Dywel, and let us not forget the price the Dywel places on the Warriors and then the Valkyries," he said with a nod towards Akneeta. "I was just told that Odive has released the Valkyries and the other female druids. I did not recognize you as one of the Valkyries. You are not showing the makings of one."

"Odive killed one of us and I believe that broke the curse. I have reverted back to my natural self,"

Akneeta informed him.

"Interesting. I'm wondering if Odive knew this would happen," he said screwing up his face in thought. "Well, that is a matter to dwell on another time. Back to the wave effect. The worst effect was that when Ifrinn and Firinn lost complete connection with each other, the magic in Alainn began to...malfunction. Firinn is dying. A great white mist is rolling in from the east, taking what magic we have left."

"Sorry to interrupt, but do the Meadhans not provide the magic to Firinn?" Akneeta asked. "And there *is* abundant energy to be found in Alainn for the Meadhan's to draw from."

"That is the truth, so you can see the conundrum. Why wasn't the circuli tres functioning the way it should?" Hueil asked in reply.

"It shifted also, perhaps?" Akneeta replied thoughtfully.

"What's the 'circu ly tress'?" Margo inquired making a face. She had picked up a piece of cheese and nibbled at it like a mouse.

"Circuli tres," Akneeta corrected. "It's French. It means the circle of three. Did you not have education?"

"Sure I did. But they don't teach that kind of thing in public high school," Margo snapped in reply.

"Could one of you, who do know, please explain what the circuli tres is," Milton urged, sighing in frustration.

"It *is* true balance, a circle made up of three parts that all work together. Alainn creates magic, Ifrinn weaves the magic and Firinn is the magic. Three is always the key."

The room grew silent, each person digesting the

new information. Furball's purrs echoed around them while they waited for Hueil to continue.

"We do not know if Ifrinn still exists, but we do know that it will not be long before Firinn is no more. The Meadhans are not providing magic into Firinn now. What we do have is brought in by the Sprites, but that will eventually cease to be effective.

"Alainn and the Meadhans are filling up with excess magic now and the accumulation of the magic will ultimately lead to a catastrophic event. It is the balance that gives life to all three realms; we *need* each other. The Sunstone was the keystone that held the realms together. It must be healed and the realms put back into alignment with each other."

"Healing this Sunstone will reverse all the other negative effects, like a backward wave?" Milton asked as he turned to study Zack. If this was the case, then this was also the answer to fixing Zack's problem. Zack locked eyes with him and Milton could tell the young man had come to the same conclusion.

"You are saying that if we heal the Sunstone, the Gorffen curse will come off me." Zack said as a smile started to show at the corner of his mouth.

"Yes, we believe so. Enchantments were cast to create the Valkyries and Warrior Druids. Those enchantments would be null if the requirement for which they were fashioned ceased to exist."

"I'm in," Zack announced jumping to his feet.

"We are glad to hear that Warrior Druid," Pert acknowledged formally. "Additional knowledge has come to us from Ivy and the Sprite that Odive had held in bondage. Ivy was able to free the Sprite and he has been able to confirm some of our theories and fill in information that we did not have."

"That's our Ivy," Margo clapped cheerfully.

"So can we go to Ivy *now?*" Zack asked impatiently.

"It would be wise for us to be out of Firinn. I'm sure the fey in this hamlet have already spread the news of your arrival. There is other information I need to provide to you, in regards to my brother. As I told you, Guyye had been sending me communiques for many turns. I kept them all and will provide them to you to read. You will gain much insight into who Odive is and what he has done."

"Mr. Hueil, where is your brother?" Margo asked, tilting her head.

"Odive realized that Guyye knew what he had done and planned on exposing him. He sought to kill Guyye. Once you read the communiques, you will fully understand this. Odive is...different, his spells and enchantments do not always work the way they should. He was successful in killing my brother, but he destroyed a Meadhan and killed many fey at the same time."

"Is that how Pert was hurt?" she asked.

"I was hurt when the Sunstone cracked. As were many others." Pert replied.

"Oh...I'm sorry, for the loss of your brother and to you Pert," she said as sadness clouded her features.

"Pert has transported Guyye's writings to the safe house. We implore you to read them as soon as possible." He rose from his chair and waited for Pert to transform into his Sprite form, appearing on Hueil's shoulder. "It is time for us to go."

"You are coming with us?" Margo asked with a frown. "Why?"

"Because Elsie has informed Pert that I will be needed…and I've always hid, too scared to put action to my words, unlike my brother. Guyye was always the first to stand up for what was right and moral and decent. I am proud to be his brother. He never hesitated to step up, even if it wasn't his responsibility. He lost his life trying to correct these wrongs and it is time for me to take up where he left off."

Milton stood and took hold of Hueil's hand and held it tight for a moment. He didn't know this fey or his brother, but he did understand that out of all the Firinn fey he had ever met, these two were ones he would like to be friends with.

The others of the group gathered their packs and readied themselves to leave. Telfer reached down and grabbed a handful of the tea sandwiches and shoved them into his mouth and began chewing loudly.

Akneeta frowned and shot him an exasperated look.

"What? I didn't want them to go to waste," he whined with a full mouth.

"Is she in a Meadhan or the realm of Alainn?" Akneeta inquired, pointedly looking away from Telfer.

"She is in Alainn. We need only to go into a Meadhan and we can transport from there to her location."

"So it's back to Rootmire, everyone." Before Milton had finished the sentence, the young people had left. Hueil placed his hand on Milton's arm and together they blinked back to the doorway in the dead hamlet. Milton unlocked the doorway and waited until everyone else had gone through, then he stepped in and quickly locked it behind himself.

Hueil was visibly taking deep breaths and when Milton came to stand beside him he put his hand on the Woodsman shoulder. "Someday I would be honored if you allowed me to visit your Meadhan. The magic here is quite overpowering and very different than what I have grown accustomed to."

"I think that could be arranged," he answered with a smile. "If you would direct our next step at blinking I will add my power to yours."

Huiel reached out with his other hand and took hold of Zack's arm. Each person hurried to connect with another and when Huiel was satisfied that they were all touching he blinked.

CHAPTER 25 – Ivy

I finally stopped crying and Marmaw made me go with Cinder to wash my face. When I came back, it was just Rave waiting for me.

"Where's Marmaw?"

"Silver got ahold of Pert, a friend who is a Sprite. He, in turn, located Derl. Everyone is with the bug, questioning him. Pert brought a bunch of letters back with him that one of the members of the Oak Triad wrote, Master Keeper Guyye. They're over there," she said pointing behind the far sofa. I saw stacks of yellowed rolls of paper. "You probably should read them; everyone is supposed to. Oh, and the Woodsman and Hueil, Guyye's brother and a bunch of others will be showing up soon...your boyfriend is coming also."

"No! He can't come here," I yelled out. I had forgotten all about Zack and the stuff that had happened between us.

"Boy troubles?" Rave ventured boorishly.

My jaw clenched. "Zack can't come near me. Something happened to him, or is happening to him, and whenever he is near me, he tries to kill me. He can't come here," I snapped.

"The Gorffen...nasty price tag for their Dywel, isn't it?"

"Really you need to stop him from coming here, or I have to leave. He tried to kill me, and I put a vine on his arm and it chokes him if he gets near me now. I'm not worried that he will hurt me, but I don't want to kill him,"

"Ingenious *and* resourceful. Good job putting the druid in his place."

"Rave, do you know how to be nice or at least helpful? You should do some soul-searching, maybe you'll find one," I snapped.

"Sarcasm is a service I give freely," she replied.

"Geez, what am I, flypaper for freaks?"

"I like you. You were like me when I was little— a douchebag," she said with a slight grin.

"I love the sound you make when you shut up." I was really starting to warm up to this. Rave sat up and seemed to be waiting for each of my very snappy comebacks.

"I like your hair, did you butcher it yourself?"

"I like yours too, still styling it with a weed whacker?"

"Don't worry if your mind wanders, it won't go far."

"A word to the wise. Oh...well...I guess that leaves you out."

"If your personality were any less colorful, you would be invisible." My mind drew a blank and after a few seconds, she started to laugh.

"Oh eat shit and die," I retorted.

"Ivy!" Marmaw called disapprovingly from behind me.

"Oh, you're in trouble now," Rave chuckled as she wagged her finger at me.

"Zack will be here soon. Has Rave told you what to do?"

I turned to Rave and she was all innocent, looking up at the ceiling. "No, no she hasn't. Rave what is it I should do?"

"Oh it's easy. I'm going to take you to another part of the safe house while he is here. Nappy time for you... or I suppose you could read a few scrolls," she said, tilting her head towards the pile of papers.

"I'll take them," I said and I set my mouth in a hard line when she smirked at me.

I ended up in a round room with a round bed and a curved chair sitting in front of a curved desk. These guys really didn't like straight lines. I had to admit, though, I rather liked it, and it was amazingly peaceful. I stuck my head though a small doorway and found a round bathroom with a round shower stall. I laughed as I quickly undressed and took a shower under a large round showerhead that hung from the ceiling.

There were light blue towels laid out on a small round stool and I was shocked to see those weren't round also. I dried off and, wrapping the towel around me, went back out to the bedroom.

Rave must have come in when I was taking the shower because there was a pair of gray leggings and an overly long blue and gray baseball shirt lying on the bed for me. Next to the bed were all the scrolls. I hurried to dress and then got to work.

I unrolled the first one and found it was written in another language. I opened a few others and all were unreadable. Crap, that was why Rave was smirking. She knew I wouldn't be able to read them. I sat there fuming for a few minutes and then it dawned on me. I really could be stupid at times. I allowed magic to build at the back of my throat and then released it as I spoke.

"Give me the power to read these scrolls."

I looked down at the first scroll again and smiled. The words now made sense and I eagerly started to read. It turned out it was a just a letter. A letter from the druid Guyye, to his brother Hueil. There were no dates on them, but each one had been numbered. I sorted them out in order and then sat on the bed and started with the scroll that had *1* written on the outside.

"My dear brother Hueil, greetings,

I know we both thought we would never be able to converse when I left Firinn.

It pleases me to introduce you to Pert. Pert is from the third generation of the original fey that ventured out into this world. He is a Sprite, a wonderful adaptation of our people. The fey of this realm have altered their very beings into such amazing aspects of feyhood. His unique abilities allow him to transport to and from Firinn. I believe that there have been many Sprites that have traveled, unknown to the Elders, and have used their new-found abilities to keep contact with those in Firinn.

He appeared to me one day when I was feeling the isolation and separation from you and our homeland. How he knew I was in distress, I do not know, but he offered his services. He freely does this as he says it is his clan's callings to use their energies in this manner. If you ever have need of his services, he will come if you snap your fingers. He is able to transport with items such as this scroll and you will find him a trustworthy friend if you wish to speak your message instead.

I have completed my first full turn among the

druids. I am safe and I am well. Time spins in this realm and unlike our life in Firinn, I find I fight to keep account of the days. The mortals account for their time by their realm's rotations around their Sun. This is a hard manner for the fey and Eilibear to log the passing time and does confuse me. As Firinn has no Sun, unlike the other two realms, there is no true means to measure time for the three races. I do not understand the calculations our Master Druids have used, but the Oak Triad has approved their assessment and have declared a universal time for all. A 'turn'...which is approximately a measurement of 53 of the Alainn years and 123 of the Eilibear durations.

I do not see the need for the accounting of time within Firinn, however here in Alainn it is useful.

The druid fey have indeed carved out a fine academy inside the land of Alainn. All your theories and speculations were very close to the facts. There is much for me to learn and now that I have you to share my thoughts with, my life is full.

I must admit I do feel small and lost among all these white-robed longbeard druids. My master let no time pass and put me to task straight forth. I am not allowed to use my energies (a sacrilege to any true-blood fey) and instead must use the art of scripting. Your training did allow me an advantage as I already had mastered the basics of reading and writing prior to my banishment.

I do very much like it here and I am told I have the natural aptitude for this vocation.

There is a greater purpose for the fey, as you stated so many times. The druid fey are humble and amazing and have taken on this task wholeheartedly. The Oak Triad is awe-inspiring. I have not yet met or seen any of the Eilibear or Alltha that represent the humans, nor met any mortal yet, but I see and hear the work progressing around me. I am told that the similarities between the races are almost inaudible, although the mortals have many turns yet to reach our level of development. They are simple beings at this time, unable to understand the plainest of learning as yet from the druids. The time will come.

Master Sorsedd has said that if I do indeed continue to progress, the turn may come when I will be admitted into the Order as a full druid and allowed to learn the Mysteries. I find I do aspire to this and am of good humor. I am obedient to my Master's wisdom and will strive to make you proud.

Deep Peace to you,
Novicate Guyye of the Druids"

I laid the first scroll down and pondered what he had written. There were not many clues as to when Guyye had written it, but if mortals were simple, and a *turn* was fifty-three of Alainn's years, then this letter must be very old. It boggled my mind how long fey had been in existence and the knowledge that they must have. What would Alainn or mortals be if the first fey had not stepped out into Alainn to share their knowledge? I picked up the next one and continued to read, awed by these new insights.

I had finished about twenty of them by the time I decided I really liked Guyye. He painted a picture of his life that was interesting and at times thought provoking. Also, now what Talon and Adar had told me was starting to make sense. I got up and hunted in the drawers of the desk for a notepad and pencil, then sat back down and started to make notes as I read.

The more I read, the more combinations of three started to appear. Three realms, three races, three types of magic, the Oak Triad were made up of three members and on and on. I made notations on all of them and when I had finally finished, I looked at what I had written.

The guys had given all the history of the Oak Triad earlier, along with the theory they had come up with about why Marmaw had been taken and what they had concluded from that. I was beginning to think they were wrong and the answer to the riddle had been in front of them from the very beginning.

I yelled for Rave who popped in before the sound of my cry had died out. She took in the pile of scrolls that I had opened and tossed to the other side of the bed and then her eyes roamed to my note pad.

"You were able to read them?" she asked narrowing her eyes skeptically.

"Of course," I said as if I didn't know that it should have been an issue.

"Learn anything useful?" she asked with a smirk.

"Yep, tons. I think I need a refresher course from Talon. Could he come and help me for a while, and maybe Derl also? I'm done with that pile if others want to read them," I said pointing.

She studied me for a moment, then nodded.

"I'll call you when Zack gets here. I'm sure he's

going to want to see you. Can you blink in near the back column that you can see from the gathering room we were in before?"

"Yeah. That should be far enough away...I hope."

She grinned mischievously back at me and reached out to touch one of the scrolls I was done with, then she and the scrolls vanished. I really had no clue what the girl was thinking most of the time. I sat down and reread some of the more interesting letters I had held back while I waited for Talon.

CHAPTER 26 - Zack

They found themselves standing by a large boulder surrounded by jungle. Parrots and Cuckoos called from overhead and when Margo shrieked, they all turned to see a large Iguana was sunning itself on the top of the boulder.

"Sorry, they are in the safe house and I thought it would be best to let them know we were here rather than just appearing," Hueil said as he lay his hand on the boulder as if waiting for a signal. In a couple of minutes, he stepped back and reached out his arm for them all to touch him.

They appeared in a large white cavernous structure.

"This is all underground?" Margo whispered, glancing up at Hueil with wide eyes.

"Oh yes. They have had many turns to transform this once cold and dirty cave into a very nice replica of their original type of dwelling."

Footsteps echoed and a lone woman could be seen walking quickly towards them. She was older, slightly plump, with rosy cheeks and the most welcoming smile imaginable—the image of the most perfect Grandmother one could conjure up.

"Elsie," Milton breathed out. He let his axe fall to the ground and raced towards her. When they collided, they seemed to melt into one entity. Zack felt tears forming and didn't care.

"This whole mortal-marriage, love-reunion thing is quite…thrilling, isn't it?

Zack looked over and saw a black-haired girl had joined them. He took in her unique appearance and then turned back to where the couple was embracing.

"Rave," Hueil said in way of a greeting.

"Hueil," she answered with a bob of her head. "Nice to see you in person, at last."

"You've never met?" Zack asked as he pursed his lips.

"Nope. But we've communicated a lot through Pert."

Margo shifted to normal size and moved to stand next to the girl, putting out her hand. "Hi I'm…"

"Don't care," Rave said.

"Rave, try to be civilized please," Hueil admonished her. "Margo, forgive her, please. Rave tends not to filter her words very well."

Rave snorted and turned her attention back to Zack. "Glad to see you kept the dreads growing. Mother will be pleased," she said.

He turned back to look at her. "Do I know you?"

"It was a long time ago. I helped Mother do that to your hair," she informed him.

He looked at her again, and thought back to the time when the old woman had first put the dreads in his hair. There had been a girl there…a girl with long braids.

"That was you? Your hair is different,"

"Have to keep up with the times," she responded by running her hand through her short hair.

Milton and his wife made their way over to them. Elsie stopped in front of Zack and took his hands. "Zack, I am so very glad to meet you. Your mother would be very proud of the man you have become," she said softly, then she turned to Margo and gathered her in her arms. "Winnie has told me so much about you. You brought sunshine back into her life, my dear."

"Elsie, I hate to break this up, but there is the ritual we need to perform," Rave called out. She had moved over to one of the columns and stood waiting for them.

When they came close, she pointed down to a bowl that was attached to the column.

"We need you to perform our cleansing ritual. It will clean all elements that could hurt us off of you. The liquid is called Varese, it's similar to water. Cup your hands, fill them with some Varese and put some on your face. When you look up, if there are words on the column, hum them."

Hueil did as she asked. He didn't hum, so he must have not seen any words. Rave handed him a small hand towels to dry his face off afterwards. Margo went next and then Akneeta. Telfer hung back, but Akneeta motioned for him to do it, so he marched up splashed the Varese on his face and then grinned sheepishly when he was done.

Milton stepped up next and when he put the Varese to his face, he started to hum in a strange rhythm and when he was finished, Elsie took his arm and they moved away.

Zack figured it had to be no big deal and walked up expecting to simply splash his face like Telfer did. The result was surprisingly different. His face and fingers started to tingle and when he looked up, there were faint words etched into the column, but they disappeared before he could read them. When he backed away, the girl, Rave, was looking at him strangely.

Without asking, she walked up and pulled his shirt from his sleeve and looked at the vine tattoo Ivy had given him.

"That is just freaking amazing," she said as she stared at it. When she looked up and saw him looking down at her, she reached up and patted him on the cheek. "Well, sweet cheeks, too bad you're taken," she said.

He figured she had to be one of the Eilibear, but she didn't look like what he knew to be the Eilibear. She was just a normal, snarky girl. They were led into a large room where several other young people waited for them. Rave was standing next to where an old woman sat. The woman stood when he came in. Rave leaned over and whispered something to her.

Mother Vondra, she looked almost exactly the same. *How weird was that?* She walked slowly over to Zack, leaning on a cane. When she stood in front of him, she reached up and took a length of one of his dreads and caressed it.

"Always knew there was something special about you, boy," she said with a toothy grin.

"It's good to see you again Mother Vondra. I've thought of you a lot throughout the years," he said as he leaned down and gave her a gentle hug.

When she pulled back, her lower lip was trembling. She turned and made her way back to the chair and sat down. Only then did she acknowledge the others in the room.

"So Hueil, we finally meet after all this time. And Woodsman, I have heard much about you from our friend Elsie. We welcome you to our family," she said greeting them. "Sit everyone, we have much to discuss."

The young people made sure that the newcomers

had places to sit before they crammed themselves onto one of the larger sofas. Everyone seemed to be waiting for someone else to start the discussion.

"So," Margo called out. "Where are the Eilibear we are supposed to be meeting?" Her eyes darted around the room.

There were a couple of giggles before Rave started to wave her hand. Margo looked over at her and then Rave pointed at herself.

At first Margo seemed confused, then her eye went round as she realized what Rave was trying to tell her.

Giving her head a little shake, she giggled. "You can't be Eilibear, you look normal."

"I am normal for an Eilibear," Rave informed her.

"Can't be. If you were, then Zack's sword thing would zap out of his arm," scoffed Margo.

Zack looked down at his arm. Margo was right. Whenever Eilibear were near, his Dywel would start to burn.

"You can't be that stupid. Ivy is one pretty smart gal and I don't think she'd have a best friend that is a simpleton. The Dywel was created to kill Eilibear *shades*, not Eilibear," she said rolling her eyes.

Zack digested that. He wasn't sure he believed her, but no one else here was contradicting her, so he figured she knew what she was talking about.

"Oh," Margo said and seemed to fold in on herself.

"It's okay, Margo. It was a good question," he said to console her. He then turned his attention to Rave. "You, pincushion girl, sorry, your name escapes me. We just learned about thirty minutes ago that there was a difference between shades and Eilibear, so you can drop the snark."

"I can see why Ivy likes you," she replied as her eyes sparked with delight. She rolled her shoulders up and rubbed her hands together. "We are going to have such fun together."

"Can we get on with whatever it is we're supposed to be doing? Where is Ivy?" he snapped with annoyance.

"Ivy is studying. Last time I checked in on her, she was almost done with all the scrolls that Hueil sent us. I took the ones she had finished reading and deposited them in the next alcove. Hueil here tells me you have been brought up to speed on most things. We think we are close to figuring out what the prophecy means and need to come up with a plan on what to do now. So it's up to you. Would you like to read the scrolls first or brainstorm on our theory?"

"I want to see Ivy so I know she's really here and okay."

"Zack, she is," Marmaw said from across the room.

Zack looked at her and wrinkled his brow. "No insult intended, but I've never met you before and I buried a person I thought was you. So just to be on the safe side, can I please see her?"

"No insult taken," Marmaw responded gracefully.

"Zack, you cannot be near her, but I can have her appear on the other side of the outer room if you wish. But no closer. We do not have a way to stop the Gorffen from taking over. She'll be over there," Rave said, motioning out of the room into the larger area.

He stood and waited. She appeared next to a far

pillar and when her eyes landed on him, her whole face lit up.

"Hey there," she called out to him.

"Hey there yourself," he called back, feeling very self-conscious with everyone watching. "Are you okay?"

"I am now. I'm sure everyone else will fill you in on what Odive did and how I ended up here. It's another of those bizarre adventures that seems to happen only to me," she called crinkling her nose. "How are you feeling," she called out again.

Her voice echoed a little in the expanse and he started to feel the need to be close to her. The familiar need he had been having all summer long.

"I think...I think we can't be near each other for a while," he stammered as he started to feel a compulsion to get over to her. Without warning his need to be near her took over, and he took a step forward and then another. His expression hardened and his brain told him she had no right to be that far away from him. It was his right as a Warrior Druid to take what he needed and it was her obligation to give it freely. He felt his lips draw back in a snarl as he lunged forward.

Her smile slipped from her face. "Love you, Zack," she said, and then she was gone.

Instantly he realized what he had done. He closed his eyes and breathed deeply, then turned to face the audience behind him.

"That is some seriously bad shit you have going on, dude," Rave said. "I'm revolted...and rather impressed at the same time." Then she turned to face the others in the room. Everyone was staring with shock at Zack. "So now we know what the Gorffen does. He doesn't have any control over it, so until we can get that enchantment removed, we keep them apart."

Milton motioned for him to come over and, feeling lower than a dog turd, he made his way to where Milton and Elsie sat. He was sure that Milton was going to tell him to get the hell away from his family and he had every right to do so.

When he got close, Milton stood and looked at him for a second and then moved forward. Zack expected to be slugged and steeled himself for it. Instead Milton hugged him compassionately and patted him on the back as if to say it would be okay.

"Don't worry, we'll figure this out, son. It was rather a shock to see you transform like that, but I know how magic can be."

Zack could feel his lip starting to tremble, and tears started to roll down his cheeks. He was too choked up to talk, so instead he nodded to thank him.

"So Zack, we proved to you she's fine, and you proved to us that you are one messed up guy. It's time to get over your own shit and help us figure out what to do now. I vote that Talon and Derl bring all you newbies up to date on Ivy and Derl's exploits first," Rave announced as she raised her hand and glanced around to room to see if anyone else agreed with her. Margo and Telfer instantly raised their hands. "It's settled. Who wants to start?"

"I will," Derl offered as he appeared on the back edge of one of the sofas.

"The floor is yours, bug."

The Sprite began to relay his story of being bound by Odive and all that he had seen and heard in condensed version throughout the years. It took some time, but he indeed had inside information on Odive. He told of seeing Ivy for the first time and what he had seen.

Talon told Ivy's story as she had relayed it to him. The room seemed to growl and tremble as he spoke and when Talon was done, he nodded to Rave.

"Ivy has read all of the letters that Master Keeper Guyye wrote. It took her most of the day. To speed your reading enjoyment up a bit, she made notes of which letters seemed to her to be the most important. There are about sixteen of them, written mostly in Fearnce, the first fey written language. A few of the more recent ones, from a few hundred years ago are written in a combination of Celtic and Latin. Ivy really did go through these and has chosen from Guyye's first writings to his last. I would speculate that the time frame spans close to two or three thousand mortal years...a mere drop in the bucket of life for fey or Eilibear. Talon, if you would please translate and read them out loud to everyone." She sat down and Talon stepped forward once more.

Derl brought him the one that Ivy had set out as the first to be shared. Talon unfurled it and started to read:

Communique from the Academy Epoch of Learning;

My dear brother Hueil,

Greetings, I know we both thought we would never be able to converse when I left Firinn.

It pleases me to introduce you to Pert. Pert is from the third generation of the original fey that ventured out into this world. He is a Sprite, a wonderful adaptation of our people...'

Zack forced himself to relax back on the sofa and listen closely to the words Talon was relaying to them. The writing and grammar were different than what he was used to, but after a while he got into the flow of the information and the unusual wording didn't matter.

Brother Hueil,

Greetings, It has been a long while since I last sat down to write to you. Pert informs me most frequently of his time spent with you. I do believe he enjoys your company more than mine.

The time of darkness is beginning to recede from Alainn. The druids have made impressive strides with bringing them into the light. I was permitted to leave these walls for a fortnight with my Master and travel the roads of the mortals. It opened my eyes to the work that needs to be done, but the Power was so deep and strong. These humans have no knowledge of what their realm holds. In Firinn, we are pure energy and it is within our very beings. We do take it for granted.

These simple mortals of Alainn do not see or feel or even have use for this power and that does bring sadness to me. The caretakers, the Alltha, who have given up their birthright and have gone out into this world to live and provide the instructions to the humans on behalf of the druids are champions. I now understand your words of dissatisfaction with the fey that reside in Firinn. Our lives were so shallow, without worry or care, as our energies provided all we wanted or needed, but we did not do anything with them. It is sobering that the fey take for granted the Power that was only created by Alainn and pulled into our realm by means of the Meadhans. I wonder if the fey would exist at all if not for Alainn.

Grave thoughts indeed.

I do miss you and my remaining friends in the hamlet. I wish you could give them my greetings, but that would mean telling all that the Sprites can come and go. I do not think the Elders would approve. I have made a new friend, a strange one, but still a friend no less. Alainn has odd feline creatures called cat and my Master brought me one newly born as a gift. He is soft and furry and makes a sound of delight whenever I am to rub him. It is my responsibility to feed and care for him. I've given him the name of Casper as he reminds me of that fey down the road with the hair that grows wildly out of his ears. You would love him. Master Sorsedd tells me that this feline will teach me more about the mortals than he can give words to. I do not understand, but I will wait to see what great wisdom this creature could possibly impart to me.

Deep Peace to you,

Novicate Guyye of the Druids

Brother Hueil, greetings.

Casper has grown to maturity quickly and walks the halls with me. He seems to know what I need before

I do, and I've spoken to Master who remains firm with the thought that these felines have no magic. I think I found one thing I disagree with the Master on.

I have made many other friends besides my Casper, a great number of Novicates are in our ranks. All are as we, having a deep belief in our calling. Only one does give me pause, one named Odive. He is a runt among fey, small and sickly. He is no friend to any and I do not know why he chose to come hence to Alainn. Many of my brother Novicates do make merry of him, saying he must have been put out by the fey in Firinn due to his uncomely appearance. Part of me doth feel for this little fey, but then he will do something callous and I take back those feelings of care. I caught him being cruel to Casper and ran him out of the halls with harsh words. Many of our daily works that we labor over so diligently, will, on the next morn, be burnt or torn to pieces and all fingers point to Odive as only his works tend to be left whole. He is a dreadful and wretched fey, malicious and untrustworthy and I do not know if he will be validated to the next level in the Order of Druids.

When this fey discovered that many of us had befriended Sprites, he demanded that he be given a Sprite as a servant also. This did not sit well with the Sprite as they are not our servants nor slaves, but our colleagues. None would work with him due to his insensitive choice of words. Odive would not let the matter go and has made life unpleasant for any that must work with him.

Enough of that now, forgive my ramblings.

Deep Peace to you,

Novicate Guyye of the Druids

Brother Hueil,

You were always the logical one. I am humbled and chastised as I find you are correct that I have not tried to make friends with Odive and he most certainly needs one. I have attempted to make amends with Odive, however he is very suspicious at my attempts. I have offered to assist him with our studies as he is not one that reading and writing comes naturally to. It took a long while for him to agree and it is a struggle for me as he is cold and supercilious towards me, even as I give my time to help him advance.

I do have sad news to impart. I have learned the lesson that Master Sorsedd said I would from my cat Casper. It was something that I had never encountered before. Casper died. He grew old and lost his lifespark and I was beset with emotions. Fey do not die. We may grow tired of our existence and allow our energies to dwindle out until we are no more – but the choice is ours. I had been told that the mortals and all the creatures natural to Alainn have a finite life span. I thought I understood until my dear Casper was gone. Oh Hueil, it was dreadful watching the poor creature just fade from being. Emotions I never knew washed over me and I was unable to function for many cycles. My eyes are open now to what this realm deals with and also to how blind and unfeeling the fey at large are.

I should tell you that Odive did make fun of my distress, and I found I could not tolerate his arrogance while I mourned. My sorrow was great until I was told that I could seek out another cat from outside our protective walls. Odive wished to go with me as he had not had the opportunity to see mortals up close. It was interesting to have this pompous fey along with me, but I did find a small farm that had newborn cats. They did not wish to part with any until I offered my services to them. I helped the mortal plow a field and it was a joyful experience. The sun beating down filled my body with power and the breeze brought the sweet harmony of magic to me. I tried to entice Odive to experience these feeling along with me, but he was scornful that I would be used as a slave by a mortal. It was no matter to me as I was given my prize as the sun set in the western sky. Two little bundles of fur, as the mortal was greatly impressed with the work I had done. I named one Casper and many laugh at my inability to let my first friend fade from my memories.

Now dear brother, hold out your hands. Pert is delivering a gift from me to you.

Deep Peace to you,

Novicate Guyye of the Druids

Brother Hueil,

Time rolls on and Odive and I have formed a strange type of friendship. I must say I am his friend in spite of his demeanor. He is not an easy fey to like as he has the uncanny ability to say appealing words and you think he is being kind, only to realize later on that you were being ridiculed. I take many deep breaths when I am with him. I have finally discovered Odive's talent. It is not magical in nature, though. He is an Orator. He does have the ability to make a point in such a manner that you are persuaded by his words. His main obstacle, though, is his own deleterious demeanor. Not many wish to be near him.

Thus my problem with attempting to be his friend. I force myself to spend time with him and I find myself doing things I would not wish to due to the words he speaks. Once I comprehended his power I found I could hear the real words he was speaking and understand his purpose behind them. I wish I could say I was immune to his words, but with every turn of the sun, he becomes more advanced at his talent.

What all others find humorous is that he is unable to do the simplest of enchantments without them going sideways. Simple, everyday bits of magic, like starting a fire or turning a light on have the most unexpected results. A fire will light, then travel in a river up a wall and explode, or a light turned on, will turn off all other lights around him. I do see why he was asked to leave the instruction chamber when we were memorizing new enchantments. I think even he realizes that he should never put his hand to such matters and even though he brazenly shouts that he doesn't care, I know he does and it weighs on him. I catch him practicing when he believes himself alone, but do not know what he is trying so hard to master.

Deep Peace to you,

Novicate Guyye of the Druids

Brother Hueil,

I truly wish that you could have attended the inaugural of the new Chamber at the Citadel. When the Elders reversed their thinking on the fey in Alainn, I was hoping that you would be one of the first to travel to visit.

Hueil, I do so desire to see you once more and have you see this place I now call home. Maybe I will come to visit sometime soon.

But the Citadel, dear brother! It is such a wonder. Never even in Firinn has there been such wondrous works as it. The construction was completed many turns ago, however it was the final work that took the longest. No element could be accomplished using our energies, as the Druids proclaimed that it was to be performed by hand. What talent these fey have, my brother. Who would have ever known that we could do labor such as this? The fey tribes of Elfs and Dwarfs lent hand to the creating.

In the outer chamber, enchantments have been made where as you pass a wall, it writes out special poems or chants, never the same one. I found myself walking around and around to see each time what would appear.

When at last I was pulled into the Citadel's main chamber, I stood spellbound and found myself unable to give voice to the amount of emotions I felt. It is so ambitious and so great a responsibility to organize all the realms together as one responsive assemblage that these fey have undertaken. And the Citadel is perfect—it sits on the point of the epicenter where the realms are joined as one, the Balance dear brother. It is this, as you well know, that led to the Druids to choose this location in Alainn to begin with.

The Chamber itself is circular and it takes me many steps to cross from one side to the other. The walls are held up by massive trunks of the oak tree and each has been carved with the most intriguing of designs. Images and landscapes of unimaginable elegance were painted onto the walls depicting all three realms; it does provide a glimpse into what Ifrinn is like. It is so very different from Firinn, with our sumptuous gardens and elegant towering palaces. It appears to have a different beauty and if ever the time comes when we are allowed to visit their realm, I would be honored to be admitted entry.

Our fey artisans outdid themselves with the creation of the ceiling images. The details are so painstakingly meticulous. At the center, there is the sun that shines on Alainn, where all Power comes from, and radiating out are three points of light that expand into portrayals of each of our realms. Brother, I tell you I can stand for hours gazing up at it and never see or comprehend all the wonderful scenes woven through it.

If all this were not enough, there are four grand fireplaces large enough for twenty of our brethren to stand in. Each is set with an enchanted, unending flame that blazes in every spectrum of color. Every piece of furniture was also handcrafted and I do not have the words to describe them all. It is the center of the area that provokes the most emotion in me though. This precious gem, a glittering diamond, is part of the world of Alainn, imbedded into its earth and is the summation of power for this world. The gem emits waves of energies and it does so remind me of the air of Firinn. Surrounding the diamond is a table of sorts, crafted from one center slab of the largest tree ever grown in Alainn. It encircles the Sunstone, creating the perimeter walking rim for the Oak Triad's rites.

Between two of the fireplaces there has been three statues carved from the wall. How they did this, I do not know as they are partway into the wall, part of the wall itself. One statue for each of the realms, a fey, a mortal and an Eilibear, all with their arms outstretched and hands cupped, holding the scepters for each realm. Crowns of glory sit on their heads, one the sun, another the moon and another the stars, all glowing with power.

The scepters themselves are works of art, dear brother. The fey's is golden, created to resemble the Elder's palace with its twists and towers. A miniature oak tree is the pinnacle at the top, encasing a diamond the width of my hand. The mortal one is a curved sword, ornately fashioned with an amethyst and the Eilibear's has a flying creature holding a star moonstone from their world. The creature's tail spirals down around the handle and looks to be too frightening to hold in one's hand. All are the most lavish creations I have ever laid eyes on.

Next to the statue there is a smaller one, of all three personages close together with their arms intertwined, their hands becoming one. And the hand holds the Orb of Balance.

I've created drawings of these four wonderful items, as my words are lacking to describe them for you.

I was privileged to watch for the first time a Rimwalk by the Oak Triad members in this chamber. It was exhilarating. They stood upon the Sunstone's rim and raised the sacred scepters over the stone and my heart sang. I was in awe of the orb bearer who had the privilege to let fly the orb and be witness to the Joining of the Three.

I am used to the ways of our bards and their use of melody to inspire and enhance our inner peace. But now that I have heard the Eilibear intone their sacred chants, I feel that our fey bards are somehow lacking.

My greatest personal news is that it was decided that since all the brethren from all the academies were to travel through Alainn to attend this distinguished occasion that one of the ceremonies would be to announce the advancement of ranks.

I have been honored to be chosen to rise to Fellowcast Druid, along with others of my Novicate friends. I have been raised to the position of Keeper. I will spend my life here, at the Citadel, the greatest of all places, and have the privilege of spending my days in the tombs of the exalted Archive of Knowledge. Others have been assigned as educators, healers, paladins, enchanters and so many more diverse callings. Odive, was given a very different assignment, one of an Envoy. He will go out to the great halls of the mortals and work with the Alltha to enlighten the mortals to higher knowledge. An odd assignment to be sure, but I am glad for him to have found a calling.

Deep peace to you,

Fellowcast Keeper Guyye of the Druids

Communique from the Archive of Knowledge - Citadel;

Brother Hueil,

I have made the move from my academy to the great hall of the Citadel. Being here now as a resident is very different than just traveling for one event. The daily activities include doing research and scribing for the Oak

Triad counsel, these honored druids, Alltha and Eilibear who work so hard for all of us.

I have yet to have the honor to meet the Oak Triad notables in person, as these great beings spend much of their time in their own realms, dealing with matters there.

I have made friends with many of the Oak Triad counsel, the Alltha and am growing used to the odor of the Eilibear. They are a dark race, powerful and deep in their thinking. I believe you would find them of interest. One stopped a moment and spoke to me, of nothing of importance, but my heart did beat wildly. It was a small female who was only seeking a quiet place to rest afore the symposium of counsel. You would have been proud of me, brother, I was able to overcome my natural revulsion to the flavor of her scent and found myself able to assist her. We have thus become of a friendly nature and she seeks me out whenever she is at counsel.

She is a funny one in that she always says what is on her mind and uses insults to relay such. It is often that I find myself having a give and take with her and the slurs do fly. Not too many of my druid friends understand this strange friendship I have gained with the Eilibear, but I do so enjoy it.

I see very little of the first friends I made at the academy. Their callings take them on other paths. Odive though, has come to the Citadel now and then throughout time. I do not know if it is to see me or for other matters. I seem to come upon him time and *again, deep in the tombs, pouring over various scrolls of the Mysteries. He has grown very self-assured, which is a fine thing, but he has lost none of his coldness and he does still have a disdain for the mortals with whom he is called to work.*

I do not know if Pert has relayed the latest news to you, but it is my hope he will as he is reluctant to speak with me regarding it...maybe to show respect. I hope he will open with you as you seem to have a close personal bond.

A minor counsel, the Diplomats, met a short time ago and unbeknownst to the Oak Triad counsel, they instilled an enchantment on the Sprite clan. The Diplomats felt that the Sprites should not have a choice whether to serve a fey or not. They cast an enchantment that forced service, if any fey should require it, onto the Sprites. On the surface, this may seem unimportant as the Sprites have always come when one has a need. But then you may remember that the Sprites would not work with Odive. I'm quite sure there were other fey also that the Sprite clan did not wish to grant services to. I felt that was their right, but the counsel disagreed. This fey counsel have crossed a line that should never have been crossed. They have, in effect, made slaves of the Sprites, taking away their freedom of choice. They did not formally announce what they had done, and it was when the Chieftain of the Sprites made a formal complaint directly to the Oak Triad counsel that it was made known.

I was in attendance that day and all were shocked. The minor counsel was called in to answer for this and it should be no surprise that Odive was a member of this counsel as his calling put him into their governorship. Odive himself spoke on behalf of the Diplomats and, brother, it was chilling to see how easy it was for his words to sway the Oak Triad counsel to his point of view. I, myself, found that I was in agreement with him as the Diplomats who travel to all parts of Alainn do have need of the ability of communiques most frequently. But then I realized that I was falling under Odive's spell and shielded myself. Others did not, and it was easily decided by the Oak Triad counsel to let this enchantment stand and they even applauded Odive for his forward thinking.

As soon as I was in private, I called for Pert and attempted to free him from the bonds. I was not able to do this, as my magic could not overcome the enchantment. Our friend Pert said it was no matter to him as he enjoyed giving his service to you and me and he is not pulled to be of service to any others. I was happy for that, but there are many others of the Sprite clan that will not be so lucky.

I spent days dwelling upon this matter and even sought out the Mysteries to see if there was anything I could do, but it was to no avail. I happened to come upon Odive at one point, sitting at a table studying a writ. A young Sprite was perched on the inkpot, standing there at attention and when I came upon them, his eyes turned to me with such sadness. I spoke greetings to Odive and then to the Sprite, asking his name as pleasantries. He just looked at me with misery and did not speak. Odive informed me that there were confidentiality restrictions for the Diplomats, and their Sprites had the ability to communicate impeded. The way he said it was so dispassionate and cruel. My eyes filled with tears, matching the little Sprite's and we shared a moment of deep sorrow. Odive dismissed me as if I, too, were a mere servant, telling me to go as he had work to attend to. I left and do so fear for what the future holds for all our races now.

Deep Peace to you,

Fellowcast Keeper Guyye of the Druids'

"Wait, you mean this guy Odive made it so all the Sprites like me were slaves to them? I don't like him at all," Margo said with a pout.

"I didn't know he had been a part of it, but that is when I was pulled into service to him," Derl replied. "I remember Master Guyye. He was very kind to me."

Talon waited for them to finish speaking before he resumed the reading;

Communique: from Archive of Knowledge - Citadel;

Brother Hueil,

Turns do seem to fly here in this realm. Pert has delivered your communiques to me in good form and my deepest apologizes that I have not sent word back on a regular basis.

So much has occurred at our Citadel. I have risen copious times in the ranks and now sit as the Master Keeper of Knowledge, holding under my charge the full Mysteries of the Druids. This is a great honor and responsibility.

My work has not been without its troubles. Our Citadel is cast with enchantments, for protection and secrecy to keep our affairs private, our work, our race and our knowledge a mystery from all.

No Being, whether mortal, fey or Eilibear should have knowledge of all there is to know and it is my job to keep the Mysteries safe. Though I am the Keeper I do not have the ability or desire to try to use the knowledge. There are so many types of Mysteries and if utilized by one untrained in that principle, anything could happen. No Druid Educator would have use for the Mysteries of music, nor would any bard have the need for a Mystery on minerology, or a Sorcerer have need of the Mysteries of mathematics. These Mysteries are not the common magic that all fey and Eilibear possess and thus must be kept safe from those uneducated in their uses.

Therein lies the woes of my calling.

Scrolls and sacred artifacts of enchantments have gone missing without traces of magic to lead us back to the perpetrator. Our protections do not allow any that would not be of druid nature to enter the holy archives, so we have to conclude that it is indeed a druid who has done this deed. The prior three Master Keepers have left their posts in disgrace, as it was their charge to protect the Mysteries. Many druids are seeking answers to how the items were taken, but I do not think normal methods will uncover the deceptions.

Odive came to see me when I was given the post. He was in good humor and slapped my back with congratulations. He told me that having a friend governing these precious records gave him great pride, but I am worried. He too has risen in position and now is the highest ranked Envoy of the Diplomats, which of course means he is the head of the Oak Triad counsel. He has direct contact with the fey Elders in Firinn now and I do worry at his ability to sway the thoughts of others.

Many catastrophes and misfortunes have been occurring in Alainn, and we are left with the haunting fear that this was the purpose for taking the missing Mysteries. I fear that Odive is behind it all, as he has always shown such contempt for the mortals and their world. That our wonderful Mysteries would be used for darkness or by one untrained is very distressing, and I had to make the call to conceal the losses while under my care.

I have formed a covert band of my most trusted fellow Keepers and together we created reproductions of all of our holdings. Pert has now brought you these items. Keep them hidden, dear brother. None can know you have them. I fear that many will be lost to us forever if I do not take these drastic measures.

In my new role, I now stand with the Oak Triad counsel inner circle. I enjoy my meetings with the Eilibear present. They are so brilliantly different. They do not use magic as we do, or at least not the type of magic we know. When the Triad is called, it is their chants and prayers that lead our governorship in peace. Our own bards have powers similar, yet so different. Seeing their ritual of the Varese, the cleansing, makes me wish that we also had a way to wash our daily iniquities away and clean our souls. And when the notes of clear song emit from them, it lifts me to a place of inner stillness and balance.

The key to all balance is of course the three. The Eilibear have need of Alainn's special aura of magic as it gives life to their realm. The Eilibear are not pure magic like the fey. It is instead their realm that is pure energy that feeds its existence from Alainn. It is so hard to explain, but know this, it is the balance of these three realms that gives life to all. The fey would not be without Alainn, the realms would not be without Alainn and the mortals and their world would not be sustainable without the fey and the Eilibears to extract the magic that is created every moment of every mortal day. Without the fey and the Eilibear using that power, Alainn would not remain stable and the power would overwhelm their realm. It would be as a pig's bladder being filled with air unceasingly, and without a leakage, the bladder would expand beyond its possibilities and would shatter into the void.

It is from my friend Vondra, an ambassador of the Eilibear, that I have gained this knowledge. She spins such tales of her people. My other Eilibear friend has also risen in stature and now is one of the Oak Triad notables. I am very proud to be her friend.

Odive has not made colleagues with the Eilibear, which should not surprise you. He is so arrogant and dismissive of them and their counsel at the meetings. Of course him telling them they smell like mortal fecal matter and expressing his aversion to their odor every chance he gets does not help. A number of my Eilibear friends at first threw their slurs against him and I believe, as it seems to be their way, that there was little understanding on their part that Odive did not see their banter as friendly. I am embarrassed by his actions and it is disheartening that the other members allow him to continue on this path.

The Eilibear are like me, though more so, and are immune to his power of persuasion. All fey heads will be nodding agreement to something he declares, while the Eilibear glare at him. It does infuriate him that they do not go along with what he proclaims. There have been many instances where he and the Eilibear have ended up in shouting matches, not a respectable occurrence for either side. I do hand it to the Eilibear, their slurs and insults can even give Odive pause. Many a time, I have been witness to such hatred in his eyes for them that I *am beset with trepidation.*

Deep peace to you, dear brother,

Master Keeper Guyye

Brother Hueil,

I did laugh so when I heard what measures you had taken for protections. You always were looking for a reason to remain apart from the "unschooled and slothful fey," your own words dear brother. I am sending along many works for you to enjoy, apart from the others. Feel free to read these. I take my calling seriously and it would not behoove any fey, Eilibear or mortal, for these works to be lost. I have had many books and other works distributed to Alainn libraries where they can be hidden in plain sight.

Tensions are running high as Odive and a few of the other lesser and even higher members of the Oak Triad counsel are now in verbal war with the Eilibear. It is not a good thing.

On another note, word has come that the new clan of the Boggarts have formed an enticement for magic. This clan formed from the Brownies, delightful little imps that always seemed to be in trouble. I have come into contact with a few, much to my dismay as their little pranks can be quite unpleasant. The Boggarts are a new breed of fey that we see coming forth, a darker side of the fey. This is a serious matter in itself, as many such adaptations are happening more and more frequently and we do not know why.

The Oak Triad counsel is putting the blame on the Eilibear (Odive does push this viewpoint), but I am not of the same mind. It could just be normal evolution that does seem to happen in Alainn.

The Boggarts did not like their clan heading into the deep darkness and so created an enchanted stone to siphon off the darker magic so that it would impede the effect on them. I applaud their endeavors but many outside of the Oak Triad counsel (we tend to keep our voices quiet around many of the fey now) are concerned with just how this, so-called, Sumair stone will control the magic it collects.

Deep Peace to you,

Master Keeper Guyye

Brother Hueil,

It was my great honor at the last Rimwalk to be the Orb bearer. I was greatly proud of the honor and, save for unkind words from Odive, about the pointlessness he feels for it all, I hold my head high.

Deep peace to you,

Master Keeper Guyye

Brother Hueil,

This is a sorrowful day for all fey. The Oak Triad

counsel has come to a full disagreement with the Oak Triad personages. They wish to formally dismiss the Eilibear as members and many of us wonder how we can have a Triad for the realms if we dismiss one of the three.

Odive has declared that the Eilibears' counsel is not needed. He put forth 'proof' that it is the Eilibears that are turning our fey to darkness. I found no validity to his claims but many did. Oh brother, this Odive's powers seem to be growing and I do not know from where they come. His power to turn the minds of many and to instill fear to all has grown beyond concern, but is now a threat to the Oak Triad and all the realms.

When he did seek to banish the Eilibear, there were a number in attendance. Many retreated, via their fold in space, back to their nearest Fearainn Eadar, through a doorway that is within the fold of the Citadel's grounds. Like our Meadhans, they have a large consortium of their population that call their lands-between home.

My friend Vondra was unwilling to give ground and continued to argue her views, declaring that Odive had manufactured this proof. Odive gave her no mind and it is my belief that he seeks to not only rid the counsels of Eilibear, but disband the Oak Triad and take the power they hold for his own end. I do fear for all my friends' safety.

Deep peace to you,

Master Keeper Guyye

Brother Hueil,

Two nights ago, we celebrated the fifth Rimwalk of the year. It seemed to be a very low-spirited meeting of the Oak Triad, their power as strong as ever, but a darkness seemed to hover over the counsel. At the Rimwalk end, Odive announced that henceforth the Fey Scepter, by order of the fey Elders, would be kept in Firinn until the time of the sixth Rimwalk and thereafter. Triad fey Cerian was much saddened to have his Scepter taken and after Odive, Edme and Freman did leave the others of the Triad, our Alltha representative and the Eilibear Sovereign stayed within the walls of the Citadel to perform a purification ceremony to heal the inner turmoil of all. Their chants were melancholy and woeful to hear. I stayed with them through the night, joining with the song.

It was in the morn that our world did shake and, with a great thunder and crash, did our Sunstone roll and then cracked across its expanse. A great ball of white-hot fire erupted from the crack and did take the lifeforce of many fey and Eilibear.

Vondra was spared as was I, though one leg is without a foot now and poor Pert has been burnt down one side. I do not think his arm will recover and one wing is gone. Vondra and I were able to transport her dead and ourselves to the safety of the tombs and when the world stilled, I was witness to true Eilibear magic. Vondra did give of her own lifeforce to as many of her people as she had the energy for. Nine she was able to bring back from death's grip. But to do so has taken a great toll on her and as she gave up her lifeforce, she did age as a mortal would and I cried. She gave me back part of my foot so I may walk, though with a forever limp now. Pert she was not able to mend, though she did heal and take his pain the best she could.

I attempted to take them to the doorway of their Fearainn Eadar but it is closed and is only a normal arch in the inner garden. I have hidden them as best I could within the Citadel boundaries.

We stayed safe until this day when I ventured out, keeping my own physical damage hidden. Odive was in attendance in the Citadel and declared the Eilibear our enemy, laying the blame on them for the destruction of the Sunstone. He is seeking all remaining Eilibear in Alainn and the Meadhans to bring them harm. I did attempt to speak on their behalf, but my words were not heard and I know that I have created a foul enemy of Odive now.

I need to find a safe location for my friends as they cannot remain here. Odive is sure to find them soon. I've asked Pert with the help of any Sprite friends he may have to seek out such a place so we can get them away from Odive's reach. I am thinking somewhere in Alainn.

Master Keeper Guyye

Brother Hueil,

Thank you for taking the time to help. Pert and I were able to get our friends to the location you found. I have helped set them up with good accommodations which they are pleased with under the circumstances.

Odive has sought me out and tried to force me to tell him where they are. How he knows that I helped them is unclear. He was unable to get the information from me and I was able to remain firm that I do not know where they have gone.

To say he was very upset with me is an understatement. He stomped off with his associates and I know my station here is in grave danger, and probably my life as well.

Master Keeper Guyye

Brother Hueil,

As Pert has relayed to you it has been extremely hard for me to send communiques. Odive has put Paladin guards on the tombs (more so on me than the tombs) and I am never alone. Today all of those same Paladins were called away and I did sneak out of my restrictions to follow.

We are at war, dear brother. For the first time, fey are at war. For countless turns I've seen fey shake their heads with confusion over why the mortals seem to *always find a new reason to fight with one another. And now here we are, part of a horrible chaos, and I believe it to be our fault.*

Alainn has been invaded with Eilibear in the form of shades, Eilibear without form, and they are instilling themselves inside of mortals and fey alike. There has been a cry for help and all Paladins and druid of any calling are being asked to come forward to help combat this threat. I was able to catch a glimpse of Odive and the fey did not look like he was taking this news in good form. He looks to me to be panicking and his loud shouting at any and all is doing little more than frightening a great many of the druids. I must say, though, that although our Paladins have always been kindly fey who only seek to keep the peace, all of them have stepped up and vowed to take up arms against this threat.

Let me know what you hear of this matter.

Master Keeper Guyye

Brother Hueil,

It is not the fey that are the cause. I know who is to blame for this madness — Odive.

In the turns since the battle started, we learned that we have no way to combat these foes. No normal weapons, nor magic, do damage to the shades or demons as they are now being called. We have lost a great many good druids on the battlefield and know we cannot continue in this manner. We all will be lost.

Odive and his associates have taken up residence in the tombs and are pouring over all the Mysteries, seeking something that might help. Odive has cast a number of spells now and invoked at least one of the remaining artifacts. A number of the surviving Palidens are with them and I am really not surprised to find they have a new rank, that of Warrior Druid. An impressive calling for sure, but still none of this would have happened if not for Odive.

If any enchantment went wrong, it had to be Odive's doing. That fey should never be allowed to cast them. And so now I sit here, unable to warn all those with him of his inabilities to cast even the simplest of spells with complete success and there is no way of knowing if what he casts will work or what the outcome will be. Hueil, I am growing so tired of all of this and wish to go back to just being a druid, and working with all three realms.

Casper is much afraid of Odive, or maybe he is in loathing of him; either way, he hisses and arches his back with his hairs straight up in such a manner as to scare even me when this fey is near. Odive has struck out at him and other than finding himself with a hand bleeding from numerous nasty claw marks, cannot catch him. Now Casper has gone and hid himself and I do hope that when Odive is gone, he will come back to me. How is it that a creature from Alainn can see Odive for what he really is, but fey cannot?

Master Keeper Guyye

Brother Hueil, greetings.

How very long it has been and I have missed my correspondence with you. I do not regret my decision to send Pert to you and do thank you for keeping him safe until such time as he deems it secure enough to return to me. We do know that there has been a sufficient lessening on the bleed of magic that is flowing into Firinn now and there is the fear that Firinn will one day run dry and, thus, fey will be no more. Pert says the mist from the east is ever encroaching on more lands and swallowing up whole cities within Firinn and draining their magic as it touches them. How many fey have we lost? How many mortals have been killed? What has happened to the Eilibear? All these questions left hanging with no answers and what remains is nothing more than the slim hope that someday there will be an end to all this lunacy.

If Odive's end game was to destroy everything and every being, he is surely on his way to doing so. He brought back the Valkyries of old, utilizing the Valkyrie stick that the wisest of druids had stolen and hid away from the mortals who had first used it. Valkyries that of course could fight and kill the Eilibear shades, but also ended up killing everyone else. So many fey and mortals lost their lives before Odive was once more brought to task and, in a fluster, he cast yet another enchantment. Please forgive my cynicism, but aren't we lucky to have

Odive on the fey's side. The Valkyries were indeed dealt with, swept away to who knows where. But then all the female druids vanished with them.

He then cast an enchantment onto the Paladins which resulted in the creation of a master group of Warriors. Wondrous swords erupt out of their arms that send out ribbons of power that can enslave the shade Eilibear and destroy them. Part of me is glad of that – but they were peaceful, helpful Eilibear and save for Odive's hatred of them, they did not deserve to be mutilated in this manner. And the poor Druids that so bravely gave of themselves to be mutated into these Warriors? There turns out to be a high price to pay for this new magic. It is being called the Gorffen, a most horrible penalty, but not from the druid but instead from any who has the bad luck to fall in love with one. They are drained of all their magic and are no more. So now we have Warrior Druids who can save us from the demons, created by fey, who must kill those they love. But wait! – oh dear brother, Odive spoke to all who complained of this and he was able to convince them that it was no worry, as the magic of the Gorffen turned off the emotion of love in the said druid so they would not and could not feel remorse at what they were called to do – all in the name of saving the fey! They accept this as truth and he felt empowered again.

He tells all that it is the Elders who cast these enchantments; at least the ones that did not work as planned. I know better. When will anyone learn that if

Odive casts a spell of any type, magic rebels?

Odive has set himself up as head of what he calls the Druid Counsel now, telling all that the Oak Triad was a mistake and should be wiped from memory. He attempted to remove the art and carvings in the Citadel that spoke of any Eilibear or of the Oak Triad. To my great relief, he was unable to do so. The enchantments the Oak Triad originally placed on the Citadel are beyond his ability to cancel. He did throw such a temper tantrum when he discovered it. It was amusing and painful to witness.

I am sending the last of the Mysteries; no copies this time. If it is the last thing I do before I stop drawing breath, it will be to stop Odive and somehow find a way to reverse what he has done.

I am also sending Casper to you, for your safekeeping, along with a number of his brethren that I have been able to round up.

Odive is seeking me as I script, I will be leaving by way of the Friar Meadhan in the Alainn land called England. It is not a Meadhan that I think Odive would think I have knowledge of.

Soon to be with you,

Master Keeper Guyye

When Talon finished all sixteen letters that Ivy had chosen, he rolled the scroll up and handed it silently to Derl.

All the Eilibear seemed solemn. Even the girl, Rave, seemed to have been affected by the letters. She was the first to speak, turning her attention to Guyye's twin.

"Hueil, your brother was a very dear friend to us. If not for his bravery, we would not still be here. For you that don't know, the Friar Meadhan imploded. One day it was there and the next it wasn't. Derl is fairly certain this was Odive's doing. Master Keeper Guyye has not been seen or heard from since, so we can only assume that Odive found him and made sure he wouldn't get into Firinn.

"Derl has provided some other information we found curious. All the fey knew when the Valkyries were created and what a fiasco that turned out to be. They also knew about how Odive supposedly saved the day by getting rid of them. Of course, somehow all the female druids vanished also. But again he managed to make everyone think this was a good thing. Just a couple of days ago, he released the Valkyries," she pointed at Akneeta.

"The female druids showed up also, which is good, I guess. Any of the females that were not Paladins, the original warrior of the druids, he allowed to remain at their original home in Aforne. All of those who were Paladins and the Valkyries were sent to an island, along with all the Warrior Druids. Derl informed us that it was Odive's plan to have the Valkyries use their Siren call to attract the remaining Eilibear shades to one place. I guess if you are fighting a war, this is a pretty decent strategy. Except that we can see that this Valkyrie has reverted to her original self, which should mean all the others have also.

"We…"—Rave motioned to the other Eilibear in the room— "know that not even a fraction of the shades were pulled to that location. So either the Sirens weren't as strong as Odive thought they would be, or now with only one true Siren Valkyrie, the call did not have enough power to draw the Eilibear shades.

"This is a good thing for the shades since with Derl's help, we now know where their bodies are to be found, even if we can't reach them at their present location. The problem is that Derl thinks that Odive plans on killing all the Paladins, Valkyries *and* Warrior Druids as soon as that first part of his plan is accomplished.

"Odive is not the brightest bulb in the bunch, but he does seem to be the most dangerous because we cannot gauge what he will do next. If he uses the same enchantment that he used to destroy Friar Meadhan, then many fey lives will be lost. The fey may be at war with the Eilibear shades, but we, the true Eilibears, are not at war with them. We do not want to see even more lives lost if there is a way to stop it.

"Zack, you found a way out of a containment field that should not have been possible to get out of. Can you find your way back in to let them know that they are in danger?"

Zack looked over at Telfer. His friend nodded back.

"Yes, my dad is on that island. We'll go, try to convince them of the danger and, even if they don't believe us, we will find a way to get them out of there."

"I will go with them. My sister Valkyries may be made to listen to reason. All of them know what Odive is capable of," Akneeta said as she stood.

"Great. You three will be taken back out of our safe house. You can't, of course, bring them back here. Take them some place you think might be safe, or even to the Citadel if you think they would be able to convince others of Odive's doings. Silver, if you would."

The Eilibear named Silver stood and motioned for the three to follow him.

CHAPTER 27 – Ivy

When Zack was gone, I rejoined the group. It was bitter sweet seeing Zack and knowing that he would probably do exactly as he had done before. I had hoped that maybe something had changed and my Zack would be the only person I saw. But I knew when his eyes started to glass over that nothing had changed.

All I could do now was hope that we could find a way to correct the chaos that Odive had created. I wanted my Zack back.

As soon as Margo saw me, she made room for me to sit down, hugging me as soon as I did.

"I am so sorry all that happened to you," she whispered as she bit her lower lip.

"I know, it was not very pleasant, as Derl is apt to say," I said forcing a smile on my face and looking back at Derl. He flew forward and sat on my shoulder.

"It is a great relief to speak of what that fey has done. I believe that if anyone can stop his bad enchantments, it is you, Only Ivy," he proclaimed sincerely.

"Only Ivy?" Margo mouthed at her.

"Private joke," I replied and truly smiled. It was good to be amongst friends again.

"So Ivy, Talon says you have your own theory for us to consider. Lay it on us," Rave said from across the room.

"Well, I know all of you have been under the impression that the Sumair stone is the key that can heal the Sunstone, right?" I asked and waited as heads nodded in agreement. Rave made a rolling motion with her hand for me to keep going.

"After reading the letters from Guyye, I think you might be mistaken. Rave can you put up the prophecy please?"

Rave gestured towards the wall, and words started to appear in blue flashes of light. When it had completely appeared, I stood and went over to the wall.

"*The balance key is the three, who are the three who know the key, to restore the balance three.* Your theory is that Marmaw, Granddad and I are the three, the three that know the key, the Sumair stone, and that it is the stone that can heal the Sunstone and restore the balance.

"I've heard you all say over and over again that three is always the key. And that is the true balance, a circle of three that all work together. Am I right?" I studied the room to see if they were in agreement.

"Derl, where is that scroll I marked? I think it's the last one." Derl flew over to the pile and retrieved the one I wanted.

"Here, listen to this: '*To watch for the first time a Rimwalk to be performed by the Oak Triad members was exhilarating. They stood upon the Sunstone's rim and raised the sacred Scepters over the stone and my heart sang. I was in awe of the Orb bearer who had the privilege to let fly the Orb and be witness to the Joining of the Three.*'

"and then this passage,

'*At the Rimwalk end Odive announced that henceforth the Fey Scepter, by order of the fey Elders, would be kept in Firinn until the time of the sixth Rimwalk and thereafter. Triad fey Cerian was much saddened to have his Scepter taken and after Odive, Edme and Freman did leave the others of the Triad, our Alltha representative and the Eilibear Sovereign stayed within the walls of the Citadel to perform a purification ceremony to heal the inner turmoil of all. Their chants were melancholy and much woeful to hear. I stayed with them through the night joining with the song.*

It was in the morn that our world did shake and with a great thunder and crash did our Sunstone roll and then cracked across its expanse.'

"and then this one, *'I attempted to take them to the doorway of their Fearainn Eadar but it is closed and is only a normal arch in the inner garden. I have hidden them as best I could within the Citadel boundaries.'*

"It seems to me that Guyye is telling us, even though he didn't know it, what Odive used to cast the *bad* enchantment. He took one of the Scepters and the next day the Sunstone was cracked and all hell broke loose on the Eilibear and one of their **Fearainn Eadar** vanished."

I looked around the room and I could see that everyone was considering this as deeply as I had.

"Now I haven't had much experience with enchanted items, but I do have my talisman that Granddad created for us. I know that nothing can negate my talisman except the same magic that Granddad used to create it...am I right?" I asked again. This part I was a little unsure about.

"You are correct. To undo an enchantment, normally the same artifact used to create it would be needed to reverse it," Rave admitted a little begrudgingly.

"So it can't be the Sumair stone, can it? It didn't

create the enchantment or crack the Sunstone or remove the Fearainn Eadar," I said in a rush. "So what if this," I pointed back at the prophecy, "is telling you that the balance key is the Oak Triad, three people, who know the key, the Scepters and how to begin these Rimwalk things that bring the balance back?" I breathed out and looked around at everyone.

"There was writing on the wall outside the Citadel, writings like you are doing here," Granddad said pointing at the wall. "One of them said something about weaving the balance."

Talon looked at Granddad, his features twisted with concentration. And then he looked over at Rave, his eyes opening wide.

"Rave, our words were not the only ones used in Rites. We formed the script wall but many of the words were invocations and prayers of the mortals or the fey. I know them all, but have not thought to remember any other than ours," Talon glanced around the room, his voice still ringing with bewilderment. "It was I that worked with the bards and the Alltha to find the words that held power to script onto the wall. They were not the full invocations, but morsels of words from each. There is only one that had what the Woodsman has spoken of. It was a prayer, not to the Sunstone, but to what the mortals worshiped— the Sun, the moon and the stars." He moved over to the wall and touched it with his finger. Blue script started to flow across the wall until the prayer was displayed.

We call on the three to weave the balance,

We give thanks to the circle three for their restoring might,

We bow to the balance derived from the three

They all read what had appeared and Rave was the first to speak.

"How Talon? How did we overlook this?" she asked, her voice rising.

"It was a mortal prayer, Rave. I would never have thought of it, if not for the Alltha Woodsman speaking of it," he cried, hanging his head in shame.

"Is it right, Rave? You called on the three to weave the balance, the three have restoring might, like healing or mending, right? And the *balance* was derived from the three?" I started to hop up and down, unable to contain myself. "That's it. That has to be it! Don't you see? We need to create the Oak Triad again and find the Scepters so they can weave the balance with their restoring might!" I said with excitement.

"It can't be that simple," Rave hissed, suddenly angry. "Why didn't we recognize this?"

"You didn't have the letters from a fey or the words from a mortal. Doesn't it always take three?" Margo asked thoughtfully.

Awe transformed Rave's face as she jerked her head around to stare at Margo. Silence hung in the air and I looked over at my friend. No one should ever discount Margo. I pulled her into a hug and she squirmed delightedly against me. I did love my little Sprite friend.

"So, do you think my theory has some validity?" I asked Rave. She pulled her eyes from Margo and nodded at me.

"I think Odive took the fey scepter into Firinn and used it there in the lower part of the Elder's palace to cast his bad enchantment. Derl said he was waving something around when he did the spell *and* I'm pretty sure I know where that one is. One of the Not Elders was waving a fancy club thing around and when he died, it fell and rolled behind the thrones. We need the Scepters, the Orb and a new Oak Triad."

"I don't know, Ivy. Odive is obsessed with the Sumair stone and you guys," Cinder interjected doubtfully.

"Odive is an ignoramus. Why would you do what he thinks is right?" Margo asked and was rewarded with a sour look from Cinder.

"The Sprite, Margo, is right. It is us that have allowed ourselves to be misled. Ivy, what do you suggest we do now?" Rave asked and for the first time, I think I saw a bit of respect behind her eyes.

"Well, I think first we need to get back to the Elders palace and retrieve the Scepter that one of the Not Elders dropped. And then we need to find a way to get to Odive and have him tell us where the other ones are and what the enchantment was that he used."

"Oh, is that all," Rave said with a roll of her eyes.

"I will go," Derl offered.

"I'll go also. I believe I have an easier way to enter the Palace," Granddad said lifting his axe. He stood, looking like he was ready for action.

"Wonderful. Maybe we can get the fey Scepter back. But how do you think you will get Odive to tell you anything?" Rave scoffed flatly at me.

"Easy, I'll let him capture me and then figure out a way to get him to tell me."

Rave gave me a long look and then shook her head.

"There is something very curious about you, Ivy. Either you are brilliant or just have a shitload of dumb luck poured out on you…but whichever it is, I'm still game. Odive *is* an idiot and I was an idiot for following his cue on the interpretation of the prophecy," she said as she hit her hand against her forehead. "I think I'll go with you on this adventure. He'd just love to get his hands on me and I kind of missed giving him shit. Between the two of us, we are the perfect bait."

CHAPTER 28 – Milton

Derl perched on Milton's shoulder like Margo was apt to do, and he led them to the doorway that would take them into Firinn.

Milton ended up standing in a jungle more tangled and wild than the one in Jamaica had been. Trees towered overhead, almost strangled by vines. The odor of decomposing vegetation was heady and smelled thick with mold and decay. It was nasty smelling and Milton worked at breathing through his mouth.

They were in front of a doorway, set in a mountain that resembled a cave opening. Milton held his axe up and touched it. The doorway shimmered and opened before them.

"We will need to be very fast if we are to get to the opening of the **Fearainn Eadar** before our magic is taken away by the rolling mist," Derl informed him with obvious nervousness.

"I think we will use a shortcut. **Hueil** said that at one time the Palace was like all other structures in Firinn, so there must have been doors. Just blink us there and I will get us in," Milton replied as he shouldered his axe.

Derl nodded, but didn't seem too optimistic that Milton's plan would work. Milton pushed through the doorway with Derl keeping pace with him.

They stepped into the thick fog and Milton could feel his magic being pulled from him. Before he could form a word to speak, Derl blinked them to the side of a blank stone wall.

"This is the palace, do it quickly!" Derl screamed

out.

Milton touched his axe to the side of the wall and yelled for it to open. The stones started to shake violently and then crumbled in a heap, leaving an opening the size of a double-wide door. They stepped inside and some of the pull on their magic subsided, but not completely. Milton turned to ask Derl which way, when he blinked them again.

They appeared in a huge chamber held up in multiple places by ornately carved pillars. What drew Milton's attention first was the chopping block, the dead fey lying next to it and his substitute axe that Odive had taken. Ivy hadn't been exaggerating when she'd told her story. There was a thick pool of blood around the fey and most of his face was smashed in. It was unspeakably hideous, and Milton had to look away. Just thinking of what these fey had attempted to do to Ivy made him want to get his hands on Odive and strangle the life force out of him. Ivy seemed to have done a pretty good job with this one, and he felt a bit ashamed that he had been treating her like a fragile child.

"Over there is Edme," Derl said pointing across the room.

A fey was slumped against the wall, shriveled like a dried-out prune. Milton felt no sorrow for the fey; he had gotten what he deserved. He pulled his attention away and saw the thrones Ivy had described. Piles of brown goop covered the seats of all three.

He hurried to them and slid between the two closest, trying not to touch the ooze that had been the fake Elders. It took only a second for his eyes to land on the Scepter. It was behind the middle throne, dirty and covered with slime.

As soon as he picked it up, Derl landed on his head and blinked them back to the doorway. Milton had never closed it so it was easy to step inside and then swing the axe behind him to close it tight.

They transported back to the jungle in Jamaica where Silver stood, patiently waiting for them. He blinked them inside the safe house and had them perform the cleansing ritual before he would allow them to join the others.

The remaining group was seated around a large table. The Eilibear were reading through all the scrolls that Hueil had sent them and now and then translating them for the ones that could not read the scrolls themselves. They all looked up when Milton laid the Scepter on the table.

"It's been a long while since I have laid eyes on that," Mother whispered in awe and reached out to stroke it reverently.

"Where's Ivy?" Milton asked, looking around.

"They decided on a plan and went to the park by the college she attends. They thought it best they didn't lead Odive here," Marmaw told him as she pulled out a chair next to her and motioned for him to take a seat.

There was nothing else he could do right now, so he sat and joined in with the odd study group.

CHAPTER 29 – Ivy

Rave and I brainstormed for quite some time and neither of us could come up with a real strategy other than to just let Odive take us. We figured that since Odive wasn't aware of my full powers, he wouldn't expect me to be able to overcome him or his magic. It may have been arrogant on our part, but we figured that I should be able to find a way to shift the events into our favor, no matter what happened.

We blinked to the park in Ashland, a place Odive would think was normal for us to be and very far away from where the rest of our group was. We lay in the sunshine and shot bits of magic out now and then, waiting. Either this guy would find us or he wouldn't. Our whole plan was really just a shot in the dark.

I woke to birds chirping and a fragrant breeze blowing around me. At first it was enjoyable, until I fully woke up. I remembered closing my eyes on the lawn in the park. Rave had been sitting next to me, crumbling up one handful of leaves after another. She was clearly getting bored. I sat up and looked around. I knew I wasn't in the park in Ashland, but there was no telling where I was now. And Rave was nowhere to be seen.

I tried to blink...but nothing happened and somehow I wasn't surprised.

I turned and looked around me. I was in a

meadow of tall grass and a stone stood at the center. It was covered with runes and looked like it had been there forever. I stood, feeling damp from the grass, and walked over to it. There was nothing really special about it, and I touched it with my finger. Suddenly my view shifted and, to my shock, I realized I was inside a sphere. The sky was there, but I could see a gray stone ceiling though it.

I climbed up onto the stone and only by standing on my tiptoes could I place one fingertip against the sphere. It was solid and cold to the touch. Jumping down from the stone, onto the grass, the view shifted again. Now I was in the meadow ringed by trees, birds flew overhead and I could hear the sound of a waterfall somewhere in the distance.

Gingerly I touched the stone again, and once more the view shifted and I was in the sphere. I spent a good long time trying to keep my touch on the stone, while reaching out to feel the wall. It was impossible. Only if I stood on the stone could I touch the thing that imprisoned me.

Where the hell was I? I sat down on the grass and leaned against the stone. That kept the sphere around me and I stared at it. It reminded me of a round snow globe I had had when I was little. Outside the sphere, there was a large old room, similar to the chamber of the Elders but of gray, not white stones. Maybe a castle? It was empty and dark, except for the light emitting from the sphere.

I didn't want to leave where I was, but I had to see if Rave was somewhere here also. Getting up, I started to walk…and walk and walk. Once I had left the stone, the sphere and the room it was in vanished from sight, and I was in another world, a Meadhan maybe. There was a wood with a pond and a quaint waterfall. I was a little excited when I found the stone house. It was solid and plain, but there was a fireplace and upstairs there were six strange beds. They looked well used and rumpled. Whoever lived here had left in a hurry. The beds weren't made and downstairs, food had been left in a pot in the fireplace.

I wondered where the people were that lived here. I went back outside and stood, surveying the area. It wasn't cold or hot...a perfectly controlled temperature for my needs and my worry increased. This couldn't be a Meadhan, at least not like mine.

I started to walk toward what I thought was the end of the area, only to have it continue to move out from me as I came toward it. The damn place was growing in size with each step. I came across deer and other creatures, along with trees with fruit that I didn't recognize. I wandered aimlessly until I found myself back at the stone house.

There was nothing to do and I was tired of walking. Inspecting the house again, I absently started to clean up when a gust of air slammed into me, taking me by surprise. A hot swoosh of air enveloped me, my stomach rolled and I found myself standing back at the stone once more.

"Ivy, I've been very anxious to meet you. How are you enjoying my home of late?" A voice I didn't recognize echoed around me. I looked at the sides of the sphere and as my eyes adjusted, I realized that *I* was standing outside. Me. There I was, with a horrible sneer on my face and I had both hands on the sphere, peering inside at me.

"I've been having a wonderful time with your boyfriend. We made love on the beach and, oh my, is he one delicious hunk," she cooed at me with a wink. Who was this version of me?

I ran over to her, realizing that the sphere stayed intact, even with me not touching the stone. Puzzled I looked back at it. Then I looked over at *me* again. I was laughing.

"Haven't figured it out? If you want to see outside, touch the stone. If we want to see inside we just touch the outside of the barrier. It is a marvelous enchantment, although I did not think so when I was locked inside," she informed me. I stared at her, at me. All of this was an enchantment…and I was locked away. Which could only mean that the *me* outside worked with Odive. Obviously he had found me…so Mother had been right that I could be found by the magic I used…or he had found another means to obtain the same results.

"So is there anything you want to tell me about Zack? Got to keep our man happy, now don't I."

This girl was very stupid…or Zack was really stupid. I was betting on her. Zack couldn't come close to me without trying to kill me, so if he could get close to this version, he would know it wasn't me. Which meant this girl was doing a horrible job of lying and attempting to bait me. It wasn't working. I stared stonily at her.

"Enough Kianna."

I recognized that voice. I turned toward it and wasn't surprised to see Odive. He was dressed in a long golden robe that flowed around his feet. It was embroidered with rich silver and gold threads that formed an intricate design down the front, and around his neck was a humongous gold pendant. His skin was pale and the gold of the robe made him look jaundiced. It was way too large for him and his skinny frame seemed lost within its folds.

He strutted across the floor toward me, looking extremely smug and pleased with himself. His garb was spectacular, but I thought he looked ridiculous and was in need of some serious fashion advice.

Touching the girl on the shoulder, she altered her physical form into another. I was exceedingly glad not to be staring at myself anymore. She was taller than me, with long silver hair and a body that anyone, girl or guy, would kill for.

"You can leave now," he informed her. She smiled wickedly at me, did a little princess wave and walked out of the chamber. I was very glad to have her leave. I switched my focus to Odive. He stood where she had, appraising me with a self-satisfied look on his face.

"So Ivy…thank you. I thought everything I had worked so hard for was lost when I discovered what you had done to the Elders and Edme…and that you had actually found a way to escape though the hidden **Fearainn Eadar**. But then you provided me with an unexpected surprise, you led me right to the Eilibear that had eluded me for so very long." He patted the sphere affectionately. "You will grow to like this place, I'm sure. Derl will be joining you soon and then you will have a companion forever…won't that be nice?"

He was a smug little weasel and I locked eyes with him, my hatred emanating outward in waves.

After a few moments, he started to fidget and I knew I was making him uncomfortable. He looked away first and I felt I had won a small battle.

"Well, I see you aren't in the mood to talk so I will leave you be." He bowed mockingly to me, then turned and strolled lazily out of the chamber. The sides of the sphere dissolved and I was once again in the meadow.

I really hated that fey.

A rustling at my feet pulled my eyes downward and I spotted a rabbit sitting a few feet from me chewing on a clover leaf. It wasn't scared of me and stayed there until I took a step towards it. It hopped off into the grasses and my eyes landed on the patch of clover it had been sitting on.

Think Ivy, I told myself. Marmaw had told me that no matter what happens, my powers will be what saves me. I need to work this out logically.

Blinking may not work, but do my other powers? I bent down and touched one of the unopened clover flowers and told it to grow. It bloomed immediately and I smiled to myself.

I turned and walked over to the stone and slapped my hand onto it. The sphere appeared. It didn't take a genius to figure out the stone was part of the enchantment. Maybe if I broke it, the enchantment would also be broken.

I felt inside myself and there was energy. I tried to pull it to my tongue, but there wasn't enough to even make a tingle. I wiggled my toes into the ground and tried to pull power. There wasn't any.

That left me with my plant magic that I had been able to use since I was very young to work with. An idea started to build and I took off running through the meadow, back to the stone house. I couldn't remember if there had been any weapons there, but there had been a wisteria vine growing up the sides of it. I needed a vine and that one would be perfect. I was out of breath by the time I reached the house, but didn't care. I pulled the largest piece off I could and then started back to the stone.

I was done in by the time I got back and fell against the stone, dropping to my knees. I hung my head as I panted and tried to catch my breath. When my heart stopped beating erratically, I looked up and hurried to dig a small hole in the ground. I pushed the end of the vine in and packed the dirt around it. I touched it gently and pushed every ounce of power I had at it. *"Grow thick and strong, encase this stone and strangle it, tighten around it and keep tightening, don't stop tightening,"* I told it. Then I stood and started to back away from it.

The wisteria vine started to quiver and then shot out new little shoots. Those began to twist and grow, slowly at first and then picking up speed until it had wrapped itself around the stone numerous times. Then it started to thicken, the vines becoming substantial branches that coiled around each other. I couldn't see the stone at all by the time the vine started to tighten.

I heard a crack, then another. I moved back further from it just as the stone shattered from the pressure. I turned my head and shut my eyes as bits of stone rained over me. The sound was deafening and then there was silence. I opened my eyes and found it had worked. I was standing in the chamber with only bits of stone scattered around my feet.

Odive was gonna to be pissed.

CHAPTER 30 – Ivy

I moved slowly out of the stone debris until I was close to the doorway Odive and Kianna had exited through. The stone floor beneath my feet was cold, but slightly soft. I looked down to see a soft layer of moss had crept partway over the stones. It actually felt good and I wiggled my toes and tested it and the stones for power. I sucked in my breath as the power leaped into me. It was different than in my Meadhan forest or out in Alainn. There, everything joyfully shared with me…here it felt like it was escaping and was excited it had found a home.

I felt rejuvenated, strong and I was not going to take any more shit from any fey.

There was no clue around me to let me know where I was. I figured it had to be some Meadhan or place in Alainn, since I didn't think Odive spent any real time in Firinn. This is where the magic was, so that is where he would be. I moved out the doorway and then up the dark staircase it led to, using the wall as my guide. The stairs ended at a wall. There was no door that I could feel in the darkness, but magic tingled around my fingertips.

Keeping one hand against the wall I rolled some magic to my tongue and whispered, *"Open."* I fell through and landed with a thud on the stone floor of the other side. Sconces were lit along the hallway and cast shadows around me, but at least I could see now. Looking up, I expected to see an open door, but instead there was only a stone wall. The little turd had used an enchantment to hide the door and keep people from wherever it led. That told me that others might be here and that he did not want them to know what he had hidden down the stairs.

Quickly I used my power to encase myself in a bubble of invisibility and started down the hallway. "I can't be seen or felt," I whispered, letting a bit of magic out.

I could soon hear voices. The hallway split off into various directions and I chose the one that I thought the sounds were coming from. Arches lined the hall and when I got to the first one, I discovered a large chamber with several fey sitting on stools at tables. They were writing and another fey was wandering among them, commenting on what they were doing. A school of some sort.

I needed to find out where Odive was, but I couldn't just go up and ask...or could I? I moved silently towards the closest fey, letting magic build. When I was standing next to him, I leaned down and softly asked him if he knew Odive.

He didn't stop what he was doing, but he nodded.

So I asked if he knew where he was. He shook his head. Cool, but not productive.

I continued to move through the chamber, asking various fey as I went. I received the same answers from all of them. I started to roam the halls and chambers, asking the same questions to any fey I came across. I had almost given up hope that this would work when a fey nodded and pointed down back down the corridor. I started to run, looking into chambers and down the hallways, continuing to ask passing fey.

I was finally rewarded for my efforts when I

found the jerk strolling with Kianna. He was chewing her out for being unsuccessful in glamouring Zack. *Good on you Zack*, I thought. I smiled knowing I had been right; she had been bluffing the entire time.

He stopped at an arch leading into another chamber, but instead of going inside, he walked close to the far wall and took a step backwards and was gone. Kianna did the same and when they had both disappeared, I touched my hand to the wall. I discovered that my fingers went through. Smiling to myself I stepped into the wall to find another staircase leading down and could see Kianna and Odive again as they turned a corner and were gone from sight.

I crept down slowly after them and when I was at the bottom of the stairs and could see inside the room, I knew I had the right place.

It was packed with furniture, piles of scrolls, stacks of books and various shelves holding an odd assortment of items. Odive was continuing to reprimand Kianna in the most derisive manner imaginable. She never said a word, just stood there taking his verbal attack with a twisted, fake smile plastered on her face.

"You have failed. I see no use for the Valkyries. You are worthless to me," he said with a sneer.

"I tried to tell you when you came to get me that I didn't see how lying to the girl would result in anything useful. I don't even know what it is you are trying to accomplish here. You released us to help fight the Eilibear and for us to keep Zaccheus occupied so that the girl would be alone and so that he would not be able to complete the Gorffen.

"We fought the Eilibear and Zaccheus has been occupied. You even caught the girl and it is not my fault that she got loose. But even now you have captured her yet again. We have done all you asked. Could you please tell me what it is you think I haven't done?" she snapped.

"You were supposed to act like Valkyries, but instead you are merely another irrelevant female. Useless to me," he jeered back at her.

"So what, do you plan on locking us back up? How? You used the containment Meadhan for the girl and the Valkyrie curse has already been broken. Everyone is aware that we and the other female druids have been released. All the Warrior Druids know of this, as well as the Druid Counsel. Just what do you think you can do to me or my sisters now?" she asked with a smug smile. From the look on Odive's face, that was the wrong thing to say.

"That containment barrier I put on the island was cast to keep all of you inside. I had expected you and your sisters to pull all the Eilibear to the island and when you had taken care of them, to do away with the Warriors. It was a brilliant plan *and you screwed it up*! You dimwitted cows *didn't* pull all the Eilibear in *or* take care of the Warriors for me. You couldn't even glamour the druid! You left me no choice but to take measures into my own hands," he sneered and then pointed at an antique clock sitting on the fireplace mantle.

The clock was quite pretty, with a china body sitting on a tarnished black metal base with claw feet. The china had been painted like the plates that Marmaw once had, with flowers and butterflies. Though it looked like a normal clock I'd see in any antique shop, there was something different about it. The hands on the clock were moving backwards.

"This worked so well when I needed to rid

myself of an old *friend* that I thought I'd use it again. Did you really think I was going to let any of you live?" He leaned close to her and I could see fear starting to build on her face.

"You have until the hands wind down to get the druid to tell you where the girl and that Eilibear have been hiding. There are more of them, I know it and we need to find all of them. He must know where Ivy would have gone, maybe all those from the Hemlock Meadhan know. They could have been harboring them this entire time. Get me that information or your fate will be the same as everyone else's on that island," he said as his lips drew back in a scowl.

The color drained from her face as she looked from the clock to him. "What happens when the clock winds down?" she whispered.

"Oh, it's already happening. As it counts down, the barrier shrinks and well before it is done, all air and life will be smashed out of any living thing. You don't have much time...Go!" he bellowed. Her face twisted in hatred for the fey and she reached out to grab him, but he flicked his hand at her and as her eyes opened wide, she vanished.

Odive wiped his hands together as if ridding himself of her and moved over to the clock.

"There just isn't time. Shite!" he shrieked and, in a fury, wiped the clock from the mantle. It landed with a crash and the china casing shattered into a million pieces. But the clock hands continued to click backward.

My mind was swirling. Derl had told them that he thought Odive was going to do something really shitty to everyone on the island and he hadn't been wrong. Zack, Telfer and Akneeta should already be there. She hoped they were safe and had been able to get everyone else out also.

"Temper, temper, piss ant. Did you screw up yet another enchantment?" Rave's voice gloated from above me. I looked up and finally found Rave. She was hanging from chains, her arms stretched out as she hung suspended between two rings from the ceiling, her feet dangling about four feet off the ground. Both of her shoulders looked like they had been twisted backwards, possibly snapped out of their sockets. That did not look comfortable at all.

Rave, though, was just as arrogant as ever, and there was nothing about her that looked frail, broken or miserable. In fact, she looked like she was enjoying herself.

"Where are the others?" he yelled up at her. He had to be the dumbest fey ever if he really thought she was going to tell him.

"The balance key is the three, who are the three who know the key, to restore the balance three," Rave chanted, a sneer curling her upper lip into a half smile.

He picked up a long staff and started to stab at her. This guy was unbelievable.

"Tell me, tell me, tell me..." he demanded with each stab. Suddenly he threw down the staff and hissed at her. I really mean he hissed, like a snake. Creepy dude.

"You thought you were so superior. I showed you, didn't I? Maybe I wasn't able to kill all of you like I wanted, but I got rid of most of you. Pulled you down from that pedestal you thought you were on, didn't I? I made you run from me in terror...and how many turns have you had to hide? I brought you down. It was me and believe me when I say I *will* find the others," he told her in a whiny voice.

He must have thought he sounded powerful, but it was more like a bratty kid saying *neener-neener-neener*.

"The balance key is the three, who are the three who know the key, to restore the balance three," Rave replied again smugly.

Odive ignored her and continued with his taunting.

"I will string all of you up like this, and there is nothing you can do to stop me. I'll lock you all up and keep you for pets. But I'm very busy, so I'll probably not have time to feed you," he laughed then, a high-pitched, insane cackle.

"The balance key is the three, who are the three who know the key, to restore the balance three," Rave said again and this time kept chanting it over and over again.

"Stop saying that!" he screamed throwing his hands up to his ears. "You think the prophecy will save you, don't you? All the fey have repeated it for turns, and no one could figure it out. You are all so stupid. Not one of you knew what it meant, but I did!" he screamed insanely. "I was the only one who had the intelligence to understand it."

Rave stopped her chant and looked up at him. "I don't believe you. If you had figured it out, then you would have corrected the balance."

"Corrected it? I'm the one that split the realms apart. There is nothing to correct, other than some of you survived. You are all but extinct and as soon as I find the others, you will be. I am killing off Eilibear, the damn Valkyries and the Warrior Druids. There is none that can stop me," he boasted. "The worlds will be mine, and I will never have to deal with the likes of you again."

"But you just said you were going to keep me as a pet. I don't get to be your pet now…I'm crushed, piss ant, really crushed."

"Stop calling me that!" he screamed.

"But that's your name, isn't it? That's what Odive means. I was just using the Eilibear translation," she answered coyly.

"You should respect my powers, Rave," he snarled at her.

"Why? What have you done that is so very awe inspiring?"

"I closed off Ifrinn. I destroyed your race. It was my great powers that cracked the Sunstone!"

"You did this? You split the Sunstone and tore my people from their forms? I don't believe it," Rave said scornfully. "You aren't that powerful."

I had to hand it to her… she knew how to get under this fey's skin. Odive looked like he might explode as he gestured around the chamber like a lunatic.

"You see all this? These are the great and terrifying Mysteries of the druids. I have them and I can use them…I have used them. And no one can stop me."

She glared down at Odive. "The balance key is the three, who are the three who know the key, to restore the balance three. You said you solved the riddle and I don't believe you. YOU AREN'T THAT SMART!" she screamed at him.

His face contorted with hatred, as he puffed out his chest with indignation. "It was so simple, yet *I* am the only one who understands it. It was the hideous fey mutants, the Boggarts that created the damn thing, and they didn't know what it really was. They knew they were being deformed and they formed the Sumair stone to siphon off the tainted magic so it wouldn't affect them. But the tainted magic *was Eilibear magic!* The damn Boggarts created an item that eventually held combined fey, mortal and Eilibear magic! Now, how asinine was that? And then the cursed Boggarts let it be stolen by none other than a freaking little fey who actually ran with the thing into Firinn and then into that damn Meadhan! If that wasn't bad enough, he let the Stone give its combined powers to two mortals and a brainless Frìth fey!" he paused and moved threateningly closer to where Rave hung. She flinched back with fake terror. She was a wonderful actress.

"You might wonder how I knew about them. Well, I'll tell you. For years Alltha fey had been complaining about the Woodsman and finally I was fed up with their whining and decided to do something about him. That's when I discovered why the fey couldn't overcome the Woodsman's powers. He was a Three-in-One and so were the other two. Their natural daughter was the unlucky one; she was filled with only Eilibear magic—she reeked of it," he said making a face.

"So you see, *I* solved the riddle. The Sunstone is what held all three realms together and created the balance. *And* the only thing that can mend it is *all* three types of magic. *And* the only object that has that, is the Sumair Stone, and the only ones who know where the stone is hidden are the Woodsman and his family. And they are the only ones that seem to have the power to control the thing. All I needed to do was make sure that couldn't happen.

"I don't care where the cursed Sumair Stone is, I

just needed to make sure there weren't still three of the Three-in-Ones! I planted the idea into the daughter's mind, broke the seal of enchantment on one of the **Fearainn Eadar** to release more of the shades and the Woodsman's mate was very nicely taken care of by them. There are now only two of them, and unless they decide to collect a bunch of humans and have the stone riddle them with magic and maybe get another Three-in-One, there is no way..." Odive's eyes grew wide as he realized the potential flaw in his plan.

"Well you may have figured out the prophecy, but I don't believe it was you that damaged my brethren or cracked the Sunstone in the first place. There is no way you could have done that. There is not enough magic in any of the realms to give you that kind of power. You always were a braggart and a little runt of a druid," Rave taunted.

"Of course it was me! I found the Shatter enchantment and only had to cast it with a powerful fey artifact,"

"So you say, but who would let you near a powerful artifact? You are a mutant fey and couldn't cast a spell that works if your life depended on it! They laughed at you, have always laughed at you, *piss ant*," she shrieked at him.

He screwed up his face as it turned crimson with rage and I was sure Rave had pushed him too far.

"I had an artifact. I took the fey Scepter and they let me. I took it right out of the hand of the fey Triad and there was no one to stop me. Me! They obeyed me!" he screamed. "After I destroyed the Sunstone and your obscene kind, I collected yours and the Alltha's also. I had all three. I even have the Orb of Power! No one is more powerful than me!" he screamed.

"You are such a liar," she said and then paused. "You *had* all three? What did you do, you little roach?"

Odive looked caught with his foot in his mouth for a second and then looked up at her.

"I *have* all of them. I just put the Alltha one someplace it couldn't be found," he insisted pitifully.

"You don't have any of the scepters. They wouldn't allow you to even touch them with your pitiful little smudge of magic. What are you? You can't be a fey. I know you must be a shifted mortal and that is why your powers are so pathetic."

A blue vein popped out in his neck and he looked like a madman. Suddenly he turned and started to leap over piles of junk until he reached a dull wooden cabinet. He flung it open and pulled out a golden Spector. Holding it up over his head, he bellowed, "I have it! I have yours right here. I kept it as a trophy to remind myself of how low I brought you." Then with his other hand, he pulled out the Orb and held it out for her to see also. "See, I have all the powers of the Oak Triad!"

While he was occupied proving how awesome he was, I inched over closer to Rave. I lowered a part of my shield and touched her foot.

She wasn't at all surprised to see my fingers appear. I moved my face up so she could see me and she glanced down at me with a smug look plastered on her face.

"Good job," I whispered. "I'll get the scepter and orb and then get you out of here." I thought she'd be happy about that, but instead she used her head to motion around the chamber. I shrugged my shoulders and looked around the area, confused by what she wanted.

Odive had moved away, still carrying the scepter and orb. When he reached a table by the fireplace, he set them down and went over to a cupboard.

"We can't leave all the Mysteries here. He could try to form another enchantment," she rasped impatiently at me. I looked around the room. There was a hell of a lot of crud here. It would be easier to just go over there, grab the two items and blink us out. But she was right, we couldn't leave Odive with anything he could use.

I decided I could possibly draw it all together, sucking it up like Granddad's shop vac used to do when he cleaned his workshop. I knew I could blink with all of it. I had blinked a house, after all. I'd have to do it extremely fast so Odive couldn't find a way to stop me. I pulled in magic from around me and filled my battery up to full, touched Rave's foot and placed my hand on the closest item.

I glanced over to see what Odive was doing and was surprised to see he was gathering items from the cupboard—cheese or something—and was actually creating a plate of food.

I shook my head in amazement. This guy had some serious A.D.D. issues he needed help with. But at least he wasn't paying any attention to me.

I took a deep breath and jerked as hard as I could. Like a mighty vacuum, the items in the room were sucked instantly towards the item my hand rested on. I heard Odive scream, Rave yell, "Nice seeing you again piss ant," and then I blinked.

CHAPTER 31 – Zack

Zack appeared standing on the dock, Telfer and Akneeta arrived just seconds later. They had decided to blink to the bit of dock that had been showing outside the barrier of the island. They hadn't expected all of them to fit on it, and steeled themselves to fall into the freezing water as soon as they materialized.

Instead there was more than enough room for them to stand on the dock. A number of the old fishing boats were outside the barrier now and on either side of the pier, they could see parts of the shoreline as the waves rolled up onto the beach.

"What the hell is this?" Telfer called out.

"I think the containment barrier is shrinking," Akneeta offered.

"Well shit. The only way in is under the water or we are going to be doing a bunch of digging," Zack said as he jumped into the water. He let the waves push him toward the shore and dug his fingers into the sand to keep himself as close to the bottom as possible. He held his breath and pulled himself forward on the sand. His lungs were bursting when he raised his head up and could see he had made it under the barrier.

He looked back and saw Telfer rise up and then Akneeta followed soon after. They made their way to where he lay in the shallow waters, panting.

"I can't catch my breath," Telfer told them.

"The air is thin. Whatever Odive is doing here will kill everyone if we don't get them out," Akneeta said as she moved to her knees and started to crawl out of the water onto the beach.

Zack tried to blink to the camp, hoping they could save time. But like before, he couldn't transport inside the barrier. He forced himself to stand and started staggering up the beach. Telfer and Akneeta followed as quickly as they could.

He found Reed on the beach in front of the camp. He was face down in the sand, gasping for air.

"Telfer, pull him out," Zack yelled back, pointing down at the druid.

He continued up the path to the camp and came across more druids that had fallen. He left them, figuring Akneeta or Telfer would drag them out. Everyone he saw had passed out from lack of air, his own head felt like it might burst at any moment. Just how small was this barrier now?

He tried to remember how many druids had come with them. There were nine counting himself, from the forest, maybe twenty-five or twenty-six of the veteran Warriors, the five Valkyries, including Akneeta and he wasn't sure how many there had been of the female Paladins, possibly close to fifty to start, but he had only seen about twenty after the battle. That made roughly fourty-five or so people they needed to get outside the barrier.

As he entered the camp, he found the bulk of them. They must have known something was happening. The Valkyries were in a tight group, but there were only three of them. He hunted around, but Kianna wasn't in the camp. He found his dad with Carmen and some of the other druids, in all, counting Reed and the ones on the path, there were thirty-five. There was a large group of the Paladins in their tents and as they had passed out huddled together, so he wasn't sure if it was all of them or not.

He picked his dad up first and carried him down to the path as Telfer was making his way up it.

"I put Reed on the dock. Let's get all of them down here. Akneeta can pull them under the barrier and we can help as soon as all of them are here. Are any of them conscious?"

"No, and I'm not feeling so hot myself," Zack replied as he continued down to the beach and dumped his dad in the surf next to Akneeta. He didn't have to tell her what to do. By the time he turned, she was already pulling his dad out into the water.

Telfer had already collected one other from the path and Zack tried to grab the next one. Back and forth they went, carrying the prone bodies.

"These guys are heavier than shit," Telfer huffed as he followed Zack down the path with another load.

"I'm sure we would be heavy, too, if someone tried to carry us like this," Zack huffed as he dumped Carmen unceremoniously face down in the water.

It took a good twenty minutes to get all of them to the water's edge, and Akneeta was having a hard time keeping up. The barrier had pulled in even more, now in just a couple of feet of water. The females were lighter and somewhat easy to maneuver under the barrier, but it was a struggle to get the large druids beneath it.

When they had all of the fey on the beach, Akneeta stayed outside the barrier and blinked the ones they brought out to the dock. Zack was pushing, while Telfer was pulling some older Warrior neither of them knew under the barrier when Zack heard a shout behind him. He stomped on the guys butt with his foot and pushed him under, then looked up at the path.

Kianna stood there, looking at him in shock.

"It's happening! He wasn't bluffing," she screamed.

Zack wasn't sure what she was talking about and didn't really care. "The barrier is shrinking. We have to get out now. Get your ass down here," he demanded brusquely.

Amazingly, she ran down to him and as she drew near, he pointed to the water.

"You can get under the barrier in the water. It's only about two feet deep right now. Get in the water and crawl under it."

Zack didn't wait to see if she did as he said. He took a deep breath and flopped down and crawled forward. He felt hands pull him and then lift him out. When he opened his eyes, Telfer was grinning at him.

"We got them all, dude," he said and put his hand up for a high five.

Zack slapped his hand wearily against Telfer's and turned to see Akneeta bringing a sputtering Kianna up out of the water. They didn't give her a chance to catch her breath before they all transported over to the dock. Akneeta had lain everyone out in a row, like a line of corpses.

Dad had just sat up and was looking around dazed. When his eyes landed on Zack, he raised one a hand to acknowledge him. Zack moved over to him and knelt down beside him.

"Dad, Odive did this. He might be looking for everyone. We need to get someplace safe."

"There is no place safe from that asshole," Dad coughed out and then spat over the side of the dock.

"We will go to the Hemlock forest. Milton has the protections back up, but I can get us in."

"How?"

"I have a talisman, Dad. I thought you knew that," Zack said and then stood, seeking Telfer. He was at the other end, talking with Trone, who was starting to come around. "Telfer, get everyone touching each other. Akneeta, help him," he called out.

Then he motioned for his dad to touch the druid lying next to him, and walked over each motionless body and locked that fey's arm with the one next to him. When he and Telfer met up in the middle of the group, he glanced over at his dad.

"Dad, touch the druid and don't let go."

He took hold of Telfer's arm, then they both planted a foot on a body near their feet. Zack looked over at Akneeta. She was holding hands with the last Valkyrie in the row and nodded at him.

He blinked and took them all with him into the private glade of the Hemlock forest. When he opened his eyes, the group had transported in the same formation. But at least now they had a chance to survive.

"Akneeta, could you go see if Winnie is still here. We need water, I think," he called out.

She nodded and blinked out. By the time she returned with Winnie and a couple of buckets of water, a few more had come around.

She and Winnie went down the line, pouring water on faces and waiting to make sure the drenched fey woke up. When they were done, they had some very wet, angry, confused fey.

Zack and Telfer pulled out the lawn chairs that Ivy had brought in a few days before they had finished the house and set them up, taking the first few for themselves, Akneeta and Winnie. The four sat, facing the fey, and waited for them to calm down before Zack started to speak.

"I'm sure you all realize by now, or at least I hope you do, that Odive set a trap for all of us and expects us all to be dead by now," Zack said. "You are in the Hemlock forest, owned by Ivy Glenwood. It is due to her and her family and close friends that you were saved."

"Now, just hold on a minute. Who the hell do you think you are to cast dispersions on Odive? He's the head of the Druid Counsel and speaks for the fey Elders. You have no right!" Carmen said, jumping up.

Zack rose and clenched his jaw. "I have every right, *Carmen*. The fey Elders are *dead*. They have been dead since the Sunstone was cracked by Odive. I'm not sure how he did it, but I know that all the facts will soon come out. Odive wanted to kill the Eilibear so he cast some enchantment that he screwed up. It pulled the Eilibear out of their bodies and created those things you've been fighting all these years. He killed the fey Elders and he yanked the realms apart.

"Firinn is dying because there isn't enough magic flowing into it. We don't know if Ifrinn is dead or not, but we do know that Alainn is in danger also. He created *you*, you asshole. I don't know why you let him mutate you into this Warrior-thing that kills its loved ones just to fight demons that he created...but you did! Or the Valkyries. Why the hell did you allow him to take your daughters and transform them? And then you let him lock them up and didn't fight him when all the other female druids disappeared. Why? Are you all that blind or just that stupid?"

"Zack." Telfer called his name and he looked back at him. "Go slow here, it's all new to them."

"No Telfer, it's time someone spoke the truth." He turned to his dad. "Can you tell me why you allowed this to happen? Or were you just going to let me kill Ivy and then tell me the truth. And you, Kianna, are you going to sit there and try to tell me that Odive didn't mean to turn you into something so horrible that he'd have to lock you up?"

Kianna stood and looked around with her lips pressed tight together. "Zaccheus is right. At least I know he is right about Odive wanting to kill us. He released us...after he beheaded Gunilla. He broke the curse and at first told us it was to help the druids fight the Eilibear, but also so I could keep Zaccheus distracted so he could kidnap the owner of this Meadhan. We went along with it, first because the Valkyrie curse was still affecting us, but also because we really wanted out of the hell he had locked us in. Then after the battle, he told all of us," she motioned at the other Valkyries sitting on the grass around her, "that he expected us to call all the Eilibear in until they were gone from Alainn...and then kill all of you. He said if we didn't, he would lock us back up. But the curse was wearing off...we weren't compelled to kill with abandon anymore.

"He did abduct the fey Ivy and then she escaped. He eventually found her, but to be honest, I think she let herself be caught by him again, along with the Eilibear sovereign. He pulled me off of the island to try to trick her into telling me where the rest of the Eilibear were hiding. He locked her in the same bubble Meadhan where he had us. Then he showed me the clock he had enchanted to shrink the island barrier *and* told me he had used it before. He sent me back to the island to die with the rest of you. I'm done with him and all his lies. Whatever you need us to do, **Zaccheus**, I am with you," she said, bowing her head humbly towards him.

"Don't trust her," Akneeta whispered as she leaned over toward Zack.

"No problem there," Zack whispered back.

"I can't believe all of you are falling for this. Look at that house. The demon Ivy brought that in by herself! What fey can blink a house?" Carmen yelled out as he pointed at the house.

Zack stiffened. "Carmen, you do realize that I, me by myself, just transported, what, close to fifty fey into this Meadhan. Just because there are a few that have powers stronger than most fey, does not make them demons. Ivy, Milton and I are not demons, we are just stronger than you are."

"How dare you speak to me in that manner? I am a Warrior Druid!"

"You are a mutant created by Odive to kill the things he created by mistake. You and many other Warrior Druids just accepted the Gorffen and what it meant to complete it. Who of you fought against it? Who of you protested when Odive first started casting enchantments on you? You sicken me Carmen. When did being fey mean that we kill? How many mortals and fey have died due to Odive? Did any of you wonder why all the enchantments he cast were so corrupt? He cannot cast enchantments correctly and it doesn't help that he has no scruples. Surely some of you were around when he was a Novicate and knew of his incompetence. He is depraved and has led you all down the same path! Can't you see this?" Zack asked, screwing up his face at them, pleading with them. "It is all on Odive, all this bloodshed! This isn't what druids are meant to be, or at least I hope it isn't." He looked out on their faces and could tell that he was getting through some. A couple of the younger druids were nodding their heads in agreement, as were all the Valkyries and Paladins, but he was only pissing off the older Warriors. They needed to hear it all.

"Margo!" He leaned his head back and screamed. "Margo! I need you and Derl!"

A couple of seconds went by and then Margo appeared along with Derl.

"Well, that was weird. Who knew you could yell for me and I could hear you?" Margo said as she landed on his shoulder and gave his ear a playful pull. "Who are these people?"

"Thanks for coming," he whispered to her. Then in a louder voice, "These are fey we pulled off the island. Derl, you were right. Odive was trying to kill them." Zack spoke first to Margo and then looked at Derl who hovered nearby.

"Derl, I'm having a hard time convincing them. Can you?"

"Of course," he said with a bow mid-air to Zack. Suddenly he shifted into a fine-looking young man about six feet tall. Margo made a whooping sound from Zack's shoulder and he didn't need to look down at her to know why.

"Fellow fey," Derl addressed them with a slight bow. "I am Derl, from the Llover Meadhan, home of the clan of Kapok, bound against my will to the fey Odive. I recognize many of you and maybe you know of me. I am no longer bound, as you can see. I will tell you my story, and as all fey know, Sprites cannot lie. Hear me."

Zack got up and went over to his dad. "We need to talk. You can hear this later," he said as he motioned for his dad to follow him.

When they were far enough away, he stood looking at his dad, waiting. His dad uncharacteristically wrung his hands nervously, as if he was trying to figure out what to say. After a few awkward, silence filled moments, his dad started to talk.

"I was a **Paladin, sort of like a knight or a guard.** I worked at the Citadel. Your mother and Akneeta lived in Firinn for a time and then relocated to where I was. Akneeta was about your age, full of life and ready to take her place as a druid. She showed great promise to be accepted as a Paladin, the same as I. I wasn't anything special, only a druid who had fulfilled his calling. Then the Sunstone cracked and we were told that the fey Elders had sequestered themselves for safety. We were told that it was the fault of the Oak Triad, that they had deceived everyone and had been working with the Eilibear to destroy the fey.

"It was only a few Alainn months later that the attacks started by the Eilibear. We were told that the fey Elders expected us to take up arms and fight these demons. We tried, Zack," his dad said.

"We couldn't fight them. Swords didn't work, nothing worked against the mists of the demons. So many of the Paladins died, hundreds, maybe thousands of them," he said shaking his head, remembering.

"Then Odive informed us that the fey Elders wished to use an enchantment on us that would give us the powers we needed. All of us that remained agreed.

It made sense. I held the sword that once was the Alltha scepter and all the remaining Paladins reached out to touch it or a Paladin that was touching it. There were still so many of us that we filled the Citadel and spilled out into the corridors, each touching to receive the power.

"Odive cast the enchantment over the broken Sunstone and the Scepter pulled the enchantment in and then thrust itself into our arms. We became the Warrior Druids and now had a weapon to fight the demons. But there were not enough of us. Odive came again from the Elders with yet another enchantment. This time he needed female druid volunteers. Only six came forward, one being your sister.

"We didn't know that it wasn't a normal enchantment, but instead one of the Mysteries, this time a curse he had unleashed...or that the Elders had unleashed, as he threw the blame on them. Your sister became a monster, along with the others. If the six arrived on any battlefield and were seen, everyone died—fey, mortal and Eilibear. The losses were so great that within two days, Odive cast an enchantment to rid the world of them and all the other female druids. Again Odive's story was that it was the penalty because of the Valkyries...and we believed him. Your mother was safe because she never took the calling of a druid and was still a true-blood fey. Years passed, we fought the Eilibear but they just kept coming, and your mother grew weaker and weaker. I needed the power to pull the Dywel and I could only get it from her. I tried to stay away from her, but I couldn't. She was close to giving birth to you and I hid. When you were born, I didn't know what to do. I wanted to be with both of you, but I was killing her and couldn't stop…and finally she gave up and let me do it."

Zack listened, stone faced. His dad wasn't really telling him much that Derl hadn't already told them. But it was the first time Zack had ever seen his dad break down into tears, and that pulled at his heart.

"So why didn't you tell me that I would do the same to Ivy?" he said, working hard to keep his voice level.

"Because I know how powerful she was, Zack. I knew she had brought this house in. I know how powerful Milton is, even though he tries hard to keep it a secret. If she was even half as powerful as her grandfather, I was sure she could stop it, or fix it, or change it. If I had told you, it couldn't play out. If I had told Milton, I knew he'd stop it. I trusted Ivy to save herself *and* you. My biggest problem is that when I'm near Eilibear, I go insane. I have to kill—that is all I think about. It's all those Warriors over there think about. Whatever the enchantment is that Odive put on us, it has taken over our bodies and our minds. I abhor Odive. I'm so petrified of that fey I can't even begin to tell you. Zack, I want this enchantment gone. From me, from you, from them," he said motioning out to the others. "I will do anything I can to help you. I'll take your lead from now on, son."

"And the others?" Zack asked.

"They will also, give it time."

"We don't have time. I think Ivy is close to figuring this out and you'd better be ready when she does."

CHAPTER 32 – Ivy

We appeared in their safe house in the middle of deafening crashes, as the stuff I brought with us, fell to the stone floor. I looked over at Rave and found that her arms were twisted almost backwards. She leaned her head to one side and closed her eyes, then quickly lifted both arms up and around. I could hear crunching. When it was done, she opened her eyes and looked at me.

"I knew you'd find a way to get to me. But if not, I could have blinked any time. Odive didn't even put a binding enchantment on me," she said shaking her head.

"Are you okay?" I asked pointing to her shoulders.

"Yeah, sure," she said. But when she turned to move away, she looked like she was walking a little gingerly.

I heard my name called and jerked around to see Margo sprinting over to me.

"Zack sent me. He got everyone out and they are back in the Hemlock forest. He thought that would be the safest place. He says that most of them are all on our side and will help any way they can," she informed me as she did a delightful pirouette.

That was a big relief.

I looked over towards Rave and noticed that Silver and Mother had joined up with her. Mother had laid her hands on Rave's shoulders and when she removed them Rave rotated the right and then the left shoulder, testing their movements. Mother must have provided some healing for her since afterwards Rave seemed more relaxed. She came back towards me and started to shift through all the stuff I had brought with us without saying a word to me or Margo.

"Did you find anything out?" Margo asked, pulling my attention back to her.

"Yep. Let's gather everyone together and we can share it with the whole group at the same time."

When everyone showed up, Rave held up the Eilibear scepter and Orb she had retrieved from the pile. Cheers rang out from the Eilibear and even those in my group were as ecstatic as they were.

Granddad held up what he had collected. The club looked nothing like what I had seen Moe holding. It was clean and glimmering in the light. He laid the fey scepter on a low round table in the center of the room and Rave placed her two items beside it. We spent a few minutes enjoying the sight of items from the Oak Triad.

"We are still missing the Alltha scepter," One of the Eilibear, Chara said with a frown.

"It wasn't with the other items, and I think Odive either lost it or destroyed it," Rave replied.

"You won't find it. Uncle Eddie told Zack that Odive used it to cast the Dywel enchantment," Margo said as sadness clouded her features.

"Well, that's it then. This whole thing was a waste of time," Chara scowled.

I studied the Eilibear girl. Maybe she was right, but that couldn't be the end of the road or why was the prophecy still in play? There had to be a way around missing one of the scepters. I moved up and placed my hand over the artifacts we did have, hoping to gain inspiration and was surprised to discover there was no magic being emitted by them.

"I don't feel any magic. Not even from the one that Odive said he used to cast the original Shatter enchantment," I said as I scrutinized the items.

"They are not magic, but conduits of magic. They intensify what magic is directed into them and then channels it into this," Rave explained pointing at the orb.

"So the orb then becomes like the Sumair stone, another three-in-one," I mumbled under my breath.

"It does, and then that power is directed at the Sunstone that in turn revitalizes our realms and resolves the balance between the worlds," Rave said, putting out her hand to me for a high five. We slapped hands, feeling quite proud of ourselves...until Chara spoke up again.

"But we still don't have the Alltha scepter," she said through gritted teeth.

"So where did these scepters come from?" I asked, raising my eyebrows at her.

"What do you mean? You brought this one and the Woodsman that one," she answered tilting her head at me. Okay, not all Eilibear are clever.

"I mean when and who created them?"

"Oh. We each created and provided our own," she replied, twisting her mouth at me. "Why?"

"Cool. So we just need to create a new Alltha scepter. We need something like the first. It was a weird sword thing and it had a gem in it, a large amethyst."

"I can obtain the amethyst, if you can find the item to attach it to," Silver offered stepping forward.

"We also need the people to hold the scepters," Margo said, chiming into the conversation. We have the Eilibear Sovereign, right?" she glanced over to Mother to confirm and Mother nodded back at her.

"And we have Hueil to stand in for his brother as

the fíor-ghlan fey, if he would be willing," Mother interjected.

"I would consider it an honor," Hueil proclaimed, stepping forward.

"So now we only need an Alltha. And I think we have the perfect one," Margo said as she turned to look at Granddad.

Granddad looked around in alarm as others started to eyeball him.

"I can't be a member of the Oak Triad," he stuttered.

"Why not, Milton? I think Margo is right. You are the perfect one. You meet the requirements to be the spokesperson for both the mortals and Alltha. And you already have the perfect tool to be transformed into the scepter of power. I can't think of anyone that would be a better fit for this position."

"Well, I'd be honored, I guess. But I am just a woodworker. I've never done politics or anything like that," he tried to explain to everyone. The Eilibear were warming to the idea, and they were talking over each other, giving their own reasons why he was the perfect choice.

Silver tapped me quietly on the shoulder and whispered that he'd be back in a few minutes. I figured he was going to collect the amethyst. I looked around for Derl and found him sitting on the back of a sofa next to Margo in her Sprite form. I motioned and caught his eye. He flew over and hovered in front of me.

"Derl, do you know of a vine that when mature would blend well with the wood on Granddad's axe handle?"

He thought for a moment and then nodded.

"Could you get me a nice piece of one?"

"Of course. I will be right back," he said as he disappeared.

Both he and Silver returned at the same time and I noticed that Derl still had a bit of moisture left from the Varese ritual on his face. He handed me a bit of lianas that I wasn't familiar with, but it looked similar to the wisteria I had used to destroy the stone, and I was sure he had chosen well.

Silver put the piece of amethyst on the table. It had crystal spears jutting out all over it and was multiple shades of purple. It was the same size overall as the gems that were part of the other scepters. Granddad laid his axe down next to it and we stood back, trying to decide where to attach it.

"I think at the top of the head," Marmaw said as she moved the amethyst to the position she thought right.

"That would work," Mother agreed.

I knelt down next to the table and put the bit of lianas at the end of the handle. I pulled some of my magic to my tongue and then softly told the lianas what I wanted it to do. I stood up and watched with everyone else to see what would happen.

The vine started to elongate, melting in with the wood of the handle until it was only slightly raised from the original wood. Then it twisted and spun, growing up the length of the axe, sending off curling tendrils in an intricate design up the handle until it reached the axe head and Amethyst. The cords of vine thinned and wove around the gem and handle, attaching it firmly, yet not impeding the original use of the axe. When it was finished, Granddad reached down and picked it up so everyone could see the full effect. It was wonderful, the most unique axe ever created.

"So we really are going to abandon our first theory and go with Ivy's?" Cinder asked the room.

"It is the right time, Cinder. Our calendar shows that tomorrow would have been the date for the second quarter Rimwalk ceremony. If we do not try this now, we will need to wait for the time of the third," Rave said.

"I don't know what that means. There are only certain times when the Rimwalk can be done?" I asked.

"Both the fey and Eilibear have forms of astronomy. The druid astronomers and the Eilibear watchers discovered that not only did our realms line up, but many of our ecliptic planes did also. Even with Firinn not having a sun, there were alignment points. The Sunstone is the keystone to all of them and our three races have celebrated solstices, equinoxes and cross quarters since the beginning of time. Even mortals, before the druids gave them help, figured out the basics. The Oak Triad performed the Rimwalk on each of these points of time and tomorrow is one of them. The next one will not be for about four weeks. We should do this now before Odive has time to regroup and I believe there is time to instruct everyone on the proper ceremonial chants and devotions," Rave replied. I could see that she was figuring out what we all needed to be taught and I bit my lower lip. I was not looking forward to more instruction from Talon and Adar.

It turned out not to be too bad. Only three hours of lectures, and then a couple more hours to learn the chants and then practice them. Granddad and Hueil had the most to memorize, but both seemed up to the task. Talon acted like a stage director for a play and had us stand in a certain place, next to a certain person. He seemed to have it all figured out.

I hadn't realized how involved the ceremony would be, but Rave assured me the only real worry was whether or not it would work to heal the Sunstone. That led us to go over our plan to gain entry and what to do if and when other fey showed up...or worse if Odive showed up.

When we were done, the Eilibear set up a wonderful meal, banquet-style. I couldn't eat. I had too many butterflies inside. I found a quiet place to rest and eventually fell asleep.

Coco woke me up, saying it was growing close to the time for us to take our leave. The safe house was buzzing with activity. All the stuff we had brought back had been cleared away, I hoped to somewhere secure. Marmaw and Mother were sitting on one of the curved pale pink sofas, reading through more of the scrolls. Both were decked out in very fancy clothes; Marmaw wore a long, pale violet dress and Mother had changed into a shimmery white robe thing that wrapped around her body and ended with one lone flap thrown over her left shoulder. Around her neck she wore a pendant with a large yellow gem surrounded by specs of smaller ones. From where I stood, it looked like the Sun with rays shooting out from it. I started to walk over to join them, but before I could, Rave grabbed my arm and dragged me in another direction.

"You can't go like that. You look like a bag lady," she informed me. I looked down at myself. I was wearing the clothes I had put on when we had set the trap for Odive to capture us. It was the shorts and tank top that Rave had first given me. They had been washed and were clean when I put them back on, but running around in that odd Meadhan had soiled them quite a bit.

I glanced sideways at her to make a smart remark about how I'd been a bit busy, but noticed that she was wearing an exact copy of what Mother had on, though hers had diamonds and sapphires sewn onto the edges and her shoulder flap was a sparkling wonder. She even had a pendant like Mother's, only larger with even more diamonds.

I was spellbound by it and allowed her to pull me along. When we reached the bedroom I had used before, she finally released me. "Take a shower, you stink. Darcy created a ceremonial gown for you to wear. It's on the bed.

She pushed me roughly inside the room, and then shut the door in my face. I was growing used to her.

I did as she asked—took a shower and cleaned the grime off of the bottom of my feet. They were black and mud had dried between my toes. They disgusted even me. Once I was clean, I picked up the garment she had left on the bed for me to wear. It was similar to what Marmaw had been wearing, but the fabric was a soft shade of green with lines of ivy winding up the edges. I pulled it on over my head and it formed to my body in ways I was sure Zack would enjoy.

When I opened the door, I could see that Granddad had returned. He was holding his newly decorated axe against his shoulder and looked every bit the Woodsman. He was wearing his familiar red and black flannel with jeans. Marmaw stood by his side, along with Margo who wore a very cute knee-length, pink chiffon party dress. The rest of Mother's family were decked out in the robe things. They all looked up when I came out.

"We are waiting on Hueil now," Rave informed me with an irritated sigh. "He wouldn't go unless he had his brother's ceremonial robes. Pert collected them for him. Hopefully he won't take too long to dress."

"I'm here, Rave," the old fey said as he hurried from a side door over to them. He had on a robe similar to what he had been wearing before, but this one was pure white and glistened as he moved.

"I checked in with Zack. They are ready to join with us. Uncle Eddie thinks all but a couple of the Warrior Druids are behind our plan. Those who aren't will be left behind in the forest so they can't make trouble. Derl went and spoke with the other female druids who were released with the Valkyries. Every single one said yes," Margo said with a wide grin. "This is going to be fun."

I hoped she was right and that my plan wasn't leading a whole lot of fey to their deaths.

CHAPTER 33 – Ivy

Rave reached out and took my hand and, one by one, each of us joined until we formed a circle. I don't know who blinked, but we appeared in a wide curved corridor. We weren't alone. From down the corridor, I heard shouts and turned to see Zack and his dad. Zack waved encouragingly at me and then motioned that he was staying where he was. He was right. We didn't need him going all psycho on me right now. His dad, along with all the druids I had come to know from my forest and a buttload of others I had never seen before, hurried towards us.

Rave nodded at Uncle Eddie in greeting, as if she knew him and then motioned for Talon to do his thing. He started to arrange the newcomers, while Rave, Granddad and Hueil took their positions, three abreast in front of a set of double doors, each carrying their Scepters.

Silver stood behind them, his arms held out straight with his hands cupping the Orb.

The rest of us formed three lines. Mother behind Rave, me behind Hueil and Marmaw behind Granddad. I looked over my shoulders and could see Talon had divided everyone up evenly and placed them in lines behind us.

"Everyone in the front is set. The female druids have arrived and will follow behind the Warriors and Valkyries," Talon informed us as he rushed back to his own place in line.

I looked back and my eyes found Zack far back in

the lines. He was standing between Telfer and a girl I had never seen before, but I knew instantly who she was. She looked just like him. Margo had told me that one of the newly released Valkyries had turned out to be Zack's sister and, with everything that was going on, I hadn't had the opportunity to meet her yet. I hoped I would have the chance to do so.

My eyes roamed further down the line and I locked eyes with another I recognized. Kianna...the girl that had tried to trick me. I didn't know what it meant that she was here; either she had come to her senses about Odive...he hadn't been all that nice to her, so maybe she was on our side now...or she was still working with Odive and all hell was going to break loose inside. Whichever it was, there was nothing I could do about it now.

"Listen up everyone, there are druids inside and probably Odive, as he leads the mock meetings now. Just walk forward and don't stop," Rave called out forcing me to concentrate on the purpose for our being here.

My heart was beating so loud I couldn't hear myself think. I watched as Granddad touched his axe to the crack between the two doors and they swung open.

We started to march forward, into a huge cathedral. The place was massive and the druids that were inside barely filled a small portion of it. I heard shouts and screams, but wasn't sure who was doing the shouting. I kept my eyes looking straight ahead at Granddad's back as we continued to march forward into the chamber. The first druids we came to must have been in shock since they parted as we moved towards them.

"Stop them!   What are you doing?   They're Eilibear!" I recognized Odive's scream. He didn't sound too happy to see us.

I rolled magic to the back of my throat and then pushed it out, *Protect us.*

No one stopped us and Odive continued to scream. We reached an odd-looking table in the center of the room and I saw for the first time the Sunstone and the crack that we planned on mending. Ornate chairs sat around the edge of it, holding fey who were busy jumping to their feet. It was a good thing since Rave flung her arm out and the chairs flew up into the air and shot across the room. I heard them hit the walls and then fall in a wave of crashes.

When she and the other two reached the rim of the table, I watched as Granddad, Hueil and then Rave blinked and reappeared standing on the rim of the Sunstone.

Silver moved forward with the Orb, waiting.

I stopped about ten feet from where they were and looked behind me. Everyone with us had begun to fan out, forming loose circles around the Sunstone, all the while pushing the other druids out of the way. Odive had been pushed back to one of the fireplaces, still screaming riotously.

Mother was standing next to Marmaw and not making a move towards the Sunstone.

"I thought the sovereign was supposed to be up there," I said out of the corner of my mouth to Cinder who was next to me.

"Rave *is* our Sovereign," she replied as the corners of her mouth turned up in a haughty grin.

Holy crap, I had told the Sovereign of the Eilibear

to eat shit and die. I was sure I was going to end up paying for that gaffe.

When we were all in our places, we started to hum the chant we had been taught. As the vibrations began to build in waves throughout the large chamber, the three members of the newly-reformed Oak Trial lifted their scepters high.

Silver was ready and as soon as energy started to shoot from the gems on each of the scepters, he threw the Orb up over the Sunstone. It seemed to bounce on currents and then connection was made from all three energies. He stepped back and joined our circle. We continued the chant, rising in tempo as the power surged through the air. Other voices joined in and I didn't know if it was the people who had come with us or the druids from the Citadel.

I glanced over at the Sunstone, its crack still long, wide and jagged, and hoped I had been right. Suddenly the Triad Orb ripped into life and started to shoot rays of magic out into the chamber, but before they connected with anything or anyone, they curved back and slammed into the Sunstone. Over and over again, the Orb released its collected magic as Granddad, Rave and Hueil continued to hold their scepters up above their heads.

The stone floor under my feet shuddered violently. I could feel power attempting to enter through my feet and pushed it back, hopefully directing it to the Sunstone. It burned white hot against my bare feet, but I didn't stop the chant. Our voices rose again to the next octave and the Eilibear started to speak the words of their cleansing chant. Suddenly I could hear Uncle Eddie's voice ring out in a deep baritone. He started to recite a poem or a chant or maybe it was a prayer, I wasn't sure.

But the melodies from the two races intermingled and overlapped as if they were meant to be sung together.

The Orb started to spin wildly as it continued to send out its magic, and when it seemed to gain its maximum velocity, it shot a pure white shaft of power down at the Sunstone. When the magic connected with the stone, it spread out like ribbons and started to weave back and forth, creating a lattice effect over the crack.

Around me the chants intensified, and I struggled to join back with them. Magic had ceased trying to find its way into me and was now congealing in thick swells towards the Sunstone.

I heard shouts from behind. Odive's voice screaming out, like a heckler in a crowd. We finished the first chant and began to say the prayer of the mortals;

"We call on the three to weave the balance,

We give thanks to the circle three for their restoring might,

We bow to the balance derived from the three..."

Our words gained volume as the druids sang them with us. I could feel the vibrations of the power coming from the words. The ambiance in the chamber was transforming, darkness departing and light taking its place. It was like everything and everyone was awakening from a long, restless sleep. As we reached the highest pitch, we started singing yet another prayer, asking the sun to provide its warmth, the moon its knowledge and the stars its wisdom. Our song cried out for healing, for peace and blessings on all who gathered. The music drowned out all other sounds and our rhythmic chant flowed gracefully around us.

My eyes started to water, but I so wanted to see if the Sunstone was healing. I couldn't focus on it.

Then the shaking began. At first, just a slight tremor under my feet, then a wave rolling across the floor, then another and another. I heard screams in the distance, but still the chant continued. The world turned upside down and the chant continued. The chamber thrashed and shook and then a blinding hot light, so bright that I could feel it in my bones, erupted from in front of me, from what I hoped was the Sunstone. It filled the chamber with its brilliance. I fell to my knees and knew all the others around me and behind me had done the same. I was bathed in a refreshing coolness. I relaxed against it and felt a deep quiet peace fill my soul.

"Hear my words!" a strong voice commanded. "Hear my words!" I looked up at the Sunstone. It was whole once more. No crack could be seen. Cool, I had been right.

Rave had turned to look out at the fey, still holding her scepter high. I glanced at Granddad and saw he had lowered his arm and was rubbing it. Hueil was doing the same, but both had turned to face outward as Rave had.

"Hear my words! Pure balance of the flowing tides to you, my brethren of the Citadel. Pure balance of the quiet wind to you, my brethren of the Citadel. Pure balance of the spinning worlds to you, my brethren of the Citadel. We three of the Oak Triad do bless and greet you," she cried out into the silence of the chamber.

She motioned at Hueil and he raised his scepter again and yelled out the same greeting. Then Granddad, looking a little haggard, raised his axe and, in his deep voice, he repeated the greeting. Then as one, their voices rang out in union.

"Pure balance of the flowing tides on you,

pure balance of the quiet wind on you,
pure balance of the spinning worlds on you.
We three of the Oak Triad do bless and greet you,
our brethren of the Citadel. "

Not a sound was heard until Odive's voice broke the peace.

"Kill them! They are Eilibear! Why aren't you stopping them?" Odive screamed in panic and anger.

No one answered him.

"I be Rave, Sovereign of Ifrinn. Hear the words of the Oak Triad!"

Rave flung out her scepter and aimed it at Odive.

"We accuse and curse the fey Odive. He did abuse the Mysteries and his actions did fracture the Sunstone and rip our realms apart. He did abuse the Mysteries and took the life energy from our friends the fey Elders," Rave called out.

"They have no right! They are Eilibear and the others traitors to the fey. Kill them!" Odive screamed as he looked at the fey around him. No one paid him any mind.

"I be Hueil, twin brother of Guyye, Master Keeper of the Druids. Hear the words of the Oak Triad. We accuse and curse the fey Odive. He did abuse the Mysteries and took the life energy from our friends the Eilibear. He did abuse the Mysteries and brought forth a mindless war with the Eilibear. He did abuse the Mysteries and formed the Warrior Valkyries and the Warrior Druids," Hueil called out after Rave.

"I be the Woodsman, Three-in-One of the Alltha, I declare my right to speak for the Mortals and Alltha of Alainn. Hear the words of the Oak Triad. We accuse and curse the fey Odive. He did abuse the Mysteries, the holy knowledge of the druids. He did abuse the Mysteries and must pay the price!" Granddad yelled.

"Silence shifted mortal! You have no right to speak in our presence," Odive shrieked and flung his arm out towards Granddad.

I was sure Odive was attempting to bind Granddad with magic like he had at our home. Worriedly I looked up at him. I needn't have been concerned though. Granddad's face was tight with anger, his brows snapped together as he angled his axe down and pointed it at Odive.

"No Odive, it is you that have no right to speak in *our* presence."

I could see a faint shimmer of magic shoot out from Granddad's axe and when it slammed into Odive he reeled backwards, flaying his arms out like pinwheels, trying to keep his balance. Fey jumped up and parted, letting him fall backwards, then moved back, hiding him from sight.

Granddad must have figured out how to fight back against whatever powers Odive had. I was proud of him and mesmerized by all three of them standing on the Rimwalk. I was sure that everyone else in the chamber was also, they were a very impressive sight. I felt a presence on my shoulder and twisted my neck to see that Derl had landed on me.

"Only Ivy, be prepared to give testimony," he whispered urgently to me. I didn't have time to respond as Odive started to scream. He had fought his way out of the crowd and was standing on the floor between Rave and Granddad. Sweat beaded his forehead and his expression was one of panic.

"It's not them!" Odive screamed. "Guyye is no

more, what do we care for this Hueil? That one is an Eilibear, our enemy…why would you listen to her? And that one…" he pointed at Granddad, "used the stolen power of the Sumair Stone to steal the Hemlock Meadhan from the fey. In fact he is still using it, look at the axe he holds. That is the object the Sumair stone contaminated, it's sacrilege for him to have that here in our holy Citadel," he screeched zealously as he moved around the Sunstone's rim and tried to engage the fey. No one would meet his eyes, and as the fey in the chamber started to get to their feet they moved away whenever he got close, as if it were him that was diseased.

"Ivy," Rave yelled down at me. When I looked up, she motioned for me to join her on the rim. I blinked up and looked out over the horde of fey who stared back at me and I felt my knees grow weak.

"Suck it up, sweet pea," Rave said, sarcastic as always. I looked at her and thought that if she could do this, then so could I.

"I am Ivy…uh…the rightful owner of the Hemlock Meadhan by decree of the…uh…honorable fey Elders and…uh… a Three-in-One of the Fey." I looked at Granddad and he nodded his approval. "Hear the words of this Oak Triad. I accuse and curse the fey Odive…" I was on a roll now. I hunted around until I spotted him and then extended my arm to point at him. "He did steal some of the druid Mysteries, but through the help of the Eilibear, we were able to retrieve them. He did abuse the Mysteries for his own twisted uses, he hated the Eilibear and wanted them dead, so he cast an enchantment, but he's a horrible fey and the enchantment went sideways. It killed the fey Elders, it broke the Sunstone, it ripped the Realms apart. It was he who sought to discredit the Oak Triad and take power for himself. He hurt the fey! He hurt the druids! If he hadn't done these things, we would not have been at war with the Eilibear; there would not have been the deaths of so many mortals and fey; there would have been no need for druids to leave their callings and become Warriors...and there would have been no use for the Dywel and uh...and all the bad stuff that happened. He's a really bad fey and should be punished," I finished rather lamely. I'd be the first to admit that I had never been a very eloquent speaker.

Odive continued to scream, but was now shouting vile things directed at me. I started to move to jump down when out of the corner of my eye, I saw Derl hovering beside me. To my shock he transformed into a very nice looking young man about Zack's age. He towered over me and I was rooted to the spot.

"I am Derl, from the Llover Meadhan, home of the clan of Kapok. I give witness to what the Oak Triad and my friend Only Ivy accuse. I was Odive's bound Sprite and saw with my own eyes the *bad* enchantments he wove. I cannot lie, I be Sprite," he declared standing proudly beside me.

"No, they lie, they all lie!" Odive screamed. I watched with sick fasciation as a great number of the fey turned on Odive and reached out their hands towards him. He disappeared from sight and I didn't know if they had killed him or just removed him, but I really didn't care either way.

At first, only hushed excited voices could be heard, but soon there were greetings being called between fey, druids and Eilibear and the chamber erupted into an ecstatic celebration.

I turned around to look at the Sunstone. The huge gem was whole and glimmered with power. I couldn't resist. Tentatively I reached out and touched it with the tip of my finger.

Oh...shouldn't have done that, I thought as I toppled off the rim and fell limply to the marble surface below. My world went dark as my head connected with the floor.

My face was suddenly struck. My head jerked sideways with the impact and I heard my neck make a cracking sound. I opened my eyes to find Rave's face filling my vision, just as she leaned back and slapped me.

"Snap out of it!" she yelled at me and slapped me again and then again. My brain was foggy, I couldn't figure out why she was there. But with each slap I found my thoughts clearer and when she went to slap me for the umpteenth time I finally came around to my normal self.

"Stop hitting me, you wild bitch." I lashed out at her. Rave leaned in close and inspected my eyes, then slapped me softly one more time for good measure.

"She's back," she yelled and then leaned down until her nose was almost touching mine. "Don't you be touching that Sunstone again unless you are told to do so."

Okay, I felt put in my place.

CHAPTER 34 – Ivy

Rave helped me up, giving me a sideways smirk. Someone should have told me she was the Sovereign of Ifrinn.

"It worked," I said, not really knowing what else to say.

"You were right. I have a feeling all those rumors about you will grow even wilder now. But at least your name will go down in history as a hero. Good job kiddo," she said as she patted my face gently, then pulled me into a hug.

"Thank you," she whispered into my ear.

Someone called her name and she moved back, winked at me and then hurried off into the crowd.

"She's weird."

I turned and saw that Margo was standing behind me. Derl was with her, holding her hand. Cute. She blushed and twisted her mouth with embarrassment.

"You did well Only Ivy. Your clan should be proud to have you as their leader," Derl said, giving me a small bow.

"Yeah, well I really don't like to do public speaking. But thank you. I hope now that everyone knows what Odive did, the fey and the Eilibear can be friends again, and all the Sprites can be free," I said. "They will be free now, won't they?"

"They are not free from the bond yet, but it is my hope that the druids will reverse the hold on us."

"It will be done," Granddad said coming up to stand next to me and throwing his arm around my shoulder. "I'll make that one of the first priorities of the Oak Triad, I promise. Ivy, we need to move outside. There's something happening in the back courtyard I think you should see."

He didn't explain, but instead started to walk towards the far side of the room. Another set of doors was open to the corridor and I could see that fey were moving excitedly out of the chamber and filling the space. We pushed our way through and when we reached the corridor, I noticed for the first time there were windows that looked to the outside.

If I had been in the Hemlock forest and seen what I was seeing now, I'd be terrified. But I knew what was happening and it filled me with joy instead. The courtyard outside was made up of flagstone paths winding their way around several plots of dirt and weeds. A stone wall surrounded the area and off to the side there was a rustic circular archway also made of stone. The wall looked ancient and the stones had not been cut, but instead had been expertly stacked to form a perfectly smooth and straight barrier. The connected round arch was another marvel of architecture. It was a free-standing circle of rocks created without the use of any mortar that I could see. The wall and most of the circle's opening were riddled with dead vines. It looked like it had stood there for a very long time with no one caring for it. In fact, the entire courtyard garden looked like it had been neglected and forgotten.

The archway was cool looking and the courtyard sad, but that's not what everyone was gawking at. The sky overhead had turned a sickly green as a heavy, thick mist blocked out the sun. Over the arch, a funnel cloud had formed and it snaked down and through the arch, disappearing as it passed the threshold.

"The Fearainn Eadar has come back," I said to myself and smiled...then my chest tightened with trepidation. I wondered how may bodies I had hurt by walking on them. I pursed my lips, considering what Derl had told me. He had said I couldn't hurt them, and I really hoped he had been right.

I could see Rave and Mother walking towards the opening, along with the others of her family. I don't know why, but I needed to be out there. Looking around franticly for a door to the outside, I felt Granddad take my arm and pull me down the corridor to the left. He must have known what I needed as I ended up at a door that several fey were peeking from. They must have been too scared to leave the safety of the corridor. Without caring what they thought, I shoved them aside and pushed the door open all the way and started to run towards the group.

"Rave!" I yelled as I ran. She turned and stopped when she saw me.

"We didn't even have to tell them...they knew to come!" she cried, looking up to the green cloud of mist.

I hadn't known her that long, but seeing tears falling down her face shocked me a bit. I guess it was very emotional for her. I couldn't even fathom how long she and her family had been in hiding, or what the loss of so many of their brethren must have been like. I would have been crying with joy also.

"How will they find their bodies?" I asked as I came up to them.

"I have no clue, but I'm sure they will. I'm going in to make sure the doorway into Ifrinn is open now. I will go home when the last of the shades finds their way here," she said. "I think it best that I lock this doorway from the other side so once they have their forms back they cannot return. There is no telling what their thoughts will be and I do not want another type of war to begin."

I understood that and was unsure what to do now. Ill at ease, I looked around and my eyes fell on the dead vines. At least I could bring life back to the surroundings for them. I reached out and touched the vine and let magic roll out. "Grow and thrive," I told it. I looked back over my shoulder at the dead gardens in the courtyard and allowed more magic to gather in my throat and then released it out towards the area.

Within seconds the vines and foliage greened. Tiny buds appeared on the vines and then blossomed into brilliant yellow roses. I heard gasps of surprise from Silver and Cinder as, before our eyes, the courtyard came alive with vibrant colors.

"Okay, that is one cool bit of magic," Cinder said as she put her hand on my shoulder. I turned to look up at her and she smiled, then moved toward the doorway and disappeared inside. One by one, the others said their goodbyes to me until it was only Mother and Rave left. I didn't know what to say and probably couldn't speak coherently anyway as I had started to cry.

Mother pulled me into a tight bear hug and I could hear her whispering something, but couldn't make it out. When she pulled away, she stroked my face and then hobbled through the doorway after the others.

"What did she say?" I asked Rave.

"An Eilibear blessing of protecting. Her way of saying thank you. I need to go, take care of yourself. Don't celebrate my leaving too much, I'll be back for the

Oak Triad meetings," she said as she moved towards the door. "Oh and I think someone over there is looking for you." And then she was gone.

I stood there blubbering like a baby. Who knew when I first met her at SOU that I'd grow to consider her a friend?

I heard my name being called and when I looked over toward the door to the Citadel, I could see Granddad standing with Zack. I wiped my nose on my sleeve—I was a slob—and started walking back towards them.

No time like the presence to see if Zack still wanted to kill me.

I kept my eyes on him as I walked forward. He didn't move from the doorway and his face was set with concentration. I hoped that meant he was keeping tabs on his emotions and actions, so he wouldn't bolt out to attack me.

When I was about ten feet away, I stopped and studied him.

"I think I'm okay, Ivy. Even having *those* close is not activating my Dywel," he said pointing up to the green sky. I looked up. The sky overhead was still thick, if not thicker, than before with the green mist. None of the Eilibear shades were angling for the fey or any place other than their doorway home.

I took a tentative step forward and then another. Nothing changed with Zack. He moved out into the courtyard as Granddad continued to hold the door open. I slowed, but didn't halt my forward progress. By the time I was within five feet of him our eyes had locked and I had forgotten all that had happened between us, the crap with Odive and crawling over bunches of Eilibear. I really had endured a crappy week. He moved closer to me, closing the distance between us in two long strides and gathered me up in his arms.

"Nothing is happening. It's gone," he said into my hair and then held on tightly as he swung me around gleefully. "It's gone!"

I heard laughing behind us and when he spun me toward the door, I found that we had an audience. Granddad, Zack's dad, his sister and the bitch, Kianna stood watching us.

"I believe our Dywels are gone for good, son. I'm looking forward to being just an ordinary Paladin again," Uncle Eddie said.

Zack put me down and I studied his dad. He had known that Zack would attack me and part of me was rather upset at him for allowing that to happen. He must have understood my look, as he moved out from the others.

"I am sorry. I've already told Zack and Milton how sorry I am. But, Ivy, you have to understand my thought process. I didn't want Zack to hurt you the way I did Elizabeth. Neither she nor I had any way to stop it from happening. But there is something very special about you, I've known it ever since I saw you powering Zack during the first battle. I put my trust in you and your powers to overcome it…and you did. A whole lot more dramatically than I had anticipated, but the end result is the right one. The war with the Eilibear is over, so there is no need for the Dywel, hence no need for the Gorffen."

"I guess I'll take that as a compliment," I replied. It was just too much work to be mad at anyone right now. However, I did wonder what the other Warrior Druids thought of all this. "Have you spoken with the other ones. Are they upset or glad it's over?"

"A few of the older druids are upset. They had grown used to their life." He hesitated for a moment and looked uneasy. "There were a couple of the newer Warriors that sided with them in the end and would not join with us to come to the Citadel to help. It may take some time for them to get over it and we couldn't leave them alone with Winnie in your Meadhan…so Milton took care of it."

At first I wasn't sure what he meant, then it hit me.

"You turned them into Wisps?" I said, trying hard not to snicker. I bet Reed was livid.

"It's always worked in the past when the fey didn't see reason," Granddad said with a twinkle in his eyes.

Akneeta stepped up and waited for me to look at her.

"I'm…"

"I know. You're Zack's sister. You look like him, minus the dreads. I'm looking forward to getting to know you," I said readily.

"And I you," she responded with a smile.

I looked behind her and could see Kianna standing apart from the others, looking awkwardly down at her feet. I moved toward her and stopped when she looked up.

"What you did was ridiculous. I knew you were lying," I said to her. I had to admit she was a beautiful fey and part of me was intimidated by her. But I needn't have been.

"I know. I'd love to lay the blame on Odive and say he made me do it, but I just didn't want to get locked up again," she said deflatedly. There was a bit of courage lacking there, but I couldn't blame her.

Suddenly she cocked her head and considered me. "How did you get out of the sphere? We were stuck there for a great number of turns, but I'm told you released yourself that same day."

"The stone. If you touched it you could see outside, so I figured it had power. I broke it and the enchantment on the thing broke also," I said with a shrug.

"I never thought to do that."

"Nor did any of us," Akneeta said.

Zack came up behind me and placed his hands on my shoulders. "Ivy has some amazing talents, one of which is never giving up."

"Kids, I think it's time we go home. It's going to be a bit chaotic here for a time and I'm told that I have to be back here in the morning for a full council meeting," Granddad said.

I looked over at Kianna. "Do you have someplace to go? You are welcome to come back to the Hemlock Forest with us if you wish."

"Thank you," she stammered in surprise. "I will be going home to Aforne, as will the others of our sisterhood, but it is a very kind offer."

We left her there and I felt a bit sorry for her and all the other released Valkyries and female druids. It had been easy for me to get out of the thing Odive had put me in…but if I hadn't been able to, would I have remained sane after being locked inside it for hundreds of years? I really didn't know. I hoped that all of them would be able to find their place again.

CHAPTER 35 – Ivy

I stood on the path leading to the open meadow. It was quiet under the foliage of the trees, but I could still hear the sounds coming from the fey. My meadow, my Meadhan, my home. They were celebrating.

Hundreds of them...true-blood fey, druids, Alltha, Eilibear and my family, and my friends. They did have a lot to celebrate. Odive was gone, all the shit he'd pulled for hundreds of years had been revealed, the war was over, the Eilibear shades had their bodies back—those that had survived anyway. Margo and Derl were almost inseparable, the fey had new Elders and the three realms had a new Oak Triad to keep watch. Most of the druids had gotten over being mad that they weren't Warriors anymore and a bunch had even decided to move to the Citadel to study with the other druids. It made sense to me. Over the years, the druids had lost their original purpose, having to deal with the war instead. With the return of the Oak Triad, they could once again regain their reputation as the keepers and teachers of all the knowledge the realms had to offer. It could be a major boon for Alainn.

Firinn was reverting to its original form now also. The heavy white mist had disappeared when the Fearainn Eadar had been pulled out from under the Elder's palace and returned to where it was supposed to be. The Oak Triad had helped pick the new Elders from the fey and Granddad thought these would be a wonderful improvement over the Not Elders. I thought anyone, or anything, would have been better than Odive's puppets.

I'd even seen Rave a few times. She was kept busy with the Oak Triad and I guess life was not as she expected when she returned to Ifrinn. It turned out that Ifrinn had not been affected by Odive's enchantment, other than being cut off from the other realms. They had no idea what had happened and ended up just putting a new Sovereign in place. The new guy wasn't so keen on Rave showing back up again or the displaced Eilibear that had finally regained their bodies. I felt for her, but there was nothing I could do to help.

And then there was Zack. He was back to normal and so were we as a couple. Even better than we had been before, even, since I wasn't tired all the time now. He had kept the vine tattoo, saying it was a good reminder to always be kind to me. The only problem was he talked a lot about training at the Citadel with the rest of the guys. Part of me thought it would be marvelous for him, another part of me felt like nothing would ever be the same again and I would be left here, expected to wait for him like a faithful mutt.

I guess it had just been a very long few weeks. So much had happened that it was hard to simply go back to being, as Derl still liked to say, only Ivy again. My forest was packed with people, which meant that there was never a time when I was alone. Granddad was the newest member of the Oak Triad and he took that post very seriously, as he should. Marmaw was back also and, if I thought having Granddad taking over the new house I had brought in had been bad, it was now suffocating with her there.

I felt like an ass. I had everything I wanted...and now I merely wanted freedom from the chatter. I didn't want to worry about Zack leaving, or missing him, or holding him back. I was restless and on edge all the time. I'd go to the treehouse and found I couldn't just *be* there with nothing to do, I needed something…a purpose. I started classes again, caught up with missing a week of school very quickly and then just as quickly became bored.

And now I stood watching all these people, fey and Eilibear, celebrating in my forest and I wanted nothing to do with them. I resented them being here.

I felt a presence behind me and didn't even care enough to turn around to see who it was.

"Hey Miss Wonderful. Would you look at this?" Rave said coming up next to me and gesturing out to the festivities. "If idiots could fly, this place would be an airport." Rave slapped me on the back.

I smiled and my lip trembled.

"What's wrong?" she said, looking at me sideways. "A little post-traumatic-save-the-day, blues?"

"Something like that I guess," I answered, shrugging my shoulders. I felt stupid for being depressed.

"Don't worry, sweet pea. I've got your back," her eyes twinkled at me. A heavy object fell on my foot. I jumped and looked down.

"You dropped something," she said, and then she was gone.

It was a book. I picked it up and had to chuckle. It was the same math book she had given me previously. I flipped through the pages to the center of the book and found the note tucked between them, just like before. Pulling it out, I flipped it over and read the words written in a flowery script;

Ivy, you don't have to stay. I won't tell anyone

but Zack and Margo. They will find you if they need you. Keep searching for your own adventure. It's out there, just waiting for you. Run now!

Odd that this Eilibear seemed to understand me better than anyone else. I dropped the note and watched it flutter away into nothingness as a smile crept over my face...and then blinked.

I'd always wanted to visit the Tianzi Mountains in China.

RUN, RUN, RUN AWAY

THE IVY CHRONICLES - 1

BY C.R. CUMMINGS

ABOUT THE AUTHOR

C.R. (Cherie) Cummings started penning her first stories in high school and completed her first novel soon after. She never published it, just had it waiting until the time was right. Her oldest sister's battle with ALS and her request that she would like to see her book published prompted C.R. to get to work.

Quest of the Evensongs was published in 2011 as an eBook and her sister was the first to receive a copy. Since that time she has published numerous works and currently is revising each for paperback. Her love of fantasy, the forest and 60's music led her to write The Ivy Chronicles.

A self-proclaimed Oregonian, she spends her free time reading, walking in the woods and hiding from the mountain of clothes that needs folding.

www.ingramcontent.com/pod-product-compliance
Lightning Source LLC
Chambersburg PA
CBHW030535260626
47157CB00006B/2034